BALLET
BOY

CLAIRE
GRUZELIER

Matador
9 Priory Business Park,
Wistow Road, Kibworth Beauchamp,
Leicestershire. LE8 0RX
Tel: 0116 279 2299
Email: books@troubador.co.uk
Web: www.troubador.co.uk/matador
Twitter: @matadorbooks

ISBN 978 1785893 599

British Library Cataloguing in Publication Data.
A catalogue record for this book is available from the British Library.

Printed and bound by CPI Group (UK) Ltd, Croydon, CR0 4YY
Typeset in 11pt Aldine by Troubador Publishing Ltd, Leicester, UK

Matador is an imprint of Troubador Publishing Ltd

For Lizzie

CHAPTER ONE

"**N**o!"

Jordan's eyes jolted off the workshop clock.

"Wait for it, fuck-wit," barked Tony, lounging with dirty boots propped on the back office desk. "Wouldn' want yer knockin' off early now, would we?"

Jordan slammed down the bonnet of the gleaming BMW Bluebird, hands coated in sticky, dark engine oil.

"Now drive 'er out onto the forecourt," ordered Tony with a malicious grin. "By then I'll have the bill ready to run over to reception. After that, yer can clear up in here – an' then p'rhaps I'll let yer shut up shop... Y'hear, boy?"

Jordan slouched off, pulling his old baseball cap down low over his eyes. No choice but to put up with this shit.

Wasn't much Tony Tyler didn't know about car engines, but the guy was a sodding racist pig. Hadn't taken two months at the garage to figure that out. No use moaning to the boss though, since Tony only took it out on him even worse afterwards – and he was just smart enough to claim they were only having a laugh together. Besides, he'd that cringing, boot-licking sidekick of his, Aziz, to back him up in any lie he cared to tell.

Jordan wiped his hands on a greasy rag from his overall pocket. Then he squeezed his long legs under the steering wheel of the BMW and switched on the ignition. Revving the engine in a burst of frustration, he backed the sports car out through the folded glass doors of the workshop and manoeuvred it slickly into one of the parking spaces on the forecourt, which lay steeped in warm September sunshine. As he climbed out and locked the driver's door, he paused a moment to finger the shiny, cobalt-blue paintwork. What he wouldn't give to own a set of wheels like this...

"Keys," snarled the ever-vigilant Tony, indicating the garage shop with one stubby thumb.

Jordan swore under his breath, but he did as he was told.

Five minutes later, as he was washing up at the grimy sink, he noticed Tony and Aziz exchanging their usual winks and nudges. So what'd be today's parting shot? As he unhooked his denim jacket from its peg, it came.

"Heard from yer mum lately?" Tony chuckled, so full of himself that he could hardly keep a straight face. "Aziz here swears he had her ten times for nothin' in a doorway last night an' left her lyin' dead drunk in the gutter. Wouldn't know anythin' about that, would yer, eh?" Tony's thick lips broke into a sadistic, gap-toothed grin.

"Can't've been her," blurted out Jordan before he could stop himself. "My mum lives in London."

Triumph glittered in Tony's pale grey eyes.

Bugger! Why did he always swallow the bait?

"I mean... That is..." Jordan stammered, squirming like a fish on a hook.

Too late. Tony'd already turned to scrawny, shock-haired Aziz.

"His mum lives in London," he repeated in a knowing voice. "Yer hear that, Aziz? Like his uncle ain't in jail an' his sister ain't a crippled half-wit."

Aziz only sniggered in response.

"She does," persisted Jordan, forcing himself to face this out.

"What a lying bastard this black ape is," jeered Tony. "He don' have no fuckin' clue where his mum lives – and he don'

2

have no dad at all. So what does that make the stupid son-of-a-bitch?"

"A lying bastard." Aziz tittered, rolling his eyes. The pair of them practically doubled up with hoots of laughter.

The hackles bristled on the back of Jordan's neck and he clenched his fists in fury. For a second Tony clearly thought he was going to let fly a punch. Their wills crossed like drawn knives in the tense silence.

Then an image of home flashed through Jordan's mind: Gran, Grace, the twins... He wavered. No way could he afford to smash in Tony's fat, ugly mug. Slowly he blinked, drew a deep breath then, turning his back on his tormentor, strode stiffly away.

"So long, black boy. See yer tomorrow..."

The threat floated after him on the soft afternoon breeze.

Hammering his fist into Tony's flabby paunch. Kicking out Aziz's crooked, yellow teeth. So far, it'd only happened in his dreams. What hurt most was that he'd just told a stupid, clumsy lie. His grandma'd brought him up decently to fear God and always tell the truth. How could he stoop to lie in front of that shit-brained, foul-mouthed bully? Why couldn't he just learn to keep his bloody gob shut?

But the worst thing about this blind alley he'd got trapped in was knowing that the same thing would happen tomorrow and tomorrow and tomorrow... How much longer could he take it?

★

"No! Absolutely not. End of story. There's no way you're ever going to talk me into this, so you might as well save your breath."

The explosion burst through the open door, flattening the two girls outside against the cold white wall of the passageway.

3

Isabelle shuddered. Her friend Mei'd been ordered to report to the Deputy Director's office once the afternoon rehearsal of Act Two of *Swan Lake* ended and she'd volunteered to come along for moral support. If only she were anywhere but here! Roland Hillier was so eminent in the dance world and such a fierce disciplinarian that she was absolutely terrified of him, like all the junior members of the company, and that afternoon he sounded in an even worse temper than usual. So who was unlucky enough to be on the receiving end of this blast?

"Now, Roy, you always fly off the handle before I can explain," protested the voice of their ballet mistress, Alicia Page. "Just consider calmly for a moment—"

"There's nothing to consider," roared back her husband, banging down his fist so hard that both girls flinched. "I'm heading up for retirement. If you think I'm going to waste a moment of the last precious year of my career on a bunch of juvenile delinquents, you're out of your mind."

"They're not delinquents," objected Alicia. "They're vulnerable young people, who're growing up under challenging conditions…"

A mighty snort of disgust and then, "You sound like a damned social worker…"

It was obviously a private conversation. They oughtn't to be listening in like this.

"Do you think we ought to come back later?" whispered Isabelle.

"And end up in an even worse fix?" mouthed back Mei, shaking her sleek, dark head. "I'm staying put."

Isabelle subsided uneasily.

"… You're too soft-hearted, Allie," Roy's voice was insisting. "In ballet we can't afford to be ruled by sentiment. These kids are nothing but vandals and drug addicts. They've been in trouble with the police since they were at primary school and now they've run entirely off the rails. Their families can't control them and neither can their college principal. So how in God's name do you think *I* can help? I'm not a magician. I can't wave a wand and perform miracles."

"No one but you can possibly make a success of this project. Barbara and I are in complete agreement..."

"What do you think this's all about?" Isabelle murmured.

"Sshh," hissed Mei, raising a finger to her lips. "I'm listening."

Isabelle drew back. She had less of an appetite for company gossip than her more streetwise American friend.

"... But you're always maintaining that we need to reach out to a wider audience," pleaded Alicia. "To raise interest among young people who've never seen a ballet before. Well, here's your big chance to open new doors and change the perceptions of a whole group of teenagers."

"I've never taught beginners' ballet to a gang of street kids before and I'm not planning to start now. Look, Allie, I'm an artist. I spent years training under de Valois and Rambert; I've worked with Ashton, MacMillan and Balanchine; I've partnered Fonteyn, Seymour, Leighton – and you! Now I've said no and I mean no. And that's my last word on the subject."

Chair legs scraped abruptly and light, exasperated footsteps swiftly approached the door. Isabelle edged away as a shadow darkened the threshold.

"You're totally impossible," Alicia paused to retort. "I can see it's no use persisting. Perhaps I should suggest the idea to somebody younger..."

And with this parting shot, she sailed out into the passageway, slamming the office door loudly behind her.

Alicia was legendary throughout the company for her skills of diplomacy: everyone approached her when they wanted a favour from Roy. But this time it seemed she'd suffered total rout.

Isabelle winced. Imagine how she'd feel in her place!

But although Alicia's clear cheeks glowed pink and the light of combat sparkled in her fine, dark eyes, strangely she didn't look that upset. In fact, her lips even wore the slightest hint of a smile.

"Hello," she exclaimed as she caught sight of them hovering awkwardly at the bend in the corridor. "What're you two doing here? I thought you'd've gone home ages ago."

Mei looked uncomfortable.

"My mobile – you remember?" she prompted. "It rang during rehearsal."

"Of course," Alicia recalled with a grimace, nodding in the direction of the office door.

Through the thin partition walls they could hear muffled sounds of irritation: a desk drawer jerking open and banging shut again, a pen skidding across the floor as Roy ricocheted around the room, muttering crossly to himself.

Isabelle and Mei exchanged embarrassed glances. The noises were difficult to ignore.

"I suppose you're wondering what on earth was going on in there," Alicia remarked, surveying them speculatively. "In fact, I was planning to ask your opinion about this scheme of mine too."

"Our opinion?" echoed Isabelle. Why would she want to consult two student trainees – the lowest of the low?

"Yes. It'd involve younger members of the company too." Then, as if suddenly making up her mind, "Well, now seems as good a time as any. Have you both got a moment? I could tell you all about it over a cup of coffee," gesturing along the corridor.

"But…" Mei hung back.

Alicia turned in surprise.

"Oh yes – the mobile," she recalled, glancing back at the now silent office. "I don't think he ought to be bothered at present, do you? He's thinking things over."

Isabelle regarded her dubiously. What she'd just heard hardly sounded like someone 'thinking things over'.

"Whyever didn't you remember to turn off that phone, Mei?" resumed Alicia. "You should know by now how livid Roy gets when rehearsal's interrupted."

Mei hung her head in silence.

Isabelle felt for her.

Alicia was ballet royalty and in class they strove to imitate her every gesture with religious reverence. Although Isabelle herself hadn't even been born till years after their ballet mistress retired from dancing principal rôles with the company, one of her most cherished childhood possessions was a blurry old video of Alicia Page dancing the ethereal spirit of Giselle, veiled in filmy white and shimmering through the gloom. She'd also witnessed her acclaimed interpretation of Carabosse during a ballet school visit to *Sleeping Beauty* and stood in awe of her dramatic portrayal of the wicked fairy with pale face and flashing dark eyes.

It was impossible to recognise those flashing eyes now in the mild gaze bent on Mei, full of motherly reproach. This was so much worse than having Roy tear strips off you in public, because you felt you'd personally let her down.

Mei was tougher than outsiders imagined from the evidence of her polite, demure exterior and the fragility of her tiny frame, which always made Isabelle feel like a gangling, ginger giraffe by comparison. But now she bit her lip regretfully.

"It was an accident," she faltered. "I was late back from lunch and I forgot in the rush. Do you – d'you think he'll send me back to school?"

"Of course not," Alicia reassured her. "His bark's far worse than his bite."

Mei's anxious face relaxed into a half-hopeful smile. Alicia must know what she was talking about.

"Just take care it doesn't happen again. What Roy says is true, you know. Mobiles are death to concentration and lack of concentration in rehearsals can lead to serious accidents."

Mei duly promised to take more care and Alicia smiled back.

"Now that's sorted, let's go and get a drink and I'll tell you about my idea…"

The coffee room, its sunny yellow walls hung with dramatic posters of old company productions, lay silent and deserted at this late hour of the afternoon. When they were seated comfortably together on the maroon leather couches among a scattering of tartan cushions and dance magazines, Alicia began.

"Yesterday on my way home from work I came across my next door neighbour unloading the boot of her car in the front driveway. Now Barbara's the principal of a large comprehensive school in Brackwell Heath—"

"Where's that?" interrupted Mei. Having attended a ballet school in London, she was still unfamiliar with the local geography.

"It's a deprived suburb west of the city centre," Alicia told her, "full of derelict factories and run-down housing estates. Anyway, while Barbara and I were chatting, she happened to mention that she was hoping to pilot a new scheme of personal development with some of her more challenging pupils – which would involve them identifying and confronting the issues that make them behave the way they do."

Isabelle leaned forward. Sounded interesting.

"She says what these young people need most is an activity to help them make sense of their lives. Something that involves a huge commitment of time and energy, that encourages concentration and self-discipline, where they can set themselves real goals to achieve rather than wasting all their creative energy on vandalism, gang in-fighting and underage sex…"

"Of course," Isabelle exclaimed. "And nothing demands more energy, commitment and self-discipline than ballet."

Mei drew back thoughtfully.

"That's a pretty tall order, isn't it?" she objected. "To take kids utterly raw off the street and try to turn them into ballet dancers."

"That's not the idea, Mei," pointed out Alicia. "We all know that demands years of dedicated training. All I'm suggesting is some way of giving these disadvantaged youngsters a chance to turn their lives around. I think the person to tackle this is Roy. He's always been brilliant at getting the best out of tough customers. But of course he couldn't handle a big project like this on his own. I was naturally planning to lend a hand. And I'd been thinking that—"

"I'd love to help," burst out Isabelle.

The others turned questioning glances upon her.

"I-I know I'm just a trainee," she stammered, blushing furiously, "but I've been talking to Boris about the educational outreach programme and this sounds such a worthwhile project. Don't you agree, Mei?"

Mei looked a little startled.

"Well – it'd take up a lot of time, wouldn't it?" she temporised. "When would you be running the classes?"

"It'd need to be every week," answered Alicia. "Hopefully starting next Sunday afternoon."

Mei groaned. "But Sunday's our one free day…"

Isabelle hadn't thought of that. Idealism running away with her, as usual. But after all, she was the girl her classmates'd voted most likely to run an international charity in later life because of her organisation of the school fundraising bazaar every Christmas…

"I mean – don't get me wrong," Mei was adding, "I'd really like to lend a hand. But I'm not sure I've got time for such a big, regular commitment at the moment, what with still settling into the company and the city and so on. I'll need to think it over… And how about when we're away on tour?"

Was that a shadow of disappointment at the back of Alicia's eyes?

But she still replied with unruffled calm. "I'd considered asking Murray Bennet from Airborne – you know, the handicapped dance workshop? – if he'd be interested in joining forces with us to cover the weeks we're out of town."

"How about Boris and Masakuni, who've been helping with the outreach programme?" suggested Isabelle quickly. "They might be interested in an opportunity like this."

"It's such a good cause, isn't it?" Alicia agreed. "Barbara's been telling me about the backgrounds of some of these youngsters. There's one girl called Lauren, who had a baby when she was only fifteen—"

"Yes, yes, I'm sure she's had a really tough time and we all feel desperately sorry for her," drawled a sarcastic bass voice from behind.

Isabelle jumped and three pairs of curious eyes flew towards the speaker.

It was Roy. He was leaning casually in the doorway with his arms crossed over his chest. How did he always appear out of nowhere like that? He was so light on his feet that no one'd heard him coming.

"Unhappily that doesn't mean she's going to be any good at pirouettes or *entrechats*, does it?" he added, surveying them over the tops of his spectacles with cynical blue eyes.

"That's not your problem," maintained Alicia, dismissing him with a shrug of her shoulders. "After all, you've refused to have anything to do with the project."

"*Romeo and Juliet*," he declared oracularly. "That's the way to hook 'em, you know. It's got everything kids like that can relate to: young love, family conflict, drugs, murder, underage sex, gang warfare, teen suicide…"

"I suppose it's an idea," admitted Alicia coolly.

"I'm not too old to come up with one now and again, you know." And he threw her a sidelong grin. Then, bounding off the doorpost, "Now if we're going to get this scheme off the ground, we'll have to start thinking about a venue. What exactly's Barbara got in mind?"

Isabelle stared up at him, amazed by this unexpected about-turn.

Alicia merely smiled.

CHAPTER TWO

As the bus rumbled along Brackwell Heath high street, Jordan leaned against a yellow pole, chewing his bottom lip morosely. He scowled through the window at the familiar row of shops: Val's fish and chip takeaway, the Black Swan pub, the pound store where Gran bought the family shoes, Caribbean Joe's café, Pets' Paradise with the usual knot of kids poking their grubby fingers through the cage wire to stroke some fluffy black and white kittens… The moment the bus doors clattered open, he swung lithely down onto the dug-up footpath near the church and set off with rapid strides up the main road.

Passing the Treasure Trove furniture emporium, he neatly side-stepped a huddle of worn armchairs spilling out over the front pavement. Old Mrs Reilly, busy wheeling a bargain book trolley back inside the hospice charity shop, gave him a quick wave. Jordan brightened a little and grinned back. He liked the kindly Irish widow, who used to lend him adventure stories when he worked school holidays at the carpet warehouse next door. Flapping in the breeze beneath its open shutter hung a few pricey Persian rugs, which the bearded Indian owner was hooking down with a long wooden pole.

"Hi there, Ranjit, how's trade been today?" Jordan paused to ask.

Ranjit leaned against the pole and made a thumbs-down sign.

"You're better off at that garage," he remarked with a gloomy shake of his head.

Jordan shrugged non-committally. Ranjit didn't have to work for Tony bloody Tyler, did he?

"Your gran need fresh veg for tea tonight?" croaked Mr Chung, the ancient Chinese greengrocer, who stood looking on in grubby cap and apron. He pointed to the wooden crates heaped with red and yellow peppers, green melons and small, round pomegranates beneath a faded red-and-white-striped awning. "Ripe plantain, fresh tomato, nice mango, big, juicy, cheap—"

"Oh yeah," Jordan suddenly remembered. "Promised Gran I'd buy some stuff on the way home…"

As he was leaving the store with a paper bag of ginger root in one hand and a coconut in the other, he bumped smack into his old friend, Eugene. Eugene was lounging his way home late from school with his shirt hanging out, a beat-up rucksack slung over one shoulder and a spire of smoke rising above the cigarette dangling from his lips. Probably been in detention, as usual.

"Hey, man," Eugene hailed him cheerfully, offering him the cigarette out of habit, since Jordan's grandmother refused point-blank to have them in her house. "Y'gonna show at Dillon's gig tomorrow night?"

"Nah, man." Jordan shook his head, stuffing the paper bag under one arm and taking a quick draw. "Workin' nightshift at the Arts Centre."

Eugene's face fell.

"Again?" he protested. "Man, ya always workin' night shift at the fuckin' Arts Centre. Ain't ya never gonna have time for fun no more?"

Jordan shrugged helplessly. Eugene had a dad with a job. Didn't need to earn a living, did he?

"Look, man," went on his friend, reclaiming the cigarette,

"if ya ain't gonna show at weekend gigs, ya'll soon get dropped from the band."

"Who cares?" retorted Jordan, tossing his head uneasily. Playing bass guitar in garage and dance hall with the band was one of the ruling passions of his life. The other was their lead singer, Elodie Simpson, with her shimmering, sequin-spangled party dresses and gold-hooped earrings, who'd so far refused to have anything to do with him. "Don't wanna play with a set of fuck-wit amateurs anyway. Got better things to do with my life."

"Hey, man, keep your hair on," soothed Eugene. "B'sides, Elodie'll be there." He made wide eyes at Jordan and nudged him suggestively. "Now she and Prince ain't an item no more, she's lookin' about her. Maybe ya could be in with a chance, eh, mate? What tits she's got on her, what an arse. Hell, I'd give five years o'my life to feel her up for ten minutes—"

"Might drop by after work," conceded Jordan, ignoring his friend's crude gestures and tossing him the coconut like a rugby ball. "But I gotta get a good night's sleep before Sunday."

Eugene executed a fair imitation of a match-saving try with the coconut. Then, pulling up short, he asked, "Sunday? What's happenin' Sunday?"

"My big break, that's what," boasted Jordan. "Gonna try out for the county basketball team."

"Nah – you're just takin' the piss. Ain't ya?"

"No way. Saw the ad in a paper at work. Said to turn up at the Arts Centre gym Sunday afternoon at two."

"Hey, man, best o'luck," exclaimed Eugene, tossing away the cigarette butt and clapping him enthusiastically round the shoulders. "All them years o'workin' out and weight-trainin'll finally pay off. Fame and fortune're gonna be yours. Well," pitching the coconut back in his friend's direction, "gotta get off to football now. Might even try out at county level myself next season. Be seein' ya."

And they exchanged the complex sequence of high fives and fist bumps that'd been their personal form of farewell since primary school.

While Eugene headed off towards the recreation ground, Jordan chose one of the narrow fenced alleyways leading towards the council estate and in another five minutes reached his own front door. As he let himself inside, the aroma of warm spices filled his nostrils: cinnamon, nutmeg, pepper, pimento... Yum. Slow-baked jerk chicken. His favourite.

"Gran, I'm home," he called out, his mouth already watering.

His grandmother's voice rang out above the din of children squabbling. "Jordan Howe. Dat you, boy?"

Before he could reply, she came lumbering out of the kitchen in worn pink-quilted slippers, wiping her sturdy hands on a vast, blue and yellow sunflower apron. "Where you been den?" she demanded, crossing her arms over her broad bosom and eyeing him up and down through her spectacles with jutting lower lip. The crown of her scarlet headscarf hardly reached his shoulder, but she would've been more than a match for him were he twice her height.

"On the way home," he began defensively. Then, recollecting what was in his hands, he held out the coconut and paper bag of root ginger like a peace offering to an angry earth goddess. "Here's the things you asked me to get."

"De tea's been standin' ready for de table dis las' ten minutes an' more," she scolded, "an' eberyone wid deir bellies rumblin'. You tink I gat all de time in de world to cook for no-good lazy-bones like you? You shoo straight into dat dere kitchen an' you jus' gat de food de good Lord sent down dat great, long neck o'yours an' doan' be givin' me no backchat." And she chased him down the hall in front of her apron like a squawking barnyard hen.

Into the tiny kitchen was crowded the whole family, except for Grandad. Grandad was an electrician by trade, but he'd been out of work for six years with a bad back. All he did the whole day long was huddle in an armchair by the front window, sad and silent, watching television and sometimes shuffling across the kitchen to make himself a cup of tea.

The seven-year-old twins, Dion and Darleen, were tumbling around the scuffed vinyl in a scrimmage of flailing limbs and tight, woolly curls, while Jordan's younger sister, Grace, sat at the table dancing her knife and fork up and down on the brightly checked oilcloth. She was a leggy twelve-year-old with big, brown eyes and a wide, shy smile, just emerging from childhood into adolescence.

Jordan dived into his place at table. But he sprang up at once as if scalded when Gran turned from the sink where she was draining rice and glared at him. Hell! Forgot again.

"Cleanliness be nex' to Godliness," she quoted, settling her ruffled feathers as he rinsed his hands under the tap. "Me 'spect you been wastin' time drinkin' hard liquor wid dat no-good Asian half-breed you workin' 'longside of. Liquor's de brew o'de Devil, boy. Doan' want no more trouble in dis house…"

"I'd never be seen dead in a pub with Aziz," protested Jordan, sliding back into his seat. "Besides, I'm under age."

"Huh," retorted Gran. "I weren' born yesterday. I know dem men you work wid done a hol' heap o'sinnin'…"

"Gran, I'm tellin' ya the truth," insisted Jordan, who knew how much she worried about him. "I don't go with those men. I just stopped to talk to Eugene."

"De Devil make work for idle hands," rapped back Gran smartly. She had an apt quotation for every circumstance. "You jus' carry dis here tray to your grandad and we be startin' our meal at las'."

Jordan did as he was told. Weren't many people in the world rash enough to disobey his grandma.

16

As soon as the twins were rounded up and penned firmly onto their bench against the wall, Gran said grace. But before he'd even seized his knife and fork, Grace, who was fairly jigging up and down in her seat, burst out, "Oh Jordan, I'm just dyin' to tell. I can' wait another minute."

Jordan paused to survey her glowing face with his fork halfway to his mouth, expecting to be called upon to admire some new piece of craftwork. Grace's legs mightn't be much use, but she was pretty good with her hands. She learned sewing and knitting at the church social circle and the house was cluttered with her creations: a crooked felt tea cosy in the shape of a country cottage; a woollen cross-stitch sampler of the Ten Commandments hanging on their grandparents' bedroom wall; a lumpy knitted dog with a grey patch over one eye, lying in pride of place on their sagging sofa. At least the objects were growing slightly less hideous as Grace's skills improved.

"There's gonna be real dancers at our school," Grace announced like front-page news. "Anyone who wants can come along and they're gonna show us how to do it too."

"Really?" grunted Jordan, supremely uninterested.

At that moment there was a loud yell from next door's baby.

They heard a woman's shrill voice shrieking, "Leo-NARD! Get off your fat arse an' tend to the child."

Leonard clearly made no response, since the baby carried on wailing.

Their grandmother seized hold of Grandad's walking stick, which she refused to let him use.

"Cut dat dere racket," she roared, banging loudly on the thin partition wall with its heavy wooden handle. Then she went on grumbling, "Dey're at it nex' door from mornin' till night. You'd tink dey could at leas' give us some peace an' quiet at tea time. Elbows in, Dion. Us not riffraff in dis

17

household." Then without a perceptible pause, "Grace's set her heart on havin' a try at dis here au-di-shun, she calls it. Mind you, I ain't ezzactly sure dese dancers are God-fearin' folk. Wid classes on de Lord's day an' wearin' dem skimpy dresses an' showin' dey legs all de way up to de panties..." She shuddered grimly. "Me need to pray to de Lord for guidance. Your mudder now, her were always dancin', dancin' an' see how it led her straight into de han's o'de Devil."

"Oh Gran, you can't stop me going," wailed Grace. "I'll just die – I know I will – if I can't see all the pretty ladies in their sparkly dresses."

Jordan buried himself in his dinner plate. This was no concern of his.

"Listen to dat dere pickney," cried Gran, shaking her head at Darleen, who was surreptitiously flicking peas at her twin brother next door. "All dis whole heap o'fuss for de sake o'some fancy belly dancers."

"Belly dancers?" echoed Jordan in astonishment. "You wanna do belly dancin', Grace?"

"No! No – it's not belly dancing – it's *ballet* dancing."

"What de diff'rence?" objected Gran. "Is jus' dancin'."

"T'ain't *just* dancin'," retorted Grace. People called her slow, but she was quick enough on the uptake when she liked. "It's – it's – you know, all them pretty, skinny ladies up on the tips of their toes, wearin' shiny gold crowns. I seen it on the telly."

"Huh," grunted Jordan, shovelling peas into his mouth. "So've I. A load o'posh poofs prancin' around in pink."

Grace's eyes blazed. "It's not. It's beautiful and I'm gonna go along. I wanna be a ballerina too."

"Sure, in your dreams," scoffed Jordan. Gran babied Grace. It was his job to teach her to face up to realities. But sometimes it wasn't easy. He shied away from pointing out the obvious hitch and instead demanded roughly, "D'you know how long it takes to be a ballerina? I heard some girls at school talkin' about it once. There's this place in Kingsbridge and they start trainin' there at five years old. So that makes you seven years behind already. Get real."

"Tell him he's wrong," Grace appealed to their grandmother. "Tell him what you promised."

"Well…" Gran shifted her weight uneasily in the creaking chair. "I said dat firs' me pray to de Lord for guidance…"

"Yes – an' after the Lord gave his blessing, then what?"

"Well… den Jordan take you to dis here au-di-shun on Sunday afternoon—"

"Now hold it right there, you two," interrupted Jordan, dropping his knife and fork with a clatter. "I'm busy Sunday afternoon and I ain't takin' Grace nowhere. Besides, I wouldn't get caught dead near fairies in pink tights. Just think what Eugene and the rest of the gang'd say."

"But Mizz Manners said we all need a grown-up with us," pleaded Grace. "Gran's got a church meetin', so if you don't come, how'm I ever gonna be a ballet star in a fluffy pink dress with a wand and a shiny gold crown?"

Jordan glared at her. Jesus Christ! Why couldn't Grace just face facts? No one with cerebral palsy, who took as long to walk to school in the morning as she did, was ever going to be a ballet star. Why did his crazy old grandmother let her build up her hopes like this?

He opened his mouth to blurt out the truth – but at the sight of Grace's brown eyes, fringed with wet lashes and glowing with enthusiasm, his courage failed. BANG! He brought his fist down hard on the table and leapt to his feet, gaping round helplessly. Everyone had stopped eating and was staring up at him, even the uncomprehending twins. He gasped for breath, as though he was suffocating like a netted flounder on dry land. Next moment he'd turned and flung out of the room.

Dark hall, steep stairs, narrow landing... He stumbled over the plastic toys Dion always left strewn about on their hand-hooked bedroom rug, slamming the door so hard behind him that the house resounded with the crash and its thin walls shuddered.

He leaned his forehead against the cold window pane, battling the tidal wave of rage that surged over him. His eyes surveyed the yard outside: chipped concrete slabs, dented rubbish bin, torn sweet wrappers and rustling crisp packets, which the wind had blown against the broken wooden fence from the side alley, defaced with graffiti and ending in a railway line that shook the whole terrace whenever a train rumbled past. He hated it all.

Hated the stink of petrol fumes and oil and damp concrete filling the garage workshop. Hated the fat, smug face of Tony and his thin, sly collaborator, Aziz. Hated being called Black Boy and Fuck-Wit and having to choke down his rage in case it lost him the only job he'd ever be qualified to hold. Hated Eugene, who could afford to smoke and stay on to the sixth form – despite having fewer exam passes than himself and nowhere near as good a grade in Maths. Hated the slut that brought him into the world, who'd dumped him and Grace with his grandparents years ago and only ever resurfaced when she was desperate for cash. Hated Uncle Wes for landing himself in jail and leaving them stuck with Dion and Darleen. Hated the house, the city, the system, the world, the universe. He'd been beaten in his struggle with life before he even drew his first breath, sentenced to have shit hurled at him every day at that bloody garage and to grind on and on without the hope of ever making anything of himself or of affording anything decent of his own, because there were always winter coats to buy for the twins and food to feed everyone's hungry bellies. He was no one, he was nothing and it wasn't fucking fair!

Jordan didn't cry easily. But as he leaned his burning forehead against the window glass, a fierce sob broke out of the depths of his misery.

Then he heard the tread of heavy footsteps labouring up the stairs and an authoritative tap sounded on the bedroom door.

"Jor-DAN," called out Gran's voice.

Jordan gulped and quickly drew a hand across his eyes. Gritting his teeth, he turned to face his grandmother, whose vast bulk now filled the open doorway.

She surveyed him with considering eyes and then she said, "Till Wes come home again, you de man o'dis family, boy. So jus' you get along down to dat dere Arts Centre. Else you gonna be late for your shift and you end up fired. And den us don' hab nuttin' to put in de bellies of de pickneys, 'ceptin' what me scrape togedder wid dese han's from scourin' dem hospital wards."

She stretched her upturned palms towards him, leathery with callouses, and his rebellious spirit died with hardly a whimper.

"Gran, I'm goin'. But you just gotta tell Grace there ain't gonna be no fluffy pink dress and fairy crown for her. It's no good her takin' that audition. Can't you see? Those dancers'll laugh their heads off at the way she walks, just like the other kids tease her at school. At least I got a chance if I try out for the basketball team," in a last-ditch effort to force her to see sense.

"You know de Lord speak to me in a special way," she replied. "Me been prayin' hard to Him 'bout what to do for de best and at las' He has spoke out loud and clear."

"Yes? And?" prompted Jordan. He'd given up on religion years ago, though he'd never dared admit as much to her.

"Dere be other try-out times," she assured him firmly. "De Lord's sendin' Grace to dis here au-di-shun on Sunday. So you is takin' her. Ain't no one else to do it."

21

"But you—"

"No buts. De Lord has spoken and Angelica Howe ain't de woman to say no to His command. Don' you forget, boy, dat you 'n' me's soljers fightin' de battles o'de Lord and I is a woman o'my word. De Lord move in mysterious ways His wonders to perform. Blessed be de name o'de Lord. Amen."

It was useless. Struggle as he would, in the end he had no choice but to submit. He could fight against bullying at work, against the hardships of poverty and against the injustices of God: but not even he could fight against the decree of his grandmother.

CHAPTER THREE

There was hardly another white face in sight, Isabelle soon realised, as she trudged along the baking pavement with her practice gear in a shoulder bag and *Swan Lake* playing on the state-of-the-art iPhone that'd recently arrived from her mother's personal assistant. Mum was too busy hosting diplomatic functions in Buenos Aires these days to remember more than a phone call for her birthday, but an expensive gift always appeared on time courtesy of the super-efficient Miss Pickering. Dad, being a hard-worked hospital surgeon in London, didn't have a personal assistant, so his hastily scribbled card and cheque were unlikely to turn up for weeks yet. She was used to it. (Couru right, three, four, arabesque – and run…)

With her engrained terror of arriving late to rehearsal, she'd allowed far too much time for this journey and during the long bus ride became so absorbed in studying the music for tomorrow's rehearsal that she'd lost all sense of time and place. So she ended by jumping off the bus in a panic as it swayed into what she took to be Brackwell Heath. Still careless and undisciplined, however hard she schooled herself. (One, two, *temps lié*…) This impulsive act had led to a hot hike along the seemingly endless high street, past a seedy fish and chip shop reeking of stale fat, a brash pound store plastered with gaudy sale posters, a carpet warehouse selling cheap imitation Persian rugs and a junk shop cluttered with bric-à-brac, all lying lifeless under a scorching afternoon sun. (Pirouette, two, three, hold…)

Too shy to ask directions from strangers, she paused to push back the damp wisps of hair escaping from her ponytail and consult her sketch map once more. (*Echappé, jeté* right, left, turn…) Must be down this road here past the church, which was where she actually ought to've got off the bus, and… yes, that looked like school gates, set into brick walls defaced with scrawls of lurid graffiti. NO ENTRY announced the forbidding sign in bold black letters, backed by a wire fence and thorny hedge.

Her heart sank as she caught sight of Brackwell Heath High: a collection of shabby buildings with blank, barred windows crowded onto the cramped site like a jumble of ill-assorted boxes. Of course a large inner-city comprehensive was hardly likely to resemble the purpose-built ballet school where she'd trained: a brand new, multi-million-pound complex encircled by cool lawns in the leafy heart of Kingsbridge. But it was still a shock to be confronted by this, its only embellishments a patch of tired grass strewn with wind-blown litter and two or three crippled hawthorns marooned in a burning waste of asphalt.

Skirting the boundary in search of the main entrance, she wondered where the school gym might be. Seemed no one around to ask. But as she hesitated in the driveway amid the swelling orchestral crescendo announcing Prince Siegfried's arrival on the shores of Swan Lake, she caught sight of a young black couple approaching across the expanse of sizzling tarmac, apparently engaged in a loud argument.

The girl must've been about twelve or thirteen. She was dressed in an ill-fitting polyester skirt patterned with garish crimson roses and a canary yellow cardigan with multi-coloured pompoms dangling from strings at the neck. Appliquéd onto its front was a slightly cock-eyed turquoise and orange parrot, his maroon-beaded claws grasping a brown branch ornamented with gaudy emerald leaves.

But it wasn't her clothes that drew Isabelle's gaze so much as the ungainly way in which the girl walked, with a kind of rolling gait as though on the deck of a ship heaving from side to side in the billows. Poor kid. She was clearly physically handicapped.

Isabelle wasted little attention on the girl's companion, a tall, loose-limbed youth nearer her own age, dressed in baggy black tracksuit bottoms and a shapeless navy hoodie. His trainers were old and scruffy and he slouched moodily along with a grey baseball cap pulled down low over his curled dark head as though ashamed to be seen here.

They were evidently on their way elsewhere. But they might be able to point out the gym to her. So as the graceless pair came shambling in her direction, Isabelle pulled off her earphones and darted towards them. She politely explained who she was and what she was looking for.

"This's the right place," the girl assured her with a big, beaming grin. "I've come along to have a go. I wanna be a ballerina, see."

Isabelle stared. But the girl couldn't even walk straight. How on earth was she ever going to dance?

"You got a problem with that?" demanded the tall boy, jutting out his jaw belligerently.

Isabelle recoiled. Towering above her like that, he looked terribly menacing. She shook her head.

"Umm – no, of course not," she faltered.

"You think it's no good Grace even tryin' out for this audition, don't you?" The boy clenched his fists defiantly. "You're just like all these white do-gooders: you say everyone's equal and then you turn round and treat us like dirt."

"I'm not saying anything of the sort," Isabelle protested, floundering as though in a marsh of quicksand.

But he gave no sign of even having heard her.

"What you come here for with your posh accent, all tarted up in that fancy gear, sayin' you wanna help out, if you're just gonna look down your nose at us? We're as good as you any day!"

The violence with which he spat out these words made Isabelle step back another pace and glance round apprehensively. Here she was: all alone, in a run-down part of town near Brackwell Heath Prison, face to face with this grubby-looking teenager, who clearly had a massive chip on his shoulder and was not only a lot taller than her but looked incredibly muscular as well: the sinews bulged in his neck like whipcords. What was she going to do?

Luckily at that moment a car engine roared up the drive behind her. A gleaming silver Jaguar screeched to a halt nearby and out of it stepped Roy Hillier in a business-like manner, carrying a folder of papers and a box of CDs.

Thank goodness! Someone she knew.

She started gratefully towards him.

"Hello, Isabelle. You're very prompt," he observed with a nod of approval.

"I'm so glad you found the venue without any trouble," added Alicia, who was climbing out of the passenger seat dressed in rehearsal gear, her long, chestnut hair pinned into a neat bun.

Isabelle's slithering feet at once struck solid ground. Squarely back in the civilised world she knew, she thanked Alicia for her clear directions. The two dancers went on to exchange polite remarks about the sweltering heat of the afternoon and then Alicia turned with a welcoming smile to the pair of teenagers, who'd been loitering uneasily at a distance without making any effort to introduce themselves. "And two of our young people here already. I've been so looking forward to meeting you all—"

"So where's this gym?" interrupted Roy, surveying the range of nondescript brick buildings bordering the deserted car park. "Barbara said she'd meet us there with the keys at quarter to. She's late."

"Here she comes now," Alicia soothed, turning to greet an elderly woman with short, grey hair, who came striding briskly towards them. Isabelle guessed this must be the school principal: she certainly radiated an air of purposeful authority.

Meanwhile another argument had broken out between the black teenager and the girl, who seemed to be his sister.

"Let's just get the hell outa here," Isabelle heard him exclaim in a furious undertone.

"So sorry I'm late," Barbara apologised matter-of-factly. "I've been leaving an email for the ground staff about the removal of that unsightly new graffiti outside the back gate. It's a recurrent problem in this area, I'm afraid. How're you, Roy?"

"Lemme go, Jordan, you big bully," burst out a sudden cross exclamation.

They all turned in surprise to find the girl stubbornly shaking her brother's hand off her arm.

At once Alicia stepped forward.

"Hello. What's your name?" she asked kindly.

The girl froze in open-mouthed embarrassment.

"Let me introduce Grace Howe," announced Barbara Manners, taking charge of the situation with breezy geniality. "She's a real star in our textiles department. Grace, this is Miss Page, a famous ballerina, who's come today to show you all how to dance."

"Now, Barbara," objected Alicia, "that was a very long time ago."

She smiled reassuringly at Grace, but Grace just stared at her neat, company-crested T-shirt and casual green leggings.

"How nice to meet you, Grace," went on Alicia, extending

27

a friendly hand to the girl. "That's a very striking cardigan you're wearing."

So poised and considerate, thought Isabelle, wincing at the contrast with her own earlier clumsiness.

But the girl still gaped back at her as though quite overwhelmed.

"What's the matter, Grace?" asked Barbara brusquely.

Grace turned to her head teacher in dismay. "That lady's not a ballerina, Mizz Manners. She ain't wearin' a fluffy pink dress and a shiny gold crown."

Barbara Manners looked puzzled for a moment and then burst out laughing.

"Grace, you silly! Don't you know that ballerinas only wear tutus and gold crowns on stage? In normal life they dress just like everyone else."

"Come on, Grace," urged her brother with a furious scowl. "I told you they'd just make fun of you. Let's split."

"Jordan?" The headmistress turned towards him questioningly. "Is that you hiding under that baseball cap? What a surprise to see you back at school. Have you come to mentor Grace?"

The tall black youth shrugged, fists plunged deep in his tracksuit pockets.

"Didn't have no choice," Isabelle heard him mutter, scuffing the toe of one grubby trainer against the concrete steps. "She was set on comin', Miss, even though I told her it was a stupid idea."

"Not 'Miss', Jordan," she reprimanded firmly. "How many times do I have to tell you to say 'Mrs Manners'?"

"Yes, Mizz Manners," he replied, bowing his lofty head like a scolded schoolboy.

"That's better. Now how're you getting on in that job of yours? Let me see, it was a garage workshop you finally went into, wasn't it?"

"Yes, Miss – Mizz Manners."

Isabelle turned away: she wasn't interested in anything that surly lout had to say.

On the other side of her, Alicia Page was making an effort to compensate for her lack of glamour in the eyes of his disillusioned sister.

"I'm so sorry, Grace, that I don't look quite as you expected. It's just that a tutu isn't very comfortable to drive around in and it's a bit impractical when you are going to take class. You can see that, can't you?"

Grace gazed straight into her eyes.

"Yes, Mizz Page," she gulped and then hesitated.

"What is it, Grace?" prompted Alicia.

"Well, I was just wonderin' if you still had your fluffy dresses at home."

"I did keep some of my old costumes after they grew too shabby to dance in any more, but mostly my daughter wore them as dressing up clothes when she was little."

"Oh, you got a little girl then?" asked Grace, her face brightening.

"Well, Emma's grown up and married now, with babies of her own. But mainly, you see, costumes belong to the companies I've danced with, because they take the wardrobe mistresses hours and hours to make. Sewing together all those layers of tulle, and hand-stitching on beads and sequins…"

"Oh I know all about that," interrupted Grace, proudly indicating the gaudy parrot on her cardigan. "I made this myself. An' I helped the ladies' circle sew loads of big banners for our church too. You should see 'em, Miss. There're loaves and fishes with green sequins for scales and sheaves of yellow silk corn and the sea with blue satin waves. An' I stitched heaps and heaps of little, sparkly glass beads onto the red poppies. They look really pretty when the sun shines through the big windows on 'em—"

"Are you coming, Allie?" broke in Roy, back from investigating the gym.

"In a minute," Alicia called after him, returning to Grace, who'd suddenly shrunk into herself like a snail at the touch of a careless fingertip. "Those banners sound most impressive. Are you coming inside, Grace?"

But Grace, so brimming with enthusiasm before, now hung back uneasily.

"I ain't sure I'll be any good at ballet dancin'," she confided to Alicia in a low whisper. "You see, I ain't so good even at walkin'. Everyone calls me handicapped because I got cer- cerberal palsy when I was a little baby."

"Don't worry, Grace," Alicia reassured her firmly. "You know, we have people with much worse impairments than yours – in wheelchairs and without any legs at all – taking part in our Airborne Dance Project."

"Yes – and you see that man over there?" urged Isabelle, pointing out Cameron Davies, a company soloist of Afro- Caribbean extraction, who was just heading in through the gym door with a rucksack on his broad shoulders.

"The one in the red-spotted head scarf?" asked Grace.

"Yes."

Grace nodded doubtfully.

"Well, he'd be a good person to talk to, because he does lots of work with Airborne."

Grace regarded her with a wavering smile.

"And perhaps one day," added Alicia quickly, "if your parents agree, that is, you could come into our company offices in town and I'll take you to meet the wardrobe mistress. Sandra's always delighted to show young people the costumes she's making."

"You mean, I could actually see someone sewing one of those fluffy pink – what d'you call them again?"

"Tutus?"

"Yeah – tutus," proudly pronouncing the strange word.

"Of course. You'd just love Wardrobe – it's packed with off-cuts of all different kinds of material and paper patterns and reels of brightly-coloured thread and little drawers stuffed with boxes of hooks and tiny glass beads…"

Grace's face lit up in anticipation.

"Do you really mean it?" she breathed.

Alicia nodded. "Of course I really mean it. But now I've got to start work. Are you coming too, Grace?" and Isabelle watched her extend her hand to the girl.

Grace, who was positively beaming at her new idol, at once reached out to grasp it. But her brother, who'd kept half an ear on their conversation while being interrogated by his old headmistress, dragged her roughly back. "Come on, Grace. You don't belong here. Let's go home. We should never've come in the first place."

But Grace shook him off determinedly. She stood gazing after Alicia, who'd clearly decided it was more tactful to leave them to their family conference and was now standing at the gym doors welcoming another group of denim-clad, gum-chewing girls with an extensive array of tattoos and body piercings.

"I'm goin' in too," asserted Grace. "Didn't you hear what Mizz Page said? About the Airborne people, who do it in wheelchairs."

"Do what in wheelchairs?" cried her bewildered brother.

"Dance of course."

"Grace, she's just havin' you on. Nobody dances in wheelchairs. It's impossible."

"That's all you know, ain't it? And she's gonna take me to see the wardrobe lady, who's got little drawers stuffed with boxes of hooks and tiny glass beads for sewing on tutus."

"Look, she's just saying that. Posh folk do it all the time. Make big promises and then nothin' ever happens. She's prob'ly forgot about it already."

31

"No. She's a nice, kind lady and I don't believe you."

"Grace—"

But it was too late. Grace had already started off in the direction of the open doors, where there was now a noisy crowd of people of all ages pushing and shoving their way into the gym.

Jordan swore loudly and finally stamped after her in fury, leaving Isabelle glowing with satisfaction at seeing him totally out-manoeuvred by his feisty little sister.

"It's a pity he comes from such a disadvantaged background," Barbara Manners commented, as she herded stragglers towards the gym doors with a capability born of long experience. "He has an excellent sense of spatial awareness and got a good A in GCSE Maths. I maintain he could've made something of himself if only he'd had the chance. I tried to talk his grandmother into letting him stay on to the sixth form, but she said there wasn't the money to pay for his clothes and then rambled on about how the Lord helps those who help themselves. There's no way you can argue logically with these religious fundamentalists, you understand. I'm sorry for the lad. He's totally wasted as a mechanic…"

Isabelle listened courteously, but she didn't believe this for one minute. He was a thoroughly mannerless, bad-tempered thug and no one'd ever convince her otherwise.

CHAPTER FOUR

Jordan snorted with laughter behind his hand as he leaned up against the wall bars near the door of the gym. What a bloody shambles! Served 'em right, those stuck-up ballet folk.

The grey-haired old bugger in glasses, who'd been shouting orders and clearly expecting the whole class to jump in instant obedience, stood at the hub of a whirlwind. He was arguing like mad with Dillon Bates, who'd been complaining loudly about the rubbish music, fancying himself an expert just because he'd written a few cruddy numbers for an amateur band. At the same time a violent dispute was raging over the point-blank refusal of hot-headed Ash Kent and Sudhir Patel, the aggressive little runt who led the Asian gang, to stand next to each other in line. Jordan could've told him that'd never work. They hated each other's guts so much that in junior school the staff'd had to put them in separate classes to stop fist fights breaking out in lessons.

Mizz Page was trying to reason with them, but they were quarrelling too furiously to listen. And Grace'd worked herself into a terrific strop because everyone was making so much noise that she and her girlfriend, Ruth, couldn't hear the music and follow the steps the dancer in the white and red-spotted headscarf was trying to demonstrate. Nicole Price'd given up altogether and was sprawled over the floor in a mass of sweaty blubber, gasping for breath.

Around the edges of the gym, stony-faced friends and relatives, who'd been lounging about boredly fanning away the heat with newspapers, suddenly jolted upright in their seats. Bickering had even broken out among several indignant women, centred upon Sudhir's mother, a small, fiery Asian lady in a mauve sari, who was rarely seen out from behind the counter of the family corner shop.

Terrified by the din, Lauren's eighteen-month-old toddler, Zack, burst out screaming right in Jordan's ear. Her colossal Auntie Zoe was having no luck at soothing him, so Lauren whisked over and began jogging the curly blond toddler up and down on one hip in a business-like manner as she remarked to her cousin, Hayley, "Wouldn't be caught dead wearin' black an' white stripes if I were her. Makes her look like a racoon."

Her catty comment was pitched loudly enough to be overheard by its intended victim, Simran, one of the slender Asian girls gathered around the stuck-up, red-haired dancer, whom Jordan had met earlier. He realised it'd hit its mark from the glare of loathing Simran shot in their direction.

"And've you ever seen anythin' like the leotard that posh ballet girl's got on?" went on fashion-conscious Hayley, tossing her bright pink fringe.

"You'd think if you were as flat-chested as that, you'd buy yourself a padded bra, wouldn't you?" observed Lauren, who was very well-endowed, stuffing Zack's dummy in his mouth.

"Thin as a stick, ain't she?"

"Apparently they've all got eating disorders, them ballet dancers, you know. Always sicking up in the toilets…"

And the pair of them sniggered together behind their hands.

Jordan saw the stuck-up red-head flush and quickly turn aside – which gave him huge satisfaction after the way she'd gazed down her long, thin nose at him earlier on and stared at Grace as though she was retarded.

Meanwhile Eugene'd taken advantage of the chaos to swarm up the wall bars and was showing off his agility in front of a cluster of admiring girls by swinging from the hanging ropes – to the concern of a wiry, sandy-haired Scotsman, who was vainly trying to persuade him down. Jordan gathered this must be Murray Bennet, the tutor from Airborne, who was reputed to teach people to dance in wheelchairs. He certainly didn't seem to be having much luck with the able-bodied, to judge by the pushing and shoving going on among big Jermaine, Jordan's best mate, Oz, and a handful of the Asians in the back row, while the tall dancer with broad shoulders and a funny accent, and the Japanese midget stood gazing on in helpless disbelief.

And then, just when things could hardly get any worse, a loud, tinny chorus of *All You Need is Love* suddenly trilled out through the gym. Ash's ringtone. As far as the grey-haired old guy was concerned, this was the final straw. His face turned bright purple and he visibly swelled with fury...

★

Half an hour later, four depressed dancers huddled round a small, green metal table in the crowded back courtyard of Caribbean Joe's, the first café they'd spotted as they stumbled out of the school gates in a daze of thirst and exhaustion when class was over. The late afternoon sun beat down out of a cloudless, blue September sky and the heat and din of conversation were stifling beneath the faded canvas awning stretched overhead. Faintly tinkling tin foil streamers and lines of coloured flags drooped listlessly, strung from side to side of the flaking brick walls in an effort to infuse a carnival atmosphere into the tiny open-air terrace. Even the gaudy advertising posters hung buckled and disconsolate on the smeared glass doors. But Isabelle was too disheartened to care.

What she'd just been through was a world away from cross-stitching ballerinas on greeting cards and charming wealthy old ladies into buying raffle tickets at the Christmas bazaar.

"Zis scheme vill never verk," prophesied Boris, a Russian of few but weighty words, as he folded his arms over his broad chest and shook his head gloomily.

"No," agreed the Japanese dancer, Masakuni, with a sigh of dejection. "They will never bother to invest the time and industry necessary to achieve success. We should not waste more valuable time."

"I can't understand what's up with these guys," moaned Cameron, pulling off his red-spotted headscarf. He tossed it onto the table top, where it lay limp and stained with sweat, and ran frustrated fingers through the dark, damp stubble of his hair, his shoulders bowed with fatigue. "It's like we were talking to a brick wall or something."

"I've never seen such blank faces and angry eyes," murmured Isabelle, shivering at her recollection of that long and terrible afternoon. She hated arguments. Harsh words. Slamming doors. Memories of her parents' bitter quarrels before they were finally separated and divorced. With a trembling hand she mechanically stirred the straw in the tall glass of iced tropical fruit juice in front of her, feeling utterly drained. A dull ache pulsed behind her eyes.

"Here you are at last," exclaimed an elated voice. "Thought I was never going to find you."

All four dancers turned a disgruntled stare upon the speaker, who paused briefly in the doorway before making his entrance. One glimpse of Alex's handsome features and lithe, slim-waisted figure and the group of bored teenage girls gossiping at a nearby table instantly rearranged their legs and skirts with a flurry of excited whispers. His arrival in a crisp, white, open-necked shirt and spotless beige chinos felt like a cool breeze wafting over a sun-baked desert.

As soon as she set eyes on him, Isabelle's wilting spirits began to revive.

"Alex," she called out, "you've come."

"Yes, well I would've been here earlier if this place hadn't taken so long to find," he grumbled, borrowing a chair from the next-door table with a smile that set several hearts and rows of eyelashes aflutter.

Isabelle deliberately looked away as she shifted her own seat to make room. She and Alex had only been going out since last week and she was just starting to realise that this sort of thing was likely to happen wherever they went.

Alex seemed not to notice. Sweeping a dubious glance over the basket of plastic peppers and dusty artificial sunflowers on the ramshackle sideboard nearby, he remarked in an undertone, "Some classy joint."

"It's all there is around here," Isabelle pointed out. How odd he hadn't realised it himself. "But their iced juices're delicious."

Alex ordered a passion fruit and custard apple crush from the attentive waitress and, adroitly avoiding the neighbours' toes, slid into the cramped space between Isabelle and Masakuni.

"So how'd it all go?" he asked brightly. Then, taking in the assembly of glum faces, "That good, eh?"

"It was absolutely awful," Isabelle confessed in a low voice. "I couldn't wait to get away."

"That class seemed to last a century and it's still only half past four now," added Masakuni, glancing at his mobile.

"I'm sure something was wrong with that gym clock too," put in Isabelle, who noticed such details.

"If I must go back zere again, I vill kill myself," announced Boris and plunged his mop of silky dark hair pessimistically into his big hands.

"Come on, man – it's not that bad," encouraged Cameron,

clapping him round the shoulders. "After all, it was only the first session."

Boris raised his head.

"Maybe also last for me. I show zem how to stand up tall and proud – and zey make silly jokes and laugh. At me. I feel big hurt inside," and Boris struck his breast in a dramatic gesture of despair.

"Look, they're just kids," reasoned Cameron who, at twenty-six, had five years more experience than the Russian dancer. "I've worked with Airborne. When teenagers like that're unsure of themselves, they cover it up by laughing and joking and acting cool. I remember doing it myself."

"But they didn't like what we were showing them at all," pointed out Isabelle. "I thought they'd be really keen to have a go, but they just stood there pulling faces at the music – and talking! Imagine daring to *talk* in one of Roy Hillier's classes. And when that mobile rang, I thought he was going to go through the roof."

She bit her lip at the memory of Roy angrily confronting a shaven-headed dare-devil called Ash with a nose-stud and a skull and crossbones emblazoned on the back of his tattered leather waistcoat. If her mobile'd rung during class, she would've sunk through the floor in mortification, but the boy just pulled his out unabashed and took the call – right under Roy's nose.

Masakuni screwed up his mournful black eyes, usually so lively and full of mischief. "These young people do not understand how to show respect for their distinguished teacher. The small payment he is receiving for this project cannot compensate for the great insult to his dignity."

"And there wasn't even anywhere decent to get dressed," added Isabelle, recalling the dank odour of the changing facilities with their dripping shower heads and dented lockers. So much so that after class she'd crept away, without the heart to do more than throw a T-shirt back on over her sweaty practice gear and was now feeling uncomfortably itchy as a result.

"Can't say I didn't warn you," commented Alex who, like Mei, had felt too committed already to take part in the scheme. "It's all very well to have high ideals and good intentions. But these're just street kids after all. They've never been exposed to classical music, or any form of dancing that isn't just jigging up and down at a club…"

"Now you hold it right there, Alex," objected Cameron, suddenly raising his head. "What about that white guy, Ash, who taught himself break-dancing from old CDs? Or Dill, who told me he'd been rapping since the age of thirteen?"

Alex raised one graceful eyebrow. "Cameron, we're talking about art here, not mere street culture."

"But that's art too. Just a different kind of art."

"Yes, well I'm sure it's very significant in its way. But it's not the sort of thing people like us should be worrying about."

Isabelle's eyes widened: she'd never heard Alex talk like this before.

"What d'you mean: 'people like us'?" demanded Cameron, leaning forward. "Who should be worrying about it if not 'people like us'?"

"Because we're *professional* dancers. Our primary concern should be our own careers. It's blindingly obvious."

CRASH! Cameron brought the palms of both hands down on the table top so hard that Isabelle jumped.

"Well it's not 'blindingly obvious' to me," he retorted with blazing eyes. "Hey, man, these people are *my* people. You may come from some posh, white, upper-middle-class boarding school. But before I got taken onto the London Dance Start programme, I was living among kids like these. I know where they're coming from. You're nothing but a smug, self-satisfied pretty boy, shooting off your mouth like the ignorant prick you are. I'm getting the hell outa here!"

And he thrust back his chair and stormed off.

Boris and Masakuni exchanged glances as they watched him burst out through the side gate.

"I think we'd better go after him," announced Masakuni diplomatically, picking up his friend's abandoned headscarf. "Come on, Boris."

They both rose. Slinging their bags over their shoulders, they hastily said goodbye and disappeared in his wake.

Isabelle was left staring at Alex over a table top scattered with discarded drinking glasses and moisture-beaded water bottles. She might've only been dancing with the company for a few weeks, but one thing she'd learned was how hard they all tried to pull together. Now even Alex and Cameron were fighting with each other. The tears prickled behind her eyes…

At this point the young waitress wiggled her way over with the passion fruit and custard apple crush. But all her efforts raised only an absent glimmer of a smile from Alex. He picked up the glass and, leaning back in his seat, took a long pull on the blue-and-white-striped straw, before muttering in indignation, "I was just trying to be practical. What's eating Cameron anyway? Firing up like this project was a matter of life or death."

"I think – to him – it is," pointed out Isabelle gently. Alex was charming, witty and thoughtful, but perhaps just the tiniest bit insensitive to other people's feelings. "To be fair, I think we're all feeling a bit depressed and irritable after a long, hot afternoon."

Alex shot her a quick glance and leaned forward in his seat.

"Look, Bella, I didn't come here to fight over a bunch of street kids," he said, setting down his glass. "I came here to pick you up – your voice sounded so tired on the phone. I told you this project would wear you out. Why don't you just forget all about it? This afternoon sounds to've been a total fiasco, so hopefully Roy'll realise he's made a big mistake and call it all off. Now, shall we head to Ed's barbecue? Or would you prefer a film instead?"

He was trying to be kind. But she couldn't forget the events of that terrible class so easily. She sat still and silent.

"Now come on, Bella, you're not going to take this too much to heart, are you?" he coaxed, sweeping aside a bottle and his half-empty glass so he could reach out one hand to clasp hers.

A familiar tingle shot through her at his touch.

"Alex," she began, suddenly recalling the sole bright spot in this tangle of disagreements. "There was one girl who I think really wanted to be there. She looked about twelve – and her name's Grace. She was the only one who listened to the music and tried hard to follow the steps Roy was demonstrating."

"You've made one convert then," encouraged Alex with a smile and a gentle pressure on her fingers.

"Yes. But… Grace has cerebral palsy. She can't even walk properly, let alone dance." And Isabelle dropped her throbbing forehead onto her up-turned palm.

Alex softly stroked her other hand.

"You've got a headache, haven't you?" he asked.

Isabelle nodded.

There was a pause and then he observed, "Bella, you're too soft-hearted. No one can take all the troubles of the world on their shoulders. You've got your life to live and they've got theirs and tearing yourself into tatters isn't going to make a blind bit of difference. After all, you're not a social worker: you're a trainee in a professional ballet company and you've got your own future to worry about. Now, aren't you going to give me a tiny smile? I really missed you this afternoon."

And he stooped his head and peered up at her with a funny, little-boy-lost look on his face.

"But…" Isabelle averted her eyes.

Alex placed a warning finger on her lips. "No more of

41

that now. Come on," he added, rising to his feet. "There'll be crowds of people at Ed's and it's too hot to shut ourselves up in an airless cinema. How about a quiet stroll along the shady river bank in Bellevue Park? Then we can pick up a pizza on the way back to my place…"

How could she resist? After all, she was the luckiest girl in the world to be going out with Alex. The rest of the corps de ballet were wild with envy because he was the handsomest man in the company and already a soloist at the age of twenty. Why repay his kindness in coming here specially to fetch her with gloom and depression? He was right in a way: you could easily get so caught up in other people's lives that you forgot to live your own.

Raising her eyes, she surveyed him as he stood holding out his hand to her in the dingy courtyard, now forsaken by the September sunshine. Pain and weariness forgotten, she jumped up, the corners of her mouth curving in response to his smile. She slipped her hand into his and they laughed out loud together for no reason except that they were both young and in love.

Alex stood back for her to leave the café ahead of him and she was just giggling over some silly joke he'd made, clinging onto his arm with one hand and swinging her practice bag in the other, when she almost walked bang into a tall black youth, striding along the pavement without a glance left or right under his grey baseball cap.

"Hey! Look where you're going," called out Alex, as the youth barged past without even apologising.

The youth whirled round and Isabelle suddenly realised who he was: the scowling thug who'd brought his sister, Grace, to the dance session earlier that afternoon. From his baleful glare, it was clear he'd recognised her too. She shrank back against Alex.

Why did he hate her so much?

After another second's shocked pause, Alex pulled her quickly away.

CHAPTER FIVE

Rage swelled inside Jordan as he realised that skinny, milk-faced, posh-voiced dancing girl was happy. How dare she be happy when his life was such hell? Just to lash out and smash his fist straight through the face of her pretty blond boyfriend – one glance was enough to tell him this was the relationship between them – to shatter his graceful, blue-eyed beauty in an explosion of mindless loathing…

For a few moments he stalked along the street, picturing himself as some supernatural demon of revenge, wrapped in fiery flames, committing horrors to pay back that green-eyed witch for the insult of her joyous smile…

And then he remembered who he was. Nobody. Nothing. Didn't even have the guts to skip his Sunday evening shift, let alone commit horrors. He slunk off in defeat and self-contempt to work.

Lounging around in the quiet office of the Arts Centre gave him plenty of time to think. He sat staring down at his hands as if seeing them for the first time, studying the traces of oil and grease that stained the network of tiny creases in his palms. It sent him sidling shamefacedly off to the bathroom to scrub them, haunted by the dancer's fleeting glance of distaste earlier that afternoon.

Rich kids like that probably couldn't even begin to understand the misery he suffered every day of his life at that bloody garage. What did dancers know about hard work? A load o'stuck-up wankers, who thought they could just waft in with some CDs of boring music and change lives by telling you to stand straight and flap your arms up and down.

Apart from Mizz Page. She was the one exception – he had to admit it – among the whole stinking pack of them, because she'd been so kind to Grace. Felt sorry now that he'd ever accused her, even in his mind, of making promises she didn't mean to keep.

The dance session'd broken up in disorder with that grey-haired old bugger bawling his head off and Dill and Ash just shrugging their shoulders and telling him where to go, then laughing and swaggering out, swearing that no fucking old pervert was gonna tell them to hold hands with those shit-eating Asian bastards.

But when the rest of the crowd had drifted away, gleefully discussing the outburst of fighting and all airing their personal opinions about the rights and wrongs of everyone else's actions, Grace stubbornly refused to budge.

"Look, Grace, I'm goin' home," Jordan finally shouted. "You can stay here if you like, but I gotta go to bloody work."

Mizz Page, who was involved in a heated discussion with several people including the grey-haired old bugger and Jordan's ex-headmistress, suddenly turned and caught sight of him battling with Grace. She at once came over to them. Jordan braced himself for a scene, but there appeared no trace of anger in her calm face.

"Is something wrong, Grace?" she'd asked in that low, quiet voice of hers.

She actually remembered his sister's name.

Grace was too overwrought to speak. So he stepped in to handle the situation.

"She won't come home, Miss," he explained.

Turning to his sister, Mizz Page asked kindly, "Why don't you want to go home, Grace?"

"'Cos I was havin' such a good time," burst out Grace. "I love dancing."

Mizz Page smiled. "So do I. It's better than anything else in the world, isn't it?"

"I wanna go on dancin' forever and ever," insisted Grace.

Mizz Page thought for a moment. "Look, Grace, I'm afraid we're all a bit tired now and probably your mum's expecting you home for tea—"

"Oh I haven't got a mum," declared Grace before Jordan could stop her. "At least I have, I think, but she ain't at home and she never 'spects me back for tea."

Why did Grace have to blurt out things like that?

"We live with our grandparents," explained Jordan hastily. Didn't want Mizz Page thinking they were no better than homeless street kids.

"Can I come back next week?" demanded Grace.

"I'm not sure about next week yet," with a swift glance at the grey-haired old bugger, who was now striding off out the door with a face as dark as a stormcloud. "But I haven't forgotten that I asked you earlier on if you'd like to visit the dance studios in town to see our wardrobe mistress. Do you think you'd be able to come one day after school…?"

★

After work the following Wednesday afternoon, Jordan found himself slouching reluctantly up Temple Street behind an excited Grace. On either side rose the high red-brick walls of grim old warehouses and disused workshops, but after a few minutes they passed a fancy theatre restaurant and at last reached the glass doors that Alicia Page had described to him on the phone. These slid magically open in front of them and a moment later they found themselves inside what looked like a business office, full of filing cabinets and potted plants.

What a let-down. He'd expected something a lot more glamorous. But check out that poster on the wall behind the reception desk of a tough gang of spiky-haired bikers in black leather bristling with silver studs. Those guys wouldn't look too out of place at a Saturday night gig in Dillon's garage. What'd they have to do with ballet dancing?

"Mediaeval barons from a recent production of *Henry II*," said the golden-curled receptionist on the other side of the desk, noticing the direction of his gaze. "Ballet's not just about men in tights, you know." She nodded brightly when she heard why they were there. "Oh yes, Miss Page is rehearsing at the moment…"

Of course. Forgotten all about them.

"… She had to fill in for a colleague at short notice, but she'll be finished in a few minutes. She said you might wait for her here in the foyer – or, if you liked and were very quiet, I could show you upstairs to the studio where they're working and you could take a peek at the dancing."

"Yes please," Grace instantly agreed.

The smiling receptionist led them through the rear door and all the way up a bare white staircase, lit by tall side windows looking out over the street. At first only the tramp of their footsteps echoed in the empty stairwell, but as they neared the top, they began to hear the distant tinkle of piano music.

"There you are," whispered the receptionist, holding the fire door open for them. "In you go. But, mind, not a word or you'll disturb their concentration."

Grace stumbled inside as quietly as she could, catching her breath in awe as she gazed around the great, high-ceilinged studio with two walls of mirrors and one of wide glass windows. It was entirely bare except for a few red plastic chairs and an upright piano in one corner.

"Oh," she exclaimed.

"Shhh!" Jordan instantly hushed her. "Siddown on that chair over there." And he steered her into a nearby corner.

Grace sank onto the seat without another word and stared with all her might, while Jordan leaned up against the door post with crossed arms, bored – and irritated too – by that feeble, jingly music. Even the rubbish stuff they'd played in class last Sunday afternoon was better than this.

At first he made up his mind to ignore the dancing altogether and gazed fixedly out of the window at the grey slate roof of the building opposite. But it was hard to stand for any length of time in a room lined with mirrors without accidentally catching sight of the moving figure out of a corner of one eye. He started. Hey! He recognised this dancer. It was that mixed race guy with the red-spotted headscarf that he remembered from the gym on Sunday afternoon. And look at the skimpy gear he had on. Nothing but a damp white vest and skin-tight black leggings. Seemed as though he'd been at whatever he was doing for a while too. He was sweating like a pig as he spun and twisted this way and that. Made you feel dizzy just watching him.

Mizz Page, kitted out today in a neat navy tracksuit, hovered around the dancer, waving her arms and shouting instructions like an athletics coach on a training field. Wow, she might be short but, man, was she bossy! Whatever the guy did, she was never happy. How could he stand having some smart-arse woman ordering him around like that? Wouldn't've put up with it himself…

Mind you, that routine was pretty ace when you studied it more closely: a kind of swift spin, followed by a high leap into the air and then a series of whirling turns around the room, a couple of jumps up and down on the spot with rapid footbeats in the air and finally a drop to the ground with a grand flourish. Ouch! Friggin' tough on the kneecaps.

But Mizz Page made the dancer repeat this routine half a dozen more times without a break and even then she still didn't seem happy. What a slave driver she was. You couldn't help feeling sorry for the poor sod. His chest was heaving as he gasped for breath, sweat glistening on his forehead and pouring down his neck.

Finally they agreed to give it up as a bad job.

No bloody wonder. The guy's vest was absolutely drenched and he was puffing and snorting like a wounded bull. Jordan's eyes followed him sympathetically as he staggered over to grab a towel from the wooden rail running all the way round the studio mirrors. But just as he was about to leave the room, the dancer noticed Jordan and Grace. He lifted up his hand and waved. Just like that. As though he recognised them. Jordan automatically nodded back. Well, you couldn't ignore the poor sucker, could you?

Mizz Page crossed over to exchange a few words with the pianist as he was gathering his music together and then she caught sight of Grace, who'd risen from her chair, looking both entranced and overwhelmed by her unfamiliar surroundings.

Jordan didn't plan to look either entranced or overwhelmed. True, there was clearly a bit more to this prancing around on your toes than he'd first suspected, but that was no reason to surrender unconditionally to the enemy, like Grace. He pulled his baseball cap further down over his eyes and lounged along behind the other two, as Mizz Page led them back down the staircase and along a maze of twisting white passages to what she called Wardrobe.

This was a big room, crammed full of sewing equipment: shelves laden with bolts of shiny cloth, tailor's dummies, ironing boards and, in the centre, a large table littered with gauze netting, paper patterns, scissors and pins. Grace uttered shrill squeaks of delight when invited to poke around in the baskets of coloured ribbons and boxes of glittering beads – but Jordan couldn't block out the vision of the figure he'd just seen whirling and spinning around the studio upstairs.

He went over and over the steps in his mind, one after another, just the way he'd seen them endlessly repeated: the swift spin, followed by the high leap into the air, the series of whirling turns, then the jumps with the footbeats and the sudden drop onto the knees. The sequence of steps hammered on his brain. Didn't look that hard really. Bet he could make a pretty good stab at it himself, given the space…

No one was paying any attention to him. They were all exclaiming together over boring, girly stuff. So no one noticed him slip silently out of the room. He threaded his way unhesitatingly back along the honeycomb of winding corridors to the white staircase and began to climb, like someone in a dream. He had this weird feeling of being invisible to the rest of the world, as though a power outside himself was pulling him towards the top of those steps.

A glance in through the round glass portholes in the studio door showed him the great room lying deserted. He slid inside with a fast-beating heart and looked round warily. No one else was there.

Alicia had turned off the studio lights, but the vast, empty space shone with a soft evening glow that made it seem even more inviting than before. The grey vinyl floor was scuffed and worn with use. Jordan sat down on it and pulled off his trainers and socks. Somehow, he needed to feel that floor beneath his bare soles, as though that way he could make contact with the steps that'd just dazzled his gaze.

He started to walk over the floor: it felt cool and slightly springy beneath his feet. He was eyeing his reflection in the mirrors ahead and suddenly saw himself stretch out his arms on either side and spin round, the way he'd watched that guy do earlier. It felt good – much better even than jigging up and down in a crush of hot bodies in Dillon's garage. He kept on whirling round and round.

He could do this. Wasn't so hard after all. And if he could

do this, then he reckoned he could manage the next move as well: that leap into the air.

He braced his muscles and had a go. But he made the mistake of twisting round, trying to catch sight of himself in the mirrors to check if he was doing it right, and this threw him off balance. He skidded across the floor and landed in a clumsy heap. His baseball cap'd fallen off, but he was too busy to bother about that now.

Smarting more from hurt pride than physical pain, he quickly scrambled up again and shook himself. At least no one'd been there to see that stupid tumble. He'd stop now, before anyone heard a noise and came in to investigate...

But then he'd never have the chance again to spin free in this beautiful, wide, grey space – never, ever again. He had to see what he could do now, because for him there was no later.

He ran to the corner of the room, as he'd seen that other dancer do, and launched himself into the air, thrusting his arms forward to help lift himself off the ground. WHOOSH! WHAM!

He picked himself up off the floor again, feeling slightly dazed and bruised, but damned if he'd let that stop him. He was gonna master this step if it killed him.

He ran back and hurled himself into the leap again and again, until he was satisfied he'd more or less got it right, and then he had a go at some of those whirling circular turns. The key to success here seemed to be something to do with whipping your arms around so fast that it stopped you toppling over backwards. The action seemed simple enough, but it certainly had him stumped. He tried several times, but he still kept on sprawling flat on his backside. Clearly wasn't as easy as it looked. But he wasn't gonna be beaten.

He picked himself up again – and out of the corner of his eye he caught sight of a figure in the mirror: the old guy with grey hair and glasses, who'd tried to take that class in the gym last Sunday afternoon. Standing quietly in the doorway watching, with his arms crossed over his chest and a thin smile on his lips.

Jordan checked himself in mid-whirl and jolted to a standstill, chest heaving and sweat prickling in his armpits, as he stared back at the intruder. Their gazes crossed like drawn swords in the tense silence. Oh God! He was about to be thrown out on his butt for being up here without permission.

The light glinted on the old guy's glasses as he nodded his head, but all he said, in a dry voice like the rustle of dead leaves, was, "You need to pull up, boy, and straighten your back and shoulders. But if you aren't careful, you'll tear a muscle. Don't you think you ought to learn how to do a warm-up before you start having a go at barrel turns?"

Was he crazy?

In one wild swoop of panic, Jordan snatched up his cap, socks and trainers and dashed headlong out of the studio.

CHAPTER SIX

J ordan stared at the hands of the steadily ticking carriage
clock in the centre of the living room mantelpiece.

It was twenty past one the following Sunday afternoon
and after a big roast chicken lunch, Gran was ceremonially
drinking tea with Pastor Lance Sheldon of the Brackwell Heath
Full Gospel Church and his earnest, community-spirited
wife, Ada. Grandad drooped, sad and silent as ever, in his
armchair beside the window, while Darleen, washed, brushed
and unnaturally tidy in her best churchgoing dress and short
white socks and shoes, perched beside Grace on the worn sofa,
wriggling with boredom whenever Gran looked away.

With his family's attention fully focussed on the problem
of choosing a new project for the church sewing circle, Jordan
felt the time had come to make his move. He'd sat on the
hard wooden chair near the door on purpose, so now he rose
stealthily to his feet and started sidling out of the room.

"Where you goin'?" Grace's suspicious voice arrested him.

She have eyes in the back of her head or something?

"Out," he mumbled, making a sudden break for freedom.

Foiled. Dion blocked the doorway, trailing back from a
visit to the bathroom with his shirt hanging untidily out of his
elastic waistband. Jordan couldn't barge past and knock him
flying, so he skidded to an abrupt halt.

"It's nearly time to go." Grace swivelled round, fixing him
with her eye. She'd thought and talked of nothing else but

dancing all week long and had been counting down the hours till half past one today.

"Go where?" asked Jordan innocently. He manoeuvred to one side of Dion, still hoping to escape.

"You know."

Dion had shuffled the same way. Gridlock.

"I ain't goin' near that gym again," Jordan announced, driven to open defiance. "An' no one's gonna make me."

When he thought how he'd been caught out doing ballet by that old guy, he felt hot and cold all over. No way was he gonna to risk turning into a fairy!

"You will too," retorted Grace, stumbling to her feet. "You'll stay here while I go an' get changed."

"Got better things to do with my time."

"Gran," Grace urgently appealed to higher authority, "I promised Mizz Page I'd be there today."

Their grandmother rolled her eyes ceilingwards.

"Jordan, how often hab I tole you dat a promise is a promise?" She glanced towards Pastor Sheldon for support.

"What's all this?" the pastor intervened in his genial, Sunday-after-lunch voice. He was a large, bald man in a dark suit and white-spotted tie with a grey beard fringing his fleshy jowls.

"It's my ballet class this afternoon," explained Grace with calculated pathos. "How can I get good at it unless Jordan takes me?"

Pastor Sheldon set down Gran's best china teacup and beamed at Jordan with a glint of anticipation in his eye. The old goat never missed the chance of an improving lesson for members of his flock whom he suspected of straying.

"Dear boy," he began, rubbing his fat hands with a large, white handkerchief, "as sister Angelica rightly points out, you are bound to respect the sanctity of your word. Think how the Lord will rejoice when you open your heart to him tonight in prayer, knowing that you have conquered the temptation of selfishness and helped your young sister to gain exercise that is not just physically health-giving, but also spiritually beneficial—"

"But…" protested Jordan, feeling himself being swallowed in the relentless maw of Christian morality, like Jonah by the whale.

" – Oh Lord, I ask You to look down upon this wayward sinner," boomed the pastor, raising his hands to heaven, assured of a direct hotline to the Almighty. "Cleanse his youthful heart of all evil and fill him with the blessings of Your infinite grace and wisdom…"

It was a relief to escape the house – even with Grace in tow.

★

Shortly after half past one he once again found himself being bullied up the road by Grace, in a stew of anxiety.

"Mister Hillier said we gotta be on time," she urged. "Lesson's startin' at two o'clock sharp."

"Well, I'll just drop you off at the gate then," muttered Jordan, struggling to ease his conscience.

"No – you gotta come in," asserted Grace. "Mizz Manners said. Otherwise I can't dance. You're my mentor."

"Your what?"

"My mentor. Mizz Manners and Mizz Scott explained it all to me."

"Who's Mizz Scott?" Jordan had never heard this name before.

"She's a new teacher at school this year, who looks like a sixth former, and she's our life coach. A mentor's what she calls the person who's agreed to help us turn up on time and do our best to achieve the goals we set ourselves each week. Ruth's mum's bein' her mentor and you're bein' mine."

"I never said I'd do that," objected Jordan. No way was he gonna be bracketed with old people like Grace's best friend's mother! "Besides, you don't need help to turn up on time. We got to school so flippin' early last week, we had to stand round for ages waitin' till Mizz Manners finally showed up. I'm sick of wastin' my whole Sunday afternoon like this. I'm not comin' in."

"We'll just see about that," declared Grace with an expression that made him blench. Sometimes she looked just like their grandmother.

Still, he felt fairly confident there'd be no dance session today. After last week's disaster, he couldn't really see the old guy coming back for a second dose of rough treatment. So he agreed to play along with Grace for the time being.

But when they turned in through the open school gates, there stood the gleaming silver Jaguar, already parked outside the open doors of the gym! If there was one thing he envied the old guy, it was that stunning set of wheels. It'd practically taken his breath away last weekend when he saw it speeding up the driveway like a vision of heavenly splendour – and he wasn't sorry to admire it up close again. Some people had all the luck – and all the money! Must've set him back a good fifty grand at least. His eyes lingered lovingly on the fancy wheel trims, the plush, grey interior upholstery, the glinting bonnet...

"I was wondering if you'd be here today," observed a dry voice.

Jordan glanced up and his eyes met those of the car's owner, who stood with crossed arms in the doorway of the gym, surveying him with a look that seemed to pierce his flesh to the very bones beneath. Oh fuck! Prob'ly about to bawl him out for attempted car theft, as well as trespassing on private property.

Jordan jerked back his hand from the shining silver bodywork as though it was red hot. Better act cool, though it felt a bit awkward when he'd just been caught drooling over the bloke's flash car.

"Yeah, well I ain't stayin'," he announced brusquely. "I just come to bring my sister."

He looked round: where was Grace?

"I think she's already inside – talking to my wife," remarked the old guy, instantly guessing his thoughts.

"Your wife?" cried Jordan, puzzled. "What's *she* here for?"

"To help with class of course. Like last week. Don't you remember? She showed you and your sister round our company buildings in town on Wednesday afternoon." He sounded equally surprised. "This whole damned business was her idea in the first place."

"Oh! But that was Mizz Page," corrected Jordan. The old guy must've got his wires crossed.

"Yes, Miss Page. That's who I mean."

Jordan stared at him. "What? Mizz Page's your wife?"

"Alicia Page is her stage name. She started dancing professionally long before we got married – when she was younger than you are now."

"Oh." Jordan gulped. "An' you said this whole business is her idea?"

"Yes. She has this bee in her bonnet about helping people. You know what women are like when they get an idea in their heads…"

Think of Grace and Gran. Jordan nodded grimly. Strange he should have anything at all in common with this rich old ballet guy. So he was actually married to Grace's idol, Alicia Page, whose name had been praised in his hearing this past week almost more often than that of the Lord. Perhaps he should at least listen to what he had to say.

"… Alicia's always been one for seeing the good in people. It's a rarer talent than I once believed…"

Rambled on a bit, didn't he? But what he seemed to be

56

saying was how much this project meant to Mizz Page. Jordan squirmed inside. Didn't care about the old guy himself of course, but think of kind Mizz Page being disappointed.

"... She's so passionately eager to help young people fulfil their potential..."

He sure used loads of big words.

"... I was telling her about seeing you dance in the studio the other evening."

Jordan recoiled. He understood this well enough.

"I wasn't dancing," he contradicted.

"I see," said the old guy with a nod of his head and a quiet smile. "What would you call it then?"

What would he call it?

"Well – just foolin' around, I guess," mumbled Jordan. "Tryin' out a few moves."

But wriggle as he might, he couldn't actually deny it. This old guy'd seen him dance. It was like your grandma having seen you naked in the bath when you were a baby. You couldn't pretend it hadn't happened because both of you knew it had. It was a fact that gave someone power over you. Jordan shied away from it, like a nervous pony from a halter.

"So did you like 'fooling around', trying out 'moves'?" went on the old guy evenly.

Jordan tossed his head. There was something he didn't care for in the tone of that deep, cultured voice – a hint of gentle teasing. Didn't care if he *was* married to Mizz Page: no one was gonna make fun o'him.

He shrugged non-committally. "'S all right, I s'pose."

"I could teach you to do it better."

Jordan started. The old guy's voice was so low, he wasn't sure he'd heard him right.

"What? You wanna teach me to dance?"

"No. Just to offer you a choice."

"What choice?"

"The choice of learning how to dance, if you want to. The chance to take control of your body and your life. That's the reason I'm here today. I was going to throw in the towel after last week's fiasco. In fact, I very nearly did." He sounded angry. "But then I saw you in the studio in town and I realised that I owed it to you to try again. To offer you my help."

"Don't need no one's help," objected Jordan. "I do things on my own."

"Yes, that's right. Every dancer's on his own – he has to make his own choices, his own decisions. He has to be tough, because it's not an easy life."

"Huh! Expect me to believe that, seein' you drive this brand new Jag," demanded Jordan, glancing back at the gleaming silver car.

"That's nothing to do with being a dancer. It's merely the result of the managerial post I hold with the ballet company now I'm too old to dance any more."

Jordan blinked. Fair point.

"When I was your age, boy, my family didn't have two pennies to rub together." The old guy wasn't smiling now. His face was deadly serious, as he sat down on a metal bench beside the gym wall. "You see, my mother was a widow, because my father died in an explosion down Stonebridge coal mine when I was five years old."

So he'd grown up with no dad either. A lump swelled in Jordan's throat. But the old guy wasn't asking for pity.

"She ran the post office in the little village where I grew up and she went without new clothes and mended her old ones so she could afford to pay for ballet lessons for my little sister and me. Every week on a Wednesday afternoon when the post office had half-day closing, we used to travel six and a half miles to class in a church hall in Pentland on a rattly old country bus. If it hadn't been for my mum, I never would've made it. She persuaded me to try for a scholarship to the ballet school in London."

He sounded proud. Proud to be poor?

Jordan sank down on the other end of the bench, eyes fixed on the ground, listening in spite of himself.

"Down in London, I started off living in a bedsit the size of a large closet in a dank basement where all I could see out of the window was people's feet walking past. Everybody wondered why I got good at dancing so fast. I was too proud to tell them it was mainly because I couldn't afford to pay for my own heating. It was easier to stay in the warm studios to practise as long as I was allowed, so I could put off going home at night. My bedsit was so cold in winter that a pint of milk'd freeze on the inside window sill, so it didn't matter that I didn't have a fridge."

"You didn't have a fridge?" echoed Jordan, glancing up. "You're kiddin' – aren't you?"

"No – and there was no TV, or washing machine, or even a sofa either. And I used to cook my tea on a single gas ring in a kind of cupboard."

"You used to cook in a cupboard?" cried Jordan, starting to consider himself pretty well off by comparison. Man, this old guy must know what it was like to have his back against the wall. He surveyed him with a glimmer of grudging respect.

"Guess you must really've wanted to make a go of your dancin' then," was all he said.

"It was my one big dream. And that's the great thing about dancing, you know. It doesn't matter where you come from, what your background is, or how much your family earns a week. No one judges you on what job your father does or what kind of house you live in. The only thing that matters is how good you are and that's entirely down to you: your talent and your hard work." There was a long pause and then he glanced at his watch. At once he rose to his feet. "Anyway, it was good talking to you. But I have to go now."

"Why?" asked Jordan, stirring as if from a dream and gazing around in surprise. They were completely alone. His mates were probably all still in bed, sleeping off last night's gig.

"I'm taking class at two o'clock and it's five minutes to now. I have to sort out the music and start my warm-up."

"But no one's here," protested Jordan. "You can't start class when no one's come to do it."

"Grace's come."

"She's only one person."

"The other dancers from the company are here. Didn't you see Masakuni and Isabelle slip past us just now?"

Jordan shook his head.

"They wouldn't dare turn up late. And my wife's here too. We're all ready for class and I always start on time. Pity you aren't staying. I could teach you how to warm up properly so you won't strain your muscles when you jump. But never mind. You've got better things to do with yourself than learn to dance."

He directed a quick nod of farewell at Jordan and turned towards the door of the gym.

What was Jordan to do? You couldn't trust strangers. But then again, this old guy was married to Mizz Page and she at least was a woman of her word. Besides, all that stuff about damp basement bedsits and rattly country buses to Pentland rang true as a bell. And what he'd said about the only thing that mattered being how good you were. That thrilled him through and through. Just like he used to feel when he was a little boy and Gran told him the story about the sounding of the trumpet on Judgement Day when the graves opened and gave up their dead…

He was most afraid of making a fool of himself in front of his friends – but if none of them were there, then they'd never know, would they?

Before he realised what he was doing, he'd started forward.

"Hey there – just a minute," he called.

"Yes?"

The old guy turned with an expression of mild questioning.

"P'rhaps I mightn't be so busy after all. P'rhaps I could come in for a minute or two – just to learn how to do a – a warm-up, say."

"Suit yourself. No one's forcing you. But if you come in, you stay till the end. Nobody leaves my class before I say so."

Jordan stared. It was like picking up a piece of old rope lying in the dust only to find yourself grasping a rattlesnake by the throat. Anger swelled in his chest: who was this old bugger to order him about? What gave him the right to drive hard bargains?

Their eyes fought a moment for mastery and then Jordan's will wavered. He'd always felt before as though every door he came to was being slammed in his face. Now somebody was actually holding the door open for him. Why refuse the offer? He made up his mind.

"OK – it's a deal," he agreed.

The old guy smiled – a thin glint of a smile.

"You're on," was all he said.

CHAPTER SEVEN

D illon's garage lay screened by a terrace of ordinary houses in a dead-end lane, which ran down to the rail bridge and the river, winding among tall poplars and cooing wood pigeons. On the opposite side of the lane a row of concrete bollards stood guard before a wilderness of honey-scented buddleias and tall grasses strewn with broken bottles, plastic carrier bags, empty cigarette packets and wind-blown newspapers. Beyond this no-man's-land lurked a crumbling factory, which for as long as Jordan could remember had served as the headquarters of their mortal enemies, the Asian gang. In years past, this wasteland had witnessed lightning raids and guerrilla warfare as the two sides wrestled for power, but after an ugly incident last spring when Ash ended up in hospital with a knife wound in his thigh, the feud was now languishing in a series of sullen truces under the watchful eye of the local police.

Jordan hadn't seen any of his mates the last few days, so he'd picked up news of Tuesday night's gig from Oz's text. Eugene's words of warning had been niggling at him and tonight he'd made up his mind to take steps to defend his place in the band that he'd co-founded eighteen months ago with Dillon, a keen fan of hip hop and bashment. Besides, since flirting with the enemy at last Sunday's ballet class, he badly needed to reassert his tribal loyalties.

He paused for a moment beside the sawn-off oak,

which'd always acted as the gang's lookout post, hearing the familiar throb of music pulsating through the still night air and flooded by a warm wave of nostalgia as he surveyed this second home of his, where he'd hung out with his mates since childhood.

The sheet-iron gates of their citadel, scrawled all over with slogans of defiance, stood firmly barred against him. But he knew the trick of scaling the rusty fence spiked with barbed wire and in a moment leapt down, soft as a cat, onto the rough concrete paving with his battered guitar case slung over his back.

Dillon's father was in the business of buying up MOT failures and accident write-offs for scrap, so the outdoor courtyard was crowded with eerie wrecks of vehicles, in some places stacked three high: wheel-less and derelict, fronted by piles of worn-out tyres. Behind these rose gang headquarters, a large corrugated iron shack. By day, this did duty as a workshop with overhead strip lighting and trailing power leads, but under cover of night it stood transformed.

By nine o'clock the gig was well underway as Jordan slid in through the front door, halted dead on the threshold by the dazzling flash of multi-coloured lights and blasting music that rocked the dilapidated building on its flimsy foundations. His nostrils swelled with the strong fumes of sour alcohol that permeated the smoke haze, while his eyes gradually began to make out a seething press of sweaty bodies lurching this way and that through the gloom. The lurid glare of a roving spotlight lit up now the swelling breasts, now the shapely thighs, now the pouting lips and coy gazes of dozens of pin-up girls posted over the grimy walls. And there was no denying the twitch in his groin at the glittering vision of Elodie Simpson in green sequin spangles, purring throatily into a microphone clasped between her scarlet fingernails. What wouldn't he give for the chance to dance with her!

As the number ended and applause broke out, he saw that

playing bass tonight was that useless white wanker, Ashley Kent. What a nerve! That'd always been his job.

His first impulse was to leap onto the makeshift stage and knock Ash straight into next Thursday. But a sudden realisation checked him. When was the last time he'd showed up for band practice? Was it really so long ago that they'd got fed up waiting for him?

As he stood dismayed, the band stopped for a break and the loudspeakers broke out into canned music. At that moment he caught sight of Eugene bobbing around the dance floor with Elodie's short, fat friend, Nicole, whose shock of hair tonight was dyed electric blue.

"Hi there," yelled Jordan above the ear-splitting din.

Eugene couldn't've heard him. And he instantly swung round and somehow managed to lose himself and his partner in the surging mob before Jordan could hail him again.

But then big Jermaine pulled away from a friendly clap on the shoulder and Dillon himself, sauntering past with Hayley hanging off his arm, stared straight through him as though he wasn't there. Jordan smelt something ugly in the air.

At this point he spotted Oscar, hunched over his mobile as usual, on an upturned beer crate in the open back doorway.

Oscar had been his faithful sidekick ever since Jordan placed himself like a riot shield in front of the skinny, runny-nosed seven-year-old on the day he arrived at Brackwell Heath Primary School. With his unruly haystack of bright ginger hair, protruding ears and a splotchy red birthmark staining one of his freckled cheeks, Oscar was not a thing of beauty. The rest of the gang had instantly set about bullying him, not just because of his freakish appearance, but also out of contempt for his physical clumsiness and obvious learning difficulties.

But Jordan, who felt an instant bond of brotherhood with anyone forced into Sunday church attendance, soon learned that Oscar's family were strict Jehovah's Witnesses and that he too was plagued by an annoying little sister. More than that, Oscar turned out to be an unexpected master of computer gaming. Jordan was popular: his sporting prowess gave him huge prestige among his peers, so a strange friendship had sprung up between the two boys, which drove Jordan to fight several pitched battles in Oz's defence before he was finally accepted into the gang. The two had remained best mates ever since and Jordan knew he could rely on him for the truth.

"So what's up, Oz?" he asked in an apparently careless tone, propping his guitar case against the damp-stained wall. He flipped a couple of coins into the kitty and seized a can of beer, struggling hard to look unconcerned.

"Split – now. 'Fore it's too late. I'm tellin' ya, split," hissed Oscar out of the side of his mouth, gazing steadfastly at the lighted screen. "You c'n make it out this door wivout nobody seein' nuffink. I'll cover for ya."

"Why?" shot back Jordan.

"'Cos everybody knows what ya done."

"What I done," Jordan echoed blankly. "What've I done?"

"On'y turned into a fuckin' fairy."

Jordan dropped the can with an unheeded crash. "Who says that? I'll show him who's a fuckin' fairy," clenching his fists in fury.

"I'm sayin' it," asserted Oscar with a defiant glare. "It's no use tellin' no lies neither. Jermaine saw ya talkin' to your new mate, the balley teachin' poof, on the gym steps Sunday afternoon. An' he watched ya go inside wiv 'im. An' he crep' up to the open back door and saw ya dancin' too. Jeez, Jordan, why'd ya do it?" in heartbroken appeal.

Jordan's heart swelled with agony. How to defend himself? He stood guilty as charged.

"It's – it's not like you think," he stammered. "Ballet's not just prancin' around in pink tights, you know. It's bloody hard slog…" A hot sweat broke out on his top lip. So this was why his other friends'd ignored him! He was being cold-shouldered, blanked, frozen out. If he didn't take the hint and slip away through the back door…

"So! Jordan Howe. What ya doin' here, ya fairy cocksucker? Thought you'd've took the hint by now and crawled back into that fuckin' dung heap you come from," announced a husky voice, dangerous as the flash of a knife edge.

Jordan spun round and found himself eye to eye with Prince Harrison, a year older than himself and one of the acknowledged leaders of the gang. Prince must've come swaggering up from behind and he now stood with his thumbs stuck in the pockets of his tattered jeans, flanked by a band of tattooed henchmen menacingly arrayed in black.

Jordan froze and all but bolted straight out the open door. But something held him back. If he turned tail and ran now, he'd never be able to hold up his head among his mates again. Sweating with fear, he knew he had at least to try to face this out. His heart was pounding, but he drew a long, deep breath. Then he squared his shoulders proudly and, crossing his arms over his chest like that tall Russian dancer, Boris, met Prince's eye head on.

Jordan was no fool. His opponent, in torn sweatshirt and matted dreadlocks, stood half a head shorter than him and, though Prince carried more weight and had some skill in martial arts, Jordan was in far better physical shape from regular weight-training and sports practice at the gym. He stood a fair chance of holding his own in one-on-one combat. But what would happen if the fight escalated into a free-for-all?

By now the dancing had straggled to a halt and everyone had fallen back in a circle around the antagonists, who fronted each other like rival bulls battling for leadership of the herd. All eyes were fixed on them, warily gauging Jordan's chances of success, as their gazes locked and each began to pit his will against the mental strength of the other.

At that moment, a figure suddenly elbowed her way to the front of the crowd. In a whirl of green sequins and a flash of gold-hooped earrings, Elodie thrust herself straight into Prince's path, planting her hands on her curvaceous hips as she defiantly confronted her ex-boyfriend.

"You lay off him, you big bully," she spat in withering contempt. "There ain't nothin' wrong with ballet dancin'. I took classes with Miss King for years an' what I say is: it's such hard work, I admire any man who'll give it a go."

Prince's mouth gaped open and a murmur of surprise rippled through the onlookers. Elodie was Queen Bee of this particular hive and her opinion couldn't simply be discounted.

"Oh shut your fuckin' mouth, Elodie," Prince retorted, struggling to reassert control. "Out o'the way. This is between us men." And he shoved her roughly aside.

Jordan started forward, but Elodie needed no feeble male defence. She wheeled, blazing, upon her ex-boyfriend with a band of indignant girls massed around her: Nicole, Lauren, Hayley, who'd sprung instantly to her side like a host of warrior Amazons.

"You lay your filthy hands on me again and you'll wish you'd never been born," she warned in a low voice that rang with authority.

Prince flinched and Jordan drew back warily.

"What I say is that this ain't just between you – *men*," Elodie declared with sarcastic emphasis, "I say it concerns us all."

"You're talkin' fuckin' bullshit," muttered Prince sulkily. But words were not his strong suit and Elodie quelled him with a single, scornful glance. Then she turned to the rest.

"My mum's been at the gym these past two weeks with my kid sister, Ruth, and she says we all oughta feel ashamed of ourselves for turnin' down what Mizz Manners's tried to offer us without a fair trial. Here we all are with a once-in-a-lifetime chance to make something of ourselves. There's this famous man and his wife, who were big stars an've danced in lots of films an' TV shows, comin' to school specially to teach us all they know. An' how many of us could be bothered turnin' up?"

She glowered round at them all with her hands on her hips in a fair imitation of her feisty mother, a local news reporter of some standing in the community. Several of the onlookers winced and lowered guilty eyes.

"That's right: just my sister, Ruth, an' Grace – an' Jordan here. Three out of the whole bunch of us."

"I was bloody well there too," pointed out Lauren bluntly.

"Mum said you showed up half an hour late."

"Well I had to wait till Auntie Zoe got home to look after Zack, didn't I? Else I woulda been there on time too. I've always wanted to do ballet."

"Yeah, well it's just fuckin' girls who go to ballet classes – apart from Jordan Howe," snarled Prince.

"Yes – 'cos he's the only one with the guts to be different," shot back Elodie, seething with spite. "Look at you: spineless wankers, the lot of you," sweeping a dismissive gesture around the crowd. "All you're fit for is collectin' garbage and government benefits. Well, my mum says Jordan's got it in him to do better than that. She saw he'd made a real impression on Mr Hillier because he shook him by the hand at the end of class. So now Jordan's had his hand shook by someone who's shook hands with queens and princes, Mum says. An' she wants to write an article about the class for the *Evening Standard* an' p'rhaps even bring a camera crew round next week to film a news item. So I ain't gonna stand by and watch a jumped-up prick like you, Prince Harrison, bad-mouthing someone that'll likely end up a big star on telly soon."

There was an audible gasp among the spectators and

68

Prince's jaw dropped. Even his henchmen shuffled their feet and began to edge nervously away.

"The rest of you can spend your lives stuck in a dump like Brackwell Heath if you like, but I got big plans for the future an' no time to waste on losers," she went on, turning her back on her ex-boyfriend in open disdain. "So not only've I decided to rearrange my ballroom class so I can go along next Sunday afternoon, but I'm gonna dance with Jordan right now." And she extended her hand to him with an inviting smile.

Jordan stared at her for a moment in a daze of disbelief. But – hey! Gotta get a grip on himself here. Wasn't never gonna get no second offer like this.

With a smirk of triumph at his defeated enemy, he reached out to grasp her hand.

"You're gonna be sorry for this, Jordan Howe. From this night on, you're a marked man."

The venomous threat, hissed through Prince's clenched teeth, sent a momentary shiver up Jordan's spine.

But everyone was flocking round him and Elodie, blotting out all sight of Prince's lone figure. Who cared about him now? His rage had shrunk to ineffectual bluster; his vows of vengeance were merely empty threats.

Jordan led Elodie shimmering and swaying onto the dance floor, his head spinning so fast that he could've soared into orbit. As she twined her two arms round his neck and sparkled up into his eyes, he felt like a king. Man, was he gonna show her how he could dance tonight!

CHAPTER EIGHT

I sabelle was dressed and ready to go. She checked the silver watch that her proud grandparents had given her when she'd been accepted into the Parkhouse School for Dance at the age of eleven. Almost twenty past one by the hands on its dainty mother-of-pearl face. Just time to sort that handwashing before Alicia and Roy arrived to pick her up…

Casting a casual glance over the rustling, golden treetops beyond their back garden, she hung out four neat rows of freshly laundered leotards and practice leggings to dry on the airing rack beside her sunny bedroom window. Hmm… (stretching out the feet of the final pair of tights), remember what her old teacher, Miss Maude, used to say about worn, grey tights being the sign of a shoddy dancer. Must order a new pack this evening…

As she turned from the window, her eye fell on the photo of herself and her smiling mother with her Prix de Lausanne certificate, which stood in pride of place on her well-ordered dressing table. A wistful sigh escaped her.

The enthusiastic applause, the flattering praise, the flashing cameras. But, eight months on, it all seemed only a dream.

Of course she owed everything to Mum, who'd always ensured that the current au pair ferried her regularly to and from ballet classes ever since she was tiny. But sometimes she wondered. Was it herself that her mother cared about? Or just that glittering array of exam medals and competition trophies standing in the glass-fronted cabinet in the grand house in Twickenham, which she hardly ever saw?

And as for Dad…

With a demanding job, young wife and new baby, what time or energy did he have left to spare for her? Not even a token birthday present this year. And life with her once close-knit class of ballet school friends seemed so far in the past now they'd all gone their separate ways. Mei was a considerate enough flatmate, but they'd only met at the end of the summer holidays and she was so self-contained, it was often difficult to tell what she was thinking.

No, Alex was the only person who really cared for her – that's why his affection mattered so much. He and the company were her family now. But at the end of her trainee year, what if she didn't get offered a job there? What would she do? Mustn't think about that now. Had to do everything she could this season to prove she was good enough…

A ringtone suddenly shrilled out. Isabelle started. Alex perhaps, suggesting they have dinner together tonight?

She flew to extricate her phone from the depths of her dance bag. Odd. Didn't recognise that number.

"Hello, Isabelle. It's Alicia," announced her ballet mistress' voice, sounding slightly breathless. "Sorry we're running a bit late. We'll turn up before too long."

"Is everything all right?" Isabelle asked.

"Yes. At least it soon will be. I'm just letting Roy load the dishwasher. Undemanding domestic tasks generally do wonders for his stage-fright."

"Stage-fright? Roy?" cried Isabelle, sinking down in disbelief on her tidily made bed.

"Yes. In a manner of speaking. He's feeling a bit discouraged about the youth project at the moment. Thinks no one's going to turn up today."

"I suppose there were only four of them last week," admitted

Isabelle tentatively, smoothing out an imaginary crease in her pink-and-white-flowered quilt. "If you count Lauren, coming half an hour late after she'd managed to find a babysitter."

"We've been through all this over lunch," sighed Alicia. And then in a wicked parody of Roy's grumbling tones, "'Don't you see how this encapsulates the whole problem with these kids? I can't teach people to dance who are busy worrying about finding babysitters for their fatherless brats or arguing at the back of the class when they end up standing next to someone of a different skin colour. They have no focus and no self-discipline. When you first put this scheme to me, I told you it wasn't going to work…'"

Isabelle struggled to smother a giggle. Alicia was a brilliant mimic.

"You know what he's like," resumed Alicia in her own voice. "Might take a while to argue him into his jacket… Oh! I can just hear the dishwasher rattling shut. See you soon – " and she was gone.

Isabelle stared at the lifeless phone in her hand. If only she could feel as confident as Alicia sounded. But secretly she had to confess to sharing Roy's misgivings.

Exactly what progress had they made at Brackwell Heath? The first class had disintegrated in total confusion. At the second, the teaching staff had outnumbered the students practically two to one. True, it hadn't all ended in chaos and shouting, but it'd left her and the other three young dancers wondering why they were even there. Was there any point in going back this afternoon? Poor Alicia. After all that effort…

★

Ten minutes later, she was gliding along the ring road behind Alicia in the purring silver Jaguar. On the plush, grey upholstered seat beside her lay a manila folder containing the student attendance register and the box of CDs Roy'd used in class last week. Hadn't taken long to realise that the detour to pick her up had only interrupted, rather than suppressed, the battle raging in the front seat of the car.

"I told the boys not to bother coming this afternoon, Isabelle," was Roy's militant greeting from the wheel as the Jaguar pulled away from the leaf-strewn kerb in front of the modern block of flats where she lived. "You should be enough to field the one or two kids who might deign to turn up today, their complex personal arrangements permitting of course. I hope you don't feel it's just a waste of your precious free time."

Isabelle opened her lips to offer some polite denial but –

"You call Grace Howe a waste of time?" demanded Alicia, ignoring his heavy-handed sarcasm.

"She's a nice kid," he admitted, with a glance in the rear view mirror prior to changing lanes. "But let's face it, she's never going to make a dancer."

"That's not the point," shot back Alicia. "And what about her brother, Jordan?"

Isabelle's eyes widened and she tried hard to concentrate on the passing trees and houses.

She'd watched the tall black boy in class last Sunday afternoon and seen how quickly he mastered the five positions of feet and arms. True too, he possessed the most amazing natural turn out. But his whole approach to dancing made her feel uneasy: it was so uncouth and primitive, like the driving hunger of a wild beast rather than the hard-won poise and self-control of a classically trained artist.

"I suppose he has a grain or two of raw talent that he might possibly turn to some account," Roy conceded cuttingly. "If he could be bothered shifting his lazy butt and attending that free evening class I told him about."

Isabelle glanced across at him. So he'd invited Jordan to the privately sponsored session of Youth Dance, held at the company premises every Thursday night?

"You haven't given him a chance to explain," pointed out Alicia quietly.

"He's an undisciplined street yob, just like the rest of them. The word 'commitment' has no meaning for him. So he doesn't show. So he doesn't make any progress. I've already pointed out that he's lagging years behind his contemporaries and he really has to get his act together if he wants to make anything of himself as a dancer. Can't think why I bothered. I knew this'd bloody well happen…"

Roy sounded bitterly disappointed. As they pulled up at a set of traffic lights, he turned on Alicia in an outburst of irritation.

"Look, Allie, why can't you just face facts? This scheme of yours and Barbara's was a good idea – and we've given it a fair go. But now it's time to admit it's not working and give up. I need some input from the people I teach – I can't make it all happen single-handed."

"You've got input from the rest of your team," protested Alicia, "if you'd only listen to what they had to say. Murray told you the first week that the music you'd chosen for starters was too highbrow."

"What's wrong with Prokofiev?" demanded Roy, revving the engine impatiently in anticipation of the change of lights. "It's a brilliant score: unconventional, off-beat, full of drama and passion."

"Yes – to us, maybe. But classical music's not what they're used to, is it, Isabelle?"

What should she say?

But before she could even open her mouth, the lights turned green, the car leapt forward and Alicia pressed on with her argument.

"Now I thought Murray's suggestion of the Philip Glass score from *In the Upper Room* might be more the sort of thing to start with."

"So you said the other day. But I feel its rhythms are far too complex for beginners."

Isabelle knew what he meant. Think of the trouble she'd had this week counting entrances to its urgent, deceptively repetitive beat!

"But they're already in tune with that kind of music," Alicia was pointing out. "You're trying to drive them too far, too fast. Expecting them to adapt to new sounds and unfamiliar movements at the same time. You can't count on them all picking up what a *plié* or a *glissé* is after a single demonstration, like Jordan. You need to reconstruct some of your exercises in more user-friendly language."

"Dumb down, in other words?" Roy exclaimed, as the car sped along the dual carriageway. "Well I won't do it. I've still got standards."

Isabelle shifted her feet uncomfortably. More wrangling. Just like her parents. Raised voices, endless recriminations, the sound of furious sobbing from inside the bedroom…

"I'm a busy man, Alicia," Roy went on. "I haven't time to rethink my entire teaching style at this point in my career. There're plenty of dancers who understand the music I choose and the language I talk in. These are the people who matter – the people I'm trained to handle."

"You're just making excuses because you're scared," exclaimed Alicia.

Roy threw her a belligerent glare before jerking his attention back to the road.

"Why should I be scared of a bunch of hooligans?" he demanded.

"Because they're upsetting your apple-cart," Alicia replied, drawing a deep breath.

Isabelle cringed. That anyone – even his wife – could dare speak to Roland Hillier like this!

But Alicia persisted, apparently undaunted.

"You're just used to everybody regarding you with reverential awe as though you're in personal contact with the Almighty. Masakuni executes a brilliant triple *tour en l'air* – and you point out that he's landed two millimetres off centre stage. Mei finally manages to accomplish fifteen perfectly centred *fouetté* turns and you say: bravo, she's only got seventeen more to go before she can dance Odile. You're getting more cynical by the week. No wonder they call you 'The Grouch' behind your back."

From a convulsive twitch of Roy's left cheek muscles, Isabelle realised this was the first he'd heard of that particular nickname. But instead of the violent outburst she expected, he replied in a tone of glacial calm, "I'm sorry you're so disappointed. But that's the way I teach. It's been good enough for hundreds of professionals – I must apologise if it's not good enough for your pack of vandals and delinquents."

"Oh don't be so pompous," Alicia shot back. "You know perfectly well what I mean. You're just stuck in a groove after all these years. Now I've been chatting to Megan Scott about some of the techniques she uses with her Youth Theatre group…"

Roy gasped as though he was about to burst a blood vessel.

"You've been discussing *my* classes with that naïve little ninny of a school teacher, who whines the whole time about how the arts have a 'mission' to be 'accessible' and 'relevant'?" he spluttered in outraged disbelief. "She's so wet behind the ears, you'd think she was still a sixth former herself."

"Of course I've been talking to her. Why not? Megan's only twenty-four – the closest in age among us teachers to our target group. I know she's a little on the earnest side—"

"A little! That girl goes round the whole time looking so

anxious and over-burdened, you'd think she was personally responsible for the conduct of every teenager on the planet. She's got zero sense of humour and hideous dress-sense. When I first set eyes on her, I thought she was a jumble of old rags that'd been dragged through a thorn bush backwards…"

Isabelle suddenly found herself repressing an urge to laugh. This wasn't the way her parents used to argue at all. It was more like the thrust and counter-thrust of a strongly choreographed *pas de deux*…

"Yes," Alicia conceded shortly, "but Megan has lots of experience with young people like ours."

"At my time of life I'm not planning to take lessons from twenty-four-year-old kids. Let's admit it: I don't know anything about teaching teenagers."

"What a ridiculous thing to say. Isabelle here's a teenager."

"Yes, but she's a professional dancer, as I keep on pointing out to you, except you never listen." Roy heaved a sigh of frustration. "Allie, I can't do this. I've tried. I've given it my best shot, for your sake. But this time I've bitten off more than I can chew. You seem to be able to talk to these kids – but I'm not on their wavelength. Why not just admit it? It's too late to teach this old dog new tricks."

At that moment Isabelle caught sight of the school gates up ahead. Their journey was nearing its end.

"At least you'll run today's class, won't you?" Alicia begged uncertainly.

"Perhaps that won't even be necessary," replied Roy on a note of bleak realism as they drew up outside the lifeless gym. "We were down to four last week. This week it wouldn't surprise me if no one turns up at all."

And he shrugged his shoulders wearily as he climbed out of the car.

★

As Roy had prophesied, when the stark black hands of the great wall clock reached the hour of two, the gym was entirely deserted. Not even Grace Howe had shown up.

Isabelle and Alicia stood struggling to exchange meaningless fragments of small talk and watching Roy pace the floor, shaking his head and pursing his lips in frustration. His eyes were riveted on the gym clock and his face was growing steadily darker and more ominous as the tense minutes ticked by.

When the hands reached five past, his rage and disappointment boiled over. He stormed out of the gym in the direction of the car park.

"He hates being beaten," Alicia whispered the moment he was out of earshot.

"Should you go after him?" suggested Isabelle.

Alicia shook her head.

"What good would it do? – Oh how can they treat him like this?" she burst out, looking white and upset. "After all he's tried to do for them, all the effort we've put in – and not even Grace and Ruth've come. What on earth are we going to say if that reporter, who rang this morning, actually turns up with a camera crew to film the news item? It'll be so humiliating..."

Even as she spoke, Isabelle suddenly turned her head. What was that noise coming from outside the open doors of the gym? Sounded like muffled voices raised in angry dispute. She and Alicia exchanged puzzled glances and together darted out to investigate.

At the top of the gym steps with his back towards them stood Roy, barring the entrance to the gym. Authority radiated from his figure, rooted firm with legs apart and arms crossed majestically over his chest, exactly as Isabelle had seen him before on stage as the Prince of Verona. But instead of a choreographed rabble of Capulets and Montagues brawling in the marketplace, he was confronting an all too real mob of at least a dozen indignant teenagers, headed by Jordan Howe in a high temper.

"I told you before: class starts at two," Roy was declaring heatedly. "This isn't school. You've chosen to be here. Either you turn up on time or you needn't bother coming at all."

"But we *were* here by two," protested Jordan. He clearly believed what he was saying. Yet how could it be true? Isabelle had read the hands of the gym clock herself.

"I told you we hadn't left enough time," Grace wailed. "Oh, Mizz Page," she exclaimed, catching sight of Alicia in the doorway. "Please help. Jordan and I've been round to all our friends' houses tellin' 'em to come to class – an' Gran's stayed home from choir practice to look after Darleen – an' she's minding Zack too, so Lauren can dance with us. An' now *he* says he won't teach us because we're late. But we were comin' up the drive before two o'clock – Jordan checked his phone an' said we'd make it on time."

"The gym clock read two more than ten minutes ago," insisted Roy with uncompromising severity. "You've only been here five at most."

"Oh, haven't you noticed yet? That old clock's been running fast for ages," pointed out a striking black girl with gold hoop earrings, whom Isabelle didn't remember seeing before. "The boys fixed it one day last summer so we could get off school early – you can't hear the bell down here – and no one's sorted it since."

So that clock was wrong after all! Isabelle half-opened her mouth to agree, but the words died on her lips. Roy looked as though he was about to explode.

Suddenly Alicia stepped in front of her glowering husband.

"Then we mustn't waste any more time, must we?" she announced briskly. "Come on inside, all of you, and let's get started." And she began to hustle them through the open doors into the gym.

But Jordan, obviously smarting with wounded pride, refused to budge. He and Roy stood eyeball to eyeball, glaring at each other, and the air between them almost crackled with the heat of their rage.

"And where were you on Thursday night?" demanded Roy contemptuously. "You said you'd be at Youth Dance. I was expecting you."

"I wanted to come," began Jordan in sullen self-defence, "but at the last moment I – I couldn't make it."

"Out clubbing with your mates, I suppose."

"I told you, I couldn't make it," repeated Jordan tersely.

"He couldn't come on Thursday night – please believe him," intervened Grace, who'd been trying to haul her resisting brother up the steps behind her by main force. "It was all Darleen's fault."

"And who exactly's Darleen?" prompted Roy, keeping his eyes fixed on Jordan and not relaxing a muscle of his sternness.

"Our cousin of course," explained Grace, clearly surprised by his ignorance. "She fell when she was playing in the park and hit her head on a concrete post, so Jordan and Gran had to take her up to the hospital and sit there for hours and hours—"

"Grace, you keep your flippin' mouth shut," snapped Jordan. "It's none o'his business."

But Roy's whole bearing had altered in an instant. His anger vanished as if by magic and he scanned Jordan's face keenly.

"Is this true, Jordan?"

"Why should you believe anythin' we tell you? You're the one who's always right," spat back Jordan.

"No. I'm sorry to say you're wrong there," Roy admitted slowly. "That gym clock *is* fast. I remember thinking last week I needed to get it sorted. I guess this means that in the heat of the moment I've been too quick to jump to the wrong conclusion – and about Thursday night as well. Please accept my apology on both counts."

Isabelle's eyes opened wide as he extended his hand to the

tall black boy. It was common knowledge in the company that Roy'd been known to maintain a petty feud for weeks rather than admit he was in the wrong. Did he really believe Jordan could be that fine a dancer?

Jordan himself could know nothing of this. He stood scowling for a moment as though he'd already made up his mind not to accept Roy's handsome apology. But then he seemed to experience a change of heart. Slowly his hand reached out to meet that of his teacher.

"Good man," exclaimed Roy, clapping him on the shoulders and sweeping him towards the gym door, totally restored to good humour. "Have I got a surprise for you this afternoon!"

Jordan threw him a questioning glance. So did Isabelle.

"I was thinking about the music I've been using," Roy went on, "like you mentioned to me the other day. I've found a score that's a lot more modern and up-beat. I hope you and your friends'll like it better…"

A few moments later, grins of recognition broke out over all the faces in the gym as the pulsating strains of *In the Upper Room* blared from the loudspeakers.

"Hey, man, this rocks," exclaimed Dillon, swaying to the beat.

Roy smiled benevolently.

"Thought you'd 'dig' it," he said, with a wink of complicity at his wife.

Isabelle glanced towards Alicia. She looked ready to strangle him.

CHAPTER NINE

One gloomy October morning, as his blind fingers groped to silence the shrilling alarm, Jordan became aware that for some time now he'd been subconsciously registering noises other than loud snorts issuing from the blocked nose of Dion, who slept in the bunk above. Seemed to be coming from the other side of the wall. One of the girls perhaps, rattling around in their bedroom next door?

Sleepily, he pulled the pillow over his head to muffle the sound of raindrops pattering on the window pane. Today, when it finally dawned, would be just like the rest of the week: cold, damp and depressing. Dripping roof gutters clogged with sodden leaves. Fans of spray from passing cars drenching the legs of his jeans as he waited, shivering, at the kerb for the bus. Ugh! How he hated dragging himself out of bed these dark autumn mornings!

He burrowed further into the comfortable warmth of his duvet. Might just drift back off for a moment or two, even if it meant having to skip breakfast and sprint for the bus...

A sudden avalanche of bedclothes swished past his nose as Dion clattered down the metal ladder, snuffling and wheezing, and Gran's voice bellowed from the foot of the stairs, "Jor-DAN! You get dem lazy bones o'yours down here right dis minnut or you gonna be late for work, boy."

By this time Grace was bawling an approximation of the

Capulet ball music in the bathroom and stamping her feet in time to its strong beats, as Roy'd taught them last week in class. (That tune was so catchy Jordan'd even surprised tone-deaf old Eugene whistling it in the gym locker room yesterday afternoon as they changed for weight-training.) Outside the bedroom door, the twins were scuffling and whooping up and down the hall. Who could sleep through this? Might as well just give up now…

Hauling on the first clothes that came to hand, he stumbled downstairs, still struggling into his sweatshirt, and sat slumped over the breakfast table, head propped grumpily on one hand. In the steamy kitchen, Gran was busy frying plantain and green tomatoes in a sizzling pan, while the twins shrieked insults at each other, squabbling furiously as they gouged channels through their milk-sodden cereal.

Grace had gulped down her breakfast and was already bouncing up from the table. Peering with bleary eyes through the clinging cobwebs of sleep, he saw her demonstrating the sequence of steps she'd learned in ballet class to their bewildered grandfather, who sat mournfully hunched as usual in his armchair in the living room.

"Deez days we can' get no rest from dancin' in dis househol'," observed Gran, rolling her eyes as she slapped a plate down in front of Jordan's nose. "What's up wid dat pickney? When me first hear dat hollerin' from outa her mouth, me thought her gettin' kilt – but den her tole me iz jus' singin'. Ain't never heard singin' like dat before."

"Grace, put a sock in it," yelled Jordan through a mouthful of breakfast.

But the twins' interest had been caught by her enthusiasm. After curiously studying her gestures of violent clan hatred and defiance, they decided to join in and began stamping energetically round the room, to the accompaniment of a thunderous hammering on the partition wall from next door. It was all too much at that time of the morning.

Jordan slammed both hands down on the table top and leapt up roaring, "CUT THE BLOODY RACKET, WILL YOU!"

But as he glowered furiously around in the succeeding silence, broken only by the dismal wailing of the neighbour's baby, a very strange thing happened.

His grandfather turned his head and grumbled mildly, "Dey's on'y habbin' a bit o'fun, boy."

Jordan started. When was the last time he'd actually heard Grandad speak? For a moment he floundered around in spluttering confusion and then subsided wordlessly into the remains of his breakfast.

Grace cavorted past the table, sticking out her tongue in triumph, and when he aimed a swipe at her, skittered clumsily out of reach. She pranced off down the hall, still humming provokingly to herself.

"What the hell's goin' on here this morning?" Jordan growled in an undertone to Gran after she'd rounded up the twins, wiped their runny noses and shooed them off to clean their teeth. "Grace's been up for ages. She sick or somethin'?"

"Ain't nuttin' wrong wid dat pickney 'cept de dancin' fever," declared Gran shaking her head darkly as she surveyed the church calendar hanging on the faded green wall. "What me tell you, boy? Her's jus' like your mudder." Her stubby finger stabbed at a date on the page and a sigh of relief rumbled through the whole of her frame like an earth tremor. "Tank de good Lord iz dat show today…"

Jordan blinked. Show! What show? What was that crazy old woman rambling on about now?

"… An' not, Grace'd clean bust into teeny liddle pieces," Gran went on, waddling over to the washing basket behind the back door.

Of course! *That* show! How could he've forgotten?

When Grace had brought home two tickets for the Midland Ballet Company's upcoming production of *Romeo and Juliet* that Roy'd given them, a look of alarm started into Gran's face. She whisked them out of Grace's fingers as though they were fifty pound bank notes entrusted to the care of a toddler.

First she propped them proudly on the television top beside the shell mermaid that Grace'd made.

"When her nex' door drop by, her'll sure see dem dere," she declared with a nod of satisfaction.

But after further thought, she moved them out of the twins' reach by sticking them with a plastic pineapple magnet to the top of the fridge door.

Next day, her brow furrowed with responsibility, she began shifting them to a series of safer and safer hiding places until at last in panic she announced they were lost altogether. After a frantic evening spent ransacking the house from top to bottom, the missing tickets finally turned up inside the pages of the imitation red Moroccan leather Bible given her as a christening present by her great aunt in Kingston.

At this point Jordan's interest flagged. He'd better things to do than worry about tickets for that stupid show. If it'd been something interesting, he might've wanted to go, but it was only *Romeo and Juliet*, a soppy love story about boring, dead people that he'd hated being forced to read at school.

All this flashed through his mind, as he watched Gran rooting around in the battered laundry basket. What the hell was she doing now?

Out of the basket she furtively drew a plastic carrier containing her best striped raffia handbag, always kept hidden at the bottom for fear of thieves who, she reasoned, would never think to search for valuables in a pile of dirty washing. She opened the bag and began rummaging through its contents: important documents like National Health Insurance numbers and certificates of birth and baptism…

Finally she uttered an exclamation as she pulled out what she was hunting for.

"All dis time I kep' deez safe an' soun'. Now iz your job to look after dem," she announced, flourishing two crumpled rectangles of card under his nose.

The show tickets. Jordan groaned aloud. He was meant to be taking Grace to *Romeo and Juliet* at the Olympian Theatre this afternoon. But what about the dance practice he'd been planning to do after work?

"Why don't you use the other ticket, Gran?" he urged hopefully. "Wouldn't you like to see a real ballet?"

"Huh! Catch me wid de time to sit down so long," she grumbled. "Iz visitin' day for Dion and Darleen. Deir farder like to see dem – even if deir no-good mudder don' care nuttin' nohow. 'Sides, de tickets was give you special by dem balley folk. It's you who's gotta go."

Sod it!

Arranging a visiting order for Gran and the twins to see Uncle Wesley in prison wasn't easy. It left him no choice. With a nod of glum resignation, he reached out his hand for the tickets.

★

By twelve-thirty the rain had cleared. There were even gleams of sunshine glinting in the puddles, he noticed, on his way home from work and Mel Parkes, the owner of Pets' Paradise, was dragging some rabbit hutches back out onto the pavement.

These days, time seemed to pass a lot more quickly than it used to. His job at the garage didn't bother him so much either, busy as he now was the whole time rehearsing dance steps in his head and struggling to match them with their French names.

He even grinned to himself at the memory of knocking-off time yesterday when Tony started in on him as usual.

"Headin' downtown to practise yer fancy, fairy footwork then?" he'd sneered from behind the office computer.

Aziz drew near, anticipating some entertainment.

For once Jordan managed to rein in a surly retort.

"Yeah," he answered coolly, unhooking his jacket from its peg, then adding in his best imitation of Roy's cultured voice, "Actually I'm workin' on *battements* and *entrechats quatre* at the moment."

Tony stared back blankly.

"Fancy comin' along?" Jordan went on with a pointed glance at his boss's spreading paunch. "Looks like you could do with losin' some o'that flab."

Tony's jaw dropped and Aziz let out a snigger, which he tried to convert into a cough when he caught Tony's outraged eye.

"I'll take that as a no then?" persisted Jordan with a cheeky grin as he set off for the bus stop, carelessly humming the tune of his Grade Four set dance.

He strode along the street with his head held high. Now he had some purpose in life. Roy'd suggested he take an exam at Christmas, so he was busy practising every spare moment, often till late in the evening...

As he opened the front door, Grace came parading downstairs in her best dress, which she and Gran'd snapped up at a bargain price from the local charity shop. She must've spent half the morning plaiting her wiry hair into that lop-sided bun crowned with a gaudy plastic tiara and instantly demanded his admiration. Jordan did his best, but deep down he felt a twinge of misgiving over this glittering confection of hot pink nylon frills.

Last week after Youth Dance he'd caught a glimpse of Isabelle floating past on Alex's arm. The filmy fabric of her dress might've been cut out of a pale dawn sky and clasped around her slender waist with a silver moonbeam, contrasting vividly with her crown of fiery red-gold hair. The dancer seemed on another level altogether, like a picture of a Greek goddess he'd once seen during a school trip, glowing on an art gallery wall.

Before this, if he thought about it at all, he would've dubbed pale blue a wishy-washy shade. After all, Elodie favoured strong, bright colours like lime green, canary yellow and cherry red and he'd always vaguely felt they suited her just fine. But Isabelle's simple, sophisticated elegance was an eye-opener.

He couldn't help turning his head to stare. But at the same time he automatically shrank back into the shadow of the coffee-vending machine, terrified she'd catch sight of him gaping open-mouthed at her. Quite unaware of his presence, Isabelle drifted off to the company party along with the rest of those remote, starry creatures, while Jordan's gaze trailed after her, retaining the imprint of her beauty long after her figure had vanished from view.

He'd struggled to wrestle his soaring heart to earth by telling himself that girl had a figure like a twig. But he wasn't stupid enough to believe this and it made him uneasy now to see Grace dressed quite so – so showily, for fear she'd be laughed at if she were noticed by certain members of the ballet company this afternoon.

At that moment their grandmother poked a head bristling with plastic curlers round the kitchen door to scold them both for keeping lunch waiting. As Grace skipped off to flaunt her peacock feathers in front of their grandfather, Jordan stared after her with a frown.

"You don't think that – that hair thing might be just a bit – over the top?" he ventured to observe.

"Your sister look like a liddle fairy princess," Gran declared without hesitation. "But your own han's so dirty, she might well feel 'shamed o'her big brudder…"

Jordan took the hint and instantly headed upstairs to wash. He scrubbed his hands after work much more thoroughly these days, since traces of grease and black oil looked so out of place in a ballet studio. Recalling Alex's immaculate appearance the other night, he even went so far as to exchange his grimy grey hoodie for a fresh navy one.

After a hasty lunch he and Grace set off, leaving their grandmother to wrestle Darleen and Dion into clean clothes for their afternoon visit. As Grace bobbed along beside him, she admitted that she'd arranged to pick up her friend, Ruth, on the way to the bus stop. Jordan grumbled loudly at being lumbered with the pair of them, but he soon changed his mind when the front door of the Simpson house was opened by Elodie herself, striking in bright turquoise with tinkling chandelier earrings. She looked dressed to go out…

"Hi there," she sparkled up at him in a welcoming manner. "Ruth's in the lounge, Grace. You wanna call her, while I go pick up my coat and bag?"

"What?" cried Jordan. "You're comin' too?"

Elodie flashed him a brilliant smile.

"Sure am. Mum's busy this afternoon, so I promised to keep an eye on Ruth. I cried buckets when we went to see *Romeo and Juliet* with school, you know. It's tragic the way they died so young. Come in. I won't be a minute…"

Jordan's spirits soared. His luck was finally in. Perhaps this afternoon wasn't going to be a total waste of time after all. He straightened his shoulders and held his head as high as Boris as he entered Elodie's door for the first time. This was practically a date!

The Simpson house was an unmistakable step up from theirs. Besides, Elodie's mother was actually said to own it herself. Jordan stood respectfully in the hallway, awaiting the girls' return. He surveyed the pale, freshly-papered walls, so unlike the scuffed brown paint in their own front hall. Instead of confronting a faded tapestry of the Last Supper, worked in wool by his great-grandmother at her church school back in Kingston, a guest here was greeted by a glass vase of silky-petalled poppies, tastefully arranged on a mirrored shelf beside a photograph of Elodie's mother shaking hands with their local MP at a political function. Added a real touch of class to the décor.

Jordan did his best to engage in polite conversation with Elodie's mother when she emerged from her office upstairs to wave them goodbye and even made a clumsy effort to imitate Alex's gallantry towards Isabelle by standing back to let Elodie through the front door ahead of him. From the glint of approval in her eyes, he realised this politeness hadn't escaped the notice of Regina Simpson.

Elodie allowed him to sit beside her on the short bus trip into town, while the two younger girls bobbed up and down with excitement on the seat in front, giggling and flaunting their fine plumage like a pair of tropical parakeets.

Under cover of their noisy chatter, Elodie turned to him with a face of concern.

"You been all right lately?" she asked in a low voice.

Odd thing to ask, thought Jordan, tingling with tenderness.

"Yeah – whyever not?" he replied with a frown.

"Just wonderin'. I been meanin' to have a word in private with you for a while."

Jordan leaned closer. Why?

"S'pose you ain't seen Prince Harrison lately?" she went on, glancing behind as though wary of being overheard.

Jordan drew back, disappointed, and slowly shook his head. His waking hours were divided between his jobs at the garage and Arts Centre and his exam practice at the ballet studios in town, places where he was hardly likely to bump into Prince.

"You better watch out," Elodie warned. "He's real mad with you after what happened that night at the gig an' he's been goin' round tellin' people he's gonna get you back, no matter how long it takes. Just thought you oughta know."

"Reckon I can handle Prince," boasted Jordan airily. "He's had all the sense knocked outa him by that drunken dad o'his if he thinks he can scare me with threats."

Deep down he felt less confident than he sounded, but he wasn't planning to let on to her.

Elodie looked impressed. She opened her beaded purse and offered him some chewing gum.

"You ain't scared of nothin', are you, Jordan?" she breathed, smiling up at him.

★

Jordan had never seen a ballet before, but he'd a pretty clear idea of what to expect from passing glimpses while Grace was watching Christmas shows on TV: a tiny, dark stage, with distant figures dressed in white tutus, gold crowns and those alarming, figure-hugging tights. They'd probably be sitting right up the back where they could hardly see anyway.

So he did a double-take when the ushers at the Olympian, after a glance at their tickets, directed them downstairs along a softly-carpeted aisle into the very front row of the theatre. But it must be right because he could see Nicole (sporting green hair but looking as lumpy as ever) and Hayley (with a new lip piercing) seated further along the same row. They waved and shifted along to say hello to the girls.

Jordan sat listening to their chatter in silence. Felt just like one long-ago, primary school visit to a Christmas pantomime.

Directly below lay a dark pit full of lighted music stands, discordant with the din of tuning instruments. Gradually he raised his eyes, measuring the full height of the towering red curtains. Then his gaze travelled around the vast dimness of the auditorium: grand boxes hung with crimson velvet and glittering chandeliers, tier upon tier of scarlet-plush balcony seats crowded with mothers and fidgety little girls in spangled party dresses, rising up towards the immense cavern of the roof, which gleamed with garlands of silver-gilt foliage.

Made him feel really small. And what a buzz from all those excited voices!

But see now. Things were looking up. Here came the rest of his mates, Oz and Eugene, Ash and Dill, swaggering self-consciously down the aisle, joking together and filling up the empty spaces in their row. Man, didn't their eyes start out o'their heads on stalks the moment they noticed he was with Elodie.

True, that film crew had so far failed to show up at Sunday dance classes. But the gang hadn't entirely given up hope of TV stardom after Regina Simpson ran a short article about the project in the local newspaper with a photograph of them all posed in a dramatic cluster around Roy and Alicia. In his mates' eyes, Jordan might've narrowly escaped disaster at gang headquarters through the intervention of a girl, but since then he'd proven in class that he could out-leap, out-spin and out-dance them all. No reason he couldn't out-face them here as well. His cool stare challenged them to ignore him now and he found they didn't dare.

In fact, Oz even winked encouragement, so Jordan grinned manfully back. He handed along one of the big candy pink-and-white-striped boxes of popcorn that Elodie'd graciously allowed him to buy on their way to the theatre. Even seeing Sudhir and the Asian gang further along the row felt oddly reassuring.

At this point a thrill of interest rippled over the audience as the lights suddenly dimmed. Jordan lolled back in his seat beside Elodie, mechanically chewing gum. Perhaps in the friendly darkness he might even steel his courage to the point of reaching a stealthy arm around her shoulders...

The outburst of clapping that greeted the arrival of the conductor faded into a rustle of expectant whispers and the orchestra struck up the opening chords of the overture. Jordan almost swallowed his gum. Hell! He'd heard that tune before. Roy sometimes played it in open class and made them march to its stately beat. But this time it was so close and loud. The booming brass and clashing cymbals seemed to blare out all around him.

Then the darkened curtain rose and he was plunged into a whole new world of light and colour. In front of his eyes, day was dawning among the market stalls of the town: it was like being right in the middle of the fruit vendors, flower sellers and girls sweeping the pavement with their brooms. If he'd reached out a hand, he could practically've touched them. He lifted his head for a better view.

He knew the story of *Romeo and Juliet* from school. But he'd always prided himself on paying as little attention in English lessons as possible, because the play was full of long, dull speeches written in words he couldn't understand. Even during the performance, which his long-suffering teacher arranged for them at the theatre in town, he'd spent most of the night fielding peanuts flicked at him by Oz next door, who'd absolutely no idea what was going on and didn't care either. Some of the girls, like Elodie, had emerged from the performance afterwards with swollen eyes, gushing about how romantic it all was. But their reaction completely mystified him.

Didn't do gushing himself and as far as he was concerned, romance was a closed book. In his opinion, Romeo was a mug who should've known better than to flirt with the enemy, and Juliet a wet blanket, whose boring speeches just held up the action. In fact, he'd ended the evening thoroughly despising the pair of them and he and Oz'd laid loud bets with Eugene at the far end of the row about which one was going to kill himself first, pointing and hooting uproariously when they saw Romeo's chest heaving after his 'death', and the dagger slip straight under Juliet's arm.

But this afternoon was different. Instead of pronouncing wordy speeches, these characters instantly showed how they felt by the way they stood and moved. Their gestures spoke straight to his heart. For the first time he could understand the rising tension between the two rival families, who were easy to tell apart by the colour of their costumes. They might've been his own mates and the Asian gang across the wasteland...

A moment later, he stiffened in his seat. Didn't that street vendor over there look just like Masakuni, the slight, nimble-footed Japanese dancer, who came to help with class on Sundays? Damn! Gone again before he could be sure. And then – mightn't that broad, upright back of the guy hauling a streetwalker across the stage belong to Boris?

But it wasn't till he caught sight of Romeo's friend in brown doublet and tights that he recognised someone for sure: that bloody wanker of an Alex Fairchild, prancing over the stage like a highly-strung stallion.

Jordan jerked bolt upright and swallowed his gum in one gulp, his eyes riveted on the unmistakable silky blond hair fanning up and down as Alex's slim, muscular frame shot across the marketplace in a spectacular show of leaps and pirouettes. Jordan's mouth fell open in grudging admiration. It looked so light and effortless and the elegance and speed were breathtaking: one blink and you would've missed it. His fingers gripped the armrest tightly and he leaned forward, his heartbeat quickening at the grace and skill and power of those flying forms: the neatly dovetailed entries of the three young men bounding and whirling and spinning over the stage on the soaring wings of music.

As the street brawl erupted in a confusion of swirling cloaks and clashing sword blades, he mentally urged on the Capulets, headed by Cameron in an unfamiliar beard and moustache and dressed from head to foot in flaming scarlet. Jordan thrilled to the urgent clangor of alarm bells and the dramatic entrance of Roy himself as the Prince of Verona, striding majestically downstairs and out into the silence-stricken crowd. He laughed out loud at the sight of slender, dark-haired Juliet darting girlishly about the stage, playing hide and seek in her nurse's skirts, and his heart swelled with pride at the dignified appearance of Alicia Page as Lady Capulet, resplendent in a pearl-studded headdress and long-sleeved gown with sweeping red velvet train.

Forgetting everything else, he gave himself up to the brilliant pageantry of the Capulet ball, his eyes eagerly tracking Isabelle's red hair as she flitted among the rose-pink cluster of Juliet's friends, weaving in and out of the intricate patterns of the dance, challenging him to pursue and recapture her in the maze of ever-shifting forms.

But now a vivid red figure dominated centre-stage: Cameron as the fiery Tybalt. A surge of sympathy flooded through Jordan: rage radiated from the dancer as Tybalt strode forward, blazing with passion. This character seemed the embodiment of all his deepest frustrations and silently between clenched teeth he willed him to victory in his clash with the pallid Montagues, applauding every motion of his strong, lithe form with its glittering crimson doublet and thin-edged sword blade.

As he fought in the second act, Jordan urged him on and when he finally fell, writhing yet still thrusting out fingers that strove to clutch his lost rapier, Jordan felt as grief-racked as if he'd experienced the death of someone he really knew. He trembled with sympathy at the violent lamentation of white-faced Lady Capulet. And then the great curtain fell.

Jordan started. Tumultuous applause broke out around him, but he sat in a daze grasping the seat arms in an effort to anchor himself to the only solid object in a whirling universe. How could this be only make-believe? It'd all seemed so real.

Beside him, Grace was bouncing up and down in her

seat, applauding wildly and exclaiming, "I'm sure they saw us. Don't you think Mizz Page and Cameron could see us, Jordan? Wasn't her headdress amazing? All those shiny white pearls. Oh didn't you enjoy it the least little bit? You're not even clapping."

Jordan blinked. Luckily at that point Grace turned back towards the stage, caught up in the enthusiastic cheering from the front row of the audience, or she would've noticed he was too choked with tears to reply.

The house lights suddenly blazed out and the audience burst into loud conversation. As Jordan staggered to his feet among the rest of his friends, who were jostling their way out of the auditorium for interval drinks and ice cream, he couldn't help glancing back over his shoulder towards the dim, all-concealing curtains. What was happening now in the only place that mattered for him – the stage?

In front of him the two younger girls were pestering Elodie, loudly demanding which dance she'd liked best and which costume she thought the prettiest. As they ran off on the hunt for leaflets to cut up for their project books, Elodie directed a world-weary shrug of her shoulders at Jordan, who was tottering unsteadily along behind her like a man in a dream.

"Kids are so excitable, aren't they?" she remarked, opening her handbag and pulling out her mobile.

Jordan watched her flick through her texts, too overwhelmed by emotion to speak. What incredible luck that she'd been there to share this with him: she whose opinion mattered to him more than anyone else's in the world. He gazed at her as she began retouching her make-up in a tiny, jewelled hand mirror. Seeing her face to face with her own reflected loveliness shot a thrill of daring through him. He finally found his voice and breathed into her ear the all-important question, "So what d'you think of it?"

Elodie glanced up. "Oh I just love the beautiful, floaty dresses the pink girls're wearing," she replied with enthusiasm. "And didn't Alicia look absolutely fabulous in that dark red velvet?"

"Sure," agreed Jordan hastily. She seemed to be missing the point here. "But I meant: what d'you think of the dancing?"

"Oh that." There was a pause as Elodie chewed her gum thoughtfully. He awaited her verdict in suspense. Then she announced, "Well, as a ballet, I like *Sleeping Beauty* better myself. But this's OK, I guess."

OK? That brilliant, eye-opening miracle was just '*OK*'?

Jordan stared at her dumbly. Of course he couldn't expect her to be as bowled over as himself, but how could anyone react so coolly to a performance that'd set his very soul on fire?

At that moment he knew the whole course of his life had been changed forever. The startling vision of an undreamt-of future flashed upon his inner eye. No matter what happened, he belonged on that lighted stage. Nothing was going to stop him straining every sinew in his body to become a dancer.

CHAPTER TEN

When that afternoon's *Nutcracker* rehearsal was finally over and everyone else had left the studio, Isabelle stayed behind to practise.

It'd been a really tiring day. Just routine things of course, starting off with a brisk walk through the raw, misty morning to jump on the bus into town. Then the usual noisy skirmish among the other girls in the crowded locker room with tights, pointe shoes and rebellious hairpins. And then the sacred ritual of company class. This was succeeded by six gruelling hours of rehearsals, enlivened today by a visit to Wardrobe to be fitted for her snowflake tutu, a hasty lunch in the staff canteen with Mei and other friends from the corps, a shoe fitting and an appointment with the physiotherapist to discuss her personal fitness regime...

Sometimes her life felt like a cross between that of a racehorse in intensive training and a nun, cloistered within the four walls of the Temple Street studios. But that was just the way things were, wasn't it? In this tough apprenticeship lay her only hope of ever reaching that distant, glittering mountain top, on which her eyes had been fixed ever since she was a little girl: the dream of becoming a principal ballerina in a world renowned company.

Whenever she managed to snatch a few moments' rest during rehearsals, Isabelle always spent it religiously watching the soloists and principals executing complex *enchaînments*.

And when there was no show in the evening, she practised these tirelessly in private after the other dancers had gone home in hope of one day achieving them herself…

"You still working?" interrupted a voice from the door of the studio.

She glanced up and caught sight of Alex, still dressed in practice gear, poking his head round the studio door.

"Is it that time already?" she cried, abruptly breaking off what she was doing. How presumptuous for a mere trainee to be caught practising the steps of a solo from *Romeo and Juliet*!

"It's after six," said Alex, pointing to the studio clock. "I'm heading down for a shower. You coming too?"

"Just five more minutes," pleaded Isabelle. "One last run through."

"Go on then. Let's take a look at you."

He leant up against the door frame and motioned her to proceed.

Not exactly what she'd intended: having a soloist's critical eye fixed upon her! But a good chance to learn something anyway. She nerved herself to perform the sequence of steps she'd been practising.

Alex stood watching, rubbing his sweaty hair with one corner of the towel slung round his neck.

"Hmmm," he observed thoughtfully, "I know there isn't much time after the *jeté-pas de bourrée* sequence, but it'd help if you paused a moment to square up before going down into the *penché*. And if you lift your right arm a little higher as your back leg tilts and look beyond the ends of your fingertips, you won't lose your line… Here, try it again with a bit of support and see if you can get the right feel."

He stepped over towards her and placed firm hands on her waist. With a light, commanding touch, he first adjusted the position of her left hip in the arabesque and then tipped her gently forwards into the *penché*.

As soon as she found herself right way up again, Isabelle smiled.

"You're right," she agreed. "That feels a lot better."

Alex's confidence was so encouraging and his greater experience acted as an endless source of suggestions for improvement. The height of her secret ambition was to one day partner him in the series of grand classical *pas de deux*: with his strong, slender physique, handsome features and silky blond hair, he was born to play the part of the fairytale prince.

She relaxed back against his chest, as Juliet did against Romeo's in the bedroom scene. How often she'd watched from the wings during last month's season! At once Alex reached out and gracefully folded first one slender arm and then the other across her breast. Then he spun her easily round to face him, bending her backwards and lifting her quite off her feet.

A glimpse of how it must feel to dance Juliet flashed through her head, as Alex drew his fingertips softly down her arms: the surrounding darkness, the swelling music, the white spotlight, the breathless rapture of the audience, the surrendering up of her whole body and soul to the exaltation of young love. Any second now she'd catch fire with the perfect poetry of the moment, when all of a sudden – "Come back, Bella," he prompted in a voice of gentle teasing.

She opened her eyes to find herself swaying in his arms and his gaze fixed on her with perfect understanding. Being dancers, they both spoke the same language. A radiant smile dawned in Alex's blue eyes and he swiftly bent and brushed her lips with his own, as he set her back on her feet. The spell was broken.

"Come on," he urged, "it's late and I'm totally knackered. I need a drink."

"Here," she replied, picking up her own half-filled water bottle shyly. "Take this." And she held it out to him.

As he was unscrewing the lid, she suddenly realised how

exhausted she felt. She sank down on the floor beside her open shoulder bag and pulled off her sweaty pointe shoes. Her legs and feet ached and she had two new raw, red blisters on her toes that needed plastering...

"Is Alicia still around, do you know?" she asked, glancing up from massaging her tired insteps.

"Yes, I saw her just now eating a sandwich in the coffee room," Alex answered, raising the bottle to his lips. "Why?"

"I just need to check what's happening this Sunday afternoon – what with Roy being away..."

Alex paused. His brows contracted into a faint frown, like a cloud passing across the bright face of the sun.

"You're not still banging on about that stupid Youth Dance project, are you?" he asked. "I thought that'd folded weeks ago."

But he knew very well it hadn't, since he was always complaining about her being busy on Sunday afternoons! Isabelle opened her lips to say so, when she noticed a certain hardening of the lines around his mouth. She bit back the words. Being deliberately provocative, wasn't he? Why did he persist in belittling this commitment of hers? Perhaps if she tried explaining how much they'd already achieved, she could persuade him of the good work they were doing.

"Far from folding, I think the project's just beginning to gather pace," she remarked quietly. "Last weekend we had a really constructive class. There must've been about twenty of them there and we even started putting together a couple of basic sequences from *Romeo and Juliet*."

Alex stopped drinking and shrugged his elegant shoulders.

"Beats me what you see in this business."

Isabelle thought for a moment as she pulled on her old soft shoes.

"It's really satisfying to watch people, who've never thought about using their bodies before, suddenly start glimpsing their potential. Some of the boys, who just messed around at the back of the class a couple of weeks ago, joking and not paying attention, have actually begun trying out some of the steps – even if they're not very good at them. And Simran, one of the Asian girls, admits she's found the warm-up exercises useful for netball too. She's hoping to train as a sports teacher when she leaves school—"

"I still don't see why you want to spend your free time doing this," interrupted Alex, wiping his mouth with the back of one hand. He screwed the lid back on the bottle and held it out it to her. "I suppose Roy might be able to drill these delinquents into reproducing a few simple routines – he's pretty persistent – but they're never going to become *real* dancers, are they?"

He pulled her easily to her feet and they headed out through the studio doors in the direction of the changing rooms.

"Oh come on, Alex," she protested, hearing their voices echoing weirdly round the empty stairwell. "That's not fair. Look at Jordan Howe. Roy thinks he's got enormous potential. Look what he's done for him already: found him a place in the Youth Dance classes and even given him free lessons during the week. Jordan's making amazing progress. Alicia said he's planning to take RAD Grade Four at the end of this term. He's often here in the evenings now—"

"Oh *him*." The scorn in Alex's voice was unmistakable. "Don't know what Roy sees in him. If you ask me, it's a complete waste of effort. After all, he's already sixteen, isn't he? By the time I was his age, I'd been dancing for ten years and was about to take my first advanced exam. You can't make up in a few weeks for years and years without proper training. In fact, I think it's grossly unfair of Roy to raise his hopes like this. Without secure foundations to his technique, Jordan'll never be more than a trained monkey performing a circus routine…"

Isabelle was about to point out that a late start wasn't so impossible for boys as for girls, when Alex swung round the banister railing and almost collided headlong with Jordan Howe himself, who stood motionless on the lower landing. For a split second the two young men hesitated in an exchange of hostile glares. *Oh no!* thought Isabelle. No way could Jordan've failed to overhear what Alex'd just said!

Alex flushed. But whatever his thoughts, he promptly pulled himself together with the air of lordly command that was second nature to him. Apparently feeling the faux pas was irreparable, he made up his mind to ignore it. So he lifted his chin and swept on down the stairs, calling back over his shoulder to Isabelle, "See you in the foyer in fifteen minutes."

Isabelle hesitated. Alex's behaviour was too high-handed. Besides, his departure left her in a hugely awkward position. Should she attempt some sort of apology on his behalf? But Jordan was glowering at her so ferociously that her gaze faltered.

"So – I guess that's what you think too," he said, rounding on her bitterly.

"What?" temporised Isabelle, edging back against the white concrete wall.

"That I'll never be more than a trained monkey performing a circus routine."

His glare of contempt as he repeated Alex's hasty words stripped her of all refuge in diplomacy. What reply to make?

"You're all the same, you ballet dancers," spat Jordan scornfully. "You say you wanna help us, but what is it you actually wanna help us do? You're just trying to make yourselves feel better by givin' us a chance to learn somethin' from you and then tellin' us we'll never be any good at doing it!"

How dare he?

"Now just a minute," she retorted, drawing herself up to

face him head on. "After all the help Roy's given you, that's going too far. I'm sorry about what Alex said just now – but he'd no idea you were there."

"It's what he thinks. And what you think too."

"What does it matter what I think? It's what you believe about yourself that matters."

"Oh yeah, that's what they all say. You're just a posh little do-gooder, who turns up her nose at the least effort a person makes to do anythin' – anything – better."

Isabelle's jaw dropped.

"Look, I don't know why you hate me so much. I hardly even know you, but you keep on attacking me as though I'm personally to blame for all your problems."

"You needn't think I didn't notice the way you were laughin' at me behind my back last Sunday," he countered, quite unexpectedly.

"Laughing at you behind your back?" echoed Isabelle. What was he talking about? "That's ridiculous. I never did any such thing."

"You sniggered when I made an arsehole of myself with that big turnin' jump," Jordan declared, the recollection of his humiliation clearly heaping fresh fuel upon his anger.

"But I didn't snigger," protested Isabelle, who only remembered wondering how he'd the confidence to attempt a *grand jeté en tournant* after only a few weeks of lessons.

"And you've been telling that wanker of a boyfriend of yours all about it too, haven't you?" persisted Jordan wildly.

Isabelle stared at him. Was he mad?

"Why should I mention you to Alex? I don't know anything about you and the way things're going, I don't want to either. I try to be polite to you in class—"

"No you don't! You just keep clear of me like I got some sort of catchin' disease," spluttered Jordan.

"All right," admitted Isabelle. "But can you blame me? The

once or twice we've ever spoken, you've bitten my head off. I don't know why you've got this huge chip on your shoulder, but you should just grow up and learn to deal with it, like the rest of us."

"Oh that's easy for you to say – you with your smart clothes and your fancy ballet training. You don't understand nothing."

By this time Isabelle was trembling with a mixture of fatigue and frustration. Her feet were throbbing, her blisters were smarting and now she was being browbeaten by a total stranger. She'd had enough of this childish wrangling.

Turning on him with eyes blazing and mouth compressed into a thin, hard line, she hissed furiously, "One thing I do understand is that I hate being yelled at by someone so moody and foul-mouthed and mannerless as you. Alex's quite right about something: you're just an uncouth yob. Don't ever speak to me again because I'm never going to speak to you!"

And she flounced off downstairs, stormed through the fire door at the bottom and hurled it shut behind her.

But even while the bang was still echoing in her ears, she stopped short in horror. What on earth had she just done? She, who prided herself on her maturity and self-discipline, losing her temper and sounding off like a cross child in front of someone she hardly knew. What was happening to her?

Worse was to follow. Appalled at the way she'd allowed herself to be drawn into an argument on the stairs for anyone to hear and infuriated by Jordan's total lack of rationality, Isabelle dropped down on a hard bench nearby and promptly burst into tears.

CHAPTER ELEVEN

J ordan stamped upstairs fuming. No one'd ever told him before to his face that he was moody and foul-mouthed and mannerless. And it was surprising how much it hurt – more even than Alex's assertion that he was nothing but a trained monkey performing a circus routine. It was easy enough to recognise the signs of jealousy. But Isabelle's taunt about being an uncouth yob who needed to grow up? That knocked him sideways. Especially when accompanied by the scornful flash of those pale green eyes. He told himself she was just a stupid girl, whose opinion didn't count, but deep down he realised that for some reason, it did.

He hesitated at the top of the stairs, so furious that for a moment he felt like facing round and heading straight back down them and never coming near those studios again. All that'd happened to him since he first set foot here was pain and humiliation.

He'd only agreed to take class with Roy because he thought he'd get good quickly. After all, it was just dancing, wasn't it? Though they insisted on using fancy French terms and treating it like some kind of rocket science. Roy was experienced and at first had seemed impressed by his performance – but now he wasn't so sure. After all, he was only entered for Grade Four in December. From what he'd overheard in the locker rooms since arriving in Temple Street, professional dancers like Alex Fairchild had taken Grade Four when they were kids of eight or nine. And from his position in the back row of the open classes that Roy insisted on him attending each week, it was clear he'd a long way to go before he even reached that standard. He felt sore and cheated.

He actually turned back downstairs, vowing he'd chuck the whole thing and head off to tonight's gig instead. What with all these ballet classes, he'd hardly had a moment to see Elodie and work out if they had a real thing going…

But the thought of Elodie stopped him in his tracks. Elodie rated success highly: she had no time for losers. This was his best chance of showing her what he was made of. But tonight he was taking no bullshit. He'd ask Roy straight out whether he was really any good or not. And if not, he'd check out the next trial times for the county basketball squad and stuff that bloody Grade Four ballet exam. So he turned round again and bounded purposefully back up the stairs two at a time.

But when he pushed open the studio door, Roy was nowhere to be seen. Jordan stared around. After all the fuss he made every week about turning up on time, where was the old bugger? The only person there was Miss Page – Alicia – standing over by the CD player.

She glanced up and flashed him a welcoming smile.

"Come in, Jordan," she encouraged. "Don't be shy."

"But—"

"Roy can't be here tonight. He's in New York."

Jordan instantly frowned. How dare Roy be in New York instead of here with him!

"Is something wrong?" asked Alicia, after studying his face for a moment.

Jordan shrugged.

"What's he doin' in New York?"

"He's flown over for three weeks to help Polis Ballet with their new production of *Prodigal Son*. He's in great demand for projects like this because he learned the ballet from its original choreographer."

"But he didn't say anythin' about it on Tuesday."

"It probably slipped his mind. He has a lot of commitments."

"Oh," said Jordan, suddenly feeling very small.

Alicia shot him a sympathetic grin.

"But that doesn't mean he forgot all about you, you know. He was most insistent that someone be here to teach you tonight."

"So who's gonna do it then?" asked Jordan, thinking that perhaps Cameron might've volunteered and looking round for some sign of him.

But Alicia only smiled.

"I'm afraid you'll have to put up with me this evening. I hope that's not a problem for you."

Jordan gaped. He could just square it with his male ego if he was told what to do in class by a man – but being bossed around by a woman?

"I'm only used to doin' what Roy tells me," he said with as much tact as he could muster. "And you're just—"

"A poor second best?" suggested Alicia.

"No… well, not exactly," answered Jordan, writhing inside as he felt himself sinking deeper and deeper into the mire of social courtesy. "But you're – you know – a woman."

Alicia glanced at him, as he lowered his voice to utter this guilty admission, and then burst out laughing.

"I've been criticised for plenty of things during my years in ballet, but never this."

"I didn't mean it like that," protested Jordan hotly. "I thought women danced different from men."

"It's all right, I'm not offended," she reassured him. "Come on, Jordan, you're an intelligent lad. You've seen me working with Cameron. In this world, we're all on a level. We're just dancers. Only some of us have a bit more experience than others. Roy's bursting with pride at what you two've managed to achieve together in such a short time and I've been really looking forward to seeing how your technique's come on."

Well, if she was gonna put it like that... Jordan preened himself a little. In the face of such artful coaxing, how could he refuse? After all, it was only one lesson. He decided to put a good face on it. So he went over and stood obediently at the barre, thanking his lucky stars that none of his mates could see him now.

They started the Grade Four *plié* exercise.

Jordan was determined to remember everything he'd been taught by Roy. But the strangeness of the situation gave him a tight, nervous feeling in the pit of his stomach, eager as he was to create a good impression. So he adopted a slightly wider second position than usual and strained to sink lower in the bends, as he imagined Alex'd be able to do.

"You're remembering the exercise really well, Jordan," Alicia observed when he'd finished, "but try to keep your back straight. And make sure your knees're over your toes. Have another go."

Jordan stiffened in annoyance at his own stupidity. Of course he knew where his knees were meant to be, but the problem was that tonight they didn't seem to want to be there. When he tried again, he happened to glance into the mirror to check his position and caught sight of himself with his bum sticking out behind.

"When you do a *tendu*, extend your leg straight behind you," advised Alicia after the next exercise. "It's wandering a bit to the right. And the tension's showing in your shoulders. Relax the extended arm..."

And so it went on.

It was one of those classes when nothing would go right. Jordan caught sight of himself again and again in those merciless mirrors making a total hash of all the basic exercises that'd seemed easy enough yesterday. He couldn't understand it. In the carefree days before he started work on these maddening, petty, repetitive exam routines, he'd been able to whirl around the room throwing off pirouettes and *grands jetés* and complex *tours en l'air* without a thought. So why couldn't he do even simple stuff tonight?

As he struggled and sweated, fighting for mastery over his wayward body, Alicia's gentle corrections seemed to act on him like the stings of an annoying wasp on a pain-maddened stallion.

When he'd practically bored a hole in the studio floor with his repeated efforts to accomplish a halfway successful *relevé*, he caught her eye and broke down completely.

"Oh fuck it – fuck the whole soddin' thing," he yelled. "I've had it up to the eyeballs with this shit. I can't do it. I can't dance. I'll never be good enough to take this fuckin' bloody exam."

He broke away and flung himself down on one of the red plastic chairs in a corner of the studio.

He knew he could dance much better than this. But how could he ever face Roy again after Alicia's report on the lesson? And what about the plans he and Roy had for him to take Grade Six in the spring and perhaps even audition for a real ballet school next year? All in the dust. He was living in a fantasy world and he might as well face it. Gran and he still had six mouths to feed on their joint wages and some small government benefits. The luxury of ambition wasn't for people like him. He buried his hot, despairing head in his hands, feeling that this was the end of everything.

After a long moment he grew conscious of someone sitting down quietly beside him. He knew it was Alicia.

"Go away and leave me alone," he moaned, burrowing his head further inside the protective cradle of his arms.

No answer came in words. But a soothing hand reached

out to stroke his arm. It felt like the tender caress of a mother, which Jordan remembered sometimes receiving from his busy grandma when he was a little boy. Alicia's sympathy was so unexpected that it almost drew a sob from him, but he managed to control it just in time. Not daring to look up, he strove half-heartedly to pull away. But she remained sitting there and he could feel her gaze burning him unbearably with pity and understanding.

"I can't do it," he confessed in a broken whisper, raising his head and staring into the mirror of her eyes, which reflected all his terror of defeat.

"Jordan, a sportsman like you should know by now that everyone has off days," she pointed out. "It's no good throwing a tantrum like a spoilt child."

Jordan winced. She didn't seem to understand that he was angry with himself because dancing meant so much to him.

"I can't do it," he repeated miserably. "It's too hard. It used to be easy. But now I've started pullin' apart all those millions of tiny movements and tryin' to do them perfectly one by one, I can't dance any more. So I oughtn' to be here, wastin' your time like this."

"Who's told you you're wasting my time?"

"The real dancers. They think my technique'll never be any good because I haven't been practisin' since I was three years old and that I'll never be any better than a performing monkey."

Alicia smiled.

How could she smile when he was in agony?

"That sounds like ballet people talking," she observed wryly. "The establishment's very conservative and hard to please. Anything a bit new or different and they're at it – sniffing and tut-tutting for all they're worth..."

Jordan raised his drooping head and regarded her questioningly.

111

"It's a highly competitive world," she went on. "These days everyone in it feels they're living on a razor edge. Careers are short and youth and impressive gymnastic feats are at a premium. Principals live in dread of the word 'retirement', soloists are pushing for more and more demanding rôles to show off their technical proficiency, first artists can't understand why they haven't been promoted already and the director's in permanent tail-spin juggling the demands of the company, the problem of funding and the challenges of keeping a balance between the tried and true warhorses of the ballet repertoire and the freshness of new creativity. If you're in this business in the expectation that people are going to praise you for what you do or that you're ever going to be satisfied with the way you do it, you might as well give up now."

Jordan stared. She used big words like Roy, though because of the energy and passion with which she spoke, it was easy enough to grasp her meaning. But he'd expected more sympathy and understanding from this supremely sympathetic and understanding lady. Instead this was what he got: more talk about never being good enough, never coming up to the mark, never making the grade. It was just like school, it was just like life. He was nothing, no one...

"It's easy for you to look down on someone like me," he muttered. "After all, you've been dancing since you were three..." The words almost choked in his throat at the disappointment of seeing his last cherished hope of hauling himself out of the sewer of his life fading, like the good fairy in a dream.

"Whoever told you that?" exclaimed Alicia.

Jordan tossed his head.

"Dunno. Guess you just look like that Isabelle girl, who comes to class on Sundays. I heard her tell Grace the other day that she started ballet when she was three years old."

"Yes, well Isabelle's mother used to be a principal with the

Royal Ballet in London. Isabelle was brought up with ballet slippers on her feet and her mother's expectations to live up to. But not me. I hated ballet lessons. My mother insisted on them because in those days it was very fashionable and she said it would improve my deportment and cure me of my tomboy ways."

What? The graceful, the elegant, the well-spoken Miss Page a tomboy?

"I have four older brothers," she told him with an infectious laugh. "When I was a little girl, I was really good at climbing trees and took great pride in loathing every moment my mother forced me to spend at dancing class. But after a while I began to be interested, because ballet's so hard to do. It's fun challenging yourself to get better and better at something every day – especially if you're a competitive little monkey like I was."

"But how long does it take to get it right?" cried Jordan.

"Do you want to know a secret?"

Jordan shrugged, but he was still listening.

"You never get it right," she said. "It's the working at it that counts, not the succeeding – because there are always fresh challenges. And somehow it doesn't matter in the end. When you're on stage, with the music and the lights and the costumes and the total rapture of the audience – that's the thing that counts. Not the petty technical concerns. Sometimes even now a curtain opens in front of my eyes and I live those moments again. I know all the hard work and pain and tears are worth those tiny glimpses of glory. Dancing may look glamorous, but it's a tough business because there's a price to pay for everyone who devotes their lives to it. I've found it a very difficult journey, but I wouldn't have missed it for the world."

Jordan looked up. She was speaking to him like another human being, not just a school kid or an employee or a moody teenager. Life was hard, but perhaps it was hard for everyone, even the people who looked as though they'd had an easy road to success.

"I guess Roy's been giving you a rough time over the past few weeks," she added kindly. "He can be a pretty grim old task master, can't he?"

Jordan nodded, unable to speak for the prickling lump in his throat.

"It's only because he cares so much deep down. He's got all this experience and he's scared because he's coming up to retirement at the end of this year and he doesn't think anyone will bother about him once he's left the company."

Roy scared? Jordan gaped at her. How could Roy be scared of anything?

"The big problem with dancing you see, Jordan, is that because it exists for just a moment, so do you. You're only as good as your last performance. I've felt that Roy's railroaded you into doing what he wants, being one of his bridges into the future. He hasn't given you time to consider. But I think it's important to know what you're letting yourself in for, because once you set your foot on the stage, it's almost impossible to take it off again. After eight weeks, you're far enough on to be able to make that judgment. If you bow out now, no one will think any the worse of you."

Who was she trying to kid? What about her and Roy? What about himself? Jordan's heart was thumping painfully in his chest as the all-important question trembled on his lips.

"But am I any good? Good enough to dance in a professional company like yours?"

There – at last it was out.

"I don't know," replied Alicia, regarding him with honest eyes.

Jordan's heart sank.

"It's too early to be sure," she went on. "But there's no

reason why not – given the proper training. A girl your age wouldn't stand a chance because the competition's so fierce these days, but for boys it's still different: so much depends on strength and determination and luck and sheer hard work. And Roy's right behind you. In fact he's been so impressed by the way you've motivated your friends into showing up on Sunday afternoons that next term he wants to put together some of the dance sequences that you've all been trying out and work towards a performance for your family and friends in the summer."

"A performance?" echoed Jordan.

"Yes. So there's no time to lose. Cameron and I have an idea for giving him a surprise when he gets home, but we'd need your help to pull it off. Are you planning to finish class, by the way?"

Jordan glanced at her, thoroughly ashamed of his childish outburst.

"But hasn't the hour run out?" he asked, struggling to respond in a more grown-up and professional manner. "Won't you need to be paid overtime?"

Alicia raised her eyebrows.

"Young people today. You're all so mercenary. You don't understand the way things really are. We older dancers never do important things for money. We do it all for love."

Jordan only realised what she meant much later on. At the time he was too busy asking questions about the performance Roy had in mind and her idea for surprising him. He begged her to tell him more as they went back to work on his pirouette preparation.

CHAPTER TWELVE

When Alicia announced to the Youth Dance group at Brackwell Heath that they could sleep in as long as they liked the following Sunday because the company was leaving for a season in London, an outburst of applause greeted her words. The loudest whoops came from the mouth of Ashley Kent, who found his powers of concentration severely taxed by the discipline demanded of him in class.

"Just think what we can do with a whole free Sunday afternoon," he boasted to the others. "I can't wait…"

Jordan wasn't so sure.

By showing him the challenges that lay ahead, Alicia's words at the dance studio in town had only made him more determined than ever to become a real dancer. He decided he needed to take an unflinching look at his life and focus everything he did on achieving this one exclusive ambition. Didn't really care that much for smoking – and drinking was bad for you anyway. Besides, if he scraped together all the cash he could save by stripping himself of these unimportant luxuries, he could probably afford a cheap ticket or two to some dance productions in town. And every night after work he'd haunt the ballet studios to practise. That exam was coming up fast.

With the company on tour, the deserted buildings fell strangely silent as only administrative and technical staff were left, who were heading home by the time he arrived to begin his long evening's work. He'd soon made firm friends with the bluff caretaker, who locked up at nights, and got used to exercising all alone in the chill, echoing studio, by now as familiar to him as his own home.

When the company were out of town, open classes were always taught by Murray Bennet from Airborne and Jordan arrived the following Thursday evening excited by the prospect of working once again under firm male control.

He left an hour and a half later feeling irritable and confused.

Easygoing Murray hadn't driven him beyond the limits of his ability like Roy, nor coaxed the best out of him like Alicia and Jordan couldn't help feeling faintly contemptuous of an adult who persisted in calling *pliés* 'kneebends'. If anyone'd told him the previous week that he'd be pacing the locker room that night after class in an outburst of frustration because a woman'd handed him over to a man for ballet lessons, he would've laughed in their face. But it was still true for all that.

On Sunday the weather was cold and squally. When Gran called him down for church, he heard gales rattling his window pane, so he promptly rolled over and went back to sleep, not waking up again till nearly noon. After a leisurely lunch, he headed into the centre of Brackwell Heath with Ash to catch up with their mates.

Keen blasts of wind whined through the bare branches of the poplars bordering the desolate recreation ground, rasping torn crisp packets along the iron railings before spiking them playfully on thorn bushes in the railway cutting. Stray leaves whirled in purposeless eddies around the children's play park, deserted that raw afternoon except for some Asian guy all muffled up in a black coat and scarf, patiently pushing a kid in a red snowsuit back and forth on one of the swings.

"Stupid bastard," muttered Ash. "Who but a complete nutter'd be out here with a kid in this weather?"

They strode closer and all of a sudden Jordan gasped out loud.

"Hey, Ash, that nutter's bloody Sudhir!"

The child, presumably one of Sudhir's nephews, looked far too big for that infant seat as he clutched onto the safety bar with his woolly-hatted head thrown back, laughing aloud. In spite of the distance between them, Jordan instantly sensed something wasn't quite right with the kid. As they passed by, his eyes met Sudhir's and he saw at once that Sudhir knew what he was thinking. But the Asian youth went on defiantly pushing the kid, who was laughing, laughing out of a dribbling mouth.

The other two strode on. But a few chilling words that he'd overheard at the garage the other day sprang into Jordan's mind.

"Say, Ash," he cried, "wasn't it Sudhir's eldest sister who committed suicide the other day by swallowing a massive overdose of sleeping pills…?"

Ash just shrugged and set his face into the bitter wind.

They came across Eugene and Oz, slouching aimlessly along the high street, and the four of them soon met up with Dill and big Jermaine idly kicking their heels against a brick wall outside the boarded-up community education centre. No one made any mention of what they usually did at this time on a Sunday afternoon and Jordan planned to keep it that way. He'd got enough odd looks when he once accidentally let slip a remark about *grands battements* and *ronds de jambe* in their hearing. Better to ignore the whole business.

The attractions of the local shops were soon exhausted. Most of them stood locked and shuttered, except the Costcutter minimart with its outdoor rack of Sunday papers sheathed in polythene to ward off the spitting rain. After the boys had sauntered up and down the shelves of crisps and beer cans for five minutes laughing and joking, they were firmly escorted from the premises by watchful Mr Singh.

Emerging glumly onto the high street again, they found themselves jostled off the pavement by a group of burly, red-nosed men in waterproof jackets with woollen hats pulled well down over their ears and shoulders hunched against the icy wind, who soon piled in through the welcoming doors of the Black Swan Inn.

The well-lit warmth of the pub was still strictly off limits, so the boys lounged across the road towards Caribbean Joe's. But they cheered up when through runnels of condensation dripping down the misty window pane, they made out the figures of Elodie and the other girls seated at a table inside. Nicole glanced up and waved back, so they decided their luck was in. They all trooped into the café just as the rain began to pelt down.

Jordan found himself squeezed into a corner beside Elodie and, after they'd all decided what to drink, was even granted the privilege of fetching her a second cappuccino from the bar. The afternoon was looking up, he decided. But not for long.

On turning back as he stood waiting for service, he caught sight of her and Nicole with their sleek heads bent together, nudging each other and giggling over some private joke. The focus of their attention made him clap his hand to his empty jacket pocket and cringe with horror. How could he've been so fazed by Elodie shifting over to make room for him as to leave his phone lying on the table? They were obviously killing themselves with laughter over the cheap, out-dated model that he generally took care to keep well hidden from public view.

On his return to the table he instantly repocketed the despised mobile, but it was too late. The damage was done. His self-conscious haste only led to fresh outbursts of giggling, which they steadfastly refused to explain. He sank down on the bench, his face burning with shame.

None of his mates paid any attention to his discomfort

because they were all too busy trying to impress the girls themselves. But after a time the conversation flagged. Oz asked what they were going to do now.

"Dunno," replied Ash with a careless shrug of his broad shoulders. "We're always at the gym this time Sunday…"

"Musta done somefink on Sunday afternoons before we did dancin'," pointed out Oz with indisputable logic.

"Can't remember. 'S too long ago."

They all sat for a moment, thinking hard.

"What about a game o'football?" asked Eugene, who'd recently surprised them all by announcing his plan to try for a place on the county team and was now training hard on Saturdays. "Rain looks like it's easin' off," he added, with an optimistic nod toward the streaming window pane.

"You blind, dick head?" Ash grunted. "It's still tippin' it down out there."

"Besides, I ain't interested in football," Elodie added, smoothing her carefully straightened hair.

"We could go to a movie," suggested Jermaine, who was a keen film buff.

"Nah. I'm skint," protested Oz.

"Let's go home and watch TV instead," urged Nicole, who always preferred the easy option.

"No way." Oz firmly vetoed this proposal. "There's never nuffink good on – just a load o'junk. Anyway, who wants to go home?" A gloomy silence followed, broken only when he wistfully observed, "I s'pose the ballet company had to go on tour, didn' they?"

"It's their job," Jordan replied, his spirits reviving a little at the mention of dancing.

"But why are they stayin' away so long? I'm bored. Wish there was a class this afternoon."

Dill and Eugene exchanged pitying glances over a guy who actually wanted to go to school on Sunday afternoon.

Suddenly Ash said, "I s'pose at least the gym's warm and dry. An' it's better'n doin' nothin'. So when're they comin' back from London, Jordan?"

Everyone's eyes turned towards him.

"Two weeks," he replied, suddenly realising just how long this fortnight was going to be.

"Two weeks?" echoed Ash. "You mean to say, we ain't gonna practise our big dance for two whole weeks? It's took us ages to get them bloody steps sorted. We'll've forgot 'em again by the time Roy comes back if we don't do no practice."

"Shame. I was just gettin' into that music too," mused Dill in a tone of genuine regret. "It's given me a great idea of my own..." And he sighed aloud.

Ash pulled a face which plainly said 'What a weirdo!'

At that moment the café door jingled open and all eyes turned towards the chattering newcomers who piled in, shaking off the streaming rain. It was Sudhir with his pretty, long-lashed girlfriend, Simran, and several other Asians, muffled in scarves and winter jackets. The sight of Sudhir made Jordan feel uncomfortable.

"What the hell're *they* doin' here?" murmured Ash with a glare of undiminished hostility.

The Asians swept a disdainful glance around, as though there was no one in the café they recognised, and colonised the table next door with a show of careless bravado.

The West Indian gang huddled together, muttering resentfully. This was where they'd chosen to hang out and their territory'd just been invaded by the enemy. They indignantly watched the Asians ordering coffees and cans of coke. It was clear they were planning to stay put.

"Let's split," suggested Jermaine warily.

"Nah. We was here first," retorted Ash. "They didn't oughta muscle in on us."

Then, without warning, he rolled his eyes and burst into an explosive fit of coughing.

In a flash Jordan'd half-started to his feet, afraid his mate was having one of his asthma attacks. But when Eugene joined in with a melodramatic display of choking, he sat back with a grin to watch the show. Ash and Eugene treated them to a bravura performance, thrashing around in their seats, clutching their throats and thumping each other violently on the back. Everyone in the café turned to stare.

"Can't you smell the rotten stink?" they wheezed, fanning their noses and glancing towards the Asians.

Sudhir pretended not to notice, but from where Jordan was sitting, he could see the back of his neck flush dully. Somehow, after what he'd witnessed in the play park earlier that afternoon, his mates' teasing didn't seem so funny any more. In fact, it suddenly felt downright sickening...

"Hey, guys, I think the stench is comin' from over there," Ash announced, with a nod in the direction of the Asians.

Jordan rose uneasily.

"Ash," he interrupted in a low voice, laying a hand on his friend's arm, "hey, cool it, man. We don't need no trouble."

But Ash shook him off.

"Why don't you bloody little curry-munchers fuck off so everyone in here can breathe clean air?" he demanded aloud.

Sudhir suddenly leapt to his feet and spun round to face his tormentor. Simran tried to drag him down again, but he pushed her angrily aside.

"Say that again, you shit-eating white bastard," he threatened, clenching his fists in fury. "It's a free country. We got as much right here as you."

As Sudhir and Ash confronted one another over the flimsy trellised partition, Jordan saw the waitress's nervous eyes flicker towards Big Joe, the West Indian café proprietor, who was leaning his ham fists on the counter as he chatted to a customer. But Big Joe, a normally placid mountain of a man with a shiny bald head and the girth of a ten ton barrel, had already scented trouble. He broke off his conversation at once and swayed menacingly over in their direction.

"Outa here," he ordered before anyone could argue. "Go on, scram, the whole bloody pack o'you. I had my eye on you louts since you first come in. What'd I tell you last time there was a fight? First sign o'trouble and you're out on your behinds. Ain't you got nothin' better to do with yourselves on a Sunday afternoon than pick quarrels with each another? Young savages. Black, white or brown, you're all the bloody same. Why don't you just grow up?"

Ash, who was reckless when his temper was roused, began protesting that they'd been here first, but Big Joe would have none of it. Even Ash was forced to back down as he measured Joe's angry bulk with his eyes. They soon found themselves hustled out into the rain along with the disgruntled Asians.

"Think it's funny, eh, Short-Arse?" snapped Ash, turning up his jacket collar and trying to soothe his own humiliation by picking on Sudhir. "If you bastards hadn't come along, we wouldn'ta been thrown out in the first place."

Sudhir confronted him in high indignation. "Whaddya mean: if we hadn't come along? We was just mindin' our own business. You were the ones who started it..."

"If the whole bunch of you guys didn't behave like a pack of stupid kids, we'd all still be in the dry," interrupted Elodie furiously, trying to shield her hair under her shiny scarlet handbag as she looked round for shelter. "Point is: what we gonna do now?"

There was an awkward silence, during which they heard only the dismal pattering of raindrops and the rush of water racing along the flooded gutters. Jordan wished he'd stayed at home.

"You know, I reckon dancing was better than being stuck

123

out here getting soaked," sighed Simran, whose eyeliner was dripping in black blobs onto her elegantly manicured hands.

"Seems a pity to waste a whole afternoon with these clowns fightin' each other, don't you think, Simran?" With a glance of sympathy, Elodie made space for the Asian girl to squeeze under cover of the shoe shop porch, where she'd taken refuge.

The two had started exchanging beauty tips in the locker rooms after class on Sundays and now stood side by side regarding the boys with open scorn.

"So why not go and practise our dance?" suggested Oz suddenly. "After all," gesturing round the huddle of drenched teenagers shivering under partial shelter in the doorway, "we're almost all here, aren't we?"

Two months ago his proposal would have been unthinkable. But now they all stared at one other, startled by the discovery that they actually had something in common: if nothing else, they'd got used to dancing together.

Roy cherished no favourites. He shouted with equal energy at everyone, regardless of race or gender, and he always worked them so hard that they'd long given up fighting in class. Lately too, Alicia'd even experienced some success in coaxing them to co-operate in time to the music from opposite sides of the gym. So no one dismissed Oz's idea out of hand.

Instead Ash uttered a scornful snort.

"How could we work on our dance, dick head, even if we wanted to? We got nowhere to go. It needs a big space – like the gym."

"So what's wrong wiv goin' to the gym then?"

Ash rolled his eyes as if humouring an idiot. "It's fuckin' locked. That's what. Man, it's Sunday afternoon."

"Yes – but…" Sudhir burst out. Then he stopped and glanced back questioningly at his friends.

"But what?" prompted Jordan, keen to stop pretending he didn't care about getting drenched.

"Oh go on," urged Eugene impatiently, "you may as well tell us."

"Tell us what?" cried Oz in bewilderment.

"About the gym," explained Sudhir, shaking the sodden rat tails of hair out of his eyes. "We've been borrowin' stuff from there at the weekend for years."

"But how'd you get in?"

"Don't you guys know about the little back window into the sports equipment store that doesn't shut properly? Tanjit here," indicating the tiny Asian girl beside him, "she's small enough to squeeze through, if we hoist her up on our shoulders, and she can easily disable the alarm because her brother taught her the code when he got too big to fit through himself. She can open the front doors from the inside."

"Wicked!"

Ash couldn't help looking impressed.

"But what if we're caught inside without a teacher?" asked Jermaine cautiously.

"Who's gonna be patrolling the grounds today?" Eugene demanded, pointing to the rain.

"Besides, we can always say Mizz Scott let us in to practise," added Elodie.

"But we got no music," objected Jordan. "We gotta have the music – or we can't dance."

This problem seemed insoluble.

At that point Dill emitted a modest cough and patted his damp jacket pocket.

"Well… I got it on my mp3 player," he confessed slowly. "Wasn't gonna say nothin' 'cos I thought you'd all laugh at me, but my big bro bought me a copy of *Romeo and Juliet* for my birthday last week. Mum's eyes almost popped out o'her head when she came into my bedroom and heard me playin' it…"

There was a moment's silence as they all stared at one another, unable to think of any further objections.

"It don't change the way things are outside class, you understand," warned Ash, clearly afraid a temporary ceasefire would give Sudhir the false idea that the rival gangs had struck a permanent peace treaty.

As Sudhir nodded in agreement, everyone began shouting at once.

"So what are we waitin' for?"

"Jordan'll know all the steps. He can tell us what to do if we forget."

"I'll go home an' fetch my speakers an' meet you at the gym in ten minutes."

"Come on, man – let's go and dance…"

CHAPTER THIRTEEN

One evening in early December on his way up to practise as usual, Jordan reached the head of the stairs and halted in surprise. There was a light on in the top studio. A curious glance in through one of the round portholes in the heavy wooden door showed him the figure of Isabelle, alone at the barre, dressed in pale blue leotard and pink tights. Jordan swiftly recoiled. What was she doing in *his* studio?

The company must be back. He'd noticed the building felt warmer as soon as he stepped inside. So it was no longer *his* studio...

He hesitated. The last thing he wanted was to bump into Isabelle. She hated him. After all, she'd said she never wanted to speak to him again, so he'd better get the hell out of there before she had another chance to insult him.

But he couldn't help wondering what she was up to. It was fascinating to see dancers dancing. He could learn new steps or even just watch their bodies adopting poses that he'd begun to recognise and call by their proper names. Perhaps he'd risk another peek in through the glass porthole – just to check.

Isabelle's back was towards him and in fact she seemed wholly self-absorbed, as she stood with the ankle of her right leg resting easily upon the barre. Her right arm was raised high above her head in a gentle curve as she balanced herself lightly with the fingertips of her left hand.

Jordan drew back again, fearing she might've glimpsed him in the mirror. Perhaps he'd better sneak off and leave her to it…

He turned and for a moment felt almost sure he could tear himself away from the vision that was still stamped on his inner eye: of the pale pastel figure in the half-lit studio, poised above her lifted leg. Was her back really as straight as he remembered it? He bit his lip and looked again.

She'd changed position. Now her body lay folded forward along her leg, her arm reaching beyond the pointed toe of her soft pink leather ballet slipper. Astonishing to see how far she could stretch: impossible that anyone could be so supple…

But just as Isabelle reached the furthest point of extension, she raised herself upright once more. The swelling arc of that lifted arm. The slightly rounded elbow, the angled wrist, the gently relaxed fingers, the sheer beauty of that fleeting gesture. Jordan gaped. He felt so clumsy and uncouth by comparison.

Inspired to imitate the perfection of her pose, he stepped back from the window and raised his own arm high in the air. But he couldn't know whether he'd caught her graceful elegance without the aid of a mirror – and besides, he longed to see what she was doing now. So he crept cautiously back to the glass pane, watching in awe as she eased her right leg further and further along the barre like the opening prongs of a compass. If he'd tried to do that, he would've broken in half. She was so flexible, like the pliant limbs of plastic dolls, which Darleen twisted into impossible poses. But those dolls were stiff and lifeless, whereas the body of this girl was alive and breathing, effortlessly able to stretch and contract itself.

Without apparent strain, Isabelle exerted pressure with her hands on the barre, tipping her weight back onto her supporting leg, then grasped the free foot with her right hand and gracefully unfolded in a *developé*. Jordan followed the arc traced by her pointing toe till she stood balanced on one leg with her ankle high above her ear. How could anyone make the impossible look so easy?

Now, with a quick rippling movement, she'd shaken herself out and was executing the mirror image of what he'd just witnessed with her left leg. Then she sank gracefully towards the ground in an immaculate set of splits. Jordan breathed a sigh.

Of course he'd seen people doing the splits before. Ash was an expert. But on the floor of Dillon's garage among the flashing lights and sweaty bodies, these lightning glimpses were mere gymnastic exhibitions. This slow, deliberate sinking towards the floor felt like the gradual opening of a window into a world of ideal beauty – no hint of glamour or showiness: it merely existed miraculously in space. Jordan ached with admiration.

How little thought he'd ever given to the possibilities of the human body – how rarely ever stopped to consider this miraculous framework of bones and sinews and muscle that carried him around…

Meanwhile Isabelle's legs had curled into a seated position, then lifted her into an effortless arabesque, which soon tipped forward into a *penché*. The dizzying height of her lifted leg. The perfect line running straight from the tip of her extended toe down her spine and head to the end of her poised fingertips and even beyond. It was so beautiful that tears pricked at the back of his eyes. And there was no one here to witness this miracle except himself.

He stepped away from the door and spread his body against the cold concrete wall of the stairwell in an effort to shock himself back into reality. But the next moment he had to look again – and when he did so, Isabelle was no longer alone.

Alex was with her, clad in the light practice gear so well suited to its purpose. Except that Alex always looked so infuriatingly elegant in his, as though the black leggings'd been moulded to his muscular calves and the tight-fitting T-shirt was a mere second skin around his shapely chest.

Jordan had done his best to find fault with Alex's physique, roundly abusing him as a wimp and a weakling to his gang of friends. But there was no doubt: the all-revealing costume of a dancer at once highlighted the least bodily imperfection and though Alex was slightly built and slender-waisted, he was strong and well-muscled, as a result of constant exercise and daily weight-training in the gym.

At first Jordan could see the pair of them mouthing words he couldn't hear and exchanging gestures he couldn't read. But the next moment Alex laid his fingers on her shoulder and, turning her towards him, hoisted her with one expert hand so easily into the air that she seemed to float above his head. Jordan gasped at the simple mastery of the lift, the bold defiance of gravity and the apparent weightlessness of Isabelle's frame, as airy and light-boned as a bird's. He watched in awe as Alex paraded her effortlessly around the studio stretching out both her arms – and he realised where he'd seen this sequence of steps before: in the blue lights of a dim, spotlit stage during the balcony scene from *Romeo and Juliet*. His memory instantly conjured up the soaring passion of the music and the dark, rose-entwined courtyard with a pair of white figures irradiating the gloom all around.

Greedily he drank in every gesture and attitude, a perfect harmonisation of the male and female forms in the ecstasy of young love. Together, those two had everything: they were the children of light. If only he could be like them!

He leaned closer and closer to the brilliant spectacle, unconsciously pressing so hard against the studio door that all of a sudden – CRASH! It gave way beneath his weight, sending him staggering forwards.

The noise caused the vision before his eyes to blur and

falter. Both dancers' faces flashed round in alarm as the heavy door swung shut again, hurling Jordan backwards onto the landing with a bang that made him see stars. Dazed and breathless, he lay sprawled on the ground, clutching his jaw in silent agony. Then, fearing they'd be on him in another instant, he dragged himself unsteadily to his feet and tore away downstairs.

★

"What was that?" cried Isabelle, roused from deep concentration and aware only of a sudden loud crash and then the rhythmical motion of the studio door swinging backwards and forwards into nothingness.

"I just glimpsed a face in the mirror," Alex replied, springing off to wrench open the door and peer out into the empty darkness. "But I'm pretty sure it was Jordan Howe, spying on us again. That guy seems totally obsessed by you. He acts like some kind of stalker."

"Stalker!" echoed Isabelle with a shiver. "What makes you say that?"

"The way he watches you dance," replied Alex, as he turned back towards her. "I noticed it while I was standing in the wings during the performance that Roy arranged for those school kids to attend. He was sitting in the front row with his eyes glued to your every move. I reckon you should stop going to those classes before they lead to trouble. In fact you know my opinion: that you should never've got mixed up with them in the first place."

"Well I happen to think differently," retorted Isabelle, setting her mouth in an obstinate line. She was fed up with Alex's criticism of what he snidely termed her 'charity work' at Brackwell Heath High. "I wasn't sure I wanted to keep going at first, but now I've got used to it, I'm beginning to understand how important this outreach project is. I've really missed the classes while we've been away in London."

"What do you mean?" Alex sounded genuinely puzzled. "Cameron says it's absolutely basic stuff. Struggling to teach them the simplest routines—"

"It may look like that from the outside, but there's a lot more to it. We're trying to use the dance routines to help them come to terms with the rest of their lives. You see, at first none of them understood the concept of self-discipline or how to work together as a team. They used to argue all the time and Roy was always yelling his head off about people turning up late and mobiles going off in class. But at the start of the last lesson before we left for London, Lauren actually went and stood at the door to remind everyone to turn off their phones as they came in and Hayley admitted to me that she was determined to take advantage of this opportunity. I'm really looking forward to seeing whether Nicole manages to make it to class on time this week…"

"Sounds terrific progress when you put it like that," scoffed Alex. "Making it to class on time. Big deal."

"For Nicole it *is* a big deal. You don't understand because you haven't been there week after week watching her fail to achieve it. These teenagers've never had a highly structured routine like ours to help them control their lives and their home circumstances sometimes don't make things easy for them either."

"Now, Bella—"

"Just listen to me a moment," she interrupted earnestly. "Let me tell you about one boy there, whose mum's a strict Jehovah's Witness."

Alex raised one sceptical eyebrow. But at least he seemed to be listening.

"She refused point blank to let Oz do class on Sundays," Isabelle persisted, feeling this story couldn't fail to win him over. "At first he came along without her knowing since he didn't want to be left out and this upset him because he and his mum're usually very close. He's not particularly well coordinated, you see, so he finds the whole idea of dance a bit overwhelming."

"And?"

"Well, a fortnight ago I stayed behind to help Oz after class and we went through the sequence they'd been learning over and over again until at last he managed to get it right every time. You should've seen the grin on his face. He said he was going to practise those steps every day while I was away so he didn't forget them. Last Tuesday night his mum caught him at it in his bedroom. Then he showed her what he'd learned and she was so amazed, she said it must be a miracle. So she's changed her mind about him coming to class on Sundays now. Isn't that fantastic progress?" And Isabelle glowed with pride and pleasure.

Alex's brow contracted into a frown. "But we've been in London for the past fortnight," he pointed out abruptly. "If this only happened on Tuesday, how do you know about it?"

"Oz texted me of course."

Alex's eyes widened. "You mean you've given your phone number to a total stranger with a religious fanatic for a mother?"

Isabelle stared at him blankly.

"But Oz isn't a stranger," she said. "And his mum needs something to keep her going apart from dressmaking. You see, his dad used to work on a big country estate, but after he was made redundant, he started drinking heavily and now he can't get employment because of the gaps in his CV. His reading and writing aren't good enough even to fill in the job seekers' forms without help."

Alex was staring at her in his turn.

"What's wrong?" she exclaimed.

"You should hear yourself. You're even beginning to sound like a social worker. Poking your nose into other people's private lives…"

"But I'm not poking my nose in. Oz trusts me. He told me all about it when we went for a coffee together after class."

There was a moment's stunned silence. Then, "I can't believe this," Alex retorted. "You mean you've actually gone out for coffee with one of those street kids?"

"Why not?" asked Isabelle. Why was he making such a fuss over nothing? "It was freezing cold outside and we needed something to warm us up, so since we both happened to be walking in the same direction—"

"Bella, how could you be so stupid?"

Isabelle drew back. Who was he calling stupid?

"No wonder Jordan Howe thinks you're fair game," Alex went on quickly, "if you behave in a way that could be so easily misinterpreted. It struck me at the outset that something like this might happen, but I thought you'd be sensible enough to steer clear of the danger—"

"Danger! What danger?" demanded Isabelle. "You're suggesting we ignore other people's problems because they happen to be poorer than us?"

"That's not what I'm suggesting at all. I just think you haven't enough experience to realise what you could be letting yourself in for."

"How can you be so patronising?"

Alex flushed.

"I'm not being patronising," he protested, "I'm simply being practical. You're a dancer. You've no idea how to handle complex problems like these. That's the job of social workers and trained experts. Being a dancer in a professional company means focussing exclusively on your career and not letting yourself be sidetracked. You've got to be strong-willed and determined."

"And blinkered?"

"If you insist on calling it that," he replied, turning aside with an irritable shrug.

Isabelle wanted to shake him for being so blind. Of course it wasn't right to ignore the problems of other human beings, whoever they were! She opened her mouth to tell him how unbelievably self-centred he was and suddenly stopped short. The set of his jaw told her it was no use. He was never going to change his mind.

For one frightening moment she didn't even like him, let alone love him. The shock was dizzying, as though he'd just hit her.

"Look," he resumed, turning back in an attempt at reconciliation, "I think we'll have to agree to differ about this business, OK? Now do you want to try that lift again?"

Just like that, as though there'd been no argument at all.

Isabelle blinked. At that point there was nothing in the world she felt less like doing than dancing. She hung her head.

"Actually I'm feeling rather tired," she murmured shakily. "If it's all the same to you, I'd prefer to call it a day…"

During the awkward silence as he opened the studio door for her, she realised that this was the first serious quarrel they'd ever had.

CHAPTER FOURTEEN

J ordan stumbled out of the company studios into the ill-lit street, his cheek still smarting with the blow from the heavy door. If he could only hide himself in the security of the warm, simple world he'd always known. Those dancers, that life they represented, were too complex and terrifying for him to understand.

Before he knew what was happening, he found himself standing breathlessly at the bus stop opposite the deserted markets. By then, contact with the freezing winter darkness had shocked him back to his senses and Elodie's old words of warning suddenly flashed through his mind. He darted uneasy glances into the surrounding shadows. What if he was caught out here alone by Prince and his gang of toughs?

But no one seemed to be around. Gingerly feeling the swelling lump on his face, Jordan forced himself to think. No use running home to a house full of squabbling kids where Gran was likely to ask him what'd happened. No. What he needed more than anything were his real mates.

He'd no idea where they were that evening, so he fumbled in his jacket pocket for his mobile. A quick call to Oscar had soon located them at Mephisto and Jordan began to breathe more easily. The club wasn't far away, so he at once set off for Dark Street.

By this hour on a cold, clear December night, galaxies of blue lights were twinkling among the bare-branched trees outside the Olympian Theatre and the frosty air, redolent of alcohol fumes and cigarette smoke, throbbed with the beat of loud disco music, as youths in black leather swaggered across the road, weaving this way and that among the cruising taxis. Elbowing his way through a knot of shadowy figures huddled in a doorway under a flashing neon sign, Jordan plunged down a side-alley towards the drab, secluded entrance that led into the cavernous basements of Mephisto.

The nightclub had long been a favourite haunt of his gang. When he'd first entered its doors while still at school, Jordan imagined that its glamorous décor, reminiscent of a Hollywood take on a nineteenth-century Parisian brothel, must be the last word in elegance. But he'd long grown used to the red flock walls and naked statues flourishing gilt candelabra and realised that its chief attraction lay in the fact that at Mephisto they weren't too particular about ID and drinks were cheap.

Jordan hadn't been there for months and that night as he walked in, wavered on the threshold, driven back by the pulsating barrier of sound, which hit him like a shockwave. He shouldered his way through the heaving sea of sweaty bodies on the dance floor and finally reached the bar. But as he ordered a pint, a vision suddenly appeared beside him of Isabelle in her pale blue party dress, shining like a star. Her radiance shed fresh light on the scene around and Jordan's heart sank. How had he never before noticed the cracked and clouded mirror panels behind the bartender's head, the battered gilding of the fake Greek temple pillars? Was the summit of his teenage ambition really nothing but a seedy sham?

He instantly suppressed the thought, but couldn't help staring at the flamboyant feathered helmet, sparkling with paste diamonds, sported by the cabaret singer gyrating around the tiny stage against a backdrop of glittering tinsel. Her heavy blue eyeshadow and overblown figure, squeezed into a short, black, beaded dress shivering with fringes, would certainly've seemed tasteless to Isabelle.

He peered through the gloom, trying to spot his mates. Eventually he caught sight of Elodie in violet spangles, seated at a table in the outer porch with the rest of the gang. So he ploughed his way over, only to find himself cold-shouldered as she straightaway rose and swept towards the dance floor on the eager arm of Dillon, who clearly fancied his chances tonight in his older brother's cast-off leather jacket.

Jordan tried to pretend nothing was wrong. Setting his beer glass down among the overflowing ashtrays on the grimy table top, he pointedly drew up a chair next to Oscar, who sat in a disregarded corner as usual, hunched over his mobile. Jordan leaned back with an air of feigned carelessness and decided to work on Oz in the hope of finding out what was up with Elodie.

"So how's it going, mate?" he asked, aiming a casual punch at Oz's thin, bony shoulder. "Any bright ideas for a new computer game?"

"Yeah, man – you said it," agreed Oscar, nodding as he glanced up from the lighted screen through straggling locks of greasy red hair. There was a glint of excitement in his eye which, through the lurid smoke haze, made him look like a wizard hovering over a simmering cauldron in an underground dungeon.

"So what's it this time?" asked Jordan, automatically helping himself to Oz's lighted cigarette, which lay on the chipped, imitation marble ashtray. "Rough terrain car rallies? Sci-fi space monsters? Taiwanese martial arts?"

"Old hat, man. Got this great new idea. Fort it up a few weeks ago, when we was watchin' that ballet show at the Olympian."

"What? You're designin' a computer game about ballet

dancers?" exclaimed Jordan, unconvinced of its appeal to a mass market of teenage youths.

"Nah. Not ezzactly. It's kinda gang warfare in the city back streets. I could see jus' what that show was on about, ya know. All the story needs is a bit of jazzin' up wiv knives and guns 'steada swords 'n' daggers. 'S got everyfink a good game needs: love 'n' death, drugs, sex 'n' violence. Ballet rocks, man."

"Hadn't thought of it like that," admitted Jordan, suddenly wondering if Alicia would approve of him smoking two days before his Grade Four exam.

"Yeah, it's give me this great idea," went on Oz decisively. "An' this time I'm really gonna be aimin' high. Before, I was just kinda muckin' round – but now I made up my mind. Like, this is a major breakthrough. I need to fink frew my concepts, get 'em down in a demo an' see if I can sell it to a company. I wanna make it big time."

"Hey, man, that sounds great," responded Jordan, rather startled by this new development and deciding on balance to replace the cigarette in the ashtray. "Best o'luck. What's sparked all this off then?"

Oz blushed over his beer glass.

"Go on – you can tell me," urged Jordan with a reassuring grin.

"I bin finkin' about the future, man," confessed Oz earnestly.

"Any reason?"

Oz rolled his eyes as though there was a lot more to it than he was letting on – but still hesitated to trust Jordan with his secret.

"Fink o'the biggest fing you can imagine happenin' to me," he hinted, lowering his voice and casting a furtive glance around. But Eugene was busy entertaining the rest of the table with an account of the football match he'd played yesterday, so no one else was listening.

"Umm – dunno," muttered Jordan, racking his brains for an important event that could possibly've happened to Oscar. "Your dad finally landed a job?"

Oz frowned. "We're talkin' the real world here," he protested.

"OK, OK, man. The real world. Er, let's see… er… Gi's a clue."

"I got my eye on this bird," burst out Oz, unable to contain himself any longer, "an' I fink she likes me too." His face shone with pride and excitement.

Jordan's mouth fell open.

No girl, as far as he knew, had ever allowed her name to be coupled with that of Oscar. Not even Nicole, who'd been known to sink pretty low in her desperate search for Mr Right. They all treated him as a kid brother or a harmless plaything like a doll or a teddy bear. No one'd ever taken him seriously as a boyfriend before.

"Really?" gasped Jordan, promptly shutting his mouth in an effort not to hurt his mate's feelings. "She – er – new at school then?"

"Well, she comes to school, but she ain't – like – at it. You know her."

Jordan mentally reviewed every girl he knew connected with Brackwell Heath High, wondering who was the emotionally starved freak, whose life was so sad as to be smitten by Oscar's charms.

"Do I?" he countered, still in the dark.

"Yeah. That ballet bird."

"Ballet bird?" exclaimed Jordan in open disbelief, feeling there must be crossed wires somewhere. "You got your eye on a ballet bird?"

"Yeah. That one who turns up to help wiv class. We had our first date a couple o'Sundays back."

"Isabelle. You had a date with Isabelle?" Jordan was

staggered. He would never've dared even to *ask* Isabelle to go out with him, let alone dream she might actually accept!

"Yep. Real stunner, ain't she? All that red hair like autumn leaves and that pretty, soft, white skin. But more than that, she's really kind. She's got nice manners like an' she calls me by my name."

Jordan gulped.

"Look, Oz," he cautioned, wanting to let him down as gently as possible, "I dunno what she told you, but she's already got a boyfriend – in the ballet company."

"I ain't makin' this up, man. You fink 'cos she's so pretty, she'd never look at a loser like me. But you're wrong. We had coffee at Caribbean Joe's. Our first date. No kiddin', man. We're gonna be an item, like you 'n' Elodie. An' I got her mobile number. I texted her this week," Oz boasted, recalling Isabelle's reply on his phone and showing it proudly to his friend.

Jordan shrugged, but he still felt there must be some mistake. Isabelle dating someone like Oz?

"So you got plans to ask her out again?" he asked aloud, fascinated by the web of fantasy that Oz's brain'd been busy spinning.

"I ain't gonna hurry this, man," said Oz quickly. "This is so big, it kinda blows your mind. Gotta save up – that's why I'm makin' big plans for the future…"

Afraid where all this might lead, Jordan uneasily reiterated that as far as he knew Isabelle was seeing someone else. But Oz'd never met Alex Fairchild and nothing Jordan could say seemed to make the least impression on him.

He finally gave up. When Oz got an idea fixed in his head, it was almost impossible to shake it out – and he couldn't bring himself to be brutally frank about his gut feeling that none of them stood a snowball's chance in hell with a posh girl like Isabelle. Besides, what other reason could she have for going out to Caribbean Joe's with his mate, giving him her mobile number and replying so promptly to his text? Wasn't always easy to work out what women wanted…

Like Elodie, who was clearly bent on giving him a hard time that night for no reason he could fathom.

He tried to speak to her when Dillon brought her back to the table, but she refused to let him close enough for words. Instead she returned at once to the dance floor, this time with Eugene, where she proceeded to wiggle her hips and flaunt her breasts so provocatively that Jordan could hardly blame the guy for prancing and strutting round her like it was the pair of them that was the item. He hardly knew himself which way to look – and Eugene wasn't the only guy in the room whose tongue was hanging out, panting.

Jordan felt the back of his neck growing hotter and hotter. He ignored it as long as he could, turning his back on the dance floor and carelessly downing several pints, as though it didn't matter to him how Elodie behaved. But when even dense old Oz finally started shooting uneasy glances at him, he decided he'd had enough of being shown up like this. Must've misread the signs he thought she was sending him. Why waste more time in this tacky joint, in the company of scabs and slags? He needed to breathe clean air.

"I'm outa here, Oz," he announced, abruptly jerking back his chair. "See you Sunday."

"Sure will." Oz nodded. "Like *she*'ll be back Sunday. Nuffin's gonna stop me turnin' up. But there's no need to head off this early, man—"

"Got a busy day tomorrow, mate. Evenin' at the Arts…"

Jordan made the usual excuses and strode angrily towards the exit. But he found his way blocked – by Elodie. He blinked. How could she be there? She'd been on the dance floor just two seconds ago with Eugene's snout glued to her cleavage… His head felt slightly fuzzy, but he knew what was what all right. Wasn't gonna show her this mattered.

He pushed roughly past and headed up the narrow staircase to the front door. His anger drove him as far as the chill alleyway outside before he realised she was following behind, clutching at his arm in an effort to drag him back. He turned to shake himself free, but before he could speak, she flared up in his face.

"Where the hell d'you think you're goin', Jordan Howe?"

"Beat it," he countered, jutting out his jaw belligerently. "I got a right to split if I want."

"Stop!" she ordered, darting across his path and turning to face him in fierce confrontation under the flood of silver light from a street lamp. "You ain't goin' no place, Jordan Howe, till you tell me where we stand."

"Thought you'd made that pretty clear already," he retorted, clenching his fists and glowering with rage. "I ain't plannin' to step in between you and your – your line of friggin' customers."

"You're drunk," she exclaimed in disgust. "Look like you been in a fight too with that lump on your jaw."

"What's it gotta do with you?" he countered. Then, afraid he'd gone too far and clumsily trying to change tack, "I thought we had somethin' going. Looks like I was wrong."

"So where you been all week?" she demanded. "Here'm I waitin' on the end of the phone for a call or text and what do I get? The cold shoulder, that's what."

Jordan frowned. "You – waitin' for a call? But I ain't even got your number. See," fumbling for his mobile with some wild idea of proving it to her.

"What d'you mean: you ain't got my number?"

She snatched the phone out of his hand and showed it to him, stored in his own directory.

Jordan gazed blankly at the screen.

"B-but how'd you know it was there?" he stammered.

"Because I put it there myself."

"You what? When?"

"Last Sunday afternoon at Caribbean Joe's. Don't you remember leavin' your mobile on the table while you went to fetch me a coffee?"

Jordan lowered his gaze in dumb assent.

"Nicole and me, we put it there for a laugh – just to see how long it'd take you to spot it. But I might as well not've bothered," she went on, raking him with furious sarcasm, "since it looks like you don't want to talk to me."

"But why didn't you *tell* me you'd done it?" he pleaded miserably.

"You dense bastard, d'you need everythin' spelled out to you in black and white? Can't you read the signs? And now everybody's laughin' at me for turnin' up tonight without you."

"But I'm here," he objected.

"Yeah – but I didn't know you were comin', did I? There's me tellin' 'em all you're busy practisin' for that ballet exam o'yours. And then what do I hear but Oz say you're turnin' up after all? You made me look stupid in front of my friends."

Light dawned at last.

"So that's why you wouldn't talk to me and you been out dancin' with Dill and Eugene?"

Elodie folded her arms across her breasts and regarded him scornfully.

"What'd you expect me to do? Sit about on my ass till you got round to explaining?"

But hadn't he been trying to talk to her and she wouldn't let him?

"Look – I dunno what I'm meant to do," he exclaimed. "One minute you're givin' me the come-on and the next you're shakin' your tits all over Dill and Eugene. What d'you want?"

Elodie stood with her hands planted firmly on her hips, gazing up at him in pitying disbelief.

"God, what does a girl have to frickin' do these days?" she declared. Then seizing him by the arms, before he even realised what was happening, she'd thrust her face up into his and kissed him fiercely on the lips.

Jordan almost toppled over backwards from shock – but luckily there was a wall behind him, as he realised when he hit it with a resounding smack. For a moment he was too dazed to respond, splayed helplessly against the roughcast concrete like a butterfly on a pin. Sure, he'd kissed girls before, but never like this – and never Elodie Simpson. It felt hard and hot and wet and not altogether pleasant.

It was fine to dream about having a girlfriend and Elodie'd always seemed the obvious choice because she was Queen Bee, the one everybody wanted. But – oh God! Now he actually had her, what was he meant to do with her?

Luckily Elodie knew. She reached for his limp hands and guided them till they rested on either side of her shapely waist. Then she clamped her mouth more firmly over his, so that his whole body seemed to ignite with the heat radiating from her passion fruit-scented skin. He felt as though his head was splitting apart as her tongue bored up into his throat.

All of a sudden, she fell off him, like ripe fruit from a tree. They stood surveying one another breathlessly in the stark, silver lamplight. Then she reached out her hand with a wide, beaming smile.

"There. That's sorted," she declared with an air of business-like satisfaction. "Now let's go back inside. It's freezing cold out here."

Jordan stared at her, too confused to do more than vaguely register a sudden, soft clicking sound behind that sent a warning shudder down his spine. What exactly did she mean by 'sorted'?

For one moment there shot through his mind a vision of Isabelle with her legs stretched wide apart, as Alex flung her into the air in a pose of utter self-abandon. Was this how Alex felt when he kissed her?

But he hated that girl. Elodie was the one for him.

He stretched out his hand to meet hers and she jerked him out of the lamplight back towards the door of the nightclub. Jordan wouldn't even've thought of glancing round except that his ears caught the slight stir of a scuffle behind. A stray cat lunging after a mouse in the gloom of the alleyway? He automatically swivelled his head and glimpsed – or did he only imagine it? – a sinister shadow slinking silently away into the darkness.

It wasn't until he'd reached the safety of the crowded dance floor that it flashed upon him how close a shave he'd just had. That sinister shadow must've been Prince Harrison, balked at the very last moment of his prey.

CHAPTER FIFTEEN

At the gym the girls' changing room was in turmoil. Handbags and plastic carriers gaped open on every peg and benches lay buried beneath heaps of discarded coats, scarves and woollen hats. Roy was due back in class that afternoon and everyone'd turned up early to prepare for the big surprise.

Isabelle found her services as wardrobe mistress in high demand, helping Hayley wriggle her rose-tattooed shoulders into a thin-strapped, black leather bodice and tugging up the zip of Lauren's skin-tight denim skirt as she stooped to fluff up her blonde-bleached fringe in the mirror. Hard to believe these were the same girls who'd made such fun of her only three months ago. Now she knew them almost as well as her friends in the ballet company and didn't think twice about rushing to Zack's rescue when he rammed his pushchair into a toilet door.

So busy was she advising Grace and Ruth on the basics of stage make-up that she'd little time to spare on her own account, so it was five to two before she even started pulling on the pair of diamante-studded jeans Simran'd lent her. Glancing hastily into the mirror, she let out a gasp of horror. Look at her hair! Wispy, red strands sticking out all over her head like straw from a haystack. Yanking at the elastic band, she snatched up her brush to tidy it back into its usual high ponytail.

"Oh don't do that," urged an awestruck voice.

Isabelle stopped short. In the mirror she caught sight of

Simran's large, dark eyes regarding her with open admiration.

"You've got such pretty hair," she breathed, indicating the luxuriant, red-gold waves tumbling over Isabelle's shoulders. "It's the colour of fire."

"I never realised you had such masses of it before," added Nicole enviously. "Why d'ya always wear it scraped back like that?"

"To stop it getting in my eyes of course," Isabelle replied, resuming her hasty brushing.

"This afternoon you really oughta do somethin' more interestin' with it," advised Hayley, as she glanced up from preening herself in the full-length mirror. "Somethin' more suited to our whole design concept, don't you reckon, Simran?"

"But I'm used to having it like this," protested Isabelle.

"You oughta wear it loose," insisted Elodie, seizing the brush with a purposeful glint in her eye. "Only needs a tiny bit of back-combing to give it more body."

"Don't worry," Lauren reassured her, "El's doin' a professional hair and beauty course. She knows what she's talkin' about." She dumped Zack onto Isabelle's lap and turned to help her friend.

A few moments later Jermaine, who'd been detailed to keep watch outside the gym, came crashing through the door bellowing, "He's here!" at the top of his voice. "The Jag's just turnin' in through the school gates. Places, everybody!"

Instant panic as the girls all dived for the door at once and scurried off to their starting positions, on fire with the critical question: what would Roy think of their dance?

★

Roy wasn't in the mood to take class that day. At home he'd attempted to cajole Alicia into doing it for him since he'd only arrived back late the night before and was still jet-lagged. But she'd sternly pointed out that this was the last class before Christmas and everyone was expecting him. He then pleaded the onset of a cold, but with her usual disheartening lack of sympathy she declared there was absolutely nothing wrong with him and he had to go because the young people were planning a surprise for him.

Roy uttered a heartfelt groan.

"Oh no. Not a surprise. You know how I loathe surprises. What is it?" unable to check a stir of interest.

"I promised not to tell," declared Alicia. "But they've been working very hard while you were away. Now I agreed to run three classes while you were in New York, Roy. Well, I've run three classes and this lesson I've arranged to do something else."

"What?" cried Roy in genuine horror. "You're not going to abandon me to that mob of teenage savages? They terrify me. And besides, I can't remember their names. You promised to stand by me, Allie, when I first agreed to help out with this lunatic scheme of yours—"

"Oh come on, Roy! I'm not wasting any more time arguing. You've just got to be a man and face up to your responsibilities…"

Roy's curiosity was piqued by the idea of the surprise the kids'd been preparing in his absence. All the way to Brackwell Heath in the car, he tried to wheedle a hint out of Allie, but she remained mysterious and uncommunicative. It drove him wild.

His trip to New York had been depressing, to say the least. In accepting the offer from Polis Ballet to advise on their new production of *Prodigal Son*, he'd been partly motivated by a hidden agenda: reaching out feelers to see whether Polis, who so often invited him over to help with the staging of their Balanchine ballets, might be interested in employing him as a resident artistic consultant after his retirement from Midland Ballet.

But the tentative enquiries he'd made among his contacts had met with blank disinterest or polite evasions. True, he'd received one firm offer of a post as archivist, but this felt like an outright insult to his highly distinguished career as a dancer and administrator. Perhaps he'd need to think again about his plan of relocating to the States. So he'd returned home feeling more despondent than ever about next summer, where at present the prospect before him was an unspeakably dreadful void.

And the short piece he'd hoped to choreograph as his swan song for the gala, which the company were 'secretly' arranging in his honour, also remained a blank. He hadn't a single workable idea. How could his ever-bubbling fountain of creativity have run dry just when he needed it most? All in all, he was hardly in the mood to waste his precious time on a load of ill-disciplined adolescents, who couldn't see eye to eye for even an hour or two a week.

So he arrived at Brackwell Heath High in a foul temper, ready to blast the first moron who turned up late or stepped out of line with the thunderbolts of his fury.

It was a cold, gloomy afternoon. Even the stunted hawthorn trees in the car park, whose spiky twigs had long been stripped of their autumn berries by the hungry birds, seemed to shiver in the rain, which drizzled despondently out of a louring sky. Roy huddled deeper into his fleece-lined jacket as he climbed out of the car and glanced round, only to find Allie'd already vanished. How like a woman. Under your feet most of the time, but never at hand when you actually needed her. There was nobody else in sight.

Stamping ill-humouredly up the steps of the gym and throwing open the glass doors, he found the building entirely deserted. Not even little Grace What's-Her-Name'd turned up today. He gazed around the lifeless desolation, his mouth set in a grim line, comparing his watch with the gym clock, which was actually right – for a change. Just in time to crucify them for their shoddy inefficiency. They probably hadn't even crawled out of bed yet. He strode towards the centre of the gym, his lone footsteps echoing eerily in the dim, cavernous silence.

All of a sudden he heard a hollow click behind. He turned warily, but before he could do more than half-register the fact that the audio system seemed to have sprung to life of its own accord, a mighty torrent of sound hit him. The opening chords of the music from the great Capulet ball. And what was this? As he whipped round, he saw the empty gym was empty no longer. At each of the four entrances had materialised a figure in black. Roy froze as the figures began to advance menacingly upon him.

But what was going on here? This wasn't the conventional choreography he'd been struggling to teach them before he left for New York. In place of echelons of richly robed courtiers gliding with majestic elegance, there stalked patched and ragged street kids with grim faces and determined eyes. A thrill of excitement shivered up his spine. It was all wrong. And yet, if he were to jettison some of his classical preconceptions…

He sensed a certain raw power and dignity in this fresh take on Prokofiev's martial parade of clan aggression. And he couldn't help being struck by the seriousness with which these kids obviously regarded this first performance of theirs. For it was undoubtedly a performance. He'd never've believed they had it in them.

It was disorienting to recognise, and yet not recognise, members of his own professional company leading these ranks of pierced and tattooed savages. Boris breathing passionate defiance at the forefront of the Asian contingent. Masakuni strutting like an impudent street urchin. Cameron blazing in black from head to toe. And heading the fourth column, if it wasn't Jordan Howe himself, straight as a spear shaft and bristling with unleashed energy.

Just look at the lad. How he'd come on! Hard to believe this was the same graceless, gangling, downward-looking beanpole he'd first encountered ricocheting in self-destructive frenzy around the walls of the top studio in Temple Street. His shoulders seemed to have broadened and his stature to have increased ten-fold now he was no longer ashamed to hold himself upright. And that proud carriage of the head, a trick he'd picked up from Boris, made him look just like a towering young warrior chief. He'd known all along that stroppy young bugger could dance. And Roy grinned at this triumphant vindication of his gut instinct.

But at that moment there burst upon the stage a column of dark furies, urged on by a flame-headed witch, whom he couldn't place for the life of him. His eyes were instinctively drawn to her, following in fascination as she swept forward, wheeling and weaving through the ranks, her tangled cloud of bright hair tossing loose around her shoulders. It wasn't...? It couldn't be... By God, it was – Isabelle Richards!

Roy's eyes bulged. The revelation of Jordan's prowess came as no surprise, but he'd never've believed this: Isabelle finally letting down her hair. Before that moment he'd viewed her as merely a well-trained and highly dedicated classical dancer. He and Patrick, the company's artistic director, had spotted her at her end-of-year school show last July, originally impressed by her superb technique and purity of line. But lately he'd begun to wonder whether she was really fulfilling her early promise. Week by week she grew technically more proficient and she remained as quiet, patient and hard-working as ever. But something was still missing. And this afternoon it crystallised in his head exactly what that something was.

Throughout the months he'd watched her dancing fairies, flowers, swans and snowflakes, he'd never witnessed much hard evidence of the dramatic passion which must've gained her that Prix de Lausanne. For all her thoroughbred genes, her lightness, her grace, her tireless striving for perfection, he'd begun to fear she'd always remain doll-like and restrained, lacking the ultimate self-abandonment that'd cause her performance to spring vividly to life. But now... He made a mental note to suggest her name when Patrick was casting the youngest of the three witches in the production of *Macbeth* he was currently creating. And at the same time the seed of a bold new idea began to take root in his brain...

But it was not just the stars that shone in this performance. What also struck him, as he stood gazing round the whirl of dancers, was the emergence among the group of a unified sense of purpose that he'd never thought they'd achieve. Each individual was finally learning to accept the subordination of their own identity to the demands of the company as a whole.

Old devil-may-care Eugene, always nipping out of class for a quick fag in the toilets, showing a forehead corrugated with concentration. That fat girl with the dyed purple hair, who was normally stuffing herself with crisps or chocolate, apparently immersed in what she was doing and even seeming to have lost a bit of weight too. Super-competitive Sudhir, who'd been forced along to the first session by his fierce little Asian mother and once told Roy that ballet was girly and boring compared with football and ice-hockey, looking as though he was having the time of his life prancing up and down with his harem. Clumsy Grace Howe managing to keep up in the rear too. And that ginger kid with the ugly birthmark, who he'd given up hoping would ever be able to tell one foot from the other, actually getting it right most of the time. Even bloody old Ash and Dill, who he remembered giving him hell during that first nightmare lesson, one hundred per cent focussed. It was a miracle.

Mind you, whoever'd devised that choreography still had a bit to learn. But that wasn't difficult to fix. Overall, it was a pretty impressive showing from a body of street kids, who three months ago didn't know a *plié* from a *jeté* and couldn't stand the sound of classical music. Everyone'd have to admit he'd showed tremendous insight there. He nodded sagely to himself as the dancers struck their final massed pose and the piece ended, leaving them breathless with exertion.

There was a moment of dramatic suspense – and then Roy began to applaud loudly. He was joined by Megan Scott and Murray Bennet, who he suddenly noticed standing beside him, their faces bright with smiles.

"Did you really like it, Mister Hillier?" burst out Grace, unable to contain herself any longer. "We been practisin' hard ever since you went away."

Roy gazed round the crowd of expectant faces, some anxious, some even half-defensive, and yet all longing eagerly for praise. His opinion mattered to every last one of them and he always prided himself on giving credit where credit was due.

"What a wonderful surprise," he announced with a broad smile. "I never thought you could pull off something so ambitious. Well done, all!"

Mayhem broke out. A spontaneous roar burst from every throat and some of the boys even hurled themselves into the air, punching each other and exuberantly slapping their palms together. The girls were hugging Isabelle and one another and even Boris, the eternal pessimist, flushed pink with pleasure.

When Roy could finally make himself heard, he asked with real interest, "Now tell me, who was responsible for the interesting new choreography?"

"Did you like it?" demanded Grace boldly. "We all helped. But we wouldn't've managed to agree if it hadn't been for Mizz Page. Where is she?" And she turned to look for her, loudly calling out "Mizz Page! Mizz Page!"

Her sharp eyes soon spotted her ballet teacher standing in the shadows behind the audio system. Grace scrambled as fast as she could towards her, while Alicia hesitantly emerged with Zack perched on her hip. In spite of her modest protestations, she was firmly hauled into the middle of the applauding crowd.

"I might've known." Roy beamed proudly upon his wife. "Not only've you successfully run my classes in my absence, but you're even ousting me from my job as company choreographer. I can see I'm going to have to look to my laurels in the future. Congratulations, my dear. You've worked wonders."

And, inspired by the burst of cheering all around, he raised her free hand to his lips and pressed an appreciative kiss upon her fingers.

"Oh!" sighed several girls of one accord.

Under cover of the enthusiasm that greeted this romantic action, Roy observed to Alicia, as he embraced her and patted Zack's curly blond head thoughtfully, "You know, after what you've done with this number, I don't see why we should stop at mere excerpts. It's always so hard to know which ones to choose anyway. Why don't we just mount the whole ballet?"

Alicia stared at him dumbly.

"In fact while I was watching, I had this absolutely brilliant idea," he went on, warming to his theme. "What about rechoreographing all the company scenes along the same lines?... Well, there's no need to look at me like that, Allie. You've always been so unambitious and lacking in vision. I don't see why we couldn't pull it off, with hard work and careful planning. It'll give me something to think about over Christmas."

"But, Roy," she protested faintly, "what about the main rôles? Romeo? Juliet? You can't stage a ballet like that without trained dancers—"

"We *have* trained dancers. Just look around you," he pointed out, improvising freely in the white heat of inspiration. "After all, Cameron danced Tybalt and Mercutio last season. And Boris played Paris in the second cast. Meanwhile, there's no sense in letting the grass grow under our feet," and he turned away, keen to start work at once. "Now, about this number you've all just put together: Murray, don't you think the end could be improved by having them file off in opposite directions before coming together for the final tableau?" And then, raising his voice so as to be heard by the rest of the cast, "Look here, kids, I'd like you to run that last section again. If you'd just take up positions from that bit about twelve bars from the finish and try it like this instead, I think it might work better. Ready? Now…"

CHAPTER SIXTEEN

"I'm so glad you've decided to join the project, Mei," Isabelle told her friend as they tramped through the snowy car park, already criss-crossed by tyre marks and a maze of footprints. "But you mustn't expect too much, you know. We're not working under the same conditions here as at the company studios. Still, they've come such a long way since last September – you wouldn't believe how far. Roy's scrapped the original system of accompanying mentors. And some of the more committed ones even turn up early these days to exercise in the gym and help with the backstage side of the production."

"Pretty impressive," said Mei, knocking her snowy boots against the door sill. "After the stories I heard from Boris and Masakuni…" She left the sentence unfinished. "Anyway, where first?"

"How about costume design?" Isabelle suggested as she keyed in the door code, keen to thaw out inside. "Last week Grace and Ruth turned up straight after lunch, so they're probably here already."

"Sounds good to me. Lead on, Bella."

After stamping off the snow, Isabelle guided her down a narrow corridor and paused briefly outside the glass windows of the PE office, giving Mei a chance to appreciate the scene of industry within.

"Sandra from Wardrobe came into school for an afternoon

session at the start of January and gave the girls' textile class some practical tips on how to create theatre costumes from recycled clothing and fabric scraps. Ruth and Grace here volunteered to take charge of the research project under the supervision of their art mistress and Megan Scott, the drama teacher, who also runs a part-time fashion accessory business. That's her writing at the desk over there. At the moment they're exploring past productions of *Romeo and Juliet*."

By this time Megan had caught sight of them in the corridor and waved, so Isabelle opened the door and ushered Mei inside.

"Hi, everyone," she greeted the girls, as they glanced up from their work. And then, indicating her companion, "This is Mei Chin, a friend of mine from the ballet company. She's come to help us rehearse the girls' dance in the marketplace scene later this afternoon, but I thought I'd bring her round and introduce her before class. How's it going, Grace?"

Grace obligingly showed them her computer screen, filled with pictures of gaudy Renaissance doublets.

"First it's important to do lots of research," she informed Mei earnestly. "Mizz Sandra told us all about it. Then we need to put together our pattern boards and our colour schemes in line with the style Mister Hillier wants for the production."

"Isn't that a bit of a tall order for girls your age?" enquired Mei, smiling at Grace, whose brow was furrowed with responsibility.

"Oh no," Grace insisted. "First of all, Mizz Sandra explained how to do it and then Mizz Armitage—"

"Our textiles teacher here at school," explained Ruth, who was drawing at the table in the centre of the room.

"Yeah, she made it into a coursework project for us," went on Grace.

"So we've got the project specifications and now we have

to come up with the solutions," added Ruth in her best grown-up voice.

Mei lingered for a few minutes, admiring Ruth's artwork and examining the detailed flip-book pages that Megan Scott showed them. Then, since the team were clearly eager to return to work, she and Isabelle said goodbye and left them to it.

As they walked back along the corridor, Mei turned to Isabelle in some surprise. "You know, they're pretty professional, that pair. How old are they? Thirteen? You wouldn't catch my kid sister doing extra schoolwork on Sunday afternoon like that – she'd be far too busy on social media."

"Ruth and Grace've really been inspired by this project. Didn't realise myself how much material they'd already collected."

"What beautiful, delicate little figures Ruth draws," marvelled Mei. "And those stunning garments, perfect down to the last lace ruffle and shoe buckle. I was totally bowled over back there."

"Amazing, isn't it? She's discovered a real talent for costume design – it's become almost an obsession with her."

"These costumes the girls'll be working on – Roy's planning to have them actually made up?"

"In the end I expect a lot of them'll probably be borrowed from the company stores for the night. But the main ones are going to be produced from scratch, according to the girls' final designs. One of the Asian girls' aunties works in the rag market in town and knows how to source end-of-line fabrics cheaply. And Grace belongs to the church sewing circle. They've volunteered to take on the bulk of the actual making. Roy wants the group as far as possible to be in charge of their own production."

Mei raised one thinly plucked eyebrow.

"Isn't that a bit risky with kids from such disadvantaged backgrounds?"

"Oh we don't use that word any more round here. They despise it and I'm not sure any longer that it even applies to them. They've all got someone who loves them and wants the best for them. In a lot of ways, that matters more than money... Look, here we are at set design."

As the girls poked their heads in through the door of the gym foyer, they caught sight of Roy huddled round a low coffee table with Oscar and Jermaine.

"Hello, you two – you're early," Roy greeted them briskly, glancing up over the tops of his spectacles.

"I just thought I'd show Mei round before this afternoon's rehearsal," Isabelle told him.

"Good, good... Now, girls, come and take a look at this," rubbing his hands gleefully together. "Isn't it fabulous? It's a model of Juliet's bedroom."

The two girls crowded closer to see.

On the table stood a stage set the size of a doll's house room. Built out of painted plywood and floor-boarded with what looked like ice lolly sticks, it was complete down to the smallest detail: perspex windows, stone fireplace and tapestried bed hangings. There was even a little plastic figurine standing beside the wooden chest with its tiny lamp.

"How beautiful," exclaimed Isabelle. "Isn't it just perfect, Mei?"

Mei hastened to agree, but she still looked slightly puzzled.

"You mean you're going to build stage sets too?" she asked.

"Yes – why not?" countered Roy airily. "I've learnt that with these guys, you have to think big. Otherwise there isn't enough to challenge their creativity. Consider these two," indicating Jermaine and Oscar, who were hanging back in embarrassment – particularly Oscar. (Isabelle had noticed by now how hopelessly tongue-tied he always seemed in her presence.) "If I hadn't asked whether anyone was interested in helping with set design, how would I ever've found out that Jermaine here'd been painting war game soldiers for years and Oz was born with a hammer in his hand? I just had to throw off a few ideas last week about what Juliet's bedroom might look like and blow me down, if the pair of them don't turn up today with this little beauty. Look here. The hours of work that must've gone into it. Apparently they started in their Design Technology classes on Monday and finished it off during their spare time. Oz's dad showed him how to make the windows so that they actually open – can you see that? – and his mum sewed the drapes out of some scraps of ribbon from her rag bag. I tell you, this school's a gold mine of untapped talent. I'm going to show it to Patrick. I reckon these guys ought to be in our own set department. They're as handy as so-called professionals any day."

And he clapped both boys enthusiastically round the shoulders before turning back to the miniature stage-set. Jermaine eagerly pointed out that there was a tiny battery in the lamp too, so it could actually light up…

The girls decided to move on, after Isabelle had paused to exchange a smile with the bashfully blushing Oscar.

"Who's he?" whispered Mei, as soon as they were out of earshot.

"Only Oz," Isabelle replied. "He needs a lot of help with dancing. I didn't realise there was actually something he was good at…"

"By the way, Isabelle," Roy called out from behind, as if the casual afterthought had only just occurred to him, "d'you think you'd fancy dancing Juliet for us?"

Isabelle stopped in her tracks. Had she just imagined this? But a quick look at Mei's stunned face showed her friend'd heard it too. She glanced round to check whether Roy was joking, but he seemed perfectly serious.

"It'd be a lot of work, I know," he went on, "but Alex tells me he was teaching you some of the *pas de deux* sequences in the autumn and I think it's time you had a challenge too. Go away. Think it over. Tell me at the end of the afternoon," and he turned back to the stage set, leaving Isabelle in a whirl of confusion. How could she possibly tackle the part of Juliet? She, who'd never danced even a tiny solo on stage with the company, let alone dreamed of undertaking a principal rôle...

"Of course you're going to say yes, aren't you?" urged Mei. "I'd jump at the chance."

She would too, thought Isabelle. Mei was ambitious – and she had nerves of steel. It'd never occur to her that she mightn't be up to the part: she had none of Isabelle's own self-doubt.

Isabelle couldn't discuss this matter, even with a friend. She needed time to think. So she hastily suggested they continue their tour of inspection, hoping to find a spare moment later to call Alex and ask his advice.

Next the two dancers visited the locker room, where a brainstorming session was taking place on the subject of publicity and marketing. Although this was nominally under Alicia's control, Simran seemed to be doing most of the talking, while Zack and Auntie Zoe also had their fair share of comments to make to Lauren, who was acting as secretary. Isabelle was too dazed to take in much of what was going on, so Mei ended up introducing herself. After that, they passed rapidly by the open door of the audio box, where a heated argument was taking place between Dillon and Elodie over which recording of Prokofiev's score they should use. Isabelle judged it wiser not to interrupt them, or the stage management meeting being chaired in the confined space of the equipment store by Sudhir, who ruled his Asian retinue with autocratic fervour.

Finally the girls arrived outside the new multi-gym, where serious fitness training was in progress. As soon as the boys inside noticed them, they instantly redoubled their exertions: Eugene accelerating the speed of his sit-ups, Ashley bobbing frantically back and forth on the rowing machine and Jordan, glistening with sweat, pounding along for dear life on the treadmill.

Isabelle had never seen him before clad only in football shorts and a sleeveless vest. What powerful thigh muscles and well-developed biceps normally lay hidden under his baggy joggers and shapeless sweatshirts! She instantly shrank back from the door. Since his profile was turned towards her and his eyes remained fixed on the wall opposite, she hoped he hadn't caught sight of them. Why did Mei have to draw attention to their presence by giggling like that? She nudged her friend in the hope of urging her discreetly away. But Mei refused to budge.

"Hey, Bella," she whispered excitedly, "who's *that*?"

"That?" echoed Isabelle, following the direction of her gaze. "Who do you mean?"

"The guy on the running machine over there," prompted Mei. "Just look at those bulging pecs and that neat little butt."

Isabelle bristled. Mei's habit of appraising male physique as so much horse flesh always seemed so at odds with her dainty exterior. And foul-tempered Jordan Howe an object of desire?

"Oh that's just Jordan," she replied. "Roy's cast him as Tybalt."

Mei's eyes almost started out of her head.

"What? Not *the* legendary Jordan Howe?"

Isabelle nodded blankly.

"I've been simply dying to get a glimpse of him. I gather he's taking his Grade Six exam at Easter."

"Already?" queried Isabelle. "Last thing I heard he was doing Grade Four. Ugh! Rather him than me." She shuddered. "I would've died of embarrassment if I'd had to take that exam at his age along with a load of nine-year-olds."

"But he didn't," replied Mei, who knew all the gossip.

"What? Didn't take the exam?"

"No. Didn't take it with a load of nine-year-olds. Roy saw to that. I heard from the Parkhouse students during *Nutcracker* how he slipped Jordan neatly in among the seniors. They were impressed he'd gone to so much trouble. Clearly thinks he's pretty special."

"Perhaps," retorted Isabelle, piqued by her friend's persistent interest in someone she preferred to ignore.

"You must've heard what the examiner said about him?"

Isabelle shrugged, but Mei hardly paused to register her lack of enthusiasm.

"Apparently she asked why he'd only been entered for Grade Four and flatly refused to believe he'd been dancing for less than a term. I gather he's an absolute sensation in open classes. Julie – you know, my medic friend who uses ballet for stress relief? – she comes back raving about him after every lesson. Says he's a natural. Picks up steps so fast that in a couple of minutes, he looks as though he's been doing them for years. And he's incredibly strong too." Mei breathed an appreciative sigh. "Tell me, has he got a girlfriend?"

"How should I know?" retorted Isabelle, who'd often seen Jordan and Elodie leaving class hand-in-hand, but refused to pander to Mei's thirst for sensation. "There's no need to drool," she added tartly. "I'm sure you can get Cameron to introduce you after rehearsal." Then, in an effort to change the subject, "Talking of rehearsal, don't you think perhaps it's time we got changed? The boys'll be here soon."

She was about to lead the way back to the locker room, when she caught sight of Alex entering the door of the gym along with the other male dancers from the company.

"Alex!" she exclaimed to Mei. "Whatever's he doing here?"

Mei threw her a surprised glance.

"You mean you didn't know he was coming?"

★

It turned out that Alex had agreed to dance the rôle of Romeo. Isabelle was aware that Roy'd suggested this to him earlier in the week, but after all his snide comments about the Youth Dance project, she never dreamed he'd actually accept. Perhaps he'd thought over everything she'd said and decided she was right after all. But in that case, wouldn't he have discussed it with her beforehand? What a hurtful lack of confidence in her to turn up out of the blue like this! It even took the edge off her realisation that it'd be him partnering her as Juliet...

"I've only just made up my mind, Bella," he confessed rather shamefacedly when they finally managed to snatch a moment alone together. "I did ring to tell you I was coming, but you didn't pick up."

"No, my mobile's switched off," she admitted, struggling to swallow her resentment.

"Called Roy at lunchtime. You know what he's like. Never lets the grass grow under his feet. He said: why not come over and meet the gang this afternoon? Well, of course I wasn't doing anything in particular, with you tied up here. So I decided, why not surprise you? Thought you'd be pleased..."

"But how did Mei know you were coming?" shot back Isabelle. "I don't see why I should be the last to hear about it."

"I never said I was definitely coming when we talked about it yesterday," he protested.

"So you've been discussing your plans with her behind my back, have you?"

"Just happened to mention it in passing. Why're you being so unreasonable?"

"And what's all this about telling Roy you've been teaching me *pas de deux* from *Romeo and Juliet*? I was learning them by myself."

"Bella, I haven't the faintest idea what you're talking about. I was just trying to offer some helpful suggestions..."

"Walking in here as though you own the place, after what you've said all along about us 'wasting our time teaching circus tricks to a bunch of delinquent street kids'," quoted Isabelle remorselessly.

At least Alex had the grace to look uncomfortable.

"Well – that was before Roy explained exactly what he had in mind," he excused himself glibly. "You see, I need to prove to him that I'm up to Romeo, so he'll mention me when Patrick's casting for next season. And only a fool'd turn down the chance of being coached by someone who learned the part under the original choreographer. You've got to look at things from every angle, Bella."

Trust Alex to be motivated entirely by selfishness!

"Besides, when he told me who he had in mind for the part of Juliet..."

So he knew about that already! And he hadn't said a word to her.

Smarting with annoyance, Isabelle shrugged off his attempts at self-justification and hurried away to change. She couldn't help mulling over her grievances as she pulled on her practice leotard among the rest of the chattering girls.

Last September, when she and Alex'd first started going out, she'd practically worshipped the ground he walked on, dazzled at even being noticed by a soloist so far above her in the company ranks. But looking back on this now, perhaps she'd just been young and pitifully naïve. It wasn't easy to remain dewy-eyed after months of close proximity to Alex's sensitive ego.

Did he really love her? Or was she merely a convenience,

someone who could be relied on to turn up with him to parties, galas and other company functions? After all, it was hard for dancers to maintain normal relations with people outside the business, since they kept such anti-social hours, and Alex's acknowledged partnership with her did have the benefit of staving off emotional threats from other predatory parties.

Originally she'd been wrung with jealousy that the two of them could never go out together without crowds of women falling over themselves to hijack his attention. But perhaps Alex enjoyed this, not because he cared to respond to their advances, but only because it focussed everyone's attention firmly on himself. A woman had to have more substantial assets than youth and eye-catching dress sense before he'd put himself out to be charming. So what was it about her that'd attracted him in the first place?

Not because she was her mother's daughter – surely? Unspeakably dreadful thought. Surely not even Alex could be that ruthlessly calculating?

She'd fought off this ugly idea for weeks. But now she steeled herself to entertain it, she found it already festering inside her like a poisoned wound.

Consider Christmas, after all. How flattered she'd felt that he seemed so keen to accept her invitation to what she called (for want of another name) her 'home' in Twickenham over the holidays. And when they'd arrived there on Christmas Eve, she was so exhausted from endless coach trips and a long season of *Nutcracker* performances in venues up and down the country that she'd actually been grateful to her mother for offering to look after him while she caught up on lost sleep next day. Christmas in their household was always a non-stop whirl of parties and festivities, the downstairs reception rooms overflowing with politicians, foreign diplomats and business contacts of her step-father, as well as famous dancers, choreographers and critics from the ballet world, come to pay tribute at the shrine of her beautiful but demanding mother.

Next thing she knew, while happily greeting Auntie Jean and turning to introduce Alex, who a moment ago had been standing right beside her, there he was instead over the other side of the crowded room being presented by her mother to the film director, Basil Pierpont. And the following morning when she came down for breakfast, she'd opened the door to find her mother and Alex with their heads together in earnest discussion, which broke off as soon as she entered. Alex instantly sprang up and spent the rest of the morning dancing attendance on her. But perhaps that was only a screen to lull her suspicions. Maybe he'd planned this all along. Using his relationship with her as a stepping stone to further his own career.

Her own insecurities at once blazed out – as always, when it came to a comparison between herself and her mother. Was she no more than a pale imitation of the real classical dancer?

Since then Alex'd seemed so tirelessly devoted that she wondered if she hadn't just been making a fuss about nothing. Until this afternoon…

★

It was a fiercely demanding class. Roy was notorious for his energetic workouts and his temper'd certainly not been improved by a Christmas break in the bosom of his family.

"He's still adjusting to the fact that he now has three grandchildren," Alicia told her on the quiet. "And he hates Christmas these days." She rolled her eyes and, with a glance to check he was out of earshot, imitated his bitter complaints. "'All this manufactured jollity. What've I got to look forward to at Christmas any more? Gone is the buzz of dancing *Nutcracker* to packed houses at Covent Garden. Now it's just a week of enforced over-eating and lying marooned on the sofa, too bloated to escape the clutches of Emma's coven of little witches, struggling to pretend there's nothing I'd like better than to watch the DVD of *Ballet Shoes* for the twentieth time running.' You know what he's like…"

Better keep a low profile this afternoon, Isabelle decided.

When rehearsal began, she and Mei were busy coaching the girls in their steps for the marketplace dance and in the pauses striving to keep warm in the draughty, cavernous gym.

Impossible to ignore the upsurge of interest that Alex's unexpected arrival had aroused among the girls. Nicole hardly took one look at him before she was exchanging excited whispers with Hayley and madly fluttering her eyelashes in his direction. And it was downright unprofessional the way he was showing off in front of them all with outbursts of complex *batterie, tours jetés, cabrioles*…

At this point Roy disappeared for a coffee break, leaving Murray Bennet to take over.

Murray had come into community dance via psychology and PE training and he soon had them all practising his favourite team-building exercises. The boys enjoyed the fun and attempted greater and greater feats of daring, stimulated by competition between the rival Asian and West Indian gangs, as well as the presence of outsiders like Mei and Alex.

But Isabelle, particularly in her current mood, could see no point in all this 'getting in touch with her inner emotions'. Who needed to fling themselves around to demonstrate the obvious point of a dancer's reliance on other members of the cast?

But while she merely had reservations about standing on the trampoline and letting herself fall backwards into a sea of willing hands, she absolutely loathed being picked up and tossed around like a ball. The whole exercise was rapidly degenerating into some sort of rough-and-tumble rugby scrum.

"Stop," she protested, struggling to steady herself. "I'm dizzy…"

But no one heard her. The boys were all yelling and cheering, stamping their feet and clapping their hands together as loudly as they could.

"Hey, guys, dampen those decibels," shouted Murray above the din.

Not a flicker of response. If anything, the noise just grew louder.

"Here, catch," called out Eugene to Alex, keen to prove he was every bit as fit and strong as a real company soloist.

It was one thing to undertake controlled lifts in a calm studio environment, but quite another to field a human football, hurtling towards him in a furious rush of speed. Alex muffed the catch.

The instant he realised what was going to happen, he scrambled with undignified haste to break Isabelle's fall. But his well-meaning effort only succeeded in jolting her awkwardly sideways.

For a second that seemed to last a year, Isabelle felt herself flying through the air, legs and arms stuck out in all directions like a starfish. Frantically recalling all she'd been taught, she fought to relax as she headed on a direct collision course with the floor, which came rushing up to meet her.

And then, as she shut her eyes against the impact, all at once she tumbled SLAM! into something hard, yet more yielding than the wooden boards of the old gym. She rolled over and over among the flailing limbs of another body, until at last they slid to a halt. Was she still in one piece? Had she broken anything?

Finally she summoned up the courage to look. She found herself staring up into the equally startled eyes of Jordan Howe.

CHAPTER SEVENTEEN

When Isabelle fell, Jordan had been half-reaching out towards her, determined to outdo the hated Alex at any cost. So it needed little more effort on his part to lunge sideways and break her fall by throwing his arms around her in a kind of rugby tackle. What he hadn't bargained for was the whole weight of her body crashing down with a force that knocked all the breath out of him. And as they sprawled over the ground, their heads banged together so hard that tears started into his dazed eyes.

Before this, he'd been under the impression that Isabelle must be light as air. When he saw Alex lifting her in the studio, she'd looked so slender that there seemed nothing of her. But in reality she felt like a lead weight! However did Alex manage to hoist her off the ground at all? Let alone parade her around high above his head as though she was floating? His grudging respect for the dancer's muscle power instantly increased ten-fold.

His second thought, as he lay there in a jumble of legs and arms, some of them apparently his own, was how hot her panting body felt against his own and – impossible to believe – how sweaty!

His imaginary ballerina, cool-skinned and light as a bird, melted into the empty air – to be replaced by a real, flesh-and-blood girl, who lay glaring up at him with baleful green eyes as though she held him personally responsible for the whole accident.

Jordan recoiled as if stung, hastily disentangling his

legs from hers and unlocking his arms from her waist in stammering embarrassment.

Next moment they were overwhelmed with a clamour of assistance. Oz reached out a hand to haul him upright and Alex sprang to help Isabelle to her feet, encircling her shoulders with a protective arm and anxiously enquiring if she was hurt. Jordan turned to gaze after her – but Alex had already shepherded her to a seat, apologising repeatedly for his carelessness.

Jordan felt torn in two. One half of him longed to claim Isabelle's thanks for cushioning her fall. The other half shrank back in fear.

Discretion won out. Tamely he submitted to being thumped and hugged by his mates as though he'd just scored a goal, his head held fast in Elodie's clutching fingers. She kissed him possessively, keen to attach herself to the hero of the hour. A sudden flash of insight told him this was all her enthusiasm meant, but how could he despise her for it? After all, hadn't she saved his skin when Prince and his gang of thugs looked set to beat him to a pulp? He owed her.

Still in a half-daze, he grew conscious of Oz's awestruck voice, whispering low in his ear, "Hey, man. You touched her. How was it?"

There was no need to ask who he meant. Jordan rounded on him impatiently.

"So who had time to feel her up?"

Oz's face fell and Jordan could've bitten out his tongue. Poor Oz. The slave of an empty dream. In the mirror of his hopeless adoration, Jordan was terrified of glimpsing the reflected image of himself.

★

Alicia was drinking hot coffee with Roy in the lobby of the gym when they heard a loud uproar inside. They exchanged questioning glances and then, since the racket persisted, they both rose and, setting down their mugs, hurried back to see what'd happened.

Inside a scene of rowdy confusion greeted them. The orderly class of pupils, whom Roy'd left fifteen minutes ago too exhausted to speak out of turn, were now jumping up and down raising an ear-splitting din. He turned disbelieving eyes upon Murray, who hastened to assure him that the situation was completely under control.

But as he went on to explain, Roy visibly swelled with rage.

"They're not getting away with this sort of behaviour," he declared.

"Now, Roy…" Alicia began, laying a soothing hand on his arm. Roy shrugged it off.

"Exactly what do you pack of clowns think you're doing?" he demanded in a voice like thunder.

Deathly silence. All celebration instantly ceased.

"The trouble with you lot is that you're entirely thoughtless," Roy went on, bristling with rage as he surveyed the startled faces turned towards him. "All you care about is yourselves. Do you ever bother thinking before you act? No. In every case, your body starts moving before your brain switches on. That's why your head teacher has to waste so much of the time and energy she could be spending on projects like this getting graffiti cleaned off the school driveway."

"That's nothin' to do with us, sir," piped up Jermaine. "It's them Asians who're to blame."

"Liar!" burst out Sudhir, starting forward in self-defence. And then, in an indignant appeal to Roy, "That's racist, that is, sir."

These magical words, which usually caused their teachers to back off nervously from every confrontation, had no effect whatever on Roy. He rounded on them all, spitting fury.

173

"Shut up, the pair of you," he bellowed. "I'm not interested in your petty squabbles. D'you see Cameron and Masakuni here wasting precious class time arguing just because they come from different countries? What does it matter which gang is responsible? There's no bloody difference between you. You're all a load of brainless, no-hoping, unself-disciplined losers. Don't you understand that your little bout of horseplay could've cost Isabelle her *entire career* as a dancer?" And he paused to allow his words to sink in, raking them all with an accusing glare.

No one could meet his eye. Not so many weeks ago, Alicia thought, Dill and Ash would've reacted to this lecture with a casual grin and a careless shrug of their shoulders. But now no one moved a muscle.

And then "Oh come on, sir," ventured Eugene tentatively, "it was an accident, see. We didn' mean to hurt no one. And she on'y took a bit of a tumble. Happens every day on the football pitch."

"That's exactly the trouble with you lot," countered Roy uncompromisingly. "Go on. Shrug off your own responsibility. Yes, on the football pitch, fine and good. But Isabelle's a professional dancer. Let me tell you, I was once present at the afternoon rehearsal before an evening show, when a very promising young artist accidentally fell during a solo and tore her Achilles tendon. She had to be carried off stage on a stretcher because she couldn't even stand up – let alone walk. Her understudy took her place that evening – and the next and the next. In fact she ended up dancing the part for the rest of the season. It was her big break: she went on to become a company principal. Meanwhile poor Jean ended up in plaster for six weeks. But that wasn't the worst of it. The worst thing was: she never danced professionally again."

A murmur of dismay arose from the onlookers. Several

uneasy glances darted back and forth and there was much shamefaced shuffling of feet.

"It happens," Roy went on. "Our company often has dancers off through injury. That's why I always insist on you doing a thorough warm-up and paying full attention. What just happened here was completely avoidable – it was the direct consequence of your own carelessness. How're you ever going to be good dancers if you don't learn to think and respond like professionals? By God, I've a mind to call off the whole show."

A stunned silence met the utterance of this threat, as his listeners struggled to come to terms with what they'd just heard. Alicia could see their thoughts mirrored plainly in their young faces. Indignation. Disbelief. Despair. After all their hard work and high hopes – to call off the whole project just like that? Nobody stirred, as they all glanced helplessly round at each other. Even Grace looked too shocked to protest.

Alicia, on the other hand, judged that enough was enough. She'd witnessed these primadonna-like outbursts countless times before and her private opinion was that eventually Roy would throw one tantrum too many and someone would call his bluff by taking him at his word. Meanwhile she refused to let his histrionics endanger the future of the project she'd worked so hard to promote. She was on the point of intervening, when someone else stepped out of the crowd.

Isabelle herself, flushed with emotion and visibly trembling at her own rashness in confronting the man who exercised so much control over her own future career.

"Please, Roy," she pleaded in an earnest voice, "you can't call everything off now. We've all worked so hard. And as Eugene says, it was an accident. That story you've just told us – about Jean – I've heard it before. You see," she turned to explain to them all, "Jean's my godmother and my mother was the understudy who took her place. But nobody was to blame

175

– and the two of them're still good friends. I last saw Auntie Jean at a party at our house this Christmas. She always says that if she hadn't ended up in hospital, she would never've met Uncle Peter, who was a junior physiotherapist there, and then gone on to study and train herself. Now they run the top clinic for dance and sports injuries in London." She paused, suddenly realising that all eyes were fixed upon her. "I – that is, we – all promise to take great care that nothing like this ever happens again, don't we, everyone?" glancing around to encourage a response from the rest.

They all clustered together in support of her appeal.

Roy appeared torn, but at least Isabelle's action had given him an excuse to reconsider his hasty words. Slowly his gaze travelled over all the eager faces turned towards him and gradually, as Alicia'd hoped, he allowed his anger to seep away.

"All right," he announced, as though granting a royal pardon. "But from now on there's no horseplay in class, no mucking around, no chatting – everyone pays full attention all the time we're rehearsing. That understood?"

"Yes, sir," they chorused.

"And the first person who loses their temper and creates any kind of scene is out on their ear – regardless of who they are," persisted Roy, spotting his chance and determined to take full advantage of it.

"Yes, sir!"

"All right. You win. I'll stay."

A tremendous cheer went up, which almost lifted the roof. Everyone crowded excitedly round Isabelle.

Alicia breathed a sigh of relief. Sometimes Roy ran the most hair-raising risks, but on this occasion she really had to hand it to him...

At that moment a shout was heard at the back of the gym. "Hey, guys – it's snowing again!"

All eyes swerved towards the windows of the building,

set high beneath the lofty roof. Outside it looked as though the louring sky had split open and was pouring down bales of white, downy feathers, which floated thickly through the still, cold air.

Half an hour ago a frantic yell would've burst from every throat and they would've all pelted outside without a backward glance. But things were different now.

All eyes turned towards Roy, who looked ready to start work again. Alicia could tell by the firm expression on his face exactly what he had in mind: none of this new-fangled, keeping-in-touch-with-your-inner-feelings slush of Murray's, but good, solid exercises that kept energetic bodies busy and youthful minds well focussed.

Roy gazed around the sea of pleading eyes and fidgeting limbs. Alicia saw the conflict in his mind. He knew he wielded power over them now. But he could also see what they wanted.

"OK," he agreed shortly. "Fifteen minutes." And he tapped the face of his watch as a business-like reminder.

There was a pregnant pause as they all stared at one another in disbelief.

"I said it. Go!"

A deafening shout of gratitude arose, followed by an instant stampede for the door.

"Carefully," added Roy, clearly picturing blood and broken legs in the scramble to be first outside into the snow. "Teenagers," he grumbled to Alicia. "Talk about a health and safety nightmare."

A moment later they were the only living beings left in the silent gym. But outside it sounded as though all the fiends of hell had broken loose. Roy shrugged at the chorus of blood-curdling whoops and yells that assailed their ears.

"Oh God. Come on, Allie. We'd better go and supervise kiddies' playtime."

The two of them hastened towards the door.

What a sight they saw! The snow was falling thickly and the teenagers, Asian, European and Afro-Caribbean, were making the most of their break, along with the company dancers.

Grace and Ruth had already set to work with Boris' help to roll a snowman's round body. Elodie and Simran were organising a gang of girls to pelt Alex with snowballs and boys were everywhere: stuffing wet slush down the back of each other's necks, catching cold flakes on their tongues as they fell and leaping around with up-turned faces and white frosting on their hair and eyelashes. Some of the Asian gang were even rolling around on the ground pummelling each other with mock ferocity.

Roy glanced sideways at Alicia and observed in a tone of profound pessimism, "They're all going to get soaked through, aren't they? D'you think I should call them in?"

Alicia laid a restraining hand on his arm and shook her head.

"Why not leave them to it? After all, you could regard this as a kind of team-building exercise, couldn't you?" with a teasing smile. "Look at Mei and Masakuni dancing with Hayley and Sudhir. It's so easy to forget they're only teenagers and that sometimes they just need to let off steam and have fun together."

They agreed to return to their interrupted coffee break.

But not before Alicia'd witnessed another little act of team-building that made her smile. Otherwise unnoticed amid all the commotion, Isabelle had slipped quietly over to Jordan Howe and was standing in the swirl of snowflakes with her face upturned to his in earnest gratitude. No need to hear a word of their conversation to understand what was happening. Their faces said it all.

CHAPTER EIGHTEEN

One misty Thursday evening, Jordan came hurtling home from work as usual. If he stood any chance of making it into town for the start of open dance class, he needed to gulp down tea and be back out that door in twenty minutes flat. He poked an enquiring head round the living room door on the hunt for Gran, but she wasn't there. Instead in the frayed armchair opposite his grandfather, tamely watching the television news sat a big, shaven-headed man. Jordan instantly recoiled.

Uncle Wes! Though it was years since he'd last seen him.

His uncle raised dull, dark eyes, but before he could say a word, Jordan ducked back out of the door. Might have to be under the same roof as that loser, but no way would he ever speak to him again!

He wheeled round and headed straight for the kitchen.

Gran might've praised the Lord when the news arrived shortly after Christmas of his uncle's official day release from the prison Resettlement Unit, but he himself had slunk quietly away, aware of a fixed desire never to set eyes on that bastard again. And the first few times his uncle'd paid them a visit, it'd been easy enough to make sure he was out at ballet practice. But now Wes'd been promoted to full discharge on parole, this was bound to happen sooner or later. How to handle it?

The kitchen was steamy with the smell of spicy mackerel and coconut stew. Pots were simmering on the stove, but one glance revealed an empty room. He stared round, growing more and more perplexed. It was so quiet. And where were Dion and Darleen, who were always yelling and squabbling when he arrived home at night?

He returned to the hall. Normally he would've bellowed out loud for Gran, but he found he couldn't open his mouth with his uncle's sad, ox-like eyes fixed dumbly on him from inside the living room. What was he doing here at this time of night anyway? He had a curfew to keep. Jordan darted him a glare of outright hostility and instantly turned away.

Noises seemed to be coming from overhead. He'd run up and ask if tea was ready: the sooner he was out of this house, the more freely he could breathe again. He bolted upstairs two at a time, calling "Gran? Gran!"

As he reached the top, he tripped headlong over something in his way.

"What's this doin' here?" he cried, aiming a disparaging kick at Darleen's pink sports bag lying on the landing.

"Dere don' be no need for all dis hollerin'," scolded Gran's voice from his and Dion's bedroom.

Jordan swung indignantly round the door and skidded to a halt. Gran stood with the lower drawers of their battered tallboy gaping open and an old, grey suitcase spread wide on the bottom bunk. She seemed to be folding Dion's clothes into the case – his faded T-shirts, patched jeans and scuffed trainers – while Dion crouched among scattered piles of junk, half-heartedly sorting through a pile of toys.

"What's goin' on here?" blurted out Jordan, glancing from one to the other. "How come you're packin' all this gear? We movin' house?"

"You ain' movin' nowheres," announced Gran, stoically going on with what she was doing. "Your uncle's takin' dese pickneys home wid him tonight, so I is packin' up deir belongings. Dem's leavin' after tea."

"What d'you mean: tonight?" cried Jordan. "Thought it wasn't till the end of February, once he got himself settled in his own place?"

Gran threw him a glance of contempt over one of her broad shoulders.

"Boy, you don' know nuttin' 'bout de days o'de week, nuttin' 'bout de months o'de year. In fact, you don' know nuttin' 'bout nuttin' no more 'ceptin' dat dere balley dancin'. You tellin' me you don' even know dis *is* de end o'Febr'y?"

And she instantly returned to her packing.

Jordan felt about two inches high. He tried to hide it by flaring up.

"You're gonna let him walk outa this house with Dion and Darleen just like that?" he demanded roughly.

"An' why not?" countered Gran in apparent unconcern. "He's deir daddy. He got de right to take'em home again. Dat's right, Darleen – " in response to the little girl's mute appearance in the doorway with a pile of frilly knickers. "You take dem to Grace an' she put dem safe in de bag. I be dere in a minnut…"

"Home?" Jordan blustered, as Darleen obediently vanished. "He ain't got no home. The twins belong here with us."

"Wes hab a flat now," Gran retorted, glancing up with a glint of maternal pride in her eye. "De probation officer help him find one up Bartlett Green way. So dese here pickneys lookin' forward to goin' home at las' wid deir own dear daddy. Ain' dat right, Dion boy?" beaming reassuringly upon the skinny seven-year-old, who was gazing uneasily up at her. At the same time she made big eyes at Jordan, motioning him to silence for the sake of the child. "Is all gonna be for de bes'—"

"But you can't let the twins go home with that crook," interrupted Jordan.

Gran heaved her vast bulk upright and turned to face him,

folding her arms majestically across her mighty bosom and jutting out her chin in her most belligerent manner.

"How many times I tole you, boy? Dat no way to speak 'bout your own mudder's brudder. Now Dion – you jus' gat along to de bathroom an' fetch your toothbrush. Right dis minnut, I say."

Dion rose to his feet, wiping his runny nose on the sleeve of his striped football shirt. Gran shooed him unceremoniously out of the room, calling out, "An' mind you bring back dat eczema cream o'yours too, boy…"

Then she gazed reproachfully at Jordan.

"Dere's no call to say dem harsh words. Dion's boddered enough about dis bizznezz already."

"And can you blame him? Sendin' him away like this with someone he don't even know."

Gran shook her head.

"Wes's done his time," she declared. "He's paid his debt and learnt hard lessons. Now is different. He's turned de corner. As de Good Book says, dere's more joy in heaven over de one sinner who repents, dan over de res' of de ninety-nine righteous folk dat don' need no repentance."

"Are you crazy?" cried Jordan. "He's stole money, used drugs an' ripped off other people's bikes and cars. You can't let the twins go home with a jailbird like that."

"Boy, I done tole you, dat's all behind Wes now. At las' he's seen de light – praise be to God. He bin tellin' me how de Lord 'peared to him in his cell in a blindin' vision and showed him de error of his ways. De Lord tole him—"

"Look, Gran," burst out Jordan wildly, "can't you see the risk you're takin' with these kids' future? You're their legal guardian. Here with us they got a chance. They go to school every day. And I'm gonna work hard to help put 'em through college. But you let 'em go now and *he'll* never send 'em off to school every mornin'. Soon they'll be out on the streets and in trouble with the cops and end up in jail too. Stop shuttin' your eyes to what's really gonna happen if you let 'em go home with this – this bum."

Gran sucked in her breath sharply and shot him a scathing glare from behind her spectacles.

"An' what give you de right to sit in judgement 'pon one of God's creatures, boy?" she demanded. "You're young and foolish – you ain' seen nuttin' yet o'de troubles o'dis big, wide world."

Why couldn't she understand plain sense?

"But, Gran, people don't get five years inside for nothin'. He's not fit to be in charge of little kids," cried Jordan, almost in tears.

"Now you hush your mouth, boy," she commanded sternly. "Your uncle's jus' downstairs and likely hearin' every word…"

"And why not?" bellowed Jordan. "No-good, filthy prison scum!"

"Dat's not what you used to say," Gran taunted with maddening calm. "I 'member you at Dion's age. You'd do mos' anything to perch a minnut on dat big motorbike o'his…"

A blaze of fierce pride. Those big, warm arms around his waist, holding him safe so high up off the ground. Rubbing his cheek against the soft linen shirt and smelling sweat and smoke and musky aftershave. Snatches of phone calls about squats and spliffs, gigs and pigs, always broken off the moment he ran up. Hot tears of misery pouring down his cheeks…

Memories exploded inside his head. He fought to beat them down.

"That's before I knew how he was gettin' those bikes and what sort o'thugs were in that gang of his," he snarled, ten times harsher than before.

"Wes jus' had hard luck," Gran claimed. "Fell in wid a bad

crowd. Wasn' all his fault neither. Dat wife o'his – her's jus' as much to blame. If her hadn' gone off wid dat no-good boss o'hers, Wes wouldna started drinkin' n' lost his job and de flat too."

"But—"

"Wes knows dis now. Him's had time to think and advice in Resettlement 'bout startin' a new life. I know my boy. He's gentle as a lamb an'd never hurt one hair on de head of dese pickneys. Us're his family, Jordan. Us gotta stan' by him and help build up his new life – not tear it down wid our own han's. Where's de Christian charity I tried to learn you? You bin listenin' to de voice o'de Devil, boy, since you got out among dese worldly folk. It's time you stopped tinkin' o'nuttin' but your own self de whole time and put on someone else's shoes and walk about in dem…"

ARRGHH! Jordan wrenched himself away. Stupid old woman! What'd she know? Religion stank. There was no God. The world was just a senseless muddle of violence and suffering.

He barged past a bewildered Dion, who was trailing forlornly back from the bathroom with his toothbrush and eczema cream, and stumbled downstairs, furious at his powerlessness – even in his own household. He shot one glance into the silent living room. No way could his uncle not've heard exactly what he thought of him. His heart swelled with disgust and hatred for the flabby, miserable outcast he'd once loved so dearly.

Wesley stared at the floor, unable even to meet his glare of accusation. Just went on sitting like a vast lump of blubber in abject silence.

Jordan flung out of the door and into the darkness of the cold, foggy night.

★

At first he'd no idea where he was heading. All he knew was that he had to run, to put as much distance as he could between himself and that house: he'd suffocate if he stayed.

Charging mindlessly round the mist-wreathed streets burned off the worst of his blind fury. Soon the clammy chill of night penetrated his thin jacket and began to seep into his very bones. His mind instinctively groped towards a vision of Elodie. The bliss of burying himself in her softness and having her kiss away this burning pain…

His feet were already veering in the direction of her house, when – wait! It was Thursday night. She'd said something about heading off with Ruth straight after school for her grandparents' wedding anniversary dinner. Their house would be empty. He hesitated in the bewildering fog.

No use heading to Dillon's garage either. He'd no idea what the rest of the gang were doing that night. In fact, now he stopped to think about it, none of his old mates'd even texted him so far this week… Besides, how could he face them feeling like this? No. He needed to work off his pain alone…

Oh God! What about that bloody open class at the ballet studios in town? No use busting a gut to get there though: it'd be half over by now. But think of the comfort of that big, wide, lighted space where he could dance himself sane again.

His steps automatically turned towards the main road and he'd soon swung aboard the first bus whose headlights loomed up through the swirling white haze.

Jumping off near the ballet studios, he half-strode, half-ran in the direction of Temple Street. His old friend, the doorman, waved him past, clearly realising what an earful he was about to get from Roy. He bounded upstairs two at a time, bent on avoiding a tiresome telling off in open class, but craving a cool floor under his bare feet and a great empty void all around him as keenly as he once used to crave a lighted cigarette.

Alone in the familiar top studio, he pulled off his trainers and at once started on one of Roy's tough warm-up routines, pausing only to strip off his outer layers when he got hot. And little by little, the frantic heaving of his chest began to subside and his throbbing pulse-rate slowed to a more rhythmic beat. Instead of racing wildly out of control, his thoughts grew calm and his breathing steadied into the controlled lungfuls needed to raise and lower his limbs. His mind sharpened and focussed, at one with his body, as he launched into a sequence of leaps and triple *tours en l'air* that tonight at last he knew he could master, soaring upwards and hanging there for a moment in space, whipping round and round like a spinning top, rebounding lightly off the floor again and again in a set of intricate entrechats…

"Bravo," called out Roy's voice, as he finally whirled to a standstill.

Where was the voice coming from?

Jordan's mind had been so bent on commanding his body that, for a moment, he stood panting and gazing around in confusion.

At last he spotted Roy standing just inside the studio door, where he'd seen him once before, but this time he wasn't alone. Beside him was Isabelle, dressed in practice gear and regarding him with unmistakable interest. A flood of embarrassment swept over him.

"What're you doing here?" he gasped, his chest still heaving with exertion.

"Might ask you the same question," countered Roy coolly, advancing towards him. "Isabelle and I're about to start work on a little idea of mine in this studio tonight."

"Oh. Guess I'd better be heading off then…"

And he bent to pick up his discarded clothes.

"Not so fast, young man." Roy's voice halted him in mid-step. "Didn't expect to see you in the building – you just missed open class."

Jordan suddenly prickled with annoyance. What right

did Roy have to track his every move like some kind of hired detective? He was a free agent, wasn't he? But then... just think how much he owed this man.

He gulped back his anger and instead replied, "Somethin' came up at home, so I was too late for class – but I wanted to do a bit of work tonight anyway."

"Since you're already warmed up, you can stay and do some more work with us if you like," offered Roy with surprisingly little resentment in his tone. "Alex is away at the moment, so we could use a male body to fill in – if you've no objection, that is?"

Jordan eyed him in surprise. 'If he had no objection?' What was with this formal politeness?

But the offer seemed genuine enough and Roy apparently decided he even owed him a little more explanation.

"It's for my surprise gala in June," he confided, motioning Isabelle to start her own warm-up. "They're all busy arranging for the great and good to come and dance famous rôles from my past for the occasion. But I've decided to contribute by choreographing them a little surprise from my present. Alex and Isabelle've agreed to help out. I've chosen the music. Shall I play it to you?"

Jordan nodded, feeling deeply self-conscious in front of Isabelle. She might've come up to him that Sunday afternoon in the snow and thanked him for saving her from crashing onto the gym floor, but he'd no idea whether this meant all earlier bad feeling between them was at an end. After all, she was a professionally trained dancer – and he was still only a level or two above a circus monkey.

But then he began listening to the music Roy'd put on the sound system. Drums. Keyboard. Electric guitar. Funky stuff. Quite different from what he'd expected. Even had a familiar sound to it somehow, though he knew he'd never heard it before. In spite of himself, his foot started tapping to the beat.

Roy smiled.

"Like it?" he asked.

"'S OK," agreed Jordan warily. What'd come over Isabelle to agree to dance to this? Wasn't she a classical dancer? A snowflake or a flower, the way he'd seen her in *Nutcracker* at Christmas from a cheap seat at the back of the balcony. "In fact," he added thoughtfully, "it's got something of Dillon's style about it."

"Not 'something of'," corrected Roy with a dry chuckle. "It's Dillon's style exactly. He composed it."

Jordan stared. "You're choreographing a dance for the gala to Dillon's stuff?"

"Why not?" Roy grinned back. "I'm broadening my repertoire. You've presumably danced to this sort of music before?"

Had he what?

"I even used to play it when I belonged to the band," Jordan admitted, remembering the good old days.

"How did you used to dance to it?" demanded Roy speculatively.

"How? You mean... show you, now – here?"

"Yes – why not? Teach us how you dance to it."

Him – teach the experts something? Were they making fun of him?

"Go on," urged Roy impatiently. "We haven't got all night."

Jordan was so used to jumping when Roy told him to that he automatically obeyed. Rather sheepishly he began swaying from side to side, feeling Roy's critical eyes boring into him with a keenness that would've been enough to make a pro freeze up, let alone himself.

"Come on, boy," snapped Roy. "Stop hopping from foot to foot like a constipated warthog. This isn't what has the girls in open class wetting themselves with excitement. Here's Isabelle ready to partner you. Let's see you – what's the modern terminology again? – 'strut your stuff'."

Jordan snorted at Roy's feeble attempt at youth-speak. He considered for a moment. What'd he have to lose? Roy'd seen him make a total arsehole of himself often enough before this. He couldn't fall any lower in Isabelle's estimation than rock-bottom. And nobody else was there to see, were they? With a reckless shrug of assent, he held out his hand to Isabelle – and they began to dance.

CHAPTER NINETEEN

I t was a revelation. Like some outside power had taken
over his body and was showing him what to do. In
Jordan's dreams, he'd often wondered what it'd be like
to dance with Isabelle, but the reality exploded all his childish
imaginings.

At first he felt horribly self-conscious in case he trod on
her foot or jerked her slender arms. At first too, she seemed
rather stiff and subdued, trying to move one way when he
wanted her to turn another. So he reached one arm around
her waist and gently guided her the way she ought to go. And
then she actually smiled and showed him how his idea might
work even better.

After a while, it seemed they could do anything together. A
slight pressure on her waist and she instinctively edged right;
a slight lift and she soared into the air like a bird. Spinning her
one way and then the other, he found she'd already anticipated
him with such quick intuition that it felt as if they'd been born
to dance together. Her graceful, flexible frame so perfectly
complemented his wiry, muscular strength that it spurred
him on to experiment – yet always centred upon her, the one
constant star in his universe, as her eyes sparkled up into his.
He was dancing with his whole body, his whole mind, his
whole soul. If only it could go on and on...

And then the music stopped.

At once all movement ceased and the two of them stood

staring at one other, panting hard. As he gazed down into her wide, startled eyes, Jordan's heart leapt. Nothing else existed in the world at that moment. He'd almost begun to reach out towards her, bewildered by an overwhelming surge of tenderness, when he heard a dry cough behind.

"Hmmm…" Roy mused thoughtfully. "Just what I was hoping to see."

With a guilty start, they remembered he was there and turned to face him questioningly.

"Well come on," he urged. "We can't stand around staring at each other all night. I've got a few suggestions…"

And the three of them started work together.

★

Jordan'd never worked so hard in his life. All the classes he'd taken up till now had been mere kid's play compared to this total immersion of self in the all-absorbing act of creation. By the time he'd executed every combination of leap, jump and turn he knew, repeated endless sequences of *assemblés*, *battements* and *soubresauts* twenty times over and hoisted Isabelle into dozens of improvised lifts, he felt dizzy with exhaustion and the sweat was pouring off him.

"Are we done yet?" he panted, believing he'd reached his last gasp.

"Oh I think we've put together one or two short *enchaînments* that might prove useful," Roy assured him. Then, observing his face more closely and appearing to notice he was out of breath, he added, "You're puffing and blowing like a steam engine and we haven't been at it all that long. In my day we could keep this up for hours. Well, off you go then. See you both back here same time tomorrow night. I don't know. The youth of today – absolutely no stamina…" And he turned away, grumbling, in the direction of the studio door.

Jordan gaped in disbelief.

"Tomorrow night?" he exclaimed. "Why?"

Roy paused and shot him an arch glance over his shoulder.

"Now you've started, you're not chickening out, are you?"

"But I thought I was just standing in for Alex," blurted out Jordan.

"Yes, but he's gone down to London for some ridiculous film audition or other – he won't be back tomorrow night. And I'm starting to generate some ideas I need you to try out."

"But what if I'm doing something else?"

"Cancel it. What could be more important than making a brand new ballet?" It was that simple, as far as Roy was concerned. "Good night, kids – see you tomorrow," and, beaming upon them with a kindly twinkle in his eye, he sailed out of the room, entirely satisfied with his night's work.

Jordan stood staring dumbly after him. Sure, Roy had a point about the importance of making a new ballet, but was that the only worthwhile goal?

"Is that guy for real?" he muttered, half to himself. "What gives him the right to treat us like we got no lives of our own?"

"Oh that's just Roy's way." Isabelle reached for a towel to wipe her glistening neck. "You should know him well enough by now." Then, glancing at him curiously as though she'd only just noticed, "Don't you have a towel with you? You're not even wearing your usual practice gear."

A sensation of increasing discomfort had begun to creep over Jordan, which he now realised was the clamminess of a sodden vest clinging to his rapidly cooling stomach. He shook his head.

"Wasn't exactly plannin' this tonight, so I didn't bring my stuff."

"Here. Borrow this then," she offered, holding out her own towel towards him.

Jordan accepted it from her hands. It felt luxuriously soft

and smelt of fresh fabric conditioner – and of Isabelle's own skin. He suddenly grew shy and utterly tongue-tied. As long as they were dancing together, they'd reacted like one body. But now she'd become a stranger again and was regarding him with some surprise.

Lost in a daydream, he was still clutching her towel!

"Sorry," he apologised, abruptly handing it back. They stood staring at one another in awkward silence.

"Guess you've better things to do tomorrow night than dance with me," she ventured tentatively. "Going out with Elodie perhaps?"

"Oh no," exclaimed Jordan. Then, in an effort to temper his over-eagerness, "That is, yes." Was that a hint of disappointment in her eyes? "I mean, I got other things lined up o'course – but they're not necessarily better than dancing with you – if you see what I mean." He stopped. How stupid that sounded. He never seemed to be able to speak naturally to this girl. His words kept tripping him up and wrestling him to the ground, sprawling him flat on his back at her feet.

Isabelle smiled. Jordan grew hot with embarrassment.

"I guess I ain't – I mean, I'm not – makin' – making myself too clear, am I?" he admitted, drawing a deep breath to steady his nerves. "Actually I can't think of nothin' – er – " he winced " – anything – else I'd rather do than come back here tomorrow night. How long's Alex gonna be away?"

"Three days. He'll be home by the weekend."

"He doin' anythin' important?" asked Jordan, picking up his clothes and trainers from the floor. As they left the studio together, he automatically reached out to flick off the lights. "Wasn't Roy sayin' something about a film audition?"

"That's right. He's taking a set of screen tests down in London for a new feature film about a dancer. My mother arranged it over Christmas. It'd be a great opportunity for him."

"Guess he wants it pretty badly then."

"I think so."

She seemed not to want to talk about it. But if he stayed silent, it'd give her the chance to end their conversation and head off to the locker rooms. If only she'd stay a bit longer!

"Your mum in with a film company or somethin'?" he asked hurriedly.

"No – she just has lots of contacts. She introduced Alex to the right people when he was staying with us over Christmas."

(Their relationship must be pretty serious if Alex'd spent Christmas with her family.)

"So you'll be dancing in this film too?" guessed Jordan.

"I don't think I'm ready for that yet," she replied quickly. "I've still got so much to learn. My mother disagrees with me." She heaved a small, tired sigh and raised her eyes to his as she went on, "In fact, we had an argument about it – as far as you can argue with my mother. She's not much interested in other people's points of view."

How could anyone who was lucky enough to have a real mother sound so disillusioned as Isabelle at that moment? But after what'd happened to him at home that evening, he could easily understand how much it hurt to have your feelings trampled on without a thought.

"I know – my gran's pretty much the same. That's the real reason I came here tonight. We had a big fight about the twins," he admitted in a sudden outburst of confidence.

"The twins?" echoed Isabelle blankly.

"Yes. Dion and Darleen."

"Of course," she exclaimed, her face lighting up. "Your little brother and sister. I remember Grace mentioning them. You're so lucky to have a family. I'd love a brother or sister."

So how must it feel to be an only child?

"They're not actually our brother and sister," he pointed out. "They're just our cousins – but they live with us. That is, they have done for a few years – while their dad's been – er – out of the country," he mumbled, regretting that he'd ever mentioned this subject. How could he admit the truth to someone like Isabelle?

"But their father's come home now, has he?" she prompted kindly.

"Yeah," he replied, leaning back against the white wall of the corridor. "Wants to take the twins to live with him. My gran thinks they oughta go, but I ain't – am – am not so sure."

"But he's their father?"

"He's been away so long, he's like a stranger."

"Well, what about their mother? Can't she help?"

"No – she and Uncle Wes split up a few years ago. It was pretty hard on him. That's partly why he – er – left the country."

"Yes, I understand," replied Isabelle feelingly. "It's always hard on the children. My parents got divorced when I was ten and still living at home. I hated it – and them."

"Your parents're divorced?" gulped Jordan. She was so honest. He longed to respond in kind. "Didn't think someone like you'd know about that sort of thing."

Isabelle laughed. "What's so special about me?"

"Well, your family's rich and your mum's a famous dancer…"

"Oh come on! Having money doesn't stop people being divorced or miserable."

"S'pose not. So what does your own dad do then?" asked Jordan, proud of her trust in him.

"He's an orthopaedic surgeon. Works at Guy's Hospital in London. He's very busy, so I don't often see him. Though he did come to watch me dance during our *Nutcracker* season in London and brought some flowers to the dressing room afterwards. Beautiful pink roses." She paused for a moment with a reminiscent smile. Then her face suddenly hardened.

"My mother remarried several years ago. Her husband works in the diplomatic service, so he's quite often posted to foreign countries and she goes with him now she doesn't dance any more. I don't like him – he treats me like a five-year-old – so I'm glad to be out of that house. I only go back there when I have to. The company are my family now…"

"You're lucky to have a good job and a flat of your own," said Jordan enviously.

"But I'm not an actual member of the company, you know," Isabelle was quick to point out. "I don't have a job that pays real money. I'm still on a studentship. If they decide to keep me on next year, then I'd start earning a bit. Dancing's not very well paid, you know. Not till you get to be a principal, that is. But no one's in this profession for the money – it's more the fulfilment that comes from doing a job we love."

Jordan stared. The concept of job satisfaction had never occurred to him before.

"But I only have myself to support," she went on, "whereas you have a whole load of responsibilities – even if the twins are going home with their dad. He must be a really brave man to come back from years overseas and plan to settle down again with two young children. What does he do?"

"He's a – a builder," murmured Jordan.

"The twins must've missed him so much," persisted Isabelle innocently. "How long did you say he'd been away again?"

"Four years."

"I remember missing Dad dreadfully when he first left home."

Jordan stared down at her. She looked so wistful. He couldn't bear the thought of playing on her emotions, hiding the real reason for his uncle's absence.

"Look, Isabelle, I haven't exactly told you the truth," he blurted out.

Isabelle threw him an enquiring glance.

"The truth about what?"

Too late to backtrack now.

"About Uncle Wes and the twins," he confessed miserably. "My uncle – he wasn't abroad. He just got out of jail. It was such a shock to see him tonight. Crouched in the chair like that. Old and beaten and ground down. He used to be so big and strong…"

His voice failed.

There was a moment of stunned silence.

He'd done it now. Blown sky-high any possibility of friendship with her – ever. She'd never want to talk to someone with an ex-convict in his family.

"So what're you starin' at me like that for?" he demanded roughly. "Don't you know you been dancin' with someone whose uncle's been locked up for nearly five years?"

Wasn't gonna wait for her to make polite excuses about hurrying off for a shower. Instead he turned abruptly on his heel and flung away, too ashamed even to meet her eye. Pulling on his jacket, he shot straight downstairs and out into the dank, drizzling night.

Excuses. That was all his grandma ever made for Wes. Bloody excuses!

Now the adrenalin had stopped pumping through his body, Jordan suddenly realised he'd eaten nothing since lunch. He was starting to feel not just hungry, but quite light-headed.

After buying a burger from a sleazy-looking takeaway, he eventually slunk home, cursing himself for opening his mouth to Isabelle about Uncle Wes. All he'd achieved by that stupid outburst was to give her the power to hurt him even more.

When he arrived home, all was dark and silent. Everyone else was in bed asleep. He let himself quietly inside and climbed the stairs to his room with a heavy heart. It felt different from normal… sort of – empty.

After he'd undressed and climbed into the bottom bunk, he lay awake for a long time, hearing the usual rumble of passing trains but listening in vain for soft snorts and snuffles from above. Dion was no longer there.

CHAPTER TWENTY

"So where the hell is he?" fumed Roy, pacing up and down like a caged lion and glaring at the studio clock. "I told him yesterday we'd be starting at seven-thirty. How come he isn't here?"

Isabelle stood with her eyes fixed on the ground. She'd been so looking forward to tonight and now…

After years of *pas de deux* classes, she must've run the entire gamut of possible partners: the brash boy who hoisted her up and down like a weightlifter heaving a set of dumbbells; the timid wet blanket, who complained how awkward she was; the obsessive perfectionist, like Alex, who criticised her height and was put out by the slightest mistiming. Until last night she'd imagined that partnering him in one of the great *Romeo and Juliet pas de deux* was the ultimate thrill dancing had to offer. But last night had blown all these notions sky-high. She'd been far too excited to sleep and spent the wakeful hours of darkness entirely reformulating her attitude towards Jordan Howe.

At first it'd felt incredibly insulting to be thrust headlong into partnership with someone younger and so much less experienced than herself and expected to improvise to such uncouth music. After all, she'd started dancing at three years old when her mother first took her to smiling young Miss Maude's pre-primary class at a church hall in Chiswick and ever since the age of eleven she'd been rigorously cultivated at the Parkhouse School for Dance like some rare hot-house orchid. She'd undergone a thorough professional training in repertoire, character, jazz, tap, mime, *pas de deux* and pointe work under the tutelage of the foremost teachers in the country, obediently submitted to every annual assessment and practised with unfailing dedication for the demanding higher awards, while also studying a wide range of academic subjects and preparing for numerous competitions and end-of-term shows. Even her evenings had been spent listening to classical music, reading ballet books, resting strained muscles, attending critically acclaimed dance productions and darning the toes of satin pointe shoes, when most young people her age were out enjoying themselves at parties and nightclubs.

But with his lithe, muscular body and instinctive recall of every step and gesture, Jordan had unleashed himself upon her, charged with a dangerous and unpredictable energy that tore gaping holes in her hard-earned technique. No wonder she felt uncomfortable and exposed, as though she was dancing naked. At first she shrank back, striving to clutch the shreds of her training around her. But suddenly she'd realised she was being as narrow-minded as Alex and gradually, inspired by Jordan's courage, she'd grown bolder and begun to take risks of her own.

Now it was as though, after living in a gloomy cave of shadows, she'd finally burst out into the brilliant light of the sun. Her whole life seemed to have been a mere preparation for the moment she'd begun to dance with Jordan. When she turned to reach for his hand, it was already there; when she leaned backwards, she found he'd already anticipated her need for support; when she sprang, he caught her easily – not just once, but over and over and over again. And – the greatest liberation of all! – she could finally forget about her height. However straight and tall she stood, she could never reach

Jordan's soaring head, not even in pointe shoes. Talk about a relief!

Naturally the mechanics of their performance needed work. But this fire they sparked out of one another far transcended the bounds of mere mechanics. All day long she'd been looking forward to reliving last night. And now – no Jordan. It was like being dealt a stinging slap in the face.

"Damn him," snarled Roy. "Damn the unreliable bastard! I'll bloody crucify him for this. You're sure you haven't seen him around tonight, Isabelle?"

Isabelle shook her head.

"Would you like me to go and look?" she offered quietly, a lump of misery swelling in her throat. Why bother? It'd all been too good to be true.

"It's OK," Roy replied. "I'll try ransacking the men's changing rooms in case he's just turned up late. It'll give me a chance to vent my fury on the bugger out of earshot of polite company. You take a coffee break and I'll come and find you in five minutes…"

Isabelle caught up her sweatshirt and headed for the empty coffee room. She pushed through the swing doors, thankful for a few moments alone to pull herself together and automatically snapping on the light switch as she entered.

The sudden flood of illumination revealed a figure crouched on the hard floor in pitch darkness. Isabelle stopped short. Jordan! Blinking in confusion like a startled owl. For a moment they both stared speechlessly at one another. Then, "What're you doing here?" she cried.

Jordan had sprung to his feet, trying to pretend he wasn't huddled with his head in his hands.

"Roy's in an absolute frenzy," she added quickly. "He's roaring around the dressing rooms looking for you. Have you changed your mind about helping us out?"

Jordan looked torn. He slowly shook his head. "No – it's not that – but…"

"But what?" exclaimed Isabelle, darting towards him. "Is something wrong?"

"I got other things to do with my life apart from waste evenings messin' around here," he retorted.

Isabelle fell back a step.

"But you're dressed in rehearsal gear," she persisted, gesturing towards the old black leggings and scruffy T-shirt he usually wore for practice sessions.

"I was gonna work on my Grade Six syllabus," he excused himself lamely.

"Then why are you sitting here in the dark?"

"Look, why don't you just get the hell outa here and stop naggin' me the whole time?" he growled, raising one arm to push her away.

Isabelle flinched. Jordan must've read fear in her face since his arm dropped limply to his side. He wrenched himself away.

Isabelle started forward. She just didn't seem able to communicate with him. "Why're you always so angry with everyone?" she cried.

"I didn't mean to frighten you," he began, half-turning back in apology.

Isabelle reached out one hand towards him.

"Jordan – won't you come with me?" she pleaded. "Roy and I can't do anything with you hiding out here in the dark."

"I ain't bloody hidin'," he asserted, which instantly assured her that he was.

"Then what *are* you doing?" she demanded. "Look, I know Roy's pretty frightening when he's in a temper…"

"I ain't scared of Roy," shot back Jordan, scornfully squaring his shoulders.

"Then what are you scared of?"

Jordan's uneasy gaze shifted from her face.

This conversation was crucial to her whole future as a dancer. Isabelle drew a deep breath and sank down on one of the well-worn sofas. Better try another tack.

"When Roy and I interrupted you in the studio last night, you weren't just practising, were you?"

"What else would I've been doin'?" countered Jordan.

"I've been thinking. You were really upset, weren't you? About Dion and Darleen."

Jordan gazed at her, stubbornly refusing to admit anything.

But she knew how much he cared deep down about Grace and the twins. That was part of it. He was ashamed to confess it and this made him lash out at everyone.

"How can I help if you won't talk to me?" she exclaimed.

"Why do you want to help? Why should you care?" he asked slowly – but not quite so abrasively as usual.

"Because I want to dance with you," she cried.

"Dance? With me?" he echoed stupidly.

"Yes. With you."

"But I'm just a trained monkey performin' circus tricks."

"Jordan, when are you going to grow up and get over what Alex said? Last night should've shown you it's gone beyond that now. Honestly, you'd think I was terrifying, the way you're carrying on."

He stared at her again.

"You are," he burst out, flushing dark red. "I can't go back into that studio. I don't know how to dance with you."

"What?" gasped Isabelle, unable to believe her ears.

"I don't know how to handle those lifts properly – the kind I've seen you and Alex do in the studio. I know I picked you up and put you down a few times last night, but it must've felt so clumsy compared with what you're used to. I know how important technique is now. I can't believe you'd want to work with me again."

What was lurking at the bottom of all this? It wasn't like Jordan to shy at high fences. Isabelle surveyed him narrowly.

"This is not just about technique, is it? After all, you must realise you can't expect perfection straight off. I know we had a few technical hitches, but that doesn't mean we can't work together to fix them."

"But it'd just be a waste of time," declared Jordan. "Alex'll come back and it'll be like I was never there."

Light suddenly dawned.

"Is this what's bothering you?" she cried, jumping to her feet. "Who cares about Alex? All that matters is you and me and Roy all working together to create a new dance. Look, Roy's one of the most gifted choreographers working in Britain at the moment, probably even in the world. And you're going to throw away the opportunity of being part of that? Other trained dancers'd give years of their career to stand where you're standing now."

"But what if I can't do what he wants me to?" Jordan groaned.

"Well perhaps you should back out then, if you're going to take that defeatist attitude," scoffed Isabelle in a fair imitation of her mother's tone when, in a crisis of panic, she'd refused point-blank to climb into the taxi that was waiting to drive them to her Parkhouse audition. "None of us knows if we've got it in us – none of us can be sure. Look at me. I'm scared to death of Roy demanding a set of *fouetté* turns I can't pull off. But just because I find them hard doesn't mean I'm going to give up altogether. I'll work and work till I succeed, if that's what he wants from me. I know how much you care about dancing – because I care about it too. But you can't get better by just sitting around in the coffee room feeling scared. You have to challenge yourself all the time. That's the way to achieve things you've never done before."

There was a doubtful pause as Jordan considered her

words and then he asked in a small voice, "Was it really true what you said back there?"

"What?" cried Isabelle.

"About wantin' to dance with me?"

"Why else would I've said it? Jordan, you're such an idiot sometimes! Last night was wonderful. I've been looking forward to this evening all day long. Please come and dance with me."

And she held out her hand to him.

Jordan glanced at it for a moment and then at her. For a moment she thought he was going to tell her to get lost – then he slowly reached out his hand towards hers.

But before their fingers could meet, the swing doors burst open and Roy erupted into the room.

"What the hell're you doing in here?" he yelled at Jordan. "I told you seven-thirty in the studio."

Isabelle, who'd spun round at the clatter of his entrance, stepped in front of Jordan like a shield.

"We both mistook the time, Roy," she announced calmly. "Anyway, I've found him here all dressed and ready for rehearsal. Are we going to start now?"

Roy was so taken aback by her air of cool rationality that he agreed as quietly as a kitten.

★

At the end of their demonstration, Alex's face was a picture. But Isabelle had no idea whether he actually liked the dance or not. He made polite, non-committal noises to Roy in the studio, but it wasn't until they'd finished discussing corrections and she was threading her way back through the labyrinth of twisting corridors to change that she learned his real opinion.

"I've no idea what's got into Roy." These words, issuing from the door of the locker room ahead, halted her at a bend in the passageway. "But he's out of his mind if he thinks I'm going to have anything to do with it."

Isabelle hesitated. This conversation clearly wasn't meant for her ears. Should she walk on and risk embarrassing Alex and whoever he was talking to or creep quietly away and pretend she'd heard nothing?

"What's wrong with it?" prompted an excited treble with a faint American twang. Mei, wild for gossip as usual.

"It's not ballet," decreed Alex. "It's vulgar sensationalism." Isabelle raised her eyebrows.

"What makes you say that?" urged Mei.

"The music for a start. Who the hell composed that load of crap? Sounds like something they'd play at one of those cheap nightclubs down the road."

Mei giggled. "I gather it was written by one of the boys from the Brackwell Heath dance project."

There was a horrified silence – Isabelle could easily imagine the look on Alex's face.

At that moment out of the corner of her eye she caught sight of Roy himself heading up the corridor with Jordan. She spun round in the hope of intercepting them, but it was already too late.

"There you are – what'd I tell you?" rang out Alex's voice in triumph. "It's a good thing Roy's retiring this summer. He's clearly losing his marbles."

Isabelle winced and glanced back at Roy, who could hardly've failed to hear this. Then she started forward, meaning to interrupt Alex before he could go on. But Roy shook his head and raised a warning finger to his lips in elaborate stage pantomime. Isabelle fell back, helpless to prevent the impending confrontation.

"But ballet has to change and develop," Mei was protesting. "We can't keep dancing just *Swan Lake* and *Sleeping Beauty* or our art'll simply stagnate. We need new choreography to provide us with fresh inspiration. At least, that's what Isabelle's begun to say lately…"

Isabelle started at the sound of her own name. What was Mei implying by that word 'lately'?

"I never said we didn't need new choreography," Alex maintained. "In fact I agree with you whole-heartedly. But one has to draw the line somewhere and Roy's overstepped it, as far as I'm concerned. I'm a classical dancer. I haven't trained hard all my life to throw away my technique on a load of bullshit like that."

"But what's the matter with it?" persisted Mei, slightly overplaying the tone of puzzled innocence, Isabelle considered. "After all, Jordan's not complaining."

She hardly dared glance at Jordan, who wore a scowl like a massing thunderstorm.

"No, well it demands a level of expertise that even he can probably attain," Alex asserted airily. "But no one's talking *me* into screwing Isabelle on a public stage."

Jordan started forward in rage, but Roy jerked him back.

"Hey, steady on, Alex," cried Mei, slamming a locker door. "I'm sure it's not meant like that."

"You just wait till you see it. It mightn't be immediately obvious – but underneath it's nothing but tasteless obscenity. I'm amazed Bella's agreed to it. In my opinion, this is professional suicide."

"Alex, aren't you slightly overreacting here?"

Isabelle heard the scrape of a key in its lock.

"Look, I've just landed the starring rôle in a major international film venture. It's going to feature excerpts from all the great Tchaikovsky classics. I won't have time to work on the gala dance now. And I'll need leave of absence from the company for the shooting later on this year – it's going to be the kind of career springboard that I've always dreamed of."

"Gosh – really? Come on, tell me more about it. I'm dying for a cup of coffee…"

The sound of their voices gradually faded as their footsteps receded along the corridor.

Isabelle hardly knew where to look. Her taste slighted, her dance partnership with Jordan so sleazily misinterpreted, even her future career apparently headed for irreclaimable disaster. And on top of that, the most unpleasant shock of all. The bitter taste of being ever so politely done down by someone she'd thought was her friend…

Her brain reeled, but all of a sudden Roy's savagely glittering eyes started out at her like blue headlights in a fog. If she felt humiliated, imagine how he must feel! His visionary creation, on which they'd all worked so hard this week, condemned out of hand. If only she could just melt quietly into thin air…

Jordan was more vocal in his indignation.

"Are you just gonna stand by, Roy, and listen to Alex say those bloody stupid things?" he snarled. "I'll go and punch his fuckin' head in." And he sprang forward with clenched fists.

All of a sudden he caught Roy's eye and stopped short. Roy was – grinning! Jordan and Isabelle exchanged uncertain glances.

"You gonna let us in on the big joke?" Jordan demanded.

"Alex is becoming such a stuffed shirt," Roy announced with more than a hint of malice in his tone. "He deserves to dance nothing but boring old princes for the rest of his career."

Isabelle and Jordan stared at him.

"Well there's no need to look at me as though I've really lost my marbles," Roy snapped. "The first night I saw you two dance together, I decided I'd have to offload Alex from this project somehow. He simply doesn't have the style or mental flexibility to bring off what I have in mind for my new piece. Now he's clearly so outraged to be asked to sully the purity of his classical technique with this tasteless – obscenity, did he call it? – that he'll be happy to bow out without further ado."

"But who'll partner me at the gala?" cried Isabelle.

"Why Jordan, of course. Who d'you think?" raising one eyebrow at her slow understanding. "Now we'll be able to start on the choreography in earnest."

Jordan gulped.

"But I thought we'd just finished," he murmured.

"By no means. Tomorrow we'll start reworking from scratch. I've been saving up all my best ideas. Alex could have something there, you know: it may just be a trifle unsubtle as it stands. Nothing like a bit of honest criticism from an informed expert, is there?"

And Roy headed off down the corridor, chuckling to himself, leaving Isabelle and Jordan entirely lost for words.

CHAPTER
TWENTY-ONE

Jordan sat hunched in his faded denim jacket on a bench outside the gym. His eyes were fixed on the ground, as he listlessly kicked the toe of one trainer against the concrete step. The hawthorn trees in the car park were bursting into pale green leaf and the birds were twittering beneath a broad blue sky, but he neither saw nor heard.

Nothing was the way he wanted it to be. When the company left on their tour of China and Japan, he'd had so much to do that he thought the month would pass in a flash. But now it felt as though the dancers'd been away for years and were never coming back. Even free time at last to spend with Elodie hadn't turned out the way he'd hoped. Instead of doing something interesting at weekends like going to see visiting dance shows, she insisted on dragging him off to town to do shopping. Why? Trailing round the city centre, watching her try on clothes was just boring. But even when he finally managed to persuade her out to Mephisto for the night, it was all just bobbing mindlessly up and down in a crush of hot bodies and they ended up arguing over nothing.

And Sunday afternoons, once the high point of his week – well, he'd soon stopped looking forward to them. Sure, he was learning lessons about character development and physicality from Megan Scott's series of drama workshops and Murray Bennet was trying hard to keep the dance rehearsals ticking over, but it just wasn't the same. He wasn't making real progress, like he did when Roy was here. Without him flying into rages and forcing him to repeat the same steps over and over again, life was just stale and – boring. And everyone was busy bitching and squabbling among themselves again, something they hadn't done for months. Nicole and Jermaine even claimed they were being sidelined and were threatening to drop out…

"You comin' in, Jordan? Time to rehearse our big number," yelled Oz's voice from behind.

Jordan raised his head. Last week the professional fight director had fobbed them off with rubber swords for the marketplace scene. It really took the edge off the fun of learning to fence. But now they were starting to get the hang of the choreography, surely today they'd move on to the real thing? Just think of the clash of metal blades like in the stage performance they'd seen at the Olympian!

Jordan scrambled to his feet and hurried after Oz back into the gym, where they found the rest of the cast assembled around a big, brown cardboard box.

One glance into the box showed there'd been no need for haste. Rubber swords again.

"What the hell good's this?" grumbled Sudhir, leader of the Capulet gang, as he bent his foil into a bow with both hands and released one end so it sprang straight again with a dull twang. "What kind of a dick head'd fight with such fuckin' useless rubbish?"

It was the first time Jordan'd ever wholeheartedly agreed with him, though over months of rehearsing together he'd grown more tolerant of Sudhir's bad-tempered and bossy side.

Aware that they'd been dealt rubber swords because they were expected to behave badly with them, the boys delighted in doing just that. The fight director persevered bravely in the face of their outright misbehaviour, but he was perspiring hard by the end of the session.

"What d'they think we are? Primary school kids?" muttered Ash with lowering brows, as the boys gathered in a discontented huddle afterwards in the changing rooms.

"All these soddin' lectures about takin' care not to hit anyone," complained Eugene. "Gettin' a whack on the head with a rubber sword ain' gonna hurt nobody."

"Man, I can't wait till Roy gets back next week," asserted Sudhir, voicing all their thoughts aloud. "Hey, d'you think if we told him how we feel, he'd do something about gettin' us real blades?"

Jordan and Sudhir were picked to head a deputation to Roy on his return – although privately Jordan saw little hope. Roy always insisted on everyone toeing the line and if he once said no, that'd be that.

In the event, they'd no chance to lodge a protest before the next rehearsal began. When Roy breezed in that raw spring afternoon, he was so busy catching up on progress with Megan and Murray that no one else had a chance to speak to him. Besides, they were all so busy welcoming back their friends, the company dancers, that before they realised, it was two o'clock and time to start class.

"Right, kids," bellowed Roy in his best regimental sergeant major voice after they'd finished warming up. "Let's get stuck in. I'm looking forward to seeing how you've got on with the first fight scene. Take it from the top and run it straight through with music."

The boys exchanged squeamish glances, but they were so glad to see Roy and feel his sure hand on the tiller once more that they agreed to give it their best shot. At least that way he'd realise they hadn't just wasted the training he'd arranged for them. So they all gathered round the cardboard box and dealt out the hated rubber foils with little audible grumbling.

Roy settled down on a chair at the front of the gym with his arms crossed over his chest, looking interested and expectant, while the rest of the company dancers grouped themselves around him. Everyone else took up their starting positions and Alicia switched on the music. But about ten bars in, Roy suddenly leapt to his feet waving his arms wildly. The dancing soon petered out and the boys stood eying one other in dismay.

Roy erupted into their midst in white-hot indignation.

"What the hell's going on here, guys?" he demanded. "Dill – hand me that bloody stupid thing. What in God's name do you call this?"

"It's a sword, sir," replied Dillon respectfully, the corners of his mouth twitching a little as he offered up his weapon for closer inspection.

Roy seized the offending object and examined it. Then he bent it into a bow with both hands and released one end so that it sprang straight again with a dull twang.

"It's rubber," he cried. "Who in God's name gave you rubber swords?"

The fight director stepped forward.

"Health and Safety, Roy," he remarked shortly. "You know the rules."

Roy looked as though he was about to explode.

"Absolutely hopeless," he spluttered. "How old do you think these kids are?"

"But, Roy—" began the fight director uneasily.

"Cameron, Alex – back me up on this," cried Roy. "Rubber swords? Whoever heard of a self-respecting production of *Romeo and Juliet* using rubber swords? The kids'll be a laughing stock. We have to hear the clash of steel on steel in time to the music. It's like trying to have a good fuck with a limp prick – you get bloody nowhere and you look a ridiculous arsehole into the bargain."

The boys exchanged grins. Roy never pussy-footed around when he got mad.

213

The fight director, seconded by Murray and Megan, drew Roy aside and tried to reason with him.

"Just consider the risks involved in using real foils," Jordan could hear him protesting in a heated undertone. "They're only kids. They could easily get injured. You should've seen them mucking around last week, whacking each other on the head."

"That's not surprising," argued Roy. "You hand them something as ridiculous as one of these and what d'you expect?"

"But they have to learn to fight properly…"

Roy rolled his eyes.

"Are you joking? They already know how to fight – they learned it on the streets. They could probably show you and me a thing or two, couldn't you, lads?"

The boys burst out in agreement.

"But the responsibility," pointed out the fight director.

"Nonsense," retorted Roy. "I'll carry the can myself. The kids'll treat those foils with such respect that no one'll get so much as a scratch. What about it, guys? What d'you say?" He turned to them all in direct appeal. "You gonna play safe, abide by the Health and Safety regulations and look like a load of simpering nancy-boys? Or are we going to thrust the maids to the wall and fight like men?"

Not a second's hesitation. A roar of approval burst from every throat. In the heat of the moment, Jordan so far forgot himself as to throw his arms in triumph round Sudhir!

*

The rest of the rehearsal flew by with everyone concentrating hard and striving to improve their performance because Roy was once more out front. By the time he dismissed them, they were all so tired and sweaty that the recently refurbished changing room showers were in great demand.

"Man, I'm knackered! How d'you guys keep this up all day, every day?" asked Jermaine, slumping down on one of the slatted wooden benches and glancing sideways at Boris, who was wiping his glistening neck and shoulders with a blue and white striped towel.

"Practice," declared Cameron stoically, as he stripped off his headscarf, damp rehearsal gear and dance belt before stepping into the shower. "Class every morning, like it or not. You build up stamina…"

The rest of his words disappeared in a gurgle as he plunged his head under the streaming water jet.

"Bet you had a great time in China and Japan. Bars, clubs, nightlife?" suggested Dillon eagerly.

Masakuni, who'd just finished towelling his hair dry, stared at him in surprise.

"Who has time or energy?" he asked innocently.

"But you must've had nights off – hit the town, score with the locals?"

Boris and Masakuni exchanged dubious glances.

"No breaks at all?" cried Dillon in dismay.

"Sadly no. Noses to the grindstone all day long. Performances every night. All we ever see is the airport, the hotels and the inside of theatres."

"Seriously?" gasped Jermaine.

Jordan glanced across at Masakuni and saw his bead-black eyes gleaming with mischief. So that's what was going on! He turned to Dillon, who was still staring aghast at this mental vision of wall-to-wall work.

"Come on, Dill," he exclaimed. "He's havin' you on, ain't he?" And he aimed a friendly punch at the dancer's arm, feeling like a giant towering over a midget.

In a moment they'd all converged on Masakuni, hoisting up his slight frame as easily as if he were a child and balancing him with arms and legs waving in the air like a beetle on its back.

"Hey, guys, quit horsing around. I'm dyin' of thirst," announced Cameron, just emerging from the shower, damp and curly-haired, with a towel draped round his waist. "Say, why don't we all go out for a drink and catch up on the latest? Where's open in Brackwell Heath on a Sunday afternoon?"

The rest eventually agreed to head off to Caribbean Joe's. But Jordan had a prior commitment.

"So long, Oz," he said, clapping his friend on the shoulder. "Keep an eye on Grace this afternoon for me, won't you? Gotta get goin' now."

Oz nodded as he tossed a deodorant into his backpack. He'd only just finished dressing.

These days dressing took Oz longer than it used to. In fact, now Jordan stopped to think about it, Oz'd cleaned up a fair bit recently – bought himself a couple of decent pairs of jeans and even some smart new T-shirts without holes, like the navy one he was wearing this afternoon. At first he'd put this transformation down to an approaching interview with the software company, who'd expressed an interest in the game demo he'd sent them. But today he realised there was more to it than that: after all, an interview was no reason to swear off weed and cut down on fags, was it? From the furtive glances Oz'd been casting at Isabelle during rehearsal, it looked as though he was still as hopelessly in love with her as ever.

Jordan knew how he felt. For his own part, he'd been dutifully practising his Grade Six syllabus work this last month under the eye of the bluff and well-intentioned Murray Bennet. But the set exercises felt flat and mechanical after the inspiring set of rehearsals he'd experienced working with Roy and Isabelle on the new dance. Good thing this boring exam'd be out of the way by Easter so he could concentrate his whole attention on the approaching gala.

Catching sight of Isabelle across the gym this afternoon for the first time in almost four weeks had brought sharply home to him just how much he'd missed working with her. Without her, these days he felt like only half a whole.

Today she'd been too busy to throw him more than a quick glance of greeting – but throughout the rehearsal he'd remained aware of her fiery head bobbing up and down among the darker ones of the other girls. It caused him a fierce upsurge of pride when he saw her stopping to exchange a few words with Oz on the way out of class. She was kind-hearted like that – and it meant so much to poor old Oz...

"Aren't you coming to Caribbean Joe's then?" demanded a familiar voice.

Jordan, who'd just emerged from the men's changing rooms with his rucksack over his shoulder, glanced up and caught sight of Elodie in an eye-catching orange jacket, queening it as usual among her gaggle of girlfriends.

"No time," he replied, checking his watch. "Due at the Arts Centre early tonight. Promised I'd do a couple of extra hours on the front desk."

"Too bad. So when'm I gonna see you again?" she asked, waving her friends on ahead. "The rest've got plans to go clubbing Tuesday night."

"Tuesday's my Grade Six class—"

"But you'll be finished by eight thirty. We'll've hardly got going by then."

"Yeah, but this week Roy'll probably want me for an extra rehearsal on the gala dance."

"So how about Wednesday? I'd love to go and see *Grave Robber* at the movies. It's meant to be really good."

"P'rhaps – but I'll prob'ly be needed for another rehearsal."

"Well, Thursday then?"

"No – I've told you before – Thursday's always out because of my open class."

"Oh you and your stupid ballet lessons!" Elodie tossed her head till her chandelier earrings jingled. "You're always

217

practising for exams or going to rehearsals. Aren't you ever gonna take any time off for fun?"

The last thing Jordan wanted was a public scene, so he tried to appease her.

"Look, I'll text you – promise – and we'll fix something up for the weekend. All right?"

Elodie stopped pouting and nodded reluctantly as she turned to follow her friends.

Jordan heaved a sigh of relief. Though it was just putting the problem off, wasn't it? Now the company were back, it wasn't going to be like the past month, when he'd had time on his hands (and a bit of extra cash, now the twins were no longer living at home) to take Elodie out to parties, films and gigs. No, it was going to be like the fortnight before the company left on tour: loads of frantic texts and missed calls, barrages of angry voice mail asking why he hadn't showed up yet and telling him to shift his butt and get the hell on down to Mephisto right now, constant temper tantrums and exhausting arguments over why he wanted to spend all his time stuck in a sweaty studio practising steps he already knew how to do. Girls! They just couldn't understand that a guy had other things on his mind apart from them, most importantly ambitions for the future. Why didn't Elodie realise that he couldn't become a dancer by rehearsing only once or twice a week?

As Jordan lingered inside the gym doorway to give her and her friends time to get clear of the building, he heard voices in earnest discussion outside. Isabelle and Alex.

"Of course I want to go," Isabelle was saying. "I'm really looking forward to hearing what Grace and Ruth've been up to while we've been away."

"But, Bella, I need to pack for London."

"Oh come on, Alex – it's only for half an hour. Don't be so anti-social."

"I'm not being anti-social. I've just got better things to do with my time…"

As Jordan passed by, Alex fell silent and stood pointedly aside.

"Oh Jordan," Isabelle called out, stepping forward. "Roy'd like to start rehearsals again on the gala dance. Is tomorrow at six-thirty all right with you?"

"Fine." Jordan nodded, secretly delighted at the thought of having her all to himself again so soon.

The reinstatement of these rehearsals clearly didn't please everyone. Alex shot him a filthy look. Jordan, aware that here at least he had the upper hand and not above rubbing it in, grinned back smugly.

"See you tomorrow then – Bella." This parting shot was aimed straight at Alex. With a friendly wave, he sauntered past the dancer's very nose. Out of the corner of his eye, he saw Alex clench his fists – and then think better of it.

But at least Jordan had the satisfaction of hearing him exclaim in a shocked undertone, "You're letting him call you 'Bella'?"

Without pausing to hear her reply, Jordan sailed on past, his heart glowing with triumph. At that moment his terror at the thought of dancing in the approaching gala on that enormous stage alongside a cast of distinguished professionals ranked a poor second to his satisfaction at getting a bit of his own back on bloody Alex!

CHAPTER
TWENTY-TWO

I t was all over in less than five minutes, but for Jordan those five minutes at the gala performance marked another clear stage in the division between the old life and the new.

Since the programme items were arranged according to their order in Roy's career, he and Isabelle spent most of the evening up in the dressing rooms. They warmed up at leisure, watching people come and go along the narrow corridors: all hurrying past with purposeful steps, often greeting each other with cries of delight and hugs of joyful recognition. Nobody recognised or acknowledged him.

When the stage manager's call finally came, he and Isabelle flew downstairs, only to stand for what seemed like hours in the darkened wings, watching soloists from Polis Ballet dance the homecoming of the *Prodigal Son*. Waiting for his entrance, Jordan felt his stomach lurch sickeningly, as though he was on the deck of a ship heaving up and down on a stormy ocean.

All at once the stage lights faded, the curtains swept apart and he heard the opening bars of music – their music! At first a terrifying numbness gripped his limbs and the weight of all the steps he'd ever learned felt as though they were pressing leadenly on his brain.

But the time for panic was past and the discipline of long weeks of practice and rehearsal took over. With a last reassuring touch on his arm, Isabelle launched herself onto the stage. Automatically Jordan followed with a mighty vault, shooting through space in a series of leaps and pirouettes calculated to make the audience jerk bolt upright.

A blaze of lights; a blur of upturned faces; a sense of the spectators straining eagerly forward in their red plush seats. The steps were streaming out of him, his body galvanised by the challenge of performance into leaping higher and spinning faster than he would ever've imagined possible in cold blood. Even the harder sequences, the lifts and mid-air catches, flew by as though they were second nature. In a burst of insight, he saw how perfectly this dance suited the pair of them: Roy had choreographed to his and Isabelle's joint strengths and the result was magic.

When they sailed off stage after the final chord, Jordan's heart was on fire. For him at that minute truly anything was possible. He hugged Isabelle to him, breathless and sweating in her filmy dress. Almost before he realised, he'd buried his face in her soft, bright hair and kissed her. She raised her eyes to his, smiling through tears.

There was no one in the world like her. By now he should've got used to holding her in his arms, but each time they danced together, it still felt like the first time…

"Come on, you two," interrupted a business-like voice behind them.

Jordan reluctantly tore his eyes off Isabelle and saw the stage manager gesturing in the weird half-light.

"Listen to the audience," she urged. "Back out there and take your bows. Now where's that young musician got to? He was standing right beside me a minute ago…"

As Jordan squared his shoulders and grasped Isabelle's hand to lead her back onto the stage, he glimpsed Dillon hovering nervously behind a ballerina in a long, white classical tutu, looking unusually smart with hair neatly combed and gelled. But before he could point him out, Isabelle had pulled him away.

As the audience caught sight of them once more, a spontaneous roar of acclaim burst forth. Jordan escorted Isabelle to centre stage, dazzled afresh by the brilliance of the spotlights and overwhelmed by the applause rolling out of the great black void like thunderous ocean breakers. God knew how many people were out there, ranged in those vast tiers of seats. But every last one of them had just seen him dance!

Jordan recalled Roy's careful instructions to step back in a dignified manner, bowing with one hand over his heart and leaving Isabelle to sink into a low reverence at the front of the stage. Then he turned to acknowledge her curtsey to himself and joined hands with her to walk forward once more. Now she broke away from him and darted gracefully towards the wings to lead out Dillon, launched towards them by the long-suffering stage manager and looking highly self-conscious in borrowed suit and shiny new boots. The clapping redoubled at the sight of the young composer, as they all three bowed together – and a moment later they were back in the dimness of the wings.

The Midland Ballet Company's artistic director, Patrick Sedley, had taken the microphone and was heading out to make the final speech of the evening. It was his job to sum up the highlights of Roy's distinguished career and acknowledge his immense contribution to the company. And he didn't fail to publicise Roy's exciting new initiative to extend the benefits of classical dance training among the young people of the city with the forthcoming performance of *Romeo and Juliet* by the Brackwell Heath Youth Dance Club in September.

Meanwhile, backstage behind the great velvet curtain, Jordan was conscious of a low hushing from the stage manager. Amid a ripple of excited whispers, rustling tutus and tapping pointe shoes, the performers hastily assembled for the final curtain call: a couple from the Danish company, who'd danced a *pas de deux* from some ballet Jordan'd never heard of called *La Sylphide*, several other international stars, who'd travelled from Europe and America to appear at the gala, as well as other ex-dancers from Roy's past, who'd delivered tributes to his long career.

One of these was Isabelle's mother, Vanessa Leighton, who'd flown back from Buenos Aires especially for the occasion. She'd introduced the famous *pas de deux* from *Giselle,* which she once used to dance with Roy herself, tonight performed by two principals from the present company.

Jordan had been hurriedly introduced to her in the dressing room before the show began and, as he towered over her, was amazed how young and luminously beautiful she still looked in her elegant black evening dress and high heels – tinier even than Alicia, who'd been charged with looking after her. Her smooth bun of neat, dark hair, her pointed, heart-shaped face and expressive brown eyes came as a real shock to Jordan, who'd pictured her as red-haired and willowy like Isabelle. But the brilliance of her smile, the graceful gestures of her slender hands and the turn of her shapely head, which set up a faint tinkle from the diamond droplets in her earlobes, proclaimed her every inch a ballerina. She'd been far too busy to do more than shake hands with him and flash an appraising glance over his entire long length, but he felt as though she'd already summed up every one of his technical imperfections. In this fiercely competitive world, it didn't take much to make you feel the lowest of the low...

Yet as the cast gathered for the curtain call, an unknown male dancer, passing by in classical black velvet doublet and tights, touched him briefly on the shoulder.

"Great performance," he whispered with a generous smile.

Jordan bowed his head in an effort to master the fierce swell of pride at his heart. He was now an acknowledged

223

dancer – a member of the charmed inner circle. It was all he wanted – just the chance to belong.

Isabelle glanced up into his face and gave his hand a squeeze of understanding.

Jordan smiled back. He could never've done this without her: her patient support, her encouraging smile when he was down, her professional suggestions about improving his technique. This dance was something they'd shared that could never be taken away, no matter what happened afterwards…

At last the great curtain rose and the massed company of performers stepped forward to acknowledge a fresh surge of applause amid a glitter of streamers and confetti. And here came Roy himself, hauled bodily onto centre stage in his evening suit to receive the appreciation of the dancers and enthusiastic ovations from the audience, who were stamping their feet and rising from their seats with loud cheers.

And then it was all over. The curtains swept down for the last time and everyone on stage burst into exclamations and embraces. Jordan turned towards Isabelle, but she'd already been engulfed by a cluster of excited older women, including Alicia and her mother. While she was being showered with admiration and congratulations, he hovered awkwardly in the background. What was he meant to do now?

People were beginning to drift off in the direction of the studio, where the gala reception was being held. He could feel the adrenalin seeping away and suddenly shivered in a chill draught, which cut through the thin material of his loose-fitting shirt, causing the sweat to run in clammy trickles down his bare back.

Where were the dozens of admirers he'd imagined flocking round to shake his hand and congratulate him? Even Dillon seemed to be commanding more attention than himself, as he stood among the trailing streamers with Roy, who was busy introducing him to the orchestra conductor in black tails.

Next moment Alex had brushed past and been instantly

absorbed into the charmed circle around Isabelle. Basking in the glory of his recent success as filmstar-to-be, Alex refused even to speak to him these days. Stuck-up prick! Why was it him dancing Romeo to Isabelle's Juliet on Sunday afternoons? No matter how hard Jordan struggled to convince himself that his own relationship with her was a special part of her life, just seeing her and Alex together showed him how much less skill and experience he possessed than a real dancer. Ironically, the more he learned, the worse he seemed to get...

A great wave of exhaustion washed over him. His limbs hung dull and heavy and lifeless. It wasn't just him and Bella and Roy any more. They didn't need him; he didn't belong here...

His shoulders slumped and he turned to creep off back to the dressing rooms. But at that moment he caught sight of a figure glittering in citrus yellow, standing in the stage doorway and waving furiously to gain his attention. Elodie. What was she doing here? He'd thought she couldn't come to the performance...

He raised an arm in greeting and at once began elbowing his way through the crush. Finally he reached her, standing on the very edge of the crowd. How good she looked with her wide, radiant smile – like a little bit of home in a strange new world!

"Elodie," he cried, eagerly surveying her beautiful face with its shimmering eyelashes and frosted lips. "You came after all."

"God – yeah. O'course, Jordan. Mum said someone oughta be here – with your gran and Grace busy at the church social and you givin' me that free ticket and all. You were just great."

Praise at last!

"Thanks, Elodie – you don't know how much this means to me..."

"Look, Jordan," she interrupted in a business-like tone, her bright yellow fingernails playing with the clasp of her sequined evening purse. "You got a moment? There's something I been wantin' to tell you."

The slight crease between her brows instantly alerted Jordan to what was coming. She was annoyed because they hadn't seen much of one another lately, what with work, shifts at the Arts Centre and endless dance rehearsals…

"Look, it's all gonna be different now," he began, seizing one of her hands and launching straight into a heartfelt apology. "I know it's been really tough for you these last weeks with me busy all the time. But now the gala's over, there're no more rehearsals for the dance. And the Grade Six exam's out of the way too. I'm gonna have some time on my hands at last. With summer coming up, we can make plans – go places…"

Suddenly he stopped speaking. Something in her eyes warned him it was useless.

Elodie lowered her gaze and her fingers slipped slowly from his grasp.

"No, Jordan," she said, shaking her head so decidedly that her chandelier earrings jingled. "That's what I've come to tell you. I really knew this weeks ago, but I didn't wanna believe it. Thought to myself: just have to hang on long enough and things'll get better. But things ain't gonna get better, are they? I mean, when was the last time I saw you?"

"Well…" Jordan racked his spinning brain. "Last Sunday. At rehearsal, like usual."

"No, I don't mean with other people. I mean to talk to – alone. Or just to have a bit of fun. You fell asleep the last film we went to an' you didn't even show at Lauren's party on Friday night."

Jordan stared down at his hands in silence. Guilty as charged.

"I felt real mad at you that night," she admitted quietly,

"an' I told Lauren I was gonna split up with you right then and there. But I haven't even seen you face to face to tell you so."

"Can't we make a fresh start?" he pleaded. Elodie was the most important thing in his life at this moment. He couldn't let her go without a struggle.

"Look, Jordan," she replied kindly. "You gotta face facts. You an' me – there ain't no future for the two of us together. I got big plans for next year – hair and beauty studies at college and photoshoots for a modelling portfolio. I like shopping and partying with my friends. But you don't have time for that no more. All you want to do is dance. What good's that to me? You gone a different way now from the rest of us. I'm not saying it's a good move or a bad move – I'm just saying that's how it is. So I've come to tell you it's all over between us and no hard feelings."

Jordan wanted to throw back his head and howl. He tried to blurt out one last protest even now – but Elodie sadly shook her head. At that moment he felt a light tap on his shoulder. It was Roy.

"Come on, Jordan," he urged. "We're all waiting. The photographer's taking some commemorative shots and I want you at the front with Isabelle."

"In a moment, Roy," replied Jordan with all the dignity he could muster when his heart felt as if it was cracking in two.

"Oh hello, Elodie," Roy remarked, noticing her for the first time. "Wasn't that a terrific performance? Don't you feel proud of Jordan? We certainly do. He's got a great future ahead of him as a dancer."

Elodie nodded brightly, her eyes glittering with tears. Then she turned and, clutching her sequin purse, headed off without a backward glance.

Jordan would've given anything at that moment to run after her. But that'd mean giving up dancing, because he couldn't have Elodie and dance as well. Had to be one or the other. And he couldn't stop dancing. He had to focus on the future, if he was going to make a go of his one big chance.

His glance wavered. For a moment he gazed longingly after Elodie's receding figure and then he turned slowly back to where Roy and Isabelle were waiting for him. There was no choice. This was the way he had to go.

CHAPTER
TWENTY-THREE

The first of the two intensive rehearsal weeks planned for the Brackwell Heath Youth Dance Club production of *Romeo and Juliet* took place in late July after the end of the school term. On Monday afternoon the sun finally emerged from behind grey clouds and continued to burn so fiercely that by Wednesday, the whole city lay panting beneath its glare. It was almost too hot to sleep at nights and the parched lawns faded and withered.

At the otherwise deserted school, the interior of the gym, where the rehearsal was in progress, felt like the inside of a furnace. Every door and window stood wide open to catch the least cross-draught and the dancers, when they weren't needed, lounged around the fire exits, looking languidly on and repeatedly draining their water bottles dry.

Jordan had settled down with Oz in a rapidly dwindling patch of shade outside one of the open doors to try out the demo of *Capulets and Montagues* on Oz's hand-held computer console. But Roy just yelled at them for distracting everyone.

The old bugger'd been in a mean mood all morning, altering blocking at random and picking holes in sequences that'd seemed fine a couple of weekends ago. Not to mention his irritation with Jordan in particular because of having to arrange the whole week's rehearsal schedule round his job.

Pretty clearly why he kept on sounding off so loudly about the subject of commitment.

And after he'd got time off work too, especially to rehearse the last big fight scene. All the boot-licking he'd had to do before Tony'd agree to him taking a whole day's leave. It was fine for the rest of them, who didn't have a living to earn, to laze around chatting while Roy and Alex argued endlessly over the finer points of entrances from right and left, but what a waste of his precious holiday to be stuck seated on his butt for ages doing sod all.

And bloody Alex watching him getting told off with that superior smirk all over his stupid face! He could see the bastard glancing triumphantly at Roy as if to say, "Well, what can you expect of an amateur like that?" and then turning away in open contempt.

Alex's handsome nose was more than a little out of joint after the sensation Jordan and Isabelle's dance had created at Roy's retirement gala and it didn't help that a repeat performance had been scheduled at a choreography competition in London in September. Alex was nothing but a dog in the manger: after refusing to partner Isabelle himself, he was obviously green with envy over the praise Jordan'd won in his place. Serve him right, the smug, self-satisfied arsehole! Him and his pretentious posing with Isabelle throughout those love duets. What call had he to stand at every pause for discussion with his arm resting casually round her shoulders or to let his hands linger on her waist whenever they were stopped by Roy after a lift? Anyone'd think he bloody owned her, the way he was always pawing her in public.

Just pretend not to care. Don't show it rubbed you raw. Especially don't even look across the gym to where Elodie stood, casually fanning herself in the doorway with a fashion magazine.

Only a couple of days after the two of them split up, he'd

caught sight of her along the high street hanging off Prince Harrison's arm as though the pair of them'd never been apart. Perhaps she'd just been using him all this time to get back at Prince. What a fool he'd been to fall into her trap like that. If only he had a girl – any girl – to take her place.

While he and Isabelle were dancing together, he'd somehow imagined he was as big a part of her life as she was of his – only to find now that she seemed not even to've noticed how he'd kissed her after the gala dance. At least she'd never mentioned it since and all the time they'd spent together didn't seem to've made the least dent in her relationship with Alex. The mere idea of that jumped-up prick having her all to himself when they left the rehearsal that afternoon made his blood boil. Why did she simply refuse to see what a shit the guy was, what a vain, narrow-minded, loathsome, smarmy wanker?

Watching them across the gym all morning only made things worse. The way Alex deliberately blocked her when she looked as if she was coming over to speak to Oz and then kept her behind practising some stupid steps when she might've gone out to lunch with the rest of them, all the time casting sneering glances at Jordan as if flaunting this achievement in his face…

By the time the two of them finally took up swords opposite one another for the final Tybalt-Romeo confrontation, Jordan was spoiling for a fight.

"OK, guys," announced Roy with the air of a commander marshalling his troops for one last-ditch offensive beneath a blazing desert sun, "now I know it's hot and you're all dead beat, so we're just going to run this straight through with the music and then take a break. I'll give you notes after you've had a chance to cool down. Ready there, Alex? Places, kids, places please. Jordan, let's start at your re-entrance…"

Jordan obediently took up his position, rapier in hand. He'd never really understood the pleasure of handling a weapon until he picked up that thin steel blade and pictured himself back in the hot, dusty marketplace of Verona. A breath of wind sighed through the open door and the sweat prickled on his skin.

The music gave him his cue and he sprang on stage to find Alex crouched over Cameron's prone body. Alex leapt to his feet with a startlingly life-like expression of fury on his face and rushed at him with such apparent strength of purpose that Jordan had to summon up all his energy to withstand the impact. They instantly engaged in the well-rehearsed sequence of blows. Intense relief flooded through him as he faced his hated enemy at sword point. This didn't require much acting on his part – and Alex probably felt the same.

There was always a certain amount of jostling and confusion in the fight sequences, which the boys loved improvising in the interests of added realism. At one point, Sudhir and Ash, who were slogging it out on opposite sides with equal goodwill, happened to stumble backwards into Jordan. The light foil flew out of his hand and, instead of skidding forwards as usual, clattered onto the ground within inches of Alex's foot.

Alex sprang back as though Jordan'd tried to stab him and the whole fight sequence wavered and began to split apart.

"Oh for God's sake – it bloody slipped," Jordan protested, bristling at the carelessness implied by Alex's disdain.

"I told Roy in the first place that it was a mistake to arm people like you with offensive weapons," retorted Alex. "You could easily've injured me."

"Wha'd' you mean 'people like me'?" countered Jordan furiously.

"Oh stop trying to play Mr Tough Guy," taunted Alex with a provocative sneer. "You'll never be any good at acting anyone but yourself. Why don't you slink back into the filthy hole you crawled out of and leave us real dancers to get on with our job?"

"You just want me off the scene so it doesn' make you look so wet and useless, pretty boy."

"Who're you calling 'pretty boy'? I've a good mind to lodge a formal complaint about your behaviour. It's not going to earn you any credit with Isabelle, you know…"

At the mention of Isabelle's name, Jordan saw red. For months now Alex'd been needling him towards the limits of his endurance and these words finally thrust him over the edge. In a flash he'd laid both hands on Alex's shoulders and dealt him a violent shove. Alex staggered backwards and fell heavily to the ground while Jordan, burning to pay him back at last, leapt on top of him and began pummelling him with furious fists.

Everything happened so fast that he was hardly aware of the shrieks of the girls and the confusion all around. Next thing he knew, he was being roughly hauled off Alex, whose nose'd begun to spurt blood.

Roy was standing over them, ice-blue eyes blazing.

"What the hell do you think you're doing, Jordan Howe?" he demanded.

"He asked for it," yelled Jordan, struggling to throw off the hands that were holding him back.

"That's no excuse," bellowed Roy. "This is a dance rehearsal – not a bloody street brawl. I don't know how you've been brought up, but this sort of behaviour's simply not on and you know it. Alex, are you all right?"

With help from Cameron and Mei, Alex had by now scrambled to his feet. But one eye was already swelling grotesquely and he was daubed all over with blood. As he rubbed his bruised knuckles, Jordan couldn't help snorting with amusement at the sight.

Roy heard and instantly rounded on him. "What d'you think you're grinning at?" he exploded. "I've never seen such a display of unself-disciplined brutality in the whole of my career. Get out!"

Jordan stared at him. No one else moved. Even Grace stood open-mouthed in amazement.

"You heard what I said," yelled Roy, his face flushed with rage. "Nobody starts a fist-fight in one of my classes. I told you what'd happen if anybody dared. Get out – now. Get out and don't come back!"

Absolute silence throughout the gym.

What was Roy saying? Jordan clenched his fists so as not to lash out. *That's right*, he thought. *Give us help and hope and then when we've started to trust you, tear it all away again.* Roy was just a fucking bastard, like all those white, middle-class company dancers. He had no choice.

"Suits me," he answered with a casual shrug, straining hard to show he couldn't care less. "I'm off back to work. Keep your fuckin' ballet. Stuff it up your arse."

And he strode out of the door without a backward glance.

He'd hardly left the gym when he heard a cry and flying footsteps behind him. Isabelle. He recognised her voice. He almost hesitated in his tracks, but then thought the better of it and kept on walking. Stuff the whole damned lot of them!

But he didn't quicken his pace and in a moment or two she caught up with him at the far end of the car park. She almost threw herself in front of him.

"Jordan," she cried out, panting for breath. "Stop!"

Because it was Isabelle, Jordan faltered and stood still. But nothing was gonna send him crawling back to that gym. He turned to face her with his arms crossed over his chest.

"Jordan, you can't walk out like this," she pleaded, white-faced with distress.

"Just watch me," he retorted.

"Come back and apologise."

"Ain't apologisin' to no one," moving to turn away.

She put out one hand to grasp his arm.

He instantly shook it off.

"Jordan, what about the performance?" she cried. "Who's going to dance Tybalt?"

He shrugged.

"But after all the work you've put in – everyone's put in. We're all depending on you. How can you let the company down like this?"

"I ain't the one lettin' you down. *He* threw me out. Fine – it's not my problem. I'm outa here."

"But what about your dancing?"

"Stuff it. Who cares? Not him – the soddin' stuck-up bastard." Then, mimicking Roy's cultured voice, "'I don't know how you've been brought up, but this sort of behaviour's simply not on... I've never seen such a display of unself-disciplined brutality in the whole of my career.' Who does he fuckin' think he is? God?"

"What did you expect him to do?" protested Isabelle. "Stand by and watch you beat Alex to a pulp?"

"Alex had it comin'," growled Jordan.

"You just listen to me. No one's got the right to attack someone else like that. You should be ashamed of yourself. Now, Alicia's trying to calm Roy down. Come back and apologise to him and to Alex. Probably if you grovel enough, Roy'll think twice about wrecking the show at this late stage. Come on, Jordan," exerting all her strength in an effort to haul him after her.

But Jordan stood like a rock and refused to budge.

"Jordan," she cried, clearly realising she was getting nowhere. "Why won't you come back?"

"It's no use. I ain't plannin' to grovel to no one – not to Roy and not to Alex neither."

"But, Jordan – you can't give up now. What about the competition at the end of September?"

"What does that matter to you? You got that pretty boyfriend of yours to dance with. You don't need me."

"But… but…" stammered Isabelle, flushing bright red.

"Look," he blustered with more confidence than he felt inside, "I don't need Roy any more. Don't need the rest of you neither. Stuff the lot of you. I can go it on my own!"

And he flung away, hardening himself against the sight of her stricken face.

CHAPTER
TWENTY-FOUR

W hy wouldn't he see sense? Isabelle had truly believed Jordan was growing more ambitious and self-disciplined as a result of the hard work he'd been putting in with Roy. But to throw it all away like this and without a moment's hesitation head back to the garage workshop! Was it impossible for someone to change the course of their life after all?

She stood watching helplessly as he strode off down the driveway and vanished round the corner. He didn't come back. The world suddenly drained of its bright colours as a cloud veiled the face of the sun. Isabelle shivered. Recalling that she was wearing only light practice gear, she turned and slowly retraced her steps to the gym.

In the lobby she met Roy and Mei supporting Alex's shaken and blood-stained figure between them.

"We're just off to A & E," Roy told her. "You coming too?"

Isabelle nodded mechanically. She ran to throw on some clothes, while Mei and Roy helped Alex out to the car.

Leaving Mei behind with Alicia to clear the gym and lock up, the three of them drove to the nearest hospital. There Isabelle spent a long, hot afternoon, doing her best to comfort Alex, who was upset as well as in pain, and also to soothe Roy's justifiable fury.

In Roy's case, her efforts were entirely useless. He was still muttering curses and abuse of Jordan as he dropped them back at Alex's canalside apartment early that evening and, having assisted Alex as far as the lift, advised Isabelle to see he got some rest.

When the two dancers finally set foot inside the flat, Alex summoned up all his strength and flew towards the great mirror on the white wall of the living room to examine the damage for himself. After peering for a moment at his reflection in the brutal glass, he drew back with a shudder.

Isabelle could hardly blame him. It was a terrible sight. The red stream gushing from his battered nose had long since been staunched and the raw weals on his forehead were hidden under a securely taped bandage. But the abrasion on his mouth was thickly crusted with blood and one puffy eye was almost closed by the scarlet and purple bruises distorting its mottled lid. The full extent of his disfigurement apparently struck home as Alex glimpsed his studio portrait hanging on the opposite wall. He threw himself onto the black leather sofa in despair.

"See what that bastard's done to my face." He groaned, plunging his head into his hands. "How can I possibly appear on stage like this? Everyone'd laugh their heads off. It'll be weeks before I can face the rest of the company and what if it's not fully healed by the time I'm scheduled to start filming? I should've known something like this'd happen when I agreed to help Roy out."

"It could be worse," Isabelle observed wearily, laying her bag on the nearest armchair and throwing open the balcony window to air the stifling room. But the suffocating closeness outside afforded no noticeable breath of relief and distant thunder rumbled along the clouded horizon. "At least it's summer break and the nurse said the cuts and bruises'd look much better after a fortnight." She fetched one of the black and white satin cushions to help make Alex more comfortable.

"What does she know?" he exclaimed in a fit of petulance, starting up impatiently and flying back to the mirror to dab at the dry blood caked on his injured lip with a cottonwool ball. "It's fine for the pair of you to talk. It's not your face. What if that sod's scarred me for life? He might even've broken my nose," feeling it tenderly with his fingers. "It's so swollen it's hard to tell what permanent damage he's done. I'll get him back for this – you'll see. Attacking me like a wild animal…"

Isabelle had heard all this and more during the course of that long afternoon at the hospital and she was fed up with Alex's endless lamentations and self-pity. You'd've thought he'd been half-killed, the way he kept going on. And she wouldn't put it past him to have exaggerated his pain in an effort to make Roy even angrier with Jordan.

"You really ought to leave that cut on your lip alone," she advised curtly. "You're only making it bleed again. Would you like a drink of iced water?"

Alex nodded.

"Besides," she threw over her shoulder as she turned to leave the room, "you can't exactly claim that Jordan's outburst was unprovoked."

Alex regarded her in blank amazement.

"What're you talking about?" he demanded, following her out into the gleaming stainless steel kitchenette.

"You should never've made fun of him in the first place," she replied, feeling that fair was fair, as she opened the freezer door in search of some ice cubes. "You know how short his fuse is."

"I see. So now you're taking his side against me. Well, I suppose it's only to be expected in view of the close understanding that's clearly blossomed between the pair of you over the past few weeks."

"And what's that supposed to mean?" demanded Isabelle, slamming the freezer door shut.

"You can't claim not to've noticed the way his eyes're always following you round the room. You blame me – but it strikes me that you're just as guilty for leading him on."

"Leading him on?" echoed Isabelle, pausing with a glass beaker in her hand. "Are you dreaming? When've I ever led him on?"

"What do you call that dance of Roy's that you've just been working on together?"

"But it's art," shot back Isabelle indignantly.

"You try telling that to someone like Jordan Howe. He's not sophisticated enough to be able to distinguish performance from personal emotions. I know you can't possibly have any serious interest in that yob – though other people might suspect it after the way you behaved this afternoon—"

"What exactly are you implying?" interrupted Isabelle, banging down the glass so hard that the ice cubes shot over the granite work surface and whirling round to face him.

"Don't you think it might've looked a bit odd to members of the company, like Mei for example, the way you just dumped me and went racing off after him like a mad woman?"

"Well, she was making such a fuss over you that I didn't think you needed me too," retorted Isabelle. "And besides, Alicia asked me."

But was that the only reason? her conscience whispered. Hadn't she already started after Jordan even before Alicia offered her the excuse?

Alex regarded her with what would've been a significant look, if his half-shut eye hadn't spoiled it by giving him a lop-sided, almost comical air.

"Anyway," he resumed on a more business-like note, "at least this afternoon's fiasco's shown Roy the impossibility of going on with this project."

"What?" cried Isabelle. "Did he tell you he was going to call it off?"

"Why should that matter to you?"

"But all the work we've put in," she murmured, biting her lip. "I know I've spent hours researching and learning the part of Juliet. And what about everyone else?"

"I doubt there's any mileage left in it now Jordan's out of the picture and I'm planning to withdraw."

"Withdraw?"

"You can't expect me to go on after this, can you? I guess it wouldn't be too hard to replace Jordan with a professional dancer – but why would one of the company principals want to waste their time dancing Romeo in an amateur show, even as a favour to Roy?" And Alex started back in the direction of the living room.

Isabelle ran after him with a bursting heart.

"Alex, you can't be serious," she cried, catching up with him in front of the handsome studio portrait of himself. "Don't you realise how much this performance means to everyone we've been working with? They've put their hearts and souls into it. What about the costumes that Grace and Ruth've designed and the church group are busy sewing? And the set that Oz and Jermaine and Oz's dad are building and all the publicity leaflets that've been printed? If the show got cancelled now..."

It was unbearable to think of the bitter disappointment to the whole community of Brackwell Heath.

But Alex seemed unconcerned. He merely shrugged his shoulders. There was a long silence and then Isabelle looked away.

"You don't care, do you?" she said in a low, trembling voice. "It doesn't matter to you what anybody else feels except yourself. How can you be so utterly selfish?"

"Oh don't be melodramatic, Bella," he retorted fretfully. "These people are none of your concern, as I've tried to point out to you—"

"These people?" repeated Isabelle on a rising note of anger. "*These people*? Why do you keep on talking about them as though they're a different species from us? And – yes – they *are* my concern: Oz and Lauren and Sudhir and Grace – over the months they've become my friends."

Alex looked incredulous.

"Bella, you're tired. Go home and have an early night and I'm sure you'll understand what I'm saying. It's no use tearing yourself to tatters over a bunch of losers. You see how easily Jordan could walk out on Roy, after all the help he's given him. No sense of loyalty or gratitude. Not even a backward glance. The guy's got no concept of right or wrong – he just responds on the basis of gut emotions—"

"But I can see his point of view," interrupted Isabelle. "He has feelings too."

"You're trying to defend the bastard who's just done this to me?" Alex demanded coldly, gesturing towards his disfigured face.

Fair point.

"I'm not defending Jordan's actions," she admitted. "I'm just saying that there're reasons why he behaves as he does. He's never been taught to express himself any other way."

"I see – and you're the one who's undertaken to give him a course in self-expression, along with so many other lessons?"

"What exactly are you implying?"

"Don't play the naïve innocent with me, Bella. Something's happened to you while I was away in London. I've been watching you since I got back and it's pretty clear what this is about – all this sympathy and understanding for Jordan Howe. He's not just been screwing you on stage, has he? I can't believe you'd throw away our whole relationship for the sake of that inarticulate ape…"

Isabelle gasped. That he should dare trail such poisonous

slime over her precious dance partnership with Jordan! But no way would she lower herself by shouting back abuse. She drew a deep breath.

"If that's the way you feel, we clearly have no relationship," she retorted icily. "As far as I'm concerned, everything's over between us."

With a glare of blistering scorn she snatched up her bag from the chair and marched out of the flat, banging the front door loudly behind her.

★

Don't cry! Don't you dare cry! she told herself as she fled from the waterside apartment block, tears pricking sharply behind her eyes.

How could Alex speak to her like that after she'd been so patient with him all that tedious, sweltering afternoon? Accusing her of disloyalty and even worse – those ugly, false insinuations about her relationship with Jordan. She was entirely innocent. In fact, if anyone was to blame, it was Jordan himself. He was the cause of all the trouble…

Ashamed of being seen like this by anyone, she swerved blindly into the first side-passage she came across and stumbled down to the canal path, heedless of the fitful spits of rain. Hurrying along with lowered head past smart restaurants fronted by bay trees in tubs and coffee bars adorned with hanging flower baskets, she eventually reached a hump-backed bridge. Here she plunged down a steep flight of steps and along a derelict alley until suddenly she found herself confronted by the towering, graffiti-daubed wall of a burnt-out factory that ran all the way down to the murky canal waters, now spotted with falling rain. There was no way out.

She halted, heedless of her brimming tears.

Where was she? A moment ago she'd been squarely in the centre of the civilised world she knew, but now…

She threw a glance over her shoulder. Should she run back to Alex's? But think how selfish and mean-minded he was. And what unforgiveable things he'd said. She couldn't go back there – even if she remembered the way.

Had she really been guilty of leading Jordan on? Surely not. But think again. Alex wasn't the only one who'd noticed his eyes following her wherever she went. Own up. She'd felt flattered, but now her behaviour just seemed – cheap. And the hug he'd given her in the wings after the gala dance. She'd told herself it was just an outburst of relief that the performance was over at last, but it might easily've meant more than that. What did she really feel for him? Might there be some truth in Alex's accusations?

She'd always known before exactly where she was heading, but now she had no idea. Her stomach lurched, as though her feet were inching closer and closer towards the edge of a steep drop into nothingness. How to save herself?

She gripped the hard iron railings that barred the entrance to the roofless shell ahead. It all felt frighteningly surreal. Smoke-blackened bricks glaring out at her from a dazzling chaos of spray-painted graffiti. Grey dots dancing in front of her bewildered eyes…

At that moment a musical trill pierced the surrounding silence.

She started violently and jerked bolt upright. With a pang of reviving sensation, she realised the moisture trickling down her cheeks wasn't just chill raindrops, but also hot tears of misery and shame. What was that sound, which rose above the pattering shower and the throb of her own fast-beating heart? Of course! Her mobile's muffled ringtone.

But why bother picking up? What did it matter? Her dazed eyes struggled to focus on the sheets of rain scouring the ruffled surface of the canal as she clutched at the shreds of swiftly fading self-revelation. But it was too late. She was squarely back in the real world.

Who could the caller be but Alex, trying to sweet-talk her back to his flat? He hated being left alone… But then – what if he was feeling ill and really needed help? She couldn't just ignore him.

The rain was pelting down now and she had no coat – not even an umbrella. She'd get soaked. Where to take shelter? She stared around. Was that a narrow gap between the crumbling brick wall of the factory and the broken down wooden fence leaning away from the water? Could she manage to crawl inside till the downpour ended?

She squirmed into the cramped space and crouched underneath the dripping slats. There was hardly room to breathe, but at least she was safe from the worst of the shower. Her mobile was trilling insistently, so finally she fished it out of her shoulder bag.

"H-hello," she quavered, smearing the tears off her cheeks with icy fingers.

"Hi there, Isabelle." It was Alicia's matter-of-fact voice. "Are you still at Alex's?"

"N-n-no." Isabelle gulped back a sob and hastily wiped her streaming nose on a crumpled tissue from her bag.

"How is he?" Alicia enquired in a tone of concern.

"N-not too bad, considering," Isabelle stammered guardedly. "I – I left him – resting."

"Are you all right?"

"Yes. Why wouldn't I be?" Isabelle straightened her shoulders, exerting all her powers of self-command to stop sniffing pathetically. No one must suspect what a grovelling fool she'd been.

"I just thought you sounded a bit odd…" Alicia lowered her voice to a conspiratorial whisper. "Jordan hasn't rung you, has he?"

"No. Why should he?" Isabelle dabbed at her swollen eyes with the wet tissue, as the violent heaving of her chest began to subside.

"Pity. Oz was going to see if he could track him down after class, but I haven't had a call from him either."

Isabelle wasn't keen to discuss Jordan.

"How about Roy?" she asked. "Any success at talking him round?"

A deep sigh at the other end of the line.

"I've tried, but he's in such a foul temper," Alicia replied. "He's out in the kitchen now, clashing pots together and chopping the heads off carrots and celery sticks."

The corners of Isabelle's mouth twitched in spite of herself. By now her shoulders had stopped shaking and the rain shower was finally easing.

"When we got back earlier," went on Alicia ruefully, "I suggested he give Jordan a ring and attempt to resolve matters, but he refused point blank. Said Jordan'd started it and ranted on about not countenancing physical aggression in his classes and so on. You know what he's like. So I asked how he'd feel if Jordan could be persuaded to beg his and Alex's pardon."

"And?"

"Huh! He just laughed in my face. Said if I thought that stubborn, pig-headed so-and-so would ever apologise to him, let alone Alex, I'd got another think coming."

"Oh no…"

"Trouble is, he's probably right. Jordan's just as stubborn and pig-headed as him." Alicia groaned. "When I think of all the time and energy he's invested in that lad, I don't see how he can throw him over like this. But that's how things stand. For the moment at least Jordan's out of the cast."

A large raindrop plopped off the broken boards onto Isabelle's nose. She shivered. Remember Alex's dark hints about Roy calling off the show altogether.

"But with no Tybalt and Alex injured, what about the rest of this week's rehearsals?" she asked in a small voice, vainly blotting the water drops oozing off tails of hair onto her neck with the soaked tissue. "Roy didn't actually want to take on this project in this first place. He wouldn't...? I mean, he isn't going to...?"

"It's all right," Alicia reassured her. "Luckily he feels we've gone too far to cancel now. After all, the production's been widely advertised. At the gala too, remember. He's already invited Virginia Seymour from the Pentland Ballet School and Patrick's keen to attend – not to mention one or two old friends, who've bet Roy he'll never pull it off. He says his reputation's at stake. Not to mention having the rest of the company to think of."

"So what's he planning to do?" asked Isabelle, breathing a quiet sigh of relief.

"Well, he thinks – and I agree with him – that no one else among the youngsters can possibly handle Tybalt."

"What about Cameron?" suggested Isabelle quickly, shifting her cramped limbs. "After all, he's been dancing the part this season."

"But then there'd be Mercutio to fill."

"Surely we could co-opt another member of the company? After all, it's just one performance..."

"Yes, but even so, our biggest problem still remains: what to do about Romeo. How do you think Alex is feeling, Isabelle? Roy reckons that, after a decent interval and once he knows Jordan's out of the picture, he might be persuaded back."

"It's a possibility," admitted Isabelle, without much conviction.

"Anyway, whatever happens, we're going ahead with tomorrow's rehearsal as scheduled. I'm going to ring everyone now and tell them."

As she spoke, a gleam of returning sunlight shot across the canal, setting the water afire with sparkling light.

"But what about Jordan?" asked Isabelle tentatively, fighting to prevent her teeth chattering with cold.

"Well… I'll have another go tonight at trying to talk Roy round. But I don't hold out much hope. I'm pretty sure he'll stick to his guns. However – and this is where you come in – I've decided I'm simply not prepared to give up on Jordan without a struggle. Surely, with Grace's help, the three of us can manage to drum some sense into him. After all, look how much he stands to lose if we don't…"

CHAPTER
TWENTY-FIVE

For once Isabelle wasn't looking forward to a dance class. Where could she find the strength and courage to get through tonight? But she couldn't desert Jordan. Unbearable to think of all that talent going to waste. She just had to grit her teeth and get on with it.

It was also in her own interests. The London choreographic competition in September was a prestigious showcase for young talent and an appearance there would be a huge boost to her own career. But she couldn't dance without Jordan. No one else could possibly fill his place. So she'd agreed to take part in this plan, which she and Alicia'd spent some time hatching together secretly with Grace.

Roy remained adamant that his terms were non-negotiable: a full and unconditional apology to both himself and Alex and a solemn undertaking never to repeat such behaviour in future. He refused to discuss the matter further and was busy making arrangements to replace Jordan in his rôle as Tybalt as though he'd never existed. Reluctantly, Alicia gave up trying to reason with him.

But Jordan was another matter. After a week's exile in the wilderness, she and Isabelle hoped he'd be ready to see sense. This had prompted them, without Roy's knowledge, to engineer a private rehearsal, apparently to work on the competition dance, but also in hope of holding out the possibility of a reconciliation. Grace agreed to be the go-between.

But Jordan refused point blank to set foot in the ballet studios in Temple Street – so Alicia came up with a neat solution. Her old friend, Sylvia King, ran ballet classes at the Brackwell Heath Arts Centre. Sylvia had attended the gala performance last month and was glad to help out when she heard what was at stake. So she booked them into the gym studio for the evening.

Isabelle wasn't convinced this was going to work, as she hurried from the bus stop to the Arts Centre. But what other option did they have?

In the mellow evening light after a day of constant rain, the Brackwell Heath Arts and Leisure Centre was not an inspiring sight. The complex, Alicia'd explained to her, had sprung up thirty years ago as part of an urban renewal project. Its huge façade, fronting the roar of the ring road traffic, had been painted by a group of local artists with an inspiring vision of all the activities they dreamed would take place there: football, gymnastics, basketball, hockey, martial arts and adult education…

But the years had passed and the mural had faded along with the hopes of the community. The cracked paint was flaking off the decaying buildings, so the jumble of ill-proportioned structures now wore a grim and unkempt air. The seats outside the car park were the resort of the neighbourhood drunks and shifty-looking characters flitted furtively past in the lengthening shadows.

Isabelle called at reception to ask the way to the studio and was directed by the taciturn night watchman up a short flight of steps and through some double doors into one of the network of drab passages honeycombing the complex. Venturing along an oppressively low-ceilinged corridor, she noted the scarred, yellow walls and scuffed vinyl, repeatedly repaired with heavy-duty black tape. What would be the condition of the dance floor in a run-down building like this?

A tinkle of piano music in the distance told her she was nearing her goal. Peering through the metal slats in the studio door, she caught sight of legs and ballet slippers belonging to Alicia, who was warming up at the barre. Isabelle quietly pushed open the door.

The studio, hung with ropes and climbing bars, was a far cry from the bright, modern facilities of Temple Street. But at least it was a good-sized space with a sprung wooden floor, a high ceiling and even a row of mirrors on the far wall. It was well-lit, both by fluorescent strips and windows set beneath the triple peaks of the roof line. But Alicia was alone.

"Jordan not here?" Isabelle asked.

Alicia shook her head.

"But it's not gone half past yet. Go and get changed. He promised to come."

Isabelle retreated to search for the changing rooms.

When she returned in rehearsal gear and pulled open the heavy studio door, the first thing she saw was Jordan's familiar figure with his back turned towards her, occupied with stretching exercises at the barre. He'd come after all! She uttered a cry of relief and almost flew to greet him.

But the moment he turned round, she pulled up short. Matters weren't going to be so simple after all. His jaw was grimly set and his eyes were sharp with pain. He brushed aside all her strained inquiries.

Exchanging anxious glances with Alicia, she fell to warming up silently at his side. Perhaps the returning pleasure of dancing together would persuade him to abandon his anger.

Both she and Alicia made a superhuman effort. They cooed and coaxed and petted his vanity with all the little ploys they could think of. Isabelle strove to conjure a smile from him by appealing to their shared memories of difficult steps, trying to lure him back into their old partnership.

But whatever she did, she found herself blocked, blundering and stumbling up against one towering, unmentionable subject. It was like struggling to dance with the shadow of Death constantly coming between them. Though Alicia tried her hardest, she was simply not Roy. Even the recorded music sounded strange and tinny on the primitive portable disc player and everything went wrong.

The lifts were mistimed. The catches were muffed. Isabelle slipped twice in Jordan's grasp – and the second time with an awkward twist as she slid down his chest. She fought to make light of the accident, forcing herself to smile, as if eager to carry on. But she couldn't disguise the fact that she was biting her underlip to restrain the tears.

Jordan surveyed her briefly, then wheeled round with his back towards her, breathing hard.

"It's all right," she assured him, darting up and laying a hand on the clenched muscles of his sweaty arm. "I'm fine. Really I am."

"You're really bloody not," he exploded, whipping back to face her. "It's all wrong. You know it's fuckin' crap. You've both done your best and I can see you're tryin' to help. It's me who's to blame."

"Everyone makes mistakes," murmured Alicia, whose cheeks were white with stress.

"Not if you're a professional, you don't," bellowed Jordan. "Face the fact: I can't dance. I'll never dance again. I'm goin' back to the garage. It's all I'm bloody good for!"

And he turned and strode out of the studio, leaving Alicia and Isabelle staring helplessly at each other.

"The waste," moaned Alicia. "The pitiful, miserable, futile waste…"

Isabelle was too upset to speak.

★

Jordan's dreams of a better life lay in ruins. The despair he felt now made his earlier torment and frustration seem like pale shadows of reality. Over and over again he wished he'd never started dancing in the first place. The one result was that his hopes had been raised, only to be dashed again from an even greater height when he saw they could never be fulfilled.

He was angry with Grace for her excitement about auditioning with Airborne, the handicapped dance project, and for continuing to attend *Romeo and Juliet* rehearsals when he was the one for whom these really mattered. He was angry with Isabelle and Alicia for their misguided efforts to keep hope alive inside him. He was angry with Roy for teaching him just enough to understand how to suffer when he was unable to learn any more. But most of all he was angry with himself. What if what he'd told Alicia and Isabelle was true? That all he was fit for was that bloody garage? Since he'd glimpsed another world out there, a world where people cared nothing for race or class but accepted him on the strength of talent alone, he'd come to loathe that garage like poison.

He stormed out of the Arts Centre after the failed rehearsal, burning a trail of fury after him as far as the high street, where he plunged blindly in through the lighted doors of the Black Swan Inn.

That Friday evening the pub was crowded and noisy and there was a new hand on the bar, who served him as a matter of course. All the doors and windows were thrown open and half the male population of Brackwell Heath had congregated there to watch a football match on the big screen. So when he turned with foaming beer glass in hand, it was no surprise to bump into Dillon's sociable older brother, Joel, celebrating a friend's stag night with his mates.

"Man, are we gonna drink this house dry tonight,"

announced Joel, his speech already beginning to slur. "You with someone then?"

Jordan shook his head gloomily.

"Ain't no fun drinkin' alone, man," Joel went on, clapping him round the shoulders. "Bring that pint o'yours over here and join us…"

Jordan needed no second invitation. Anything to blot out the memory of Alicia's white face and Bella's stricken eyes. Eugene's cousin, Malory, offered him a cigarette and he soon began to feel better. This was more fun than being stuck in a dance studio, sweating and straining after unattainable perfection.

After a while he realised he had a week's pay in his pocket, so he stood a round of drinks for the party, who'd rapidly become his best mates. Soon he stopped counting how many glasses he'd drunk. Nobody'd be waiting up for him at home, would they? Bugger the whole world. He was gonna have fun tonight…

★

As he groped his way towards consciousness next morning, his head felt like it had split apart and his mouth was full of baking desert sand. He half-opened bleary eyes, shrinking away from the blinding brilliance of a ray of sunshine, which streamed in through a wide crack in the hastily-drawn curtains.

Where was he? The dingy ceiling of this room, where he found himself lying with his cheek pressed up against the paint-chipped skirting board, looked nothing like the white, polystyrene tiles of his bedroom at home. A nearby moan made him shift his head and strain to focus on the blurred body stretched alongside him. Dillon's brother, Joel, stirring feebly in a trance-like stupor. The vague recollection darted through his brain of doing vulgar impersonations of ballet dancers on a table top... But this couldn't't've been while they were still at the pub. Must've happened after closing time, when they'd come staggering back to Joel's mate's flat to carry on smoking and drinking late into the night. Someone'd offered him a joint...

Confused memories came flooding back. A smell of sweet, cloying smoke in his nostrils and the weird impression of a sea of disembodied faces hanging in the air around him, ebbing and flowing like the tide. The shock of finding his wallet practically empty when he could've sworn it'd been full of cash... Wait! This was Saturday morning, wasn't it? What was the time?

He fumbled around the stained carpet tiles for his watch, oversetting an ashtray of cigarette butts, until he eventually spotted it on his wrist. He squinted at the blurred figures on its face. Eight forty-five. On a Saturday morning. Christ – he was already late for work!

At first he crawled, then stumbled to his feet, picking his way unsteadily through the puddles of beer and wreckage of bodies, some snoring heavily on their backs and others lying motionless where they'd passed out the night before. With his head still spinning dizzily, he blundered into the kitchen and helped himself to a quick cup of black coffee, which he swallowed almost in one gulp, scalding the inside of his mouth raw.

Rank with sweat in yesterday's clothes, he floundered out through the door of the flat, only to find himself trapped in a back alley. After roaming helplessly up and down for several minutes, barging into rubbish bins and knocking over several potted plants with loud clatters, it struck him that he must've come out through the back door. Eventually he wove his way to the high street, where he managed to jump on a bus to work.

Falling into a fitful doze against the yellow pole, on which he'd leaned his aching forehead, he almost missed his stop. But a lucky jolt jarred him awake and he lurched off the bus in the nick of time, making for the garage on the street corner beside the Brackwell Heath Tavern.

"Head down, boy," warned Aziz, as he caught sight of him tottering in through the back door of the workshop. "Tony's had a row with his missus. He's in a furious strop."

But it was no use.

"So what time o'day d'yer call this, Nigger?" demanded Tony, who'd instantly spotted him stripping off his jacket and skulking round the back of the workshop in a feeble effort to pretend he'd not just that moment arrived. "We already got a big backlog after yer little 'holiday' last week and now yer puttin' us even further behind, yer dick-brained mother-fucker."

Jordan shrugged and growled under his breath. Didn't see why he had to make excuses to him.

"So – yer plannin' to do some work today?" Tony went on with heavy sarcasm. "Or yer just come in for a rest? We're ready to MOT that Ford Escort out in the forecourt. Get yer bloody black arse into gear and drive her in or I'll put my fist through yer face."

"You just try it," muttered Jordan mutinously.

"What yer say, fuck-wit?" demanded Tony, rounding upon him with a threatening frown.

Jordan scowled and hung his head, shifting his feet uneasily and making no reply. Back at square one again.

"That's right, Black Boy," Tony taunted him savagely. "Just remember yer place here, right at the bottom of the pile." He took a closer survey of Jordan's face and his lips parted in a malicious grin. "Lookin' a bit the worse for wear this mornin', eh boy? Been out on the town, have yer, with some o'them filthy friends o'yours? P'rhaps yer'd like to do us one of yer little fairy dances. Hey, Aziz, over here! Our young balley star's gonna show us a bit o'the arse and thigh that's turned all the girlies' heads round here. My missus an' her bloody sewin' circle can't talk o'nothing else. Come on, big boy – show us your stuff then…"

Before he even knew what was happening, Jordan had lashed out at his tormentor, lunging at him so suddenly that Tony flew backwards, hitting his head with a mighty crack against the solid concrete floor. After a moment's stunned disbelief, he struggled to his knees, practically gobbling with rage.

"Yer vicious black bugger," he howled, his double chins quivering violently. "Yer just try a trick like that again and I'll strew yer brains over the ground. Aziz – go fetch the manager – right now, y'hear? Tell him Sambo's turned up late for work, reekin' of drink and drugs and laying about him like a madman…"

Aziz scuttled away, but Jordan saw and heard no more. The fury swelled inside him, driving him to action. He sprang at the older man, looming over his trembling figure and hauling him forcibly to his feet by the scruff of his grubby shirt.

"So I'm a dick brain and a cocksucker, am I?" he snarled, tightening his fingers around Tony's bull neck. "You're gonna pay for all the shit you've ever vomited out of that stinkin', evil gob o'yours…"

Tony, whose flabby cheeks were by now mottled an angry puce, choked in Jordan's grasp. Through a red haze of anger, Jordan could see the yellow whites of his bulging eyes and feel the fat fingers clutching at his hands, as Tony struggled to prise apart the stranglehold on his throat, uttering desperate gurgles of terror. Then with a violent twist, he managed to aim a glancing blow at Jordan's shin and jerked up his knee to catch him in the groin.

"Yer throttlin' me," he finally managed to splutter. "Leggo. Aziz. Help! Murder!" With a convulsive exertion of strength, he finally wrenched himself free and tried to take to his heels. But Jordan was too quick for him. Without a moment's hesitation, he swung back his fist and punched Tony's stubbly jaw so hard that he cannoned straight back into the folding doors of the workshop. The opaque panel of toughened glass instantly shattered into a spider's web of splinters.

"Yer bastard," roared Tony out of a bloody mouth, grovelling around on his knees and shaking his fist in fury at Jordan. "Yer'll pay for this. Yer out of this workshop right now – and I'll make damned sure you never set foot in it again!"

Jordan felt he'd gained at least a foot in stature. He positively glowed with freedom.

"Don't bother," he retorted. "I'm outa here. You take your fuckin' job and you know where you can stuff it? Right up your fat, hairy arse!"

And he made an obscene gesture and stalked off without a backward glance.

CHAPTER
TWENTY-SIX

"So how's fings wiv you, mate?" asked Oz, settling himself comfortably behind his can of Coke in a corner of Caribbean Joe's café, since it was far too cold and rainy to sit on the outside terrace. "Long time, no see."

"Never been better," Jordan lied, as he leaned back against the discoloured wall plaster. Of course he was bound to bump into an old friend on the high street one day. He'd long been half-looking forward to, half-dreading it.

"Heard you got the sack," Oz remarked, taking a swift swig from the can and wiping his mouth with the back of his hand.

"Well you heard wrong then," retorted Jordan. "I quit."

"Some story goin' round 'bout you bustin' Tony Tyler's head and pitchin' him frew a glass door." Oz threw a searching glance at him over the top of his can.

Jordan stared back uneasily. Should he try to put him off?

"The bugger was askin' for it," he murmured at last.

"He gonna press charges?"

No choice but to tell the truth.

"Cops came round to ours an' asked a few questions," he admitted in a low voice, still smarting at the memory of Gran's sorrowful face. "But the big boss said he didn't want no trouble, so he settled it with 'em. In the end they let me off with a caution an' told me to keep my nose clean in future."

"Whew! Lucky break, man. Got another job yet?"

"Been followin' up a few leads," remarked Jordan guardedly.

How could he tell Oz the truth about this? With few qualifications and no reference from his previous employment, he was finding it harder than he'd imagined to land another job as a mechanic. Even in garage workshops outside the neighbourhood, every position he turned up to ask about seemed mysteriously to've just been filled. Or suddenly they didn't need a junior after all. Hadn't taken long to work out that Tony'd been onto all his contacts in the business, systematically blackening his name.

"So – you goin' back into a garage?" asked Oz, who could know nothing of all this.

"Nah – decided against it. Rather make it with my dancing."

"You said it, mate. We'll soon be seein' your name up in lights in the West End, eh?"

"P'rhaps," Jordan replied, feeling slightly more positive about the future by sharing his plans – if only with Oz. "Got an audition tomorrow for a show at the Olympian. Just a stop-gap – fillin' in for a dancer who's gone off injured. But it'll pay and it's only till I land a place at performin' arts school. Think I'll have a pretty good chance if I can get an audition, so I'm busy checkin' out the web sites and sortin' some applications."

"So what ya gonna do for money meantime?"

Jordan drew a sharp breath. Why'd Oz keep on asking such awkward questions?

"Oh – bitta this, bitta that," he temporised airily. "Extra evenin' shifts at the Arts Centre, labourin' jobs for my Uncle Wes and some of his mates… So how's things with you? We gonna see *Capulets and Montagues* on sale in time for Christmas?"

"*Capulets and Montagues*'ve sure done the business for me, man," Oz declared, a broad grin overspreading his freckled face. "It's gonna be big online. So the firm've offered me a job on their design team."

"You havin' me on?"

Oz shook his head firmly. "No way, man. 'S a real job. Decided to say yes. Got big plans for the future. Make a killin' on the computer games market, ya know. Chances are I'll hit the jackpot one day if I just keep pluggin' away at the old ideas fing. Gotta lot to be fankful to them ballet people for—"

He stopped short – as though dimly realising this mightn't be the best topic to raise in front of Jordan.

"I got no hard feelin's," lied Jordan with studied carelessness. The topic was bound to surface in the end, but he didn't plan ever to let on to anyone how he felt about his exclusion from the dance project.

"You know, man," Oz went on, encouraged by this reassurance, "I cleaned up my act a lot 'cos of what they've taught me. My mum – she really keeps me goin', you know – she says she blesses the day I started that dancin' business. An' like it's made a big diff'rence to Dad too. When Roy found out what the old man could do wiv a hammer, he pulled a few strings at that company o'his, an' all of a sudden Dad found hisself in a job again. He's started work at the scene construction department – an' he just loves it. Don't wanna come home nights. Got a big job on the new sets for *Macbeth* what's premiering in November. But you've prob'ly heard all about that."

Jordan was famished for a single crumb of news about his old friends – but no way was he going to admit it.

"Guess I heard somethin'," he murmured.

"Yeah, s'pose you get all the news from Isabelle, bein' your dance partner an' all…"

Isabelle. Jordan hadn't seen her in weeks – not since that terrible night at the Arts Centre studio. Neither she nor Alicia'd tried to contact him again. P'rhaps he'd left them little choice. But at least they could've gone on trying.

"S'pose she keeps you up to date wiv what's happenin' wiv *Romeo and Juliet*," went on Oz, throwing him a sideways glance. "An' Grace too, if she's anyfink like my little sister. Chatter, chatter, chatter…"

"You bet. But shoot anyway," Jordan urged, anxious not to appear over-eager. These days he never spoke about the show with Grace, who'd stopped trying after a couple of bristling repulses. "How's rehearsals then?"

"Last big push's comin' up in free weeks' time when the company get back from their late summer tour, wiv our big night at the end of it. You gonna come along?"

"What, me?" The idea'd never occurred to him. "Sit in the audience? No way, man."

"Fort you'd wanna cheer us all on. All your old mates like."

"I been down to Dill's garage a couple of evenin's lately," Jordan began with seeming irrelevance. "No one was there – it was just dark and lonely and kinda spooky…" His voice faded away.

Oz looked concerned. "But I woulda texted you if there was gonna be any action," he protested loyally.

"Chill, man. Wasn't lookin' for action. Just rememberin' the old days. Seems a long time ago."

Oz sighed deeply. "We all been so busy, I guess we ain't had no time for gigs lately."

"Busy?" echoed Jordan. He could hardly remember what being busy felt like.

"Yeah – wiv the show and so on. Girls're all holed up at each other's places, sewin' on sequins and pearls an' stuff. Hayley's doin' front o'house work experience at the Olympian an' Eugene's helpin' out at sports camps for little kids at his uncle's place. Dill an' the band've played a few gigs at pubs an' clubs in town – didn't you hear about them ones at Mephisto?"

Jordan slowly shook his head. No one rang him any more and even texts were few and far between.

"S'pose someone else is dancin' Tybalt?" he murmured with a sick feeling in the pit of his stomach.

"Oh yeah – you 'member Cameron? Pretty hot stuff – ya know – bein' a real dancer and all."

A blow upon a bruise. Cameron dancing Tybalt? Fiery, passionate Tybalt – the rôle that belonged to him…

"And Roy's coachin' Masakuni to do Benvolio," added Oz, swallowing another mouthful of Coke.

Roy. At last. The name Jordan'd been shying away from for weeks…

"So how's the old bugger?" he asked wistfully.

"Oh – mean as ever. You know what he's like…"

Yes, Jordan knew exactly what he was like – a stony-hearted, sinew-cracking tyrant. Suddenly a great, empty nothingness seemed to yawn open inside him. He'd never understood what that old sod meant to him till he wasn't there any more. Didn't think he'd ever even thanked him for all he'd done – not once. He and Alicia'd treated him far better than his own dad and mum when they didn't even have to. What'd Isabelle once said? "I don't go back home very often. The company are my family now…"

"Man – you oughta turn up to the big night," Oz urged, breaking in on his thoughts. "It's gonna be the greatest. Don't you wanna see Isabelle dance Juliet?"

Jordan swallowed hard. Wouldn't he've practically torn the heart out of his body to see Isabelle dance again? Especially in her début as Juliet, for which she'd worked so hard. But it was no use. She'd tried to help him, she and Alicia, even after everyone else'd turned away, and he'd thrown her kindness back in her face. He was no one – he was nothing – he was lower even than nothing…

"You wouldn't believe how pretty she looks in that balcony scene," Oz rambled on, growing almost poetical. "Saw her havin' a costume fittin' last Sunday. Her dress's made out o'this light, floaty stuff. Looks like an angel…" He breathed a deep sigh of pleasure. "Gonna be a real stunner on stage. She 'n' Alex make a great-lookin' couple."

Jordan's eyes opened wide. "Alex? You mean Alex's back?"

"Oh yeah. Haven't you heard? Didn't look too good the first Sunday he showed – you sure gave him a massive shiner on his eye. But the bruise's fadin' pretty quickly now – be all gone by the big night. Ya know, Jordan," hesitating slightly, "I once fort you had the hots for Isabelle yourself. An' I don't mind tellin' ya, I was pretty gutted at the time you and she were hangin' round together doin' that gala dance. But I guess we both gotta look at it this way: she's too classy for blokes like us. 'Specially now she's been took on."

"Took on?" Jordan gulped.

"Yeah. Got a permanent job in the company. Didn't she tell you? She's on her way to bein' a star. I mean, what would guys like you 'n' me do, even if we did ask her out for real? You can't see her at a gig in Dill's garage like the rest o'the birds we know. She's different. On a higher plane – like Alex. He comes from her world, he knows what to say to her. I never did. Like that time I came here wiv her – remember?"

Jordan nodded slowly. It was like suffocating by inches.

"Tried talkin' to her 'bout music 'n' ballet and so on. But I didn't know nuffink about 'em. An' she didn't know nuffink about computers. So we really didn' have too much to say to each uvver. Tried makin' out like we'd gone on a date. But it wasn't true. It was all just make-believe. It's better as it is – her wiv Alex an' so on…"

Jordan bowed his head, unable to meet Oz's gaze. For Isabelle now it was as though he'd never been. But every moment of every day he looked out for her, wondering if he might meet her at a street corner on her way to rehearsal at Brackwell Heath gym – even on week days when she couldn't possibly be there. And every night she came to him in dreams, just as he remembered once holding her in his arms. A slight pressure on her waist and she instinctively edged right; a little lift and she seemed to soar into the air like a bird. He'd lain awake for hours hearing trains rumble by, straining to recall the exact shade of her fire-bright hair or the elusive greenness of her eyes. And what frightened him most was that he was actually beginning to forget what she looked like. Whenever he found himself walking behind a red-haired girl in the street, he'd try to get ahead of her somehow, just to catch a glimpse of her face. But none of them were Isabelle. He'd never see her again. He'd had his one big chance and he'd blown it.

Worse even than that – hard though it was to imagine anything worse – was not dancing any more. Hadn't noticed at first because he was so busy being sore at Roy. But gradually he'd begun to feel like a drug addict with withdrawal symptoms. There was nothing to do during the hours of every day that he used to spend dancing. Tuesday came – and there was no Grade Seven syllabus lesson with Roy. Thursday – and no open class either. No prospect of heading into the ballet studios after work to practise alone just for fun. And most terrible of all were Sunday afternoons.

Grace, who'd rather die rather than be scolded for missing a single rehearsal, would set off for the gym, leaving him sprawled on the sofa in front of the TV trying to pretend he was so engrossed in watching a film that he hadn't even noticed she was leaving. He'd wait till she'd turned the corner, then fling off in the direction of the recreation ground to pace moodily up and down the barren, grassy waste for hours. Once he'd tried using the banister railing outside his bedroom as a barre, but their upstairs hall was too narrow for a decent *plié* – the worst thing about dancing was how much space it needed. So he gave up and headed down to the Arts Centre. But now when he tried to give himself a lesson in the empty studio, it just wasn't the same.

He fretted about losing what little technique he'd managed to claw together and getting more and more out of condition. But no matter how he threw himself into workouts in the multi-gym or even made up his mind to return to the basketball squad to start training all over again for the county trials, it wasn't like dancing. He missed dancing so much he thought he'd go mad and, as he aimlessly wandered the back streets of Brackwell Heath, he couldn't help remembering what Alicia'd once told him about setting one foot on the stage and never being able to take it off again.

His meeting with Oz made him realise he'd have to take steps as far as the future was concerned. After all, Roy wasn't the only dance teacher in the city. What about the ballet school at the Arts Centre? He wasn't proud. He'd do anything to take class again.

But when he approached Miss King, he discovered she was an old friend of Alicia's and – worse – that now he'd no settled income, he couldn't afford to pay even her modest rates.

All that was left was to sink into the oozing mire that'd long been waiting to claim him and for its slimy, black mud to close over his head.

CHAPTER
TWENTY-SEVEN

A blaze of lights; a blur of upturned faces; the spectators straining eagerly forward in their red plush seats. Jordan felt all eyes riveted on him as he threw off a triple pirouette and an extempore *tour en l'air,* then attempted a couple of *grands jetés,* for which there was hardly room on that tiny platform. Ending his final number of the evening with a half-hearted flourish, he fled off stage, too overcome by shame to heed the outburst of raucous cheering in his wake.

"Go on. Take a bow," urged Derek, the nightclub's business-like lead dancer, shooing him back from the wings, where he stood poised for his entrance in the shabby bird-of-paradise turban and transparent pantaloons of a harem slave.

Jordan obeyed in a daze, steeling himself to acknowledge the applause of the audience, who'd risen to their feet braying with enthusiasm: a heaving sea of luridly painted faces and bodies decked out in gaudy spangles, reeking of cheap liquor and stale perfume. Then he shot off stage, deaf to the suggestive compliments of a couple of tap-dancing sailors lounging behind the purple curtains.

Reaching the privacy of the cramped dressing room, cluttered with costume racks, clothes hangers and dilapidated make-up benches, he threw himself into a chair breathing heavily, his head bowed almost onto his chest.

"You get used to it. After a while you don't even notice any more," advised a sympathetic voice from behind.

Jordan glanced up and in the mirror caught sight of a weird-looking creature in a scanty costume of black leather and gold sequins. Jesus Christ! It was himself. What would Isabelle say if she could see him now? In a passion of self-disgust, he tore off the garish, scarlet-feathered headdress and flung it down on the make-up bench. His flesh crawled. How could anyone ever get used to this?

Ignoring the concern on David's face, which hovered behind him in the mirror, Jordan locked himself in the shower room and hurriedly exchanged the rest of his tawdry costume for a pair of comfortable old jeans, a faded T-shirt, his denim jacket and grey baseball cap. The memory of the date he had after work that night helped him feel more himself again. Choked by lack of fresh air, he bolted along the dingy corridor without a backward glance, slipping out through the rear exit into the all-screening darkness of a warm summer night.

★

The Fallen Angel stood barely three streets away from Temple Street where the ballet studios were located, but it might as well've been in another world. Here Jordan had finally managed to secure a job when every other door seemed closed against him.

He'd honestly struggled to make a go of his dancing by emailing enquiries to several ballet schools. But they'd demanded so many professional references, records of previous experience and staggering audition fees that he soon realised he'd need help even to make an application. So he ended up slamming down the phone or tearing up the polite advertisements of audition times for next year's intake. No one seemed to understand that he wanted to start now and that what he needed most of all was a job. No one except the lead dancer of the Fallen Angel cabaret. Derek had agreed to hire him the same day on the strength of a brief audition, but even then he warned that it was only on a trial basis.

Jordan's heart sank when he understood what the cabaret consisted of, but he'd no choice but to accept. One or two of the old hands, like David, were kind-hearted. They took him under their wing, teaching him the routines and complimenting him on being a quick study and would've volunteered more of their companionship if Jordan'd been less bristly and stand-offish. He couldn't nerve himself to confess to his family where he was really working and said instead that he'd found an ushering job at the Olympian Theatre. Besides, this was just a stop-gap till he managed to land a part in a real stage show.

That night after work Jordan had arranged to meet Oz and some of his other mates at Footlights, a bar close to the Olympian. When he emerged from the rear door of the Fallen Angel, the streets were throbbing with noisy disco music and bright with the flashing neon lights of the neighbouring pubs and clubs. Glow-worm cigarette tips betrayed knots of drunken party-goers loitering in darkened doorways as acrid whiffs of smoke drifted towards his nostrils on the breeze.

He started out at a brisk pace with his baseball cap pulled well down over his lowered head. In that area there was a real risk of bumping into someone he knew from the ballet company, so he soon turned down a side street, striving as far as possible to keep among the shadows cast by the high walls of the old, disused warehouses and modern apartment blocks.

As he was hurrying past the shuttered windows and graffiti-blackened rear entrance of an adult cinema, two figures suddenly staggered straight into his path. One was a tall black woman, dressed in a glittering pale green negligée, her frizzy red hair wound into a tangle of pearl beads. Her shorter companion, a platinum blonde with pouting cherry lips, wore an electric blue mini dress and thigh-length leather boots. Clearly a couple of hookers.

Two nights at the Fallen Angel had taught him not to stare, but he couldn't help starting when the black woman accosted him in a deep bass voice.

"Hey, didn't we just see you on stage in the Fallen Angel?" added the platinum blonde, eying him with interest.

"Dunno what you mean," countered Jordan evasively. "Now look here, um – ladies, I'm meeting friends and I'm already late…" And he made to pass on his way.

The platinum blonde giggled coyly, but the owner of the green negligée gathered the front of Jordan's denim jacket into the grasp of one massive fist.

"Think again, big boy," she advised. "That's no way to address a lady…"

Jordan tried to edge aside, but the pair grew more insistent. He was struggling to loosen their grip on his clothes when he noticed a group of black youths, clearly on the lookout for amusement, turn up the otherwise deserted side alley and saunter in the direction of the undignified scuffle.

As they came nearer, Jordan realised with a jolt of horror that their leader was none other than Prince Harrison. The next moment Prince recognised him too. He grinned unpleasantly.

"Well, well, well. If it ain't Jordan Howe – fairy cocksucker supreme," he said with a sneer. "Fancy bumpin' into you in this part o'town – along with your two lady friends here."

"Them's no ladies," tittered one of his dreadlocked henchmen, who'd been surveying the green negligée in fascination. "Them's guys with falsies."

Prince's band of toughs instantly burst into loud laughter, cracking crude jokes and threatening to tell Jordan's mates about the company he was keeping these days.

Jordan knew he needed to keep his cool. Prince was just

a barnyard cock crowing on a dung hill. Now he had Elodie back, perhaps he'd be content merely to gloat over his fallen rival. So he grinned ingratiatingly and ground his teeth in private, on the lookout for the first chance of escape.

Meanwhile, the green negligée and the platinum blonde had taken offence at the insults being hurled at them and started hustling Prince and his gang. Spotting his moment, Jordan exerted all his strength and wriggled out of the loosened grip of the green negligée, darted down the nearest alleyway and sprinted as fast as he could round several corners. No shouts of pursuit came from behind. After a couple of minutes it seemed likely that Prince and his gang were too busy skirmishing with the prostitutes to chase after him.

Heaving a sigh of relief, he set a fresh course for the theatre bar. Thank his lucky stars he'd got off so lightly. The loss of a baseball cap was a small price to pay for throwing Prince off his scent. Hastening up the dimly-lit side alley, he scanned each shadowy figure flitting past. Only let him reach the safety of Footlights and the company of his friends!

But just as he was emerging onto the main thoroughfare opposite the entrance to the bar, he ran smack into Prince and his gang again.

"Thought you mighta headed up this way, Jordan." Prince smiled, squarely blocking his path. "Seen you in this fancy joint before. So how's about takin' a little walk with us instead?" And he slipped one hand under Jordan's arm in the friendliest looking manner.

Jordan instantly shook himself free. His mouth was dry with fear, but no way was he going to let Prince see it.

"Thanks for the invitation, guys. But I'm meetin' friends just across the road here. Next time maybe." And he grinned cheekily, spurred on to rashness by the sight of Oz and Sudhir seated at a round metal table on the open-air terrace under a string of coloured lights. They were thirty metres away at most. If Oz'd only just turn his head!

"Hey, man, wait up," urged Prince, nodding to his men, who instantly encircled Jordan. "We got some unfinished business."

"I ain't got no business with you," Jordan insisted. Thank God! Oz'd glanced round to check if he was coming and clearly noticed what was happening on the other side of the road. He rose and seemed to be alerting the others seated round the table. Jordan just needed to keep Prince talking a little longer…

"You ain't forgot that night at Dill's garage?" Prince was asking, his back to the street.

"Exactly what night d'you mean?" temporised Jordan, struggling not to bat an eyelid as he saw Eugene, Dill, Ash and Sudhir too, shouldering their way through the crowd behind Oz.

"That night we were broke in on just as things were gettin' interestin'," persisted Prince, his thumbs stuck in his tattered waistcoat pockets.

Jordan gave ground a little. "Yeah – well, you won out, didn't you?" he admitted with uncharacteristic humility. "You got Elodie back, no sweat. So what's the big deal?"

His mates were just about to cross the street when a couple of cars swept past.

Prince thrust his face into Jordan's. "Yeah, the best man won out. But I got a long memory an' I made up my mind then and there that what you needed was a lesson, Jordan Howe. I been keepin' an eye out to teach it to you, only you ain't been hangin' round the usual joints too much of late."

"Oh yeah?" growled Jordan, falling back till he felt a solid brick wall behind him.

"I been waitin' a long time for tonight, man, and now it's come, I'm gonna teach you a lesson you won't never forget."

"And what if I don't wanna learn it?" demanded Jordan, breaking out in a hot sweat.

"Oh you gonna learn it, man, 'cos I gonna make you."

"How you gonna make me?"

"Like this."

With one swift motion Prince pulled something out of the inner pocket of his denim jacket. A blade-edge glinted in the veering car headlights. Jordan fixed it with a wide-eyed stare as his mates came pelting across the street towards them.

"Watch it! He's got a knife," he yelled and at the same moment, with a convulsive struggle, ducked out from under Prince's arm.

Everything happened at once. All Jordan knew was that as he started running, Prince lunged after him and grabbed him by the shoulder. At the same moment Oz caught hold of Prince's arm to seize the knife. There was a fierce scuffle of flailing limbs and all of a sudden a terrible cry as Oz sagged to the ground.

Prince was still gripping the knife, but its gleaming blade had turned dark. Jordan let out a yell and leapt forward to wrench the weapon out of his grasp, but Prince'd already panicked and dropped it. He and his henchmen took to their heels, fleeing down the side passage with Dill and Ash in hot pursuit. Jordan refused to budge.

He fell to his knees beside Oz's motionless figure.

"Oz. Hey, man. You all right?" he cried, raising the slumped body in his arms. Oz's head fell back limply across his shoulder, his face with its disfiguring birthmark deathly white beneath the hail of freckles in the silver light of the street lamp. Jordan saw red blood staining his pale shirt. He glanced up at Eugene, standing open-mouthed beside him. "Quick, man. What you waitin' for? Call an ambulance – now!"

★

273

Jordan crouched in one corner of the police holding cell, his bowed head cradled in his hands. He was shaking all over. A reaction to the attack from Prince and his gang or to his treatment since at the hands of the police? He'd no idea.

When a paramedic had turned up at the scene on his motorbike, Jordan was still holding Oz in his arms. The burly officer's face looked grave under his yellow crash helmet and he at once started routine procedures without reference to Jordan, who hovered at his elbow, helpless and disbelieving. A crowd of curious bystanders from the nearest bars and clubs had gathered on the pavement and the air shrieked with sirens as an ambulance came bowling round the corner and screeched to a halt, closely followed by a police car.

Jordan watched Oz being loaded into the back of the ambulance on a stretcher while the rest of their friends stood by, staring dumbly at one another. Then he felt a heavy hand on his shoulder. Spinning round, he found himself confronting a pair of tall police officers. He shrugged off the restraining hand, growling that he'd get Prince back for this if it was the last thing he did. Why were they just standing around while that bastard was high-tailing it out of danger?

"Now look, son," suggested the older police officer in a voice of authority, "why don't you just come with us?"

"But Prince'll get away," protested Jordan, straining like a greyhound on a leash.

"Yeah, well, we'll need to hear the whole story and then we'll know what's what," insisted the officer.

"You don't understand! What's happened to Oz?" cried Jordan.

"He's on his way to hospital – everything's under control. Now you just come along quietly…"

But Jordan refused – at the very least he thought he ought to go with Oz. When the officers tersely repeated their order to climb into the police car, he threw off their detaining hands and a brief scuffle ensued, until they finally pinioned his arms roughly behind him and thrust him into the back seat. He sat in silence, jammed into one corner, along with Eugene and Ash, who both wore scared and solemn faces.

When they finally reached the police station, they were herded inside like cattle. They had to turn out their pockets, received an official caution about making statements and were asked if they knew a lawyer. Cameras flashed in their faces and DNA samples were swabbed from their mouths. Jordan kept yelling that he wasn't a bloody criminal – but no one took any notice. Gazing around the benches of faces just like his, some scared, some bored, one even fast asleep with his curly brown head lolling back against the shabby wall, he saw that he was just one more teenager causing trouble on the city centre streets that Friday night – and he already had a police record. He shut his mouth.

Finally he found himself bundled into a cell with a noisy drunk yelling on one side and an angry prostitute demanding her rights on the other. A lawyer would soon arrive to help him make his statement. Meanwhile he had the right to make one phone call. Who did he want to speak to?

He automatically dialled his home number. It rang and rang. Where was everyone?

"Yas?" Gran's sleepy voice answered at last.

He stammered out where he was and what'd happened.

There was a moment's silence and then he heard a heavy sigh.

"What trouble you got yourself into, boy?" she demanded.

"Look, Gran," he cried, "it ain't none of it my fault. There was a fight. The cops think it was our gang against the Asians from across the wasteland. But Sudhir was with us. It was Prince and his toughs caused all the trouble. He pulled a knife on me. Oz was hurt under my arm. But no one'll tell me what's happened 'ceptin' he's got took to hospital. Looked in a pretty bad way. For God's sake, find out what's goin' on."

"Me try de best me can. An' you – don' you say nuttin', I tell you, widout no lawyer. He dere to help you make de statement."

How'd she know about the lawyer?

"They're askin' if I want anyone with me when he comes," Jordan went on miserably.

"You wantin' me to come along down to de perlice station?"

"Gran, I need someone. They tell me I'm in big trouble for what's called resistin' arrest."

"You jus' keep quiet, boy. Me see what's to be done…"

Jordan was left staring at the phone lying dead in his hand.

Suddenly light dawned. No wonder Gran knew the ropes. She'd been through this all before with Uncle Wes! Jordan plunged his head back into his palms. What would she say if he ended up in jail too?

He huddled on the cell floor, shivering like a little child. There was a racket of angry voices all around. Telephones rang, computer keys tapped. The drunk in the next cell was roaring abuse at no one in particular and the prostitute on the other side had resorted to whining and whimpering to go home. It felt like hell.

Impossible to tell the passage of time, since his watchstrap had broken in the scuffle and his mobile'd been confiscated. Couldn't understand what was going on anyway. It all seemed like some terrible nightmare, from which he'd never wake up.

After a while he was hauled out of the cell and questioned, with some smart, smarmy-looking legal guy on hand to tell him what to say. He sat sullenly on the hard chair. Why were they asking him all these stupid questions about Sudhir and the Asian gang when what'd happened was so bloody obvious? What he did dimly grasp was that they all thought he'd done it, because he'd been left with the knife, holding Oz. How would he ever face Gran standing in the prisoner's dock in court on a charge of murder? His heart would burst with shame.

At last after a very long time, he heard the rasp of a key in the lock. He raised his weary head just high enough to see the door swing open. Feet creaked into the cell wearing shiny black shoes.

"Come on, sonny. Up you get," urged the business-like voice of one of the station officers. "You're free to go."

Jordan raised dull eyes to the stern face. Impossible that these words could be addressed to him. Surely they didn't release suspected murderers on bail?

"Look lively, son. You're outa here. Someone's come to take you home."

The police sergeant stepped aside and Jordan's wondering eyes caught sight of the large, shambling, bear-like figure behind him.

"Uncle Wes," he cried.

His uncle looked desperately uncomfortable. He shuffled his big feet and stared at Jordan with a swaying nod of his huge shaven head.

Jordan shot him a glance of mute questioning.

"Let's get outa here, boy," his uncle muttered.

Finally the police sergeant managed to convince Jordan that he was being released without charge – he really was free to go.

In a daze Jordan held out his hands for the jacket and belongings being returned to him and stumbled out of the station leaning on his uncle's strong right arm. But as they were heading down the steps to the car park, he started out of his stupor.

"Oz. How's he doin'?" he demanded. "Anyone ring the hospital to find out?"

Wesley shook his great head gravely.

Jordan's heart skipped a beat.

"Look, boy – it's no use," his uncle told him. "Your mate, Oz – before the ambulance could reach the hospital, he was already dead."

CHAPTER
TWENTY-EIGHT

O z's coffin lay in the middle of the small chapel with a wreath of white chrysanthemums on its gleaming surface. The building overflowed with mourners: Jordan could see Oz's weeping mother and grim-faced father in the front pew next to his skinny, red-haired little sister, who'd read a passage from the Bible about the resurrection of the dead on Earth and broken down in tears at the end. With them sat his grandma from Essex and a whole raft of relations Jordan'd never even known he possessed.

Packed close together around the walls with solemn faces and wearing formal dark suits stood all Oz's mates from school: Eugene, Dill, Jermaine and Ash. Hayley and Lauren supported a blubbering Nicole while Elodie and her mum, dressed in black, sat with their arms around the shoulders of Ruth and his sister, Grace, who'd refused to stay at home. Elodie'd publicly vowed she'd never see Prince Harrison again.

On the instructions of Sudhir, the Asian gang had turned out in force. And all the ballet people were there too. Alicia's trim figure in a simple, dark dress and Roy in a suit and tie, seated together in a pew a long way in front, together with other dancers from the company: Mei and Alex and, on the other side of them, Isabelle's flame-coloured head bowed in silent mourning. Masakuni and Boris stood propping up a nearby pillar and Cameron rested his hands on the back of a pew, his brown eyes dark and serious.

Jordan had arrived late after everyone else entered the building, so he slid in at the rear just as the service was beginning. He listened to the bland, measured words of the church elder, relating the simple facts of Oz's short life and reassuring his audience that the current world order was soon to be destroyed at Armageddon, when thanks to the sacrifice of Jesus Christ, the dead would be raised and they would greet their loved ones again in paradise on Earth…

It was some comfort that the police'd finally caught up with Prince, hiding out in a filthy squat in London – but whatever happened to him, it wasn't going to bring Oz back, was it? Who gave a damn for the words of these do-gooding ministers of religion, advising the wronged constantly to look to the next world and preaching that vengeance lay in the hands of the Lord? There ought to be payment for sins on Earth too and he'd be quite happy to deal out some to Prince in person, if only he could lay hands on him.

At the end of the funeral, after the final hymn and prayer, everyone began filing out of the chapel into the dank and gloomy afternoon. Jordan skulked behind a pillar, watching the ballet dancers leave: Alicia, gracious as ever, pausing at the door to offer a word of sympathy to Oz's parents; Roy, upright and stern-faced, shaking hands with Oz's dad. Didn't think they'd seen him and he planned to keep it that way. If only he could've spoken a word to Isabelle. But she was hemmed in by friends: Boris had his arm round her shoulders and all the rest of the dancers seemed like an escort, barring his approach.

He watched her pause in front of the curtain, which now hid the coffin from view, and stoop to lay down something she was carrying. But, clenching his fists resolutely, he willed his longing heart to let her go – out of his sight, out of his life.

Wouldn't've known what to say to her anyway. Better for all concerned that things should stay as they were.

After everyone else'd left the building, he finally emerged from behind the pillar and walked slowly up the deserted aisle. He stopped in front of the curtain to say a last goodbye to his old mate, fixing his eyes on the single, pink, long-stemmed rose that Isabelle had laid on the carpeted step: Oz would've liked that.

As he stood with his head bowed and the helpless tears pricking behind his eyes, he swore to Oz that he'd pay Prince back for this, however many years he had to wait. Couldn't live on in this world, knowing his old mate'd died in vain. He swallowed hard and turned to leave the chapel in stony determination.

But just as he stepped outside, pulling up his coat collar against the drizzle, there stood Roy in front of him. Jordan started and hastily turned away. Where to hide?

"Jordan," called Roy's voice after him, deep and stern like the voice of his grandmother's God.

Jordan hadn't lost the hard-learned habit of unquestioning obedience to that voice. He stopped in his tracks. What did Roy want with him?

"Thought you'd be here," Roy pursued neutrally. "I haven't seen you round lately."

"Been busy," replied Jordan, half-turning back but keeping his eyes fixed on the ground.

"You still dancing?"

Jordan's heart quivered at the sound of that word. He struggled to say yes, but he couldn't. What he did at the Fallen Angel wasn't in the same league as what he used to achieve with Roy. No way could anyone ever confuse the two. So even as his mouth was forming the word "Yes", he shook his head in bitter defeat.

"Pity," returned Roy evenly.

Hope flared inside Jordan as he looked up at Roy, longing to glimpse in his face an offer of forgiveness and rescue. But it faded at the sight of the steely glint in Roy's eyes. Mad to suppose even for a moment that Roy'd take him back into the company without a full apology. His heart sank because he was too proud to say words he didn't mean.

He started to slink away, but Roy's voice halted him once more.

"All that rage and hatred and violence and revenge lead to is waste," the voice said quietly. "You know that, don't you, Jordan? We're all losers. Oz's gone and nothing can bring him back. But you owe it to him not to waste the talent that's in you out of stupid pride and stubbornness."

Jordan glanced back over his shoulder and saw Roy watching him with the same expression on his face as he'd worn the previous September, that day on the steps of the gym when he'd refused on principle to teach Jordan because he vowed he was late to class. And then Roy'd found out he was mistaken... Jordan almost let out a sob, unable to speak for the pain that was swelling up and choking him. But he could still act.

Slowly he stretched out a trembling right hand towards Roy, struggling to imitate the generosity he'd learned from his example.

"You were right, Roy," he admitted in a low voice. "Rehearsals aren't the place for fist fights. I was totally out of line. I'm – I'm sorry."

It was as if the closed door he'd been vainly kicking against in the dark all his life suddenly swung open and light came pouring in. The words were hardly out of his mouth when he felt Roy seize the offered hand, his face alight with fierce exultation.

"Good man," he exclaimed, clapping him on the shoulder. "I knew you could do it. Now, our second intensive rehearsal week starts on Monday morning at nine-thirty in the gym, but I'll meet you there at eight o'clock sharp…"

"W-what for?" faltered Jordan.

"You've got some ground to make up, haven't you? If you're going to dance Tybalt at the performance next Friday night. Allie, come here – the prodigal's returned. Cameron, go and call Alex. Jordan has something to say to him. Might as well get it over at once, like foul-tasting medicine…"

Jordan watched in numb bewilderment as people shot off in obedience to Roy's commands. His eyes were still fixed in wonderment on the older man's face and his heart swelled with the big question he'd never asked before. Another moment and it'd be too late. Cameron was already approaching with Alex in tow. The sight drove him to speak out.

"Roy, why're you helping me like this?" he whispered.

Roy half-turned back, smiling his thin, wry smile.

"We come from the same place, Jordan," he replied. "Haven't you noticed yet?"

★

Jordan crawled home late that afternoon, exhausted. How to cope with this confusion of joy at having so much restored to him and, at the same time, of grief that Oz wasn't there to share it?

From the evidence of the shouting and banging he could hear as he pushed open the front door, he guessed the twins were there – probably playing games upstairs with Grace. This meant Gran must be home from work. When he poked his head round the kitchen door to tell her he was back, there she sat at the table drinking a cup of tea with Uncle Wesley. They seemed to be involved in earnest discussion.

"You lookin' dead beat, boy," she remarked with a trace of

283

sympathy in her voice as she glanced up and caught sight of him. "Come in an' drink a cup o'tea wid Wes and I."

Jordan shook his head slowly. "Thanks, Gran. But I think I'd rather just go upstairs and be by myself for a while."

"I say, you come in an' sit down right here," she insisted, tapping the table top with a light of purpose in her eye. "Your uncle – him got someting to say to you."

Jordan glanced questioningly at Wesley, unable to blot out the memory of the mighty surge of relief and gratitude that'd flooded through him the other night when he caught sight of his uncle's familiar face at the door of the police cell. He'd felt as happy as a child when he realised Uncle Wes was there to take him home. But it wasn't easy to be overjoyed to see someone and fiercely ashamed of him at the same time. So since then he'd gone on struggling to ignore his uncle as usual. What could he have to say to him now?

Wesley shifted his great bulk uneasily on the kitchen chair, which creaked as if in protest at the unwelcome task before him. But Gran shook a warning head and he at once shrank back in silence. She heaved herself to her feet, clearly meaning to leave them alone together to talk what she regarded as men's business.

Jordan eyed his uncle hopelessly as she lumbered out of the room, pulling the kitchen door shut behind her. Both of them saw it was no use trying to avoid this conversation. Even though she was no longer there and they could hear her stumping upstairs calling out to Grace and the twins, they both knew they had to do as she said. Jordan heaved a deep sigh and dropped into the seat opposite his uncle. He might have to be physically present at this talk, but that didn't mean he had to take an active part in it. He sat and waited sullenly.

His uncle seemed apologetic and even more uncomfortable than himself. For a long time, he merely shuffled his big feet under the table and uttered a series of preliminary coughs and throat-clearings. Jordan remained stubbornly silent.

"Jordan," his uncle blurted out at last, clearly groping for every word, "Ma's tole me I gotta have this talk with you. 'Bout the trouble you've got yourself into."

"I ain't in any trouble," Jordan was quick to protest. "The cops let me go without pressing charges."

"Yeah," agreed his uncle succinctly. "They lemme go like that too – the first time."

"Things're different now," Jordan assured him with rising impatience. "I've decided my life's gonna change."

"Yeah – that's what I said too," answered his uncle with a weary sigh. "Look, boy – you think I'm just some worn out old has-been – yeah, you do," as Jordan opened his mouth in automatic protest, "but here at least I know what I'm talkin' about. I been in your shoes and I made mistakes and I paid for them. I don't want you to make them same mistakes."

Jordan tossed his head resentfully. No chance whatever of him making the same mistakes as Uncle Wes. His uncle clearly read his mind because he thumped his mighty fist down on the table top and went on with renewed purpose.

"Look, boy, we all believe it ain't gonna happen to us – that we're different, special like. Everyone thinks it's hard to go wrong, but I know it ain't – it's easy. It's like one o'them slides in the play park. You're at the top and life seems great. But then you start comin' down faster an' faster till you shoot straight off the end. You hurt yourself – an' you hurt other people too – people that love and depend on you."

Jordan must've gone on regarding his uncle with an unconvinced expression, because at that point Wesley leaned forward over the table.

"Look, Jordan, I know. I remember standin' in that prisoners' dock in court – and it wasn't the sour, kick-arse, snotty-nosed judge that I cared about, who doled out my sentence in this posh voice as though I was mud in the gutter. And it wasn't the sight of them smart lawyers on fat salaries shakin' hands after the trial and sayin' how sorry they were they couldn't get me off, but it could've gone a lot worse for me – and snappin' shut their briefcases at the end of another day. It wasn't even the cops or the prison bars or hardly ever seein' the twins that bothered me most. No, it was the look on Ma's face on the other side of the courtroom when they sentenced me to five years inside. It'll haunt me till the day I die. I don't want you to go where I been, boy. Believe me, it hurts more than just your pride. Climb off the slide, Joey. For your grandma's sake. She's had a whole heap of troubles: she don't need no more. Pull up, while you still got time…"

Jordan stared at his uncle's earnest face. Perhaps they had more in common than he'd thought. Remember how he'd felt, crouched in that prison cell, worrying how upset Gran'd be when she found out what'd happened to him. The world wasn't just black and white: the goodies and the baddies, like they tried to make out on TV or in films. Everyone had some power of action in them. The difference lay in how they chose to use it.

"You bought any old motorbikes lately?" he suddenly asked out loud.

Wesley wrinkled his brow and nodded, clearly puzzled at the connection between this query and the painful advice he was struggling to impart.

"Yeah, man. Guess so," he admitted. "Got a great little 1925 Douglas CW/24 up on blocks in the car port. Needs a bit o'work though."

Jordan looked him straight in the eye.

Wesley shrugged. "OK then, a lot o'work."

"Remember how I used to give you a hand when I was a little kid?" Jordan went on quietly.

"You were my best mate," his uncle told him with a trace of pride in his voice.

There was a moment's silence as they both thought back

to the old days and even Jordan was surprised when he heard himself ask, "Mind if I come round and take a look at the bike next Sunday after the show's over?"

Wesley flashed him a broad grin.

"Guess you could do just that," he said.

CHAPTER
TWENTY-NINE

The Youth Dance Project's keenly anticipated performance of *Romeo and Juliet* finally took place on a hot Friday evening in early September. Everybody who was anybody in the local community was there and even the long-awaited camera crew arrived to shoot film footage for the regional news.

The Brackwell Heath High School gym was packed with families, friends and well-wishers. Extra seats had to be squeezed in on the ends of rows to accommodate late arrivals begging for tickets and a knot of curious bystanders even gathered outside the fire doors, which had been flung wide to admit more air into the crowded building. The noise inside was deafening.

Jordan loitered restlessly behind the makeshift stage, peering at the audience through a narrow crack in the curtains. He watched Roy, on top form tonight as the company's front man, shaking hands with various dignitaries and personally escorting Isabelle's mother, along with Patrick Sedley, the artistic director of the Midland Ballet Company, and a thin, blonde woman, whom Jordan had never seen before, to their reserved seats beside the school principal. He'd never known business-like Mrs Manners in such a flutter of proud smiles: she seemed as on edge as the performers.

Murray Bennet was sitting with his wife further along

the same row, looking hugely uncomfortable in formal collar and tie, while Megan Scott had just caused a major sensation among the girls by her arrival in a stunning silk shift with a handsome boyfriend in tow. Near the front of the audience Jordan also spotted Pastor Sheldon and his wife, who'd organised the costume-making team. They were seated next to Regina Simpson, conspicuous in a peacock blue suit, fanning herself with a programme and chatting pleasantly to the city mayoress.

Everyone's parents were there, Asian, black and white, even Oz's mother, father and little sister, who'd insisted that Oz would've wanted the performance to go ahead regardless. The ladies of the Brackwell Heath Full Gospel Church sewing circle had come to admire the results of their handiwork on stage and Auntie Zoe was fulfilling Lauren's strict instructions to sit on the end of a row so Zack had the chance to watch his mother perform in the street scenes, but could be swiftly removed if he started to make a fuss.

The members of the audience on whom Jordan's gaze lingered most lovingly were an ill-assorted little group on the left-hand side several rows from the front. Bear-like Uncle Wesley, his arms crossed over his broad chest, sat silent and uncomplaining as the lively twins clambered round, hanging off either side of him as though from a human climbing frame. But Jordan's heart swelled with even keener pride at the sight of his grandmother, who always refused to stir from the house at night except on church business, occupying a chair next to his grandfather, who never went anywhere at all, but had firmly announced his intention of coming to see Grace dance in the performance she'd told him so much about. They looked an incongruous pair: Gran's enormous bulk swathed in a vast tent of gaudy orange poppies, with her best striped raffia handbag and green straw Sunday hat, wreathed in artificial sunflowers; his grandfather with hunched back and thin, drooping shoulders, squeezed into an unregarded corner, leafing patiently through his programme and looking as bemused as if it were written in Chinese characters.

Tingling with nerves, Jordan turned from the chink in the curtains to survey his fellow performers.

Backstage all was tension and excitement. The boys had buckled on their sword belts and were strutting round in leather jerkins and skin-tight leggings, self-consciously warming up their muscles or rehearsing last-minute steps. The girls were whispering and giggling together, checking their make-up and shoes and rustling their brightly coloured skirts. Alicia, overseeing the stage management crew all in black, was running a series of last minute checks with Sudhir and Dillon, who was in charge of the music.

The professional dancers from the company were scattered almost indistinguishably among the rest of the cast. Mei, as wardrobe mistress, was busy sewing a final adjustment to the glittering white and gold chiffon party dress that Elodie wore for her first appearance as Lady Capulet. Cameron in the cobalt blue waistcoat of Mercutio was lightly jogging on the spot, while Boris, towering head and shoulders above the rest like a giant among dwarves, stood with his arms folded majestically across Paris' silver and white tunic, passing a low comment to Masakuni, who was about to dance his first Benvolio.

Alex, true to form, stood preening himself in the stage-side mirror. Grudgingly Jordan had to admit that he looked every inch the part of Romeo with his slender figure and pale, smooth complexion, entirely restored to his usual good looks and bearing no trace of the injuries he'd dealt him.

Not far away, beside an admiring Nicole in her ample nurse's outfit stood Isabelle, clad in a gauzy blue shift, quietly grinding the toes of her pale satin pointe shoes into the rosin box. Jordan knew how much this performance meant to her. With Patrick Sedley in the audience watching her début as

Juliet, she stood the chance, if she danced well, of convincing him to try her in the rôle of the youngest witch in his upcoming production of *Macbeth*.

She suddenly glanced up, as though feeling someone's eyes fixed upon her. Jordan nodded good luck and she flashed him a quick smile.

They'd had no time to talk this last week, which had sped by in an endless succession of practices, costume fittings and runs on stage, followed by technical and dress rehearsals and culminating in the performance this evening. But he'd heard from Mei that she and Alex had split up soon after his own dismissal from the company. Seeing them dance together since, no one would ever've suspected it. True professionalism, he supposed, striving to imitate it in his own dealings with his old enemy…

At that moment someone brushed past. Jordan glanced round and caught sight of Grace, heading towards her first entrance. Her dark eyes sparkled in the dimness.

"Good luck, Jordan," she said, reaching up to adjust the set of his jerkin with neat, professional fingers. "You know, I think you're the handsomest big brother in the world. I was sure you'd look amazing in that shade of red." And she gave his costume a final pat of approval. "Looks miles better on you than it would've on Cameron."

Jordan grinned at her unconcealed bias and gazed after her, as she stumped away towards the stage. Without her stubborn persistence he wouldn't've been standing here today. He'd more than one reason to be thankful to his feisty little sister.

But now it was time to focus on the coming performance. This was his big chance to justify Roy's belief in his talent and prove he was worth all the effort his teacher had spent on him over the last year, as well as showing his family and friends there was something he could do after all. Tonight that audience was going to see a Tybalt to die for.

Alicia was making hushing signs and calling for the starters to take their places. The house lights faded, the buzz of audience chatter died away, the opening chords of the overture sounded. The performance had begun...

★

Isabelle skimmed down the ladder from the balcony in a blaze of exaltation.

After a year's experience in a professional company she was used to leaving her identity behind in the dressing room along with her pre-performance nerves, steadied by the routine ritual of make-up, hair, costume and warm-up exercises. She knew too that dancing a dramatic rôle demanded far more than the competent execution of its thousands of individual steps and that all her hard work and long hours of rehearsal were just the springboard to launch her into telling a story with the aid of the music. But nothing had prepared her for the miracle of this evening's transformation. Tonight she *was* Juliet.

As soon as Alex entered the stage, she could see he was on brilliant form and his assurance had fired her with the confidence to match him step for step. Together they'd accomplished feats in that balcony *pas de deux* that she would never've dreamed possible, lifted out of themselves by the music, the lights and the excitement of the audience. She'd once imagined that what she and Alex danced on stage would be a mere reflection of their own personal happiness. But the reality far transcended any imagination. It was like an ecstatic reaching out of the soul towards ideal beauty, making her feel clean and new and strong.

"Bella!" breathed Alex, eyes glowing as he emerged from the shadows at the rear of the raised set. "What a performance! I've never seen you dance so well."

Alex did not deal out praise lightly. Isabelle was too

overwrought to reply in words, but she reached out her hands to meet his, her heart on fire with joy and pride.

Blind to everything around her and only anchored to earth by his firm grip on her fingers, she floated along the corridor towards the changing rooms, feeling as though her satin-slippered feet were barely touching the ground. Faces she only dimly recognised streamed past, as everyone hurried to get ready for the second half: Elodie regarding her with increased respect, Jordan throwing her a half-defiant glance of wonder, Grace pausing an instant to finger the folds of her gauzy dress with shining eyes...

Isabelle squeezed her hand hard, knowing it was Grace's own determination and hard work which had set her firmly on the road to independence. It was a timely reminder of reality.

Alex lingered at the door of the changing room, reluctant to let go of her hand.

"No regrets?" he whispered, raising it to his lips with all the old tenderness alight in his face, attended by a new glimmer of professional esteem.

A giddy madness seized hold of Isabelle. With one gesture now she could instantly revive their lost relationship. To go back to the way things used to be!

Memories of happy times flooded her mind: feeding each other slices of pizza out of a cardboard box on the floor of Alex's sitting room, walking hand in hand along the sunny river bank in Bellevue Park when he came to fetch her after that first dreadful Sunday afternoon class in this very gym, practising lifts together in the top studio in Temple Street, dancing under garlands of lights at Mei's eighteenth birthday party... How good it'd felt to have Alex to relax with in lunch breaks and after evening performances, to share the ups and downs of the day, to sympathise with her fears and ambitions. Particularly after two long months of feeling the emptiness of life without him. Surely she could forgive the stupid things they'd quarrelled over so they could go on dancing together just like tonight?

But then – had Alex ever really sympathised with her fears and ambitions? Her eyes narrowed. Remember his total inability to comprehend her interest in the Youth Dance classes. How he'd only joined the company because he believed it would promote his own professional interests with Patrick. And how he'd accompanied them to Oz's funeral because it looked good, not because he really cared whether Oz was alive or dead. Think too of the bitter things he'd said to her about Jordan Howe. These she could not forgive.

She shook her head quietly.

"I'm too tall – remember," she said. "You're better off dancing with Mei."

After the briefest second of hesitation, Alex dropped her hand and nodded.

"You're quite right of course. London beckons... Well, must go now. Big scene coming up."

And he smiled brightly and disappeared in the direction of the men's changing room.

Isabelle turned away with a tight throat. How it hurt to admit that everything was finally over between them. But it made her even more determined to prove herself in the challenging scenes ahead...

★

With an infinite exertion of effort, Isabelle's lone, white figure seemed to haul itself by painful degrees across the surface of Oz's lovingly crafted tomb. She reached out one yearning arm towards the body of Alex, who lay where he'd fallen in death and after this poignant farewell, sank gracefully to rest. For a long moment the stage lighting illuminated the final stark tableau of the lifeless lovers and then faded slowly into darkness.

A breathless hush gripped the entire auditorium.

Jordan, still quivering from the heady excitement of his own performance, had been following the last act with keen attention from the wings. In the long moment of silence after the music ended, he breathed a deep sigh and the tears pricked behind his eyes. From what he'd seen tonight, not just on stage, but in their rapturous reunion off-set which he'd witnessed with a sinking heart, it was clear to him that Isabelle and Alex had got back together. Oz'd been right after all: she was too classy for guys like them...

Applause thundered out on every side. Everyone was roaring approval, starting to their feet to welcome back the cast for curtain calls. Each group of performers summoned forth rising bursts of enthusiasm, as the audience cheered Masakuni's mischievous Benvolio and Boris for his dignity as Paris. The shouting and stamping of feet that greeted the appearance of himself and Mercutio was ear-splitting, while the emergence of Romeo and Juliet almost raised the roof.

With a lump of emotion burning in his throat, Jordan watched Isabelle and Alex step gracefully forward, applauding everyone else's performance. Then his eyes sought out Roy, who sat in the audience beaming with unmistakable pride. Good old Roy. He'd never let him down.

Next Alex drew a misty-eyed Alicia from the wings to accept a huge bouquet of lilies and Isabelle darted forward to welcome Roy onto the stage for the presentation of a rubber sword and a magnum of champagne.

"Speech! Speech!" roared everyone, until he was finally forced to take centre stage for the first time that evening. As the noise died down, Roy swept his eyes over the rows of expectant faces.

"Well," he began with unassuming directness, "I don't mind admitting that when a proposal was made to me this time last year by my wife," (indicating Alicia, close beside him) "that I should lead a course of ballet classes at Brackwell Heath High School, I had severe misgivings. After the shambles of that first harrowing session, (and don't think I'll ever forget the humiliation you inflicted on me, Dill and Ash, because I won't!)" with a grimace at the pair who'd been his tireless right-hand men throughout the whole of production week, "after that first session, I wouldn't have believed these young people here could ever possess enough commitment and strength of purpose to see a single class through, let alone an entire year's programme. And the idea of undertaking a full ballet would never even've entered my head."

A murmur of self-conscious laughter rippled through the cast at this point and several of them pulled wry faces.

"How wrong I was," Roy declared, glancing round in warm approval. "I can't pretend we haven't had our fair share of ups and downs, our set-backs and even, in some cases, our violent disagreements," directing a meaningful glance at Jordan, who blushed at the memory of his own shortcomings.

But Roy was already admitting with more sober honesty how there'd been times when he seriously thought this evening would never take place, particularly after the untimely death of the former cast member, to whom tonight's performance was dedicated. He warmly praised the heroism of Oz's parents, who'd insisted the show go ahead in spite of their tragic loss, and then declared with quiet sincerity how over the months they'd worked together, these youngsters had grown as dear to himself and his wife as members of their own family.

"Most of these kids started off last September knowing nothing at all about ballet," he went on. "But in a single year, they've grown confident enough to stage this entire performance practically on their own. They've devised and built the set, with advice from some of the parents and friends I can see out there among you. They've designed and sewn the majority of the costumes with the help of other relations and supporters. They've organised publicity, music, stage management and even choreographed some of the dances you've watched tonight. My wife, Alicia, my colleagues, Murray and Megan, my devoted handful of young company dancers and I myself, who've merely been responsible for providing the experienced guidance, have watched them learning to work together and responding with developing professionalism to every challenge they've encountered. Our grateful thanks are due to Mrs Barbara Manners, whose original idea this was and who's keenly supported the project from its inception, and also to a variety of groups and trusts listed in your programmes, who've provided the much-needed funding. But I'm sure no one will disagree when I say, kids," turning to the cast who were clustered around him, "that without all of you, nothing could ever've happened. And if you can achieve this, then you can achieve anything. The world is waiting for you. Go out there and give it all you've got!"

The roar that rose from the throat of every single cast member was deafening and the building resounded with a mighty storm of applause.

★

Amid the exchange of handshakes and courtesies that took place after the performance, there was a certain pre-concerted arrangement in which Jordan had a vested interest. But what if Roy got so distracted by all the people who wanted to speak to him and all the compliments that were being showered upon him as to forget the favour he'd promised faithfully to perform: to speak about Jordan's dancing to his grandparents?

He hovered anxiously in the background, watching Roy out of the corner of his eye and paying less than full attention to the congratulations of passing well-wishers, as his family gathered round him, awe-stricken by the discovery that their ugly duckling had turned out a swan.

But Jordan's teacher did not fail him. Displaying the charm and easy grace with which he performed every public duty, Roy, as if by chance, paused to acknowledge the Howe family in his lap of honour, accompanied by the well-dressed woman with cropped blonde hair and the unmistakable poise of an ex-dancer, whom Jordan had noticed seated beside him during the performance. Roy began by casually introducing the woman as Virginia Seymour, an old friend of his, who reached out to shake Jordan's hand with glowing eyes and a warm smile of approval.

"You must allow me to tell you how impressed I was by your performance tonight," she began with a generous smile.

Jordan grinned gratefully back and murmured that it was all thanks to Roy.

"Actually this's the second time I've had the privilege of watching you perform," she went on and then, in response to his questioning glance, "I saw you dance earlier this summer at Roy's retirement gala. It was an unforgettable experience. And this evening in the final duel: that dazzling leap from the head of the stairs, the electrifying sense of struggle between yourself and Romeo. When you finally fell, I was convinced you were going to grasp that sword your fingers were straining after…"

"Oh Jordan likes to keep us guessing," observed Roy with an ironic smile. "But he always comes up trumps in the end." He cast a sideways glance at Jordan's grandparents as if to gauge their reaction to what was being said. "Of course I knew the first time I saw him dance that this was a young man of exceptional talent and I am glad to say he's proven himself hard-working and determined as well. I think he has a great future in dance ahead of him. But what he clearly needs now is full-time professional training."

Jordan watched Gran's eyes widen as she grasped the meaning of Roy's seemingly off-hand words.

"Dere ain' no way dat we can afford no expensive fees to fancy balley schools, Mister Hillier," she began in the respectful voice she usually reserved for addressing Pastor Sheldon and other church dignitaries.

Jordan's heart sank. She'd made a similar reply when Mrs Manners had pleaded with her to let him stay on into the sixth form. A certain stubborn expression always settled over her face as she said no, it was the will of God. Why, after he'd struggled so hard and come so far, was the answer always no?

"No, I appreciate your position," replied Roy, fixing Gran directly with his keen eye. "But if it were possible for Jordan to receive a scholarship to a first-rate ballet school, surely you wouldn't prevent him taking it up by withholding your consent?"

After a moment's pause, Gran slowly shook her head.

"In that case," went on Roy with lightning swiftness, "may I have the pleasure of introducing to you Miss Seymour, the directress of the Pentland Ballet School? She happens to have one place left to fill this term and she's keen that Jordan should start at once…"

Jordan's head was in such a whirl that he could hardly take in what followed. And when Roy and his honoured guest finally continued on their triumphal progress, he was left behind staring in stupefaction at his grandmother. All he could grasp was that at last someone had said yes.

"You mean you'll really let me go to Pentland?" he blurted out dubiously. "I can't believe I could ever be so lucky."

"Huh!" Gran gave a contemptuous sniff. "Dis ain' no luck, boy. Dis here's de will o'de Lord. Remember all dat dere fuss you made at de start of dis dancin' bizznezz 'bout takin' Grace to her balley class?"

Jordan nodded slowly. "Yes, but—"

"Dere ain't no buts about it. God has spoken an' I is a woman o'my word. Me tole you den you was to do jus' dat and see now de blessin's what's flowed from it. Grace here's full o'joinin' dat Airborne Dance Company an' she gonna study dressmakin' an' design for her career. An' at las' your feet are turned back towards de paths of righteousness. You recall what I done tell you? De Lord move in mysterious ways his wonders to perform. Blessed be de name o'de Lord. Amen."

CHAPTER THIRTY

Alicia wasn't convinced that the part-time administrative post Roy'd rashly accepted in the company's new education outreach office at Brackwell Heath Arts Centre was the right move for him. So she waved him off to work on his first morning with some misgivings and spent most of the day worrying about how he was getting on. She caught a bus home straight after the end of the *Macbeth* rehearsal, fully prepared when she arrived back to find him slumped in the living room in profound depression and to have to spend the rest of the evening soothing a storm of complaints about the miseries of retirement.

She smiled grimly at the fulfilment of her predictions on letting herself in through the front door to find the house pervaded by a tomb-like stillness and no aroma of dinner preparations wafting to greet her, as Roy'd faithfully promised over breakfast that morning. She peered apprehensively round the hall door, but the living room was empty. So she checked the kitchen and conservatory, but no one was there either. After calling upstairs and receiving no answer, she concluded that the house was entirely deserted. Far from sitting around moping, Roy hadn't even arrived home yet. Where on earth could he be?

As she stood gazing round the unoccupied dining room in puzzlement, she suddenly heard the familiar drone of an approaching car engine and out of the corner of her eye saw a silver streak flash up the driveway. The Jaguar roared abruptly to a halt outside the garage. Then the car door opened and slammed shut again. Darting to the window, she realised in amazement that Roy was actually whistling as he came striding up the side path and in through the back door.

Unable to bear the suspense any longer, she poked a wary head round the kitchen door and found him humming to himself as he switched on the kettle.

"Hello there," he greeted her briskly, glancing round from the open cupboard with a mug in one hand. "Do you want a cup of coffee?"

"Um – yes," she faltered and then, thinking she might as well know the worst at once, "Er – how was your day?"

"Absolutely first rate," he retorted, as he clattered the mugs onto a tray in high good humour.

"Wonderful," she remarked, brightening. "I never thought you'd settle so easily into an office job…"

Roy turned to stare at her.

"What're you talking about?" he demanded.

"You know – you've never had too much patience with computers and so forth, have you?"

The penny finally dropped.

"Oh I soon got bored with that dreary administrative business," he assured her with a dismissive wave of his hand. "The secretary needs something to keep her occupied after all. No, no, I've done a lot of thinking since this morning. I've been on the phone to Barbara Manners and that friend of yours at the ballet school – and Patrick too, with an exciting new scheme."

Alicia looked hard at him, already harbouring serious doubts about the nature of this 'scheme' of his.

"You see, I was going through the programme of outreach events first thing this morning," he hastened to explain, "and it struck me that after the brilliant success of last Saturday night's performance of *Romeo and Juliet*, why should the Brackwell Heath Youth Dance Project stop there?"

Alicia tried to interrupt, but he was already sailing under full canvas.

"It's true that some of those kids are now perfectly happy to call it a day. Eugene, for one, hasn't time for dance rehearsals since he's made the county football team and Ash was telling me after the show that for some unknown reason I've inspired him to join the army. I gather Hayley's been offered a front-of-house job at the Olympian and Lauren's decided to swap shop-lifting for a college course on childcare. But what'll happen to Grace's design skills if she's left to stagnate in some tedious GCSE dressmaking class, learning how to stitch buttons on men's shirts? Or Sudhir's superb organisational mind, if he ends up wasting his energies on the tactics of gang warfare? How's Dillon ever going to compose a worthwhile ballet score if there's nobody to dance it? You saw the expressions on their faces last Saturday night when they realised that this was the end of the production and of the company too. I've been thinking over the weekend: why should it be the end of the company? Why shouldn't it just be the beginning?"

"So what do you have in mind?" Alicia enquired slowly, sinking into a chair at the kitchen table.

"Well, we've outgrown Barbara's gym – that's quite clear. But that elderly friend of yours with the ballet school at the Arts Centre, who's thinking of retiring…"

"Sylvia King?"

"Yes – her. Managing the school alone's getting to be too much for her, but she doesn't want to give up teaching altogether. She told me so on the phone today. So I put it to her: what about refounding it as the Brackwell Heath Youth Dance Company and running it as an out-of-school-hours project working towards a performance each year in September? More than one possibly. Maybe even one a term, once we get all the organisation in place. We could offer accredited qualifications in dance, involve the whole community, start fundraising to renovate the complex as a brand new performing arts centre, enlist Sylvia, Cameron, Isabelle and anyone else from the company who's interested in improving their own teaching experience to come and help tutor on Sunday afternoons... That way I'd be able to build up a company of well-trained dancers capable of performing the new ballet I have in mind"

"New ballet?" echoed Alicia faintly. This was the first she'd heard of a new ballet.

"Yes. You see, I've learnt a lot myself over the last year. I used to think my inspiration had to come from literature: poetry, plays, stories and so on, but now I've realised it's not the only way. Ballet needs to reach out to young people if it's going to survive – and the inspiration is right there in their own lives."

"But I thought you didn't know anything about teaching teenagers to dance," she pointed out with a hint of irony.

"What rubbish you talk sometimes," countered Roy, pouring the boiling water decisively into the coffee maker. "I've been teaching teenagers to dance for years. Now I was just thinking, Allie, that you could handle the girls' classes. I've been most impressed by the way you relate to them, as well as how you've come on as a choreographer this year. What d'you say to joining forces with me in this venture?"

"But I already have a full-time job as company ballet mistress," she protested wearily.

"Retire. Best move I ever made. I tell you, retirement gives you a whole new lease on life..."

"Let's talk about it later this evening," she hedged, as he set a coffee mug down on the table in front of her.

"I don't like to hurry you," he remarked, "but we need to eat dinner soon because I'm rehearsing with Jordan and Isabelle in town at seven tonight. It's the choreographic competition next week. What d'you say to lamb steaks with red onion and aubergine salad?"

Alicia nodded in bewilderment. And she'd thought that when Roy retired, he might be spending more time with her. Fat chance!

"Oh Roy, why does it have to be you who does this?" she protested.

Roy paused to consider for a moment as he reached for the refrigerator door handle. Then he turned and said, "Well, if I don't, who else will?"

★

After an hour and a half's rehearsal Jordan felt practically light-headed with exhaustion. By the time Roy grudgingly called it a day, his heart was thumping frantically inside his ribcage and his chest was heaving as he gasped for breath. He doubted he could've danced another step if his life'd depended on it.

Roy hardly seemed to notice.

"'Bye then, kids. See you next week in London," he called over his shoulder, as he breezed cheerfully out of the room. He'd been brimming over with enthusiastic plans for his new youth company all lesson long.

Jordan staggered weakly towards the barre and reached for a towel. His T-shirt was wringing wet from the sweat pouring down his neck and chest and his black leggings clung clammily to his shuddering thigh muscles. He pulled a wry face at Isabelle, who'd sunk to the floor in exhaustion. She smiled faintly up at him.

"There's nothing you can do," she remarked, wiping the perspiration off her neck with the towel he'd just tossed her. "He's always the same. But where would we be without him?"

Jordan shrugged, but less resentfully. He had a pretty good idea himself.

"So you've got what you wanted then?" he asked, changing the subject as he stretched out one hand to swing her to her feet. "Patrick's decided to give you a go at Third Witch?"

"Yes. Only in the second cast of course, but it'll be a great opportunity to learn from Andrea, who's actually having the rôle created on her. We've been rehearsing all afternoon. That's why I'm so dead beat. It's going to be an amazing show."

Jordan watched a gleam of pleasure reawaken in her tired green eyes.

"And I'll be there on opening night," he responded eagerly. Even if he had to stand at the back of the balcony right underneath the roof.

There was an awkward pause as Isabelle bent down to pick up her water bottle.

"So you're heading off to Pentland tomorrow?" she resumed with lowered eyes, her slender fingers playing thoughtfully with the blue plastic lid.

"Yes, first thing in the morning. I'm all packed." This new venture was exciting but also a bit worrying, since he'd never been away from home for more than a couple of days at a stretch before. He also remembered with a jolt that these were the last moments he'd be spending with Isabelle. "But I'll be seein' you in London at the competition next week."

Isabelle nodded. "I'm so pleased you'll have the opportunity to train properly."

"Yeah. It's the best thing that's ever happened to me."

"You know," she admitted, glancing around the great, empty studio. "I can't imagine what this building's going to feel like without you. I'm so used to bumping into you round every corner… Still, I guess you won't be missing it."

Was it his imagination or was there a slight note of regret in her voice?

"Bella, you can't mean that," he exclaimed. "This studio's the place where I started out. I remember Roy standin' over by the door there makin' some wise-crack about learnin' to do a warm-up before I had a go at barrel turns." He could remember a few other humiliating lessons he'd also learned here, which he didn't particularly want to think about now. "This is – I know it's stupid to say it – but it's like my other home and the company are like my other family. I'll be back – perhaps even as a member of the company myself one day."

"Then we might be able to dance together. You know, Jordan…"

"Yes?"

She raised honest eyes to his.

"I once thought my greatest ambition was to dance the grand classical *pas de deux* with Alex. But I've changed my mind. Of course I'd still like to dance the great classics, but I'd rather dance them with you."

A thrill of joy shot through him. He tried to steady his dazzled gaze, like a diver on the brink of a sunlit pool, moistening his dry lips with his tongue in an effort to force speech out of his tight throat.

"But I thought after seeing you two dancing *Romeo and Juliet* the other night that you must've – you know – got back together," he murmured in a low voice.

Isabelle shook her head.

"Jordan, that was just acting," she pointed out quietly. "Alex and I split up a couple of months ago. I think he's going out with Mei now."

(So that accounted for the slight coolness he'd noticed between the two girls.)

"At first," she went on with lowered eyes, "I admit it didn't make the *Romeo and Juliet* rehearsals very easy. But we've managed to work through it. Alex's a fine dancer – but he's not interested in anything but himself. Besides, he's leaving the company. He's going off to film in London and when that's over, he's accepted a contract with the Royal Ballet."

She sounded quite business-like about it.

Suddenly Jordan realised the constriction in his throat had vanished. He straightened his slouching shoulders, feeling as strong and confident as he did when soaring through the air in a mighty leap.

"Look, Bella," he exclaimed, "I'm thirsty and starvin' hungry. You got any plans after you leave here? I mean, you – are you goin' anywhere tonight?"

Isabelle shook her head. "Just out to eat before I head home."

Jordan looked her straight in the eyes, rolling all his courage up into one ball. "I suppose you wouldn't – I mean, I was wonderin' if you'd like to – that is, if you had time – whether you'd come and have somethin' to eat with me?"

There! After all these months, it was finally out at last.

But what answer would she make to his clumsy suggestion? – Isabelle, the delicate, the graceful, the highly-trained ballerina, to him, the circus monkey, the uncouth yob still smelling of garage grease? Jordan's pounding heart almost suffocated him as he waited breathlessly for her reply.

Without a moment's hesitation, she simply smiled and said, "Yes."